Hot Ménage

An anthology of sexy short stories

EDITED BY
LORI PERKINS

BLACK
LACE

Contents

1 3 5 7 9 10 8 6 4 2

First published in the US by Ravenous Romance as
Once Upon a Threesome (2010) and *Threesomes* (2009)

First published in the United Kingdom in 2012 by Black Lace Books,
an imprint of Ebury Publishing
A Random House Group Company

The Random House Group Limited Reg. No. 954009

Addresses for companies within
The Penguin Random House Group can be found at:
global.penguinrandomhouse.com

A CIP catalogue record for this book is available from the British Library

Penguin Random House is committed to a sustainable future for
our business, our readers and our planet. This book is made from
Forest Stewardship Council® certified paper.

Printed and bound in Great Britain by Clays Ltd, Elcograf S.p.A.

ISBN: 9780352346827

To buy books by your favourite authors and register for offers, visit:
www.blacklace.co.uk

Barabbas, Give Me Back My Barabbas

by Jen Bluekissed

"Rivka bat Eran," my neighbor called out to me with a warm smile. *"Chag Pesach Sameach."*

"Chag Pesach Sameach," I replied, genuinely wishing her a meaningful Passover, for what was left of it.

"Your pain will lessen, Rivka. Barabbas ben Pesech fought for a just cause, and our people will never forget the sacrifices he made in the attempt to free us from Roman rule."

For her there would always be prayers and family, unleavened bread and wine, a remembrance of our people's past, and a steadfast longing for our freedom from the Romans. She still lived with the hope of many generations' struggle and fortitude to one day not only be the chosen people, a nation with men and women as numerous as the stars of the sky, but also with the freedom to rule itself.

For me, the Passover held nothing but bitterness. My husband, Barabbas, rotted in a prison after being captured during the insurrection he'd spent his entire life planning. He had been completely sure our men could overpower the Romans. He was sure enough of his cause that he risked everything important to me. Not only was he captured, but my two sons had died the same day when the soldiers crushed the poorly armed men under the weight of their horses' hooves. Their metal scaled armor, the *lorica squamata*, protected them from the force of our men's blows.

All the insurrection accomplished was to leave me childless and with a husband who was scheduled to be crucified among thieves. I still slept with a roof over my head, but I had no idea how long even that would last. How would I eat after Barabbas's execution? He had rounded up even my brothers and uncles for the insurrection. Those who survived the Romans' wrath were left maimed or half dead. My neighbor could wish me well, but her well wishes wouldn't put food in my stomach. Those who presently took pity on me would soon tire of it. *Then what will I do?*

I returned to my house, a sack of wheat under my arm. After the Sabbath and Passover were finished, and after Barabbas was executed, I would grind the grain into flour. No doubt my tears would mix with it. At least I would have something to keep my hands busy while mourning. No doubt the Romans would deny me Barabbas's body or delay his release for burial. Pontius Pilate and the other officials would surely want to report their savagery back to Caesar.

With nothing to do but weep, I entered the house I

used to share with Barabbas and our sons. After storing the sack of wheat, I lay on my bed, longing for Barabbas's heat. If my situation were different, he would have known how to comfort me. He would hold me, and everything would seem better. But, as I remembered for the thirtieth night since the failed attempt to overthrow our tormentors, I was bound to sleep alone.

Or so I thought. Overcome with my own thoughts, I had completely missed her presence. Shoshana bat Hadar, wife of Judah ben Adon, stood in the shadows approximately fifteen cubits away. Judah had already been executed, the first of many organizers the Romans arrested the same day as my Barabbas. They were saving my husband for last in order to make a statement regarding the timing of his crucifixion. Shoshanah was without family like me, and she was the one person I was glad to see inside my house without being invited.

Shoshana looked at me with a desire I'd never noticed in her before. With deep brown eyes the color of dried figs, she settled her gaze on my face while licking her upper lip. Her hair was covered, as was mine, but I knew it was an even deeper brown than my own. I wanted to stroke it, to take Shoshana in my arms and share both my grief and my carnal longings. Since Barabbas had been in prison for over a month, my body longed for intimate contact. She stepped forward, but as she walked into the light, a look of hesitancy crossed her face.

"I know what you want, and I don't care that it's forbidden," I said, hoping to ease her from her doubt. *I need this as much as you do.*

To reassure her, I brushed my veil to the side so she could glimpse my hair. Not daring to remove my head covering completely, I pulled out a large wisp of hair. It was the color of sandalwood and fell about my shoulder in wavy lock, curling at the end near my breasts. Shoshana's eyes moved down to the tip, drinking in the curve beneath it.

She crossed the remaining space between us while freeing her arm of the outer mantle draped across her body. Standing before me in nothing but her inner tunic, the silk belt wrapped around her waist holding it closed, and a pair of dusty sandals, she waited for me to shed my outer garments.

"I'm sorry about Barabbas."

"Don't. Just comfort me," I said, slipping my arms out of my own mantle. "Neither of us can change the past. What I need now is to know I'm not alone."

Shoshana removed her sandals while whispering, "Neither of us will ever be alone as long as we remember what we've both been through."

She sat at my side while bending down to remove my sandals. When my feet were bare, she glided her fingertips up my calves, my thighs, and then between them. I lay back onto my bed, unable to contain the gasp upon feeling a woman's touch there. Her fingers were unlike Barabbas's calloused ones. They were slim and smooth, gentle and patient, but deliberate in their caress.

I wanted to watch her eyes as she lifted my inner tunic with her free hand, kissing the insides of my legs, but the will to keep my eyes open faltered. Barabbas had only ever felt for my wetness. Shoshana felt for my pleasure, for the place I didn't dare ask Barabbas to touch. My hand balled up the hem of my inner tunic that was now bunched around my waist, unable to stay still while she exercised carnal wonders where my flesh parted.

After I was too sensitive for any more of her caress, I sat up, hoping to show Shoshana my gratitude. I reached for her breast, wishing to lift her inner tunic higher than she had lifted mine so that I might take her nipple into my mouth. About to do so, we were both startled by a loud knock on my house's wooden door. Too shocked to ignore it, we both scrambled to properly cover ourselves. We were barely presentable when my neighbor burst into the house.

"Rivka, take to the street! Quickly! The Roman governor is speaking to the people about Barabbas. He's giving the crowd the choice between releasing the Nazarean or your husband."

I strapped the sandals about my feet and ran hand in hand with Shoshana to avoid being separated in the sea of people. *The governor has no reason to release my Barabbas. He is known to have killed many Romans during the Insurrection. There has to be something else behind all of this.* I didn't dare hope for Barabbas's release, yet I found myself shouting in chant with the people surrounding me, my neighbors and friends. I spoke to the governor from a place deep within my heart, unlike the people around me who were caught up in the politics of the unfolding events.

"Give me Barabbas! Give me back my Barabbas!" I went hoarse quickly from the pleas; my throat felt aflame but I continued shouting nonetheless.

Shoshana gripped my hand as if she was afraid to ever let me go, but she shouted the request just as loudly as I. "Give us Barabbas!"

When the governor washed his hands in front of the crowd and ordered the soldiers to release my husband, I nearly fainted from exhaustion and relief but I forced my limbs into submission as I greeted Barabbas. Shoshana refused to release my hand, so Barabbas embraced us both.

"Be careful, Woman," he said as my free hand wrapped around his back.

It was then that my mind registered that my hand was resting in an open wound. The skin of his back was hanging in shreds from the prison guard's brutal whip. I inspected his back more closely, tearing my hand out of Shoshana's grasp. What they had done to him was worse than I had imagined. The implement they used couldn't have been an ordinary whip. There had to have been metal or glass affixed to the end as they had lashed at him.

Shoshana and I carefully helped Barabbas back out our house. He was not only bloodied, but his legs gave out several times. Finally, one of the men of the crowd took my place and then another took Shoshana's place—it was improper for her to be so close to him in public—supporting his weight while we returned to the house. Once we were there, I gathered a basin, water, and clean rags before bidding the men to leave.

"I must care for him now."

No one except Barabbas and I noticed Shoshana's continued presence. She helped me clean his wounds, then used all the spare cloth available in the house to stop his bleeding. He covered his lap by folding his inner tunic over his legs after removing it and his outer tunic so that we could attend to his back. For as badly as he had been scourged, I was amazed he was lucid and without fever. He sat upright, the damaged skin too scattered around his body to find any relief in reclining.

"Rest, Husband," I said as I stroked his beard.

He leaned toward me, kissing my mouth before saying, "I am in too much pain to rest comfortably."

"Then Shoshana and I will sit with you."

Shoshana cast her eyes downward after briefly holding my gaze. Her cheeks flushed as she sat on Barabbas's right side. I sat on his left. Her proximity to my husband was overtly improper, but Barabbas smiled as he witnessed the seductive way she set her eyes upon me before looking at the floor. Nothing about my husband had ever been strictly proper. He drew pride from his flaunting of our people's customs. Even those who knew him but had never met him were aware he was a radical.

"I am glad to see you've chosen to comfort Rivka," he said to Shoshana, "and to comfort me."

Barabbas lifted the outer tunic from where it rested over his legs so that he wore nothing but a loincloth. His legs were almost as badly damaged as his back. Shoshana and I washed the wounds on his legs with the rest of the remaining clean water. He grimaced every time we rubbed the dirt and sweat out of his battered flesh, but as we worked up his legs, his lips curled upward.

"There is only one part of me the Roman soldiers left untouched."

I reached across Barabbas's lap to untie the loincloth, but he shook his head. Motioning for Shoshana to kneel between his legs, he said, "I would like it very much if the two of you distract my body from the pain it suffers. Let Shoshana remove all of her clothing, then you, Rivka. My eyes have seen nothing but the sting of sweat and blood for this past month. Let me watch you pleasure each other."

Shoshana slowly removed her outer mantle, her inner tunic, her sandals, and her head covering so she stood, then knelt before Barabbas, completely naked. Then she reached for his loincloth, revealing that he had spoken the truth. The Romans had not been brutal there, the sight of Shoshana's nakedness displaying that every bit of the flesh once hidden under the loincloth was intact.

I also removed everything, even my head covering. Barabbas had been so savagely tortured that I felt he deserved to see both Shoshana and me without a strip of cloth to cover our bodies. By the time I knelt behind her, Barabbas was already touching Shoshana's large breasts. I pressed mine into her back before reaching around her hips in search of the place she had so expertly caressed on my body hours earlier. A sigh escaped her lips when I found it, and Barabbas smiled at me.

Both of us could see my husband's body was too covered in torn skin for him to want to plunge himself into either of us. He stroked Shoshana's hair while guiding her head closer to where the Romans had the decency not to flog. She licked the length of him while moaning from my touch where her flesh parted and slickened.

"He likes sucking even more than licking," I said from behind as I kissed Shoshana's neck, then shoulder.

Barabbas grunted his approval as she circled her mouth over him, down his length and then up it, over and over again. Shoshana also moaned as my fingers dipped inside, then returned to the little place I'd been caressing gently, then more quickly. She finished moaning before Barabbas, her body free from the distraction of recent torture, but she continued encircling him with her mouth patiently until she was assured by his body's release that he was finished.

"I'm glad to be home," Barabbas said, his frame slumping against the bed. Exhaustion from the day's events overtook him, and I was relieved we were able to give him rest.

I had my Barabbas back in my life, and I vowed to Shoshana as he slept that I'd never let either of them go again. She returned the vow to me. Her peaceful expression coupled with Barabbas's deep sleep assured me he would never let either of us go again either, Roman rule or no Roman rule. He was once again mine.

The Untold Riches of
the Holy Lands

by Jay Hughes

Geoffrey the Blademaker sat in the middle of camp, stropping his broadsword blade across a whetstone. His blade had reached maximum sharpness quite some time ago, but the feeling of Toledo steel against stone was soothing somehow.

Sir Walter the Penniless's Crusade army had been marching through the mud, sleet, and rain of the Holy Roman Empire for days. Lacking proper maps, they'd been going in circles through the Black Forest for at least a week, and they were no closer to the Holy Land than they'd been a fortnight ago. Rations were running low, shoe leather and patience were running thin. Geoffrey had begun to have second thoughts about taking the cross and following Sir Walter in his fight to lead a peasant crusade to free Jerusalem from the Saracens, even if the promise of Oriental riches and worldly fame was quite tempting, and the only real way a landless peasant rogue like him could make his fortune.

He finally set the whetstone aside and tested the blade against the fine blond hairs that stood out on his forearm. The broadsword edge sliced them off as cleanly as the best of Spanish razors, and then some. A small patch of clean new skin now gleamed from the layers of Black Forest dirt that now coated Geoffrey from head to toe.

Like any good Christian peasant, Geoffrey rarely bathed—since it brought the soul devilishly close to carnal lust, it was an activity reserved only for high feast days or appearances before His Lordship at court. Or so the priests and monks who followed Sir Walter's army preached, anyway. In reality, it was more a combination of a lack of clean water and the high price of soap. But today even his usually filthy and flea-bitten hide was itching for a good scrub.

Geoffrey sheathed his sword and walked towards the end of camp, where the army merchants and camp-followers gathered. If memory served, there were several bathhouse wagons among them, along with the usual shepherd's pie vendors, puppetmasters, and the rank, reeking brothels-on-wheels. It had been many months since Geoffrey had partaken of the services of a lady of the night, but the notion of bedding a pox-ridden, toothless camp-follower didn't appeal to him at all. Even though he definitely had itches to scratch in that department, he thought it best to wait until they reached Venice before partaking of such pleasures. After all, he'd heard from none other than Sir Walter himself that the Venetian courtesans were well worth the wait—and the price.

He fingered the worn leather pouch that hung from

his belt. It was heavy with gold and silver that the army had gathered on its travels eastward, having collected everything from alms from devout noblemen to commissary requisitions of merchant stores to out-and-out pillaging of villages and monasteries loyal to the King of France and his Templars. Nothing was sacred in war, not even Christ. And when it came to claiming hold of the riches in the Holy Land, the old rivalries between England and France, not to mention nobility and peasantry, died hard.

He skipped past the first two ragtag rolling bathhouse wagons for the final and most expensive one: Assad's, a glossy, black-enamel paneled coach painted with exotic lettering and images of the Far East. Owned by a mustachioed, perfumed Turk, Assad's provided the balms, unguents, and steaming hot baths of the godless Saracens to the very armies that planned to conquer them. Assad was nothing if not a shrewd mercenary—he cared little for who paid him their palmfuls of pillaged gold and silver, so long as he got paid.

As a blacksmith and swordmaker by trade, Geoffrey was only a few steps above a mud-grubbing serf. Hardly the type to seek out exotic steam baths, not to mention balms and unguents literally worth their weight in gold. But after abandoning his blacksmith shop in Essex to take up the cross, forging sword and dagger blades for half of Sir Walter's armies and trudging hundreds of miles across the Continent, Geoffrey felt he deserved this luxury. And he carried a prince's ransom on his belt, so why not play the role of the prince as well?

He knocked on the shiny black Dutch door to the wagon, and shook his purse of gold to announce he meant business. After a proper pause, Assad the Turk opened the top door, his long black mustache gleaming with fine oil.

"Ahhh, greetings, fair Christian soldier," Assad oozed in his heavy Saracen accent. "Have you business with me?"

"A bath," Geoffrey grunted. He emptied a few gold coins into his palm. "The finest you can offer. I can pay. Name your price."

The Turk salivated at the sight of so much gold. "I am happy to serve you, Christian," he said. "The standard price is five gold pieces. But alas, there are already two customers ahead of you in the bath. You will have to wait." He paused, raised both his bushy dark eyebrows. "Unless . . . you don't mind sharing with others?"

Geoffrey shrugged. He'd grown up the son of a blacksmith with six siblings. He'd shared plenty of baths in his life, had shared plenty of other things too. "As long as the water is hot and the unguents are fine, I shan't mind," he said. A bath, even a shared one, would be refreshing. God only knew when he'd have another chance. Sir Walter had ordered the armies to be on the move again on the morrow, and now that the hapless general's mapmakers had finally figured out where they were, the upcoming route was through rough country—over the German and Italian Alps, moving southward towards the port of Venice. From there, it would be passage on crowded, dirty ships for the Holy Land, and possibly months before his hide saw hot water and soft fragrant oils again.

He handed over the gold, and Assad the Turk pocketed

it into the folds of his greasy linen robe. "Follow me, Christian soldier," he said, and opened the bottom panel of the Dutch door that led inside the wagon.

The mobile bathhouse's dark interior was filled with fragrant steam, and surprisingly spacious. Geoffrey inhaled deeply of the hot, aromatic mist, savoring scents he'd never experienced before: saffron, myrrh, sandalwood, even near-priceless frankincense. As his eyes slowly adjusted to the dim lighting, he could just make out two dark figures seated on wooden benches on the far end of the wagon. Assad handed him a bundle of expensive Egyptian cotton toweling and motioned for Geoffrey to join the other two guests. "Come, please, enjoy," said the Turk. "Disrobe and leave your clothes here on this ledge. You will find a selection of balms and oils and fine washing linens waiting for you on the benches inside. For an extra three gold pieces, I will launder them for you while you bathe, and polish your boots in the bargain. At that price, the bathhouse is yours to enjoy for the next three hours."

Without a word, Geoffrey dropped the required three gold pieces into Assad's palm, then stripped off his dirty tunic, jerkin, and tights and thrust them into the Turk's waiting hands. He left his boots and braces in a pile for his host to polish and oil. With that, he strolled nude through a beaded curtain down the wagon's tiny dark hallway, which opened up into a larger room lined with cedarwood benches. The two dark shadow figures were there, but he could still barely make them out through the thick clouds of pungent steam. The only sound was the misty whistle of the large copper kettles in which perfumed water boiled, and the occasional crackle of the hot cinders burning beneath them.

Well, if he couldn't see his bathing partners through the mist, he might as well be bathing alone. *Maybe this was a bargain after all*, he thought. Geoffrey smiled softly to himself, settled back against the smooth cedarwood bench, and inhaled deeply of the fragrant steam. He reached beside him, searching for the promised balms and unguents, but located only a pile of damp linen toweling. He reached out further, exploring up and down each end of the bench, and eventually his hands stumbled upon something smooth and damp.

But what he'd found wasn't a jar of myrrh, olive oil, or even priceless frankincense. It was the smooth, bare thigh of one of his fellow bathers.

"If it's the olive oil you're searching for, I have it right here," came a clear voice through the mist. It was a male voice, deep and rough around the edges with the hint of a Welsh accent. "But if you want the frankincense or the sandalwood comb, you'll need to ask me mate. Cedric, could you pass it over? Slide on down here, mate."

The shadow of a huge man suddenly filled the empty space just to Geoffrey's left. A smaller, leaner shadow slunk in to his right. As his eyes adjusted further to the misty darkness, he could just make out the features of his two fellow bathers. They were typical Welshmen, both of them—tall, fair-haired, blue-eyed, with rough beards and firm, muscular bodies. Cedric the leaner and younger of the two men, rubbed his firm chest with a thick hunk of a fragrant, waxy substance that Geoffrey supposed must be frankincense. He rubbed and scratched it into his chest with the sandalwood comb, which left deep red scratches in the man's skin.

"Hand over the 'cense to our friend here, Cedric," the deep voice boomed. "I get the feelin' he ain't never had the pleasure o' such stuff before. It's silver 'cense, the very best grade, mixed in with ambergris. That's the fat of the sperm whale, and 'tis just as priceless. Rub it into your skin, then scratch with the comb. Makes a nice pleasant burning tingle, it does. 'Twill get ye most clean, too."

The older man, thick of both chest and bicep, had the powerful body of a mace-and-battering-ram soldier, one of the many varieties of Welsh mercenaries who hired their services out to the highest bidder. Right now, the highest bidder happened to be Sir Walter the Penniless. Next month, it could be the Knights Templar.

Geoffrey took the chunk of frankincense-laced ambergris and passed it over his body, watching as his fellow bathers washed themselves with a combination of olive oil, myrrh, balsam, and tincture of chamomile. Chains, armbands, and rings of heavily wrought gold and silver hung about both men's naked bodies, and the bigger man also sported several tattoos of a strange flowery script Geoffrey couldn't read.

They were prosperous mercenaries, these men, and likely already veterans of multiple expeditions to the Holy Land. They had a clear appreciation for the finer things in life, along with the expectation that there would always be plenty more of it to be had in the future.

The large man reached out a meaty hand for Geoffrey

to shake. "Name's Tym ap William," he said. "I come from Cardiff, and me mate Cedric's from near the Cornwall coast. Sir Walter took us on just a few weeks ago, when ye'uz passin' through Augsberg. We was returnin' from the service of Hugh of Antioch, aimin' to return to Wales, but Sir Walter made us an offer we couldn't refuse. So here we are, off fer 'nother jaunt. Cedric an' me, we have a real taste for gold and spices, we just couldn't turn it down. Could we, Cedric?"

"Nay," was all the younger man said.

During this little exchange, Geoffrey had been so distracted by the beefy man's story that he hadn't realized both men had stopped rubbing the valuable Turkish unguents into their skin, and had started rubbing them into his own—Tym taking Geoffrey's chest, Cedric his back. They rubbed and kneaded the oils and balms into his skin with their strong, muscled hands, massaging him, washing him clean, working at the knots in his neck and shoulders. Geoffrey instantly relaxed, so engrossed was he in the pleasure of their ministrations that he scarcely had a chance to think about it. He'd never in his life been plied naked by two strange men. Indeed, he'd always been taught by the parish priests, not to mention the lads round the village, that such a thing was completely unnatural. But here in this moist, hot, fragrant place, it hardly seemed unnatural at all. Before he knew what was happening, the two men were rubbing him all over, kissing him, nuzzling his neck, even kneading his cock and balls.

"You look like a man who could use a good healthy thumping," Tym whispered in his ear. "An' I don't mean with a club, neither. Will ye let me show ye some o' the great pleasures o' the East, lad? The untold riches of the Holy Land?"

By now Geoffrey was so relaxed, so lost in the heretofore unknown pleasures of touch, scent, and heat, that all he could do was give a slight nod. Tym took that as his cue to unleash a river of sensual pleasure the likes of which a simple blacksmith from Essex had never known.

In one smooth, swift motion, Tym placed both his meaty hands on Geoffrey's sides and turned him round so his back faced the larger man. Then the huge Welshman slid his hands round to Geoffrey's buttocks, and parted them like the Red Sea. He fingered Geoffrey's tight red rosette, which was already slick with a mixture of steam, olive oil, and perspiration. Geoffrey opened like a spring rose in bloom, and Tym thrust his huge member forward, filling the younger, smaller man in one swift, hard jerk. Geoffrey cried out in a delectable mixture of pleasure and pain as Tym thrust hard and deep into the dark recesses of his body.

The quiet, introspective Cedric positioned himself in front of Geoffrey, then bent over, leaning against the bench on the opposite wall. The motion spread the lean young man's buttocks wide in a gesture of invitation. Without even thinking, Geoffrey thrust forward in perfect counterpoint to Tym's rhythm, and filled Cedric with his long, hard, throbbing essence.

The three of them moved and bucked in a perfect ululation of pleasure, bumping and grinding out the tension, fatigue, and frustration of the preceding weeks' long muddy march through the Black Forest. The muck, the sleet, the aching feet, even the clear and present danger of war in the mythic Holy Land all dissolved. All that existed was the hard and fast pleasure of this dark, misty moment.

The three of them exploded all at once, their sweating, streaming bodies collapsing into one another. The scent of sweat, sex, and the exotic East filled the air like perfect, pungent incense. The only sound was boiling water and heavy breathing.

Once the afterglow had dissipated, the three men stood, returned to their spots on the benches, and resumed their bathing rituals as if nothing had happened. A silent understanding formed between them, a wordless agreement that promised no one would ever speak of this incredible moment in time ever again.

They sat in silence for another hour or so, until all the balms and unguents were used up and the perfumed water in the copper kettles boiled away. Assad the Turk appeared just on the other side of the beaded curtain, shaking a few of the beads to announce his presence. "Alas, gentlemen, your time is up," he said. "Did you three Christian soldiers enjoy your baths? I hope you will partake of my services again."

"We'll be back," Geoffrey said. "Tomorrow morning, first light, before the army leaves for the road. And any other time the garrison stops, and the three of us are free. Won't we, lads?"

The three men nodded and smiled. 'Twas a gentlemen's agreement among soldiers, the only kind that ever went unbroken.

Inamorata
by Kristabel Reed

Venice, Italy 1690

Antonio Tulon, Conte di Brindisi, followed her through
the crowded streets, deftly avoiding merrymakers cele-
brating spring. The afternoon sun still floated high in the
sky, and a cool breeze drifted over the canals. The spring
festival, with its brightly dressed people parading by, held
little interest for him.

All he cared for was the woman who teased him.

Her bright green eyes laughed at him and she offered
a suggestive wink before turning her head away. She
slipped to the left and over the bridge. Picking up his pace,
Antonio weaved through the revelers, crossed the bridge,
and chased her down the streets. She played a game with
him, one they'd engaged in before.

A favorite of theirs, this chase brought both anticipation
and ultimate pleasure. Antonio enjoyed stalking this wisp
of a woman; everything about her caused his blood to boil.
The heady gasps once he caught her, the feigned terror in

her sparkling eyes. He felt drunk on merely her scent.

He'd never wanted a woman more than he did her. Now that he had her, despite these games through the streets of Venice, he refused to let her go.

She vanished behind a group of revelers. Speeding up, he crossed the street, cutting her off before she could disappear once more into the crowd.

Tugging her into an alley, he pressed her against the wall.

"No, no, no," he whispered, kissing the corner of her smiling mouth. "I detest losing sight of you, my love."

"Antonio." She laughed, a bright sound tinged with breathlessness. "We'll be seen!"

Fingers drifting lightly over skin exposed by the low-cut gown, he kissed her. Immediately, she opened for him, sighing her acceptance, winding her arms about his neck. His fingers dipped below the stiff bodice, lifting her breast from its corseted binding.

Her skin tasted magnificent, warm from their chase through the crowd and fragrant. Running his tongue along her collarbone, across her shoulder, he dipped lower.

"Antonio," she breathed again, "someone may see."

"I'll not allow you to deny me, Elisabeta." Pulling back, he looked into her eyes, pinched her already hard nipple. Her heart pounded, her chest heaving, and despite her words, she ran her hands down his doublet, over his aching cock. "Not after you toyed with me all afternoon."

He easily picked her up despite her voluminous skirts, and carried her several steps further into the shadows of the alleyway.

Before she could utter another word, he kissed her
again, lips hard as they branded her. She whimpered
in need, acquiescence, hunger, surrender. The heated
sound she always made when they were alone together.
Or not, as the sounds from the festivities drifted around
them.

"As you wish, Senator," she said coyly, fingering his
chain of office. With deft movements, Elisabeta untied the
string of his breeches and pushed them around his hips.

Once more lifting her to the wall, Antonio pushed her
skirts out of the way, running his hands along her silk-clad
legs. She rolled her hips against his hand, slick with need.
Her legs tightened about his thighs as she hovered over
him.

Antonio held her still, though his body strained to be
buried in her heat. Shaking his head once in a vain attempt
to clear his mind, he looked at her. Elisabeta stared down
at him with passion-drugged eyes, lips swollen from his,
face flushed. Several strands of blond hair had come loose
from its curled confines, clinging to her cheek.

"Antonio," she whispered, eyes going soft with love.

He kissed her slowly, hands digging into her bare
derrière as he tried to control his unquenchable lust for
Elisabeta. It didn't work. It never did.

Bringing her down hard on his cock, he entered her.
She shuddered around him but didn't break the kiss.
Deepened it, clung to him. Much slower than he wanted,
Antonio lifted her, held her above him with only the top
of his cock inside her warmth. Straining against him, she
broke the kiss and arched back.

Teeth closing over her nipple, he bit the luscious point even as he slammed into her welcoming body.

"Please." Her voice was a harsh sob, her hands gripping his head as her lips found his again. "Harder!"

Every ounce of frustration he felt at not having her every night in his bed, over his impending marriage to another, over his ever-deepening feelings for Elisabeta, manifested themselves in their lovemaking.

He pounded into her, uncaring of her dress against the wall, of her appearance, of aught but the feel of her surrounding him. Her emotions played across her face, helpless in the passion between them. Love, ecstasy, wholly abandoned in this moment between them. Inner muscles tightened around him, and his fingers found her nub.

Elisabeta's breath hitched, and she cried out once before biting the fabric of his doublet to silence her pleasure, shaking as her orgasm washed over her. He spilled his seed within her, knowing he should withdraw, but unwilling to deprive himself of this. Of her.

It took him moments to regain his senses, to pull them away from the wall. Elisabeta still shook in his arms, he could feel her inner walls fluttering about his cock. Tenderly kissing the side of her neck, Antonio evened his breathing. With a saucy smile, she pushed his shoulders, trying to release him.

"No more of these games," he growled. "It is as I say."

Her smile told him of her compliance and she nodded before resting her forehead against his shoulder. Thrusting into her, though only semi-hard, Antonio moved a hand to her hair, pulling her back so he could see her. Watched her eyes close, her breath catch. She moaned, rocking her hips against his.

"Do not ever push me away."

"I would not," Elisabeta said, her hand cupping his cheek. "But your passions overwhelmed me."

"Accustom yourself," he said, as if they hadn't been lovers for months now.

"Why should I need to?" she demanded with an impudent smile. Straightening, she pulled back but made no move to stand on her own. "You're to marry another within the year."

His hand tightened on the nape of her neck and he brought her head down so she could not mistake his words. "The state of my marriage is undetermined and I may yet find a way to break the contract." Lowering his voice further, lips a breath from hers, he said, "My want of you is never undetermined. There will be an arrangement between us, in one fashion or another."

She was silent for a long moment before nodding. They'd had this discussion before. His family was in need of money and hers was even poorer than his. A marriage between them would never work out, no matter how little he cared for this existing contract or the status of their respective estates.

"Tonight," he said, slipping out of her and setting her gently on her feet. "Come to me tonight."

"You know I shall," she said, straightening her bodice and tidying her hair as best she could.

With a final kiss, he let her go, watching her mingle with the crowd drifting past. Disappearing from sight.

*

He hated being summoned. Once Antonio returned to his own house, a house along the Rio della Madonnetta, near the Rio di San Polo, his valet ambushed him with a note from his father demanding his presence. At once.

It arrived hours earlier, and Antonio, in no rush to see his manipulating bastard of a father, had waited still another hour before venturing across the Grand Canal near Rio di San Luca and the Grimani palazzo. Though not as grand, nor as recently built, Palazzo di Brindisi mimicked its owner.

Austere, elegant, yet untouchable. Distant. His father sat in his library, seeming calm as he went over ledgers. The instant Antonio entered the room, however, he knew otherwise.

"Good, good," Christofo Tulon, Conte di Brindisi, said. It surprised Antonio, so free from reproach was his greeting. "I didn't need the servants to scour the streets and canals for you. I almost regret," his father continued in, what was for him, a rush, "the day I allowed you to purchase your own house."

Suspicious, Antonio demanded, "What is the urgency, Father? Why have you summoned me? I've matters to attend to this eve."

"You forget," Christofo said, waving a hand in dismissal, "about that little Viadro girl. At least for now. It's time to attend to your duties as my son."

Narrowing his eyes, wary of this change in the old man, Antonio asked, "What is it?"

"Giacomo d'Artusio is here with his daughter,"

Christofo said. Antonio's plans for the night with Elisabeta crumbled before his eyes.

Angry at this change of plan, he hissed, "They weren't to arrive for months yet. What are they doing here now?" Then he added, "I don't want this contract."

There was a change in Christofo's stance. It softened for the first time in Antonio's memory. "I've spoken to them about releasing the contract," he admitted, shocking Antonio to his very soul. "However, the d'Artusio family wants this—wants our title in their family line. They refuse to accept otherwise. They want this, and I agree. You must do this for the family."

Holding his temper in check, hands fisted behind his back, Antonio clenched his jaw so as not to rehash old arguments. His father knew how he felt about this, but still willfully proceeded with his plan to align their families and to buttress the di Brindisi fortunes.

In the end, much as he hated it, it was the only choice.

"Your fiancée is in the upstairs parlor," he said, gesturing for Antonio to precede him. "Come."

Feeling like a prisoner sentenced to death, he followed his father. He wanted to leave, should have left. But the demands of his position forced him to ascend the stairs. Only a few moments, it seemed like the longest of his life, then he stood before her, Bianca d'Artusio.

Dark hair and eyes, lily-white skin, she held herself straight and proud. Her figure and stature seemed close to that of his Elisabeta. Medium height, rounded hips, Bianca's breasts were smaller than Elisabeta's, and frankly, despite these superficial similarities, Antonio preferred Elisabeta's attributes. Though her gown was of undoubtedly finer quality, a deep burgundy he only noticed for the way the color reflected the jewels about her neck.

Christofo and Giacomo greeted each other, talked for several moments, then excused themselves. Resigned, Antonio turned to Bianca.

"I'm certain," he said with a slight bow, "this is all very unnerving, Signorina d'Artusio. Would I be a bit presumptuous in assuming you wish to return to your native city?" He couldn't be bothered to remember where she came from, certainly not Venice though Antonio knew his father worked to grant her citizenship here. "Perhaps," he continued, "to a gentleman there?"

Casting him a demure look, hands folded before her, she said, "It's lovely here in Venice."

"Yes," he agreed, still pushing. "Venice has its charms, but it cannot be anything like home to you. These marriage contracts were made for us, but there is no reason why they can't be altered."

Another demure look, a sweet tone. "You are not pleased with my appearance?" she asked, dark head bowed in submission. "Is your intent not to honor the contract?"

Suspicious now, wary of her reserved manner, he watched her for a heartbeat. If he broke the contract, the di Brindisis lost more than they could afford. If Bianca broke the contract, the d'Artusio family would settle a considerable sum on him. Under no illusions as to the consequences of breaking the contract, Antonio nonetheless hoped for just such an occurrence.

He was selfish and knew it—he wanted only Elisabeta,

not this prim slip of a wife. However, with too many bad years in trading, and the wars with the Ottoman Empire, this marriage was the only saving grace of his family.

"You are a beautiful woman," Antonio allowed, "but we are in a unique position. Unlike many others, with simply a word we could dispense with the agreement between our families."

"Do you not mean with a word from me?" she asked, her reserved manner slipping. "Since it is my family who holds the advantage over yours."

Where had this come from? Taking a moment, he wondered at the sudden change in her behavior. Before he could comment, Bianca continued.

"Why would I care to dispense with our marriage contract?" Bianca stepped closer, unclasping her hands and squaring her shoulders. "There are certain freedoms afforded a married woman."

"You will have no freedom as my wife," he snapped, making sure she understood. He gripped her chin, forcing her to look up at him. Her dark eyes acknowledged that, but continued to hold a hint of delight. "I'll keep you cloistered in a room where your only task will be to produce an heir for me. Should," he added with a sneer, "I choose to visit you. You'll not find this marriage between us a pleasant one."

Bianca's fingers skimmed down his chest, cupping his cock. He remained flaccid in her hand. "Pleasure," she purred, "is exactly what I desire." She stroked him, dark eyes gazing up with interest. "I don't want to join our families in war. I'd rather we create something different.

Your threats are hollow, Conte di Brindisi. My family will not allow you to imprison me like a nun in a cloister. A single word from me will ruin all you have and all you know."

Antonio admired her manipulation of the situation, but that was all. Once married, interference from her family would be negligible. And, too, she could always die in childbirth.

"I do not react well," he said, removing her hand and flinging it from him, "to such threats."

"There is no threat, simply fact" she said, amusement in her voice. I don't want contention between us. But I don't want to be tortured by a neglectful husband."

Gripping her shoulders, he picked her up and pushed her several steps until her back hit the wall. Holding her there, Antonio once more forced her head up, ensuring her complete attention.

"I'll be whatever kind of husband I choose. As my wife," he continued, unsurprised to see the stirrings of desire in her eyes, "you will obey and keep silent."

The back of her fingers grazed his cheek, slid down to rest over his heart. "There's only one reason for such ardor in a man, for I am comely and willing." Her hand slipped lower, but didn't take his cock again. "There is another desire in your life. Either another man . . . or another *woman*."

Antonio released her chin, stepping back. He didn't care that she knew he had a mistress, only what she would do to Elisabeta should she ever learn her name. The d'Artusios were powerful, and if Bianca made true with her threat on him, that anger easily could transfer to Elisabeta, should she desire.

"Ah." There was satisfaction in her one word, but she didn't move. "As I'd hoped."

Jerking his head back to look at her, he saw lust mixing with triumph in her dark eyes. Shock stiffened him, but only for a moment. Arousal and intrigue came hard on its heels, hardening his cock with interest.

"And why," he asked, lazily crossing the space between them, "is that a hope of yours? Most wives detest the mistresses their husbands keep."

"I shall not be most wives," Bianca whispered, standing still as he circled her. "I would be happy if you would share her."

He could admit to being stunned, but not repulsed by the idea. "*She is mine.*"

"I will also be yours," she reminded him. "Think of it, Antonio. The three of us enjoying each other's flesh. But, if that thought—the thought of seeing your wife enjoying the most intimate parts of your mistress—does not tantalize, then I would hope you allow me my own mistress."

The thought tantalized. Antonio was tempted. Loath as he was to share Elisabeta with anyone—man *or* woman— this suggestion captivated him. Elisabeta's beautiful long limbs wrapped around Bianca's—

"My wife and my lover?" He'd never before given this thought, but hardened at her proposal.

"We would *all* be lovers," Bianca said, and he saw *she'd* given this considerable thought. "We would be there to please you . . . and you can watch as *we* please each other."

"What do you want with her?" he demanded, eyes narrowed.

"I want to kiss and suck her supple breasts." This bold statement further aroused him. "I want to lay my soft body atop hers. I want to feel her rapture moisten my face."

Stepping off her private barge, one of the few luxuries still afforded her, Elisabeta went up the steps and entered the familiar set up of the house. When it came to Antonio, she had no shame, no concern for her reputation or her future. She knew Antonio needed to go through with this marriage, and while she might wish to stop him, knew she wouldn't. If given the chance to marry to improve her family's fortunes, Elisabeta knew she would accept.

Antonio met her in the front parlor, where heavy blue draperies were open to the sunlight of the spring day. Taking a moment to brace herself, for all Venice knew his betrothed had arrived two days prior, Elisabeta took in the room she'd seen dozens of times. What she didn't know was whether this was to be their last meeting.

Though he'd sent several letters round to her describing Bianca d'Artusio's arrival, several further negations as to that impending marriage, and, in arousing detail, all he desired to do to her next they met, he hadn't visited.

Blinking those thoughts and several useless tears away, Elisabeta looked at the tapestry that hung against one wall. The hunting scene meant nothing to her; she remembered it solely as the backdrop to the first time Antonio had taken her.

Several oil paintings from one of Venice's many artists adorned the room and a pair of sculptures added to the feel of wealth. Everywhere she looked, color greeted her. Where once she hadn't cared, now she realized how vast the gulf separating them was.

Her family's decline began several generations ago and would end with her death, the last of the Viadros. Antonio's would end with his marriage.

"Are you to abandon me now that your future wife has arrived?" she asked, striving to keep the bitterness from her voice. Elisabeta was pleased to hear she was successful—just the right balance of inquisitiveness and amusement.

Antonio moved stealthy across the room, the graceful predator. His hand smoothed wisps of hair from her face, held the back of her neck. "No," he whispered, passion darkening his brown eyes to black. "I won't do that. I don't ever want that."

Quirking an eyebrow, arousal pooling low in her belly at his look, his touch, the heat in his words, she forced herself to ask the question. "How?"

"You'll be my mistress," he interrupted, leaning down to rest his forehead against hers. "As we discussed."

"Your wife will be a very powerful woman," she whispered, as if any could overhear them. "As a new bride, she will not take kindly to me."

Though she didn't not like it, certainly didn't wish to, Elisabeta wondered if she needed to find a new lover. A new protector. She loved Antonio and he'd never paid for her, but he did give her money so she could care for her delirious mother. She wasn't a courtesan, but—

"Let's find out," Antonio said, taking her hand. He kissed the palm, sending a shiver of need through her. "She wants to meet you."

Elisabeta shook her head, shocked. "No, Antonio," she said, surprised he'd suggest such a thing. "I can't meet her. 'Tis not the way things are done."

Backing her up until she hit the back of the settee, he lifted her slightly so she rested against it. Kissing between her breasts, he suckled the sensitive skin there, tongue tracing along the cut of her bodice. Elisabeta entwined her fingers in his hair, holding him closer. She wanted him now, it was always so with them.

Kissing up her neck, his mouth was hard and hot on hers, and she lost herself. His hands held her face still as he took, devouring her mouth, hungry for more. She met him equally, nails digging into his head, ankles hooking about his legs to try to draw him closer.

Abruptly he broke off the kiss. Still holding her, he pulled back, breathing heavily. He took a moment to speak, and Elisabeta was smug in knowing she caused that. "She's insistent on meeting you," he finally said. "I think you should. It would please me greatly."

"Antonio!" she began, but he didn't give her time to protest further.

"She's upstairs in my chamber."

Shaken, disturbed, Elisabeta tried to pull away. Antonio held her tight, his black gaze boring into hers. "She's in this house?" Pushing him away, she demanded, "What sort of trap have you brought me to?"

Antonio grabbed her arm, gentle not forceful as he

turned her to face him. When he spoke, his tone brooked no argument. "Go to see her."

Elisabeta wanted to run away, but the look on his face told her he'd only come after her. There was a flicker in his eyes, she couldn't be sure what it meant, but she slowly nodded. He released her arm and for a heartbeat, she debated fleeing. That wasn't in her nature, and she ascended the staircase. Turning down the hallway, she stopped before Antonio's room, hesitating.

Curiosity warred with fear. Bianca d'Artusio was an unknown player in the game. Antonio seemed to think this meeting was harmless, but Elisabeta wasn't so sure. Bianca could harm her, attack her, have her killed the moment she stepped out of this house and onto her barge.

Curiosity won. Arousal still hummed through her veins, made her thighs slick with need. For Bianca to be in Antonio's private chambers, requesting to see her— Elisabeta opened the door.

Scanning the room, she saw no one. Stepping further in, Elisabeta looked toward the windows, moved in that direction.

"You're as lovely as I imagined you'd be."

The voice drifted from beside the bed. A lovely young woman, dark hair, pale, pale limbs, stood in a gossamer chemise. Her hair hung loose about her shoulders as she walked slowly across the room.

"Antonio asked me to see you," Elisabeta said, lowering her gaze. He'd already slept with the woman, then.

"Your gown is ordinary." Bianca's fingers danced

distastefully over the sleeve. "We shall have to rectify that."

Elisabeta's gaze jerked up, confused by the other woman's words. One nail traced the bodice of her gown, teasing the lace there, but not touching her skin.

Her fingers danced over her breasts, lingering just a moment to cup her chin. Standing through this scrutiny, skin treacherously tingling from where Bianca touched her, Elisabeta waited. Pride kept her eyes on Bianca's, her spine straight, her mouth closed. This woman held money and power, but Elisabeta was from an ancient family and no matter their current situation, that standing had not completely died.

"I can see why Antonio is so taken with you," Bianca whispered, and Elisabeta could see naked lust in her dark gaze. "Your beauty is intoxicating."

One finger lightly traced her breast, circling the mark Antonio had left.

"Hmm, this must be from my betrothed." Her nail scraped delicately over the mark, and Elisabeta suppressed a shiver of need. "And what is *his*," Bianca said, leaning forward, "is *mine*."

So saying, she kissed the exact spot, tongue laving the mark, tasting along the line of her bodice. Elisabeta sucked in a breath, shocked at the feel of another woman's mouth on her. She fisted her hands in her skirts, ashamed, cursing Antonio, and waited.

"I wanted to lay eyes on you myself," Bianca said, straightening.

Elisabeta thought for only a beat and accepted the challenge. She ran the back of her hand over Bianca's cheek, a slightly amused, slightly disdainful smile twisting her lips. "You're quite lovely yourself."

Offering a wicked smile, Bianca took her hand, drawing her closer. Though intrigued, she didn't appreciate Antonio offering her up for his wife. Still—still, she *was* attracted enough to want to indulge. For her own sake, her own passions, to sate her own need that first Antonio, then Bianca, stirred.

"However," she said, taking charge of her own fate in this game, "I'm sure Antonio expects me downstairs."

"Oh." Bianca laughed. "He'll join us shortly. But I convinced him to allow us time together, to get to know one another. After all," she continued, and Elisabeta allowed her to lead them to the bed, "we'll all be in the same household."

Stopping at those words, Elisabeta had only a moment to fully realize them before Bianca tugged at the ties holding her gown. It loosened, falling open to her hips.

"Will we?" Elisabeta asked, but made no attempt to cover herself.

Her nipples were hard, ached for a touch, but she didn't try to cover her breasts, but rather merely watched the other woman. Glancing at the door, shut against inquisitive servants, her attention was brought back to the matter at hand when Bianca pinched her nipple. Desire flooded through her, heating her blood.

"Elisabeta," Bianca said, seriousness replacing arousal for only a beat. "This would be a very beneficial arrangement for you. Don't disappoint me."

Watching her eyes, Elisabeta slowly nodded. Though

Bianca seemed to think she held all the power, Elisabeta knew otherwise. She knew this game all too well. With a soft smile, she complied. "I do not want to disappoint."

"Undress," Bianca commanded, climbing onto the bed.

With careful precision, Elisabeta did so, taking her time to tease the other woman, to slide her sleeves over each shoulder, along her arms, off slim wrists. Down her hips, gathering all her underskirts in one move. Clad only in her silk stockings, garters, and shoes, Elisabeta swayed her hips, walking slowly and gracefully toward the bed.

"Lie on your back." Bianca ordered her, but there was a catch in her throat, and Elisabeta saw her swallow hard, chest heaving.

She heard the door open then. She knew it was Antonio, and that was what Bianca had meant about being the same household. Elisabeta looked at him, a steady gaze that revealed nothing. He gave her an anxious look, there and gone in a heartbeat, replaced by one of pure lust. With an almost imperceptible movement of her eyebrow, she indicated her agreement.

"Further on the bed," Bianca ordered, hands gripping her thighs, but they shook as she removed Elisabeta's shoes.

Turning her attention back to her, Elisabeta did so. The other woman missed the exchange between the lovers, so intent on Elisabeta's body. A warm flush washed over her at that knowledge.

Bending her knees, Bianca rested her feet along the edge of the bed, exposing her. Opening her to Antonio's and Bianca's hungry gazes.

The position intensified Elisabeta's arousal, and she desperately wanted to touch herself, to satisfy this burning need. Breathing hard, she curled her hands into the bedding, but didn't speak. She heard Antonio undress. She knew her lover all too well to think this anything other than what it seemed. This was no trap, but an afternoon of pure sex between the three of them.

Biting her lip on a whimper, she waited. She was not disappointed.

"Only a woman can know all the intimate secrets of another woman," Bianca whispered.

Her hands fluttered along her thighs, one finger slipping into Elisabeta's core. Moving her hips, desperate for more, still she said nothing, tried to breathe. But Bianca's single finger moved in and out, teasing, tormenting her with the feel, with what was to come.

"How to touch her and cause her body to shiver." Bianca leaned over, finger moving leisurely in and out. "I shall teach you how to make me ache for you, as you will for me."

Meeting her eyes at that, hips raising in silent plea, she let herself go. "I already do. I already see what the three of us can enjoy."

It was hard to miss the pleased expression in Bianca's eyes, her smile. Scooting onto the bed, kneeling between her legs, Bianca kissed her. Long, deep, passionate, so very different from Antonio, but utterly gratifying. To her surprise, Elisabeta realized she wanted Bianca, and deepened the kiss.

"It pleases me to hear you speak thus," Bianca whispered.

"It is my desire to please you both," she said, making sure her voice carried to Antonio. So saying, she cupped the back of Bianca's head in one hand and brought her lips back to hers. Tracing Bianca's lips with her tongue, she enjoyed the sensation, the feel of Bianca atop her.

With a gasp, Bianca broke the kiss, only to make her way down her throat, tasting her neck, sucking on her nipples, biting down on one. Elisabeta arched back, bringing Bianca's mouth harder against her. She could feel her orgasm just out of reach, and strained closer, but Bianca would have none of it. She continued down her body, nipping along her hip, swirling her tongue in her belly button, lower.

Bianca's tongue circled her nub, and Elisabeta, so close to the edge, thrust her hips against her face.

She felt Bianca's stiff tongue enter her. Crying out, Elisabeta arched her back, legs wrapping around the other woman's shoulders. Fingers thrust deep into her, Bianca's tongue returned to her nub, flicking it with increasing speed.

Antonio's hand caressed her belly, and Elisabeta opened her eyes. Blinking to clear them, she saw him gaze at her with their familiar hungry expression. Struggling for breath, she arched against Bianca, heart pounding until all she knew was desire. He took her hand, still buried in the bedding, and wrapped it around his hard, thick cock.

Elisabeta, desperate for release, to feel Antonio deep within her, to feel Bianca's mouth on her, scraped her nails over him, saw him shudder, heard him growl so close to the edge himself. The look he gave her was different now as he watched the tableau before him, hand covering hers as he, *as they*, stroked his cock.

She opened her mouth in silent release as her orgasm broke over her, inner muscles tightening around Bianca's fingers as she climaxed. She felt Bianca's tongue continue to stroke her, her fingers pump deep into her body. Her hand tightened on Antonio's cock, but she barely noticed when he moved.

Before her orgasm subsided, before she returned to her senses, Antonio entered her in one hard stroke. Elisabeta struggled to open her eyes, to focus on him. She felt his hands on her thighs, bringing them about his waist as he drove deep into her. Bianca was beside her, turning her head to the side, forcing her gaze upon her.

She kissed her then, and Elisabeta could taste herself on Bianca and licked the other woman's lips. With a satisfied moan, Bianca's fingers pinched her nipples hard, nails scraping the sensitive peaks.

Still Antonio pounded into her. Hard, deep, fast—claiming her, she thought, as he bit her other nipple, sucked her neck. Meeting him thrust for thrust, Elisabeta could feel her orgasm coil tighter, straining for more even as her body accepted this delectable onslaught. His fingers tweaked her nub, teasing for he knew her so well. She was close, so very close, but he refused her this release.

She wanted to beg, but Bianca settled herself over her fingers. The slick heat felt delicious on her hand and Elisabeta curled her fingers within her, causing Bianca to shudder and thrust down hard. She moved in and out of the other woman, even as Bianca guided her movements.

One last pinch from Antonio's talented fingers sent her crashing over the edge. She heard Antonio roar his completion even as the world went white, as she gasped for breath, body shuddering from this luscious assault, craving it. Bianca held her fingers within her body, riding her own wave of pleasure.

The next Elisabeta knew, Antonio collapsed to the bed, one arm draped across her stomach, pulling her close to him as he panted for breath. Opening her eyes, she felt rather than saw Bianca lick her fingers. She wanted to taste her own pleasure again, but before she could retrieve her hand, Bianca had moved.

Lying atop Elisabeta, Bianca pressed her own sex hard against hers. Never letting up, Bianca pushed repeatedly down on her, rocking her hips in hard, even movements. Antonio pinched her nipple, tugging it the way she loved, and before she could stop it, another orgasm exploded through her.

She gasped, hips meeting Bianca's, breasts simultaneously aching for further pleasure and simply aching. Elisabeta didn't stop. She rode her orgasm, and knew Antonio wouldn't release her nipple until she could climax no further, and she didn't want him to. She hungered for this, desired all they did to her and wanted ever more. She didn't want Bianca to stop, wanted to feel everything this woman did, all she wanted to do.

Bianca screamed her release, pressing harder against Elisabeta as she orgasmed, and the feeling was so exquisite, she wanted it to continue. Grinding her hips against the other woman's, Elisabeta grabbed Bianca's derrière, pressing her down harder, wringing every sensation possible. Wanting it all.

When she opened her eyes this time, chest heaving, limbs weak, it was Antonio's fingers soothing her nipple. She turned her head to look at him, smiled and gently kissed him.

"I do not know," Elisabeta said, feeling Bianca curl against her other side, "if I shall survive the two of you."

Antonio offered a deep chuckle, mouth gliding along her throat. Elisabeta clasped his hand with hers, and wondered how he felt about this, if he wanted Bianca. He hadn't touched her, but that meant naught. This was her initiation, she understood that. Loved every minute of it and anticipated further pleasures.

For now, Elisabeta didn't care. Her questions could wait until later. Shifting so her hand caressed Bianca's smooth, rounded hip, she looked at her other lover.

"*Cara mia*, our mistress," Bianca whispered. "This is only the beginning."

Lord Barclay's Seduction

by Em Brown

A mantle of unease settled upon Jonathan Weston the instant he looked up from his cream-and-truffle soup and glimpsed the exquisite form standing in the doorway to the dining hall of Lord and Lady Dancaster. His gaze drank in an intelligent brow, deep enigmatic eyes, and a masterful jaw. It was more than envy of how these features fit in perfect proportion, of a masculine structure blended with enough feminine touches—smoother cheeks and shaped brows—to render the face easy on the eyes, that caused Jonathan to grip his spoon more tightly. The effect was visceral. He felt it deep in his bones, his pulse, his groin. It did not aid his disquiet to hear Lord Dancaster murmur, "Husbands, guard your wives."

Glancing across the dinner table to Genevieve, his wife of a twelvemonth, Jonathan noticed that she was the only one among the ten dinner guests who was not staring in some manner of awe at the newcomer. Instead, she seemed entranced by her soup, in which Jonathan earlier had found nothing of interest despite his best attempts to glean some distraction in his meal while their generous but tedious hostess recounted in excruciating detail her witness of the latest fashion at the court of King Louis XVI.

"Phineas! How delightful that you have come!" Lady Dancaster exclaimed, squealing like a girl half her age as she extended her hand to the man. "But how naughty of you to be late! I shall have to regale you another time of how my trip to Paris was interrupted by the dreadful unrest there."

The responding voice was a smooth low baritone, the feel of velvet made auditory. "How uncharitable of the French proletariat to inconvenience a good Englishwoman in her attempt to acquire the latest offerings of Parisian mercers."

Jonathan marveled at the bland irony with which the statement was delivered. Did the speaker, this Phineas, mean to express his sympathy or his contempt? Or quite possibly both?

Her gaiety unruffled as she accepted a kiss upon her hand, Lady Dancaster turned to her guests. "Now we are assured a merry evening! I think most of you know of my dearest and most beloved cousin, Lord Barclay."

It seemed a collective blush spread itself among the women and a collective frown among the men.

"Your only cousin, madam," the exalted guest clarified.

"Hence, my favorite! Though you have been known to exasperate me at times, such that I am tempted to introduce you as merely a *dear* cousin and not my *dearest*. Do have a seat with us, Phineas."

Though he knew not this cousin of Lady Dancaster, Jonathan found himself hoping this man would not stay. He should never have accepted the Dancasters' invitation to spend a sennight at their country estate. But Genevieve, his young wife, had insisted upon going, lauding the lavish dinners the Dancasters were wont to host, beguiling him with prospects of fox hunting with Lord Dancaster and his fine breed of hounds, and then, when Jonathan remained impassive to these enticements, accusing him of lacking any sense of amusement and threatening to burst into tears for the prospect of boredom might as well have been a death curse to her. As was his custom, Jonathan had relented, hoping the trip would put her in good spirits and that her cheery disposition would continue into the bed chambers.

His hope had faltered early when, after agreeing to the Dancaster invitation, he had attempted to capture her onto his lap. Before his lips could brush her cheek, she had pulled away, declaring with an imperial shake of her golden curls that she had to devote much time to the packing of her portmanteau, for she wished to be prepared for any occasion at the Dancaster estate, and as she could not bring the entirety of her wardrobe, the packing necessitated considerable deliberation. Jonathan had been tempted to declare that he would hire two additional coaches for the sole purpose of relieving her task if she would only do right by her duty as his wife.

"Good sir, is that a fan you carry?" one of the older guests asked once Lord Barclay had taken a seat next to the hostess.

"Indeed," Barclay responded with a trace of hauteur, as if one had to be plebian to even ask.

Overly dressed in embroidered silk, Barclay was dangerously on the order of a popinjay but for the *command* that exuded from his tall and imposing frame. With a flourish, he unfurled his fan, a remarkable article made of mother-of-pearl, decorated in the chinoiserie, and set by a fiery ruby in the rivet. The fan was as ornate as its owner, who sported powdered hair in single curls above the ears and whose cravat was an intricate cascade of ruffles. Even his silk stockings, revealing the most enviable and muscular calves were embroidered down to the silver buckled shoes, polished to perfection.

"Ah, but I think you are unfamiliar to my friends the Smartwoods and the Westons," Lady Dancaster said.

Lord Barclay held up his quizzing glass to inspect the referenced couples. He inclined his head in acknowledgement but dropped his quizzing glass rather quickly, as if finding nothing much of interest. Jonathan had expected the man's gaze to linger appreciatively on Genevieve. It was a boon and a curse to be married to a woman of countenance. He enjoyed the envy of others when they looked upon her, yet wished concurrently to shelter her beauty solely for himself. She was a treasure that prompted vigilance, diminishing the joy one would expect to reap from such a prize. Bothered that he had not received the proper acknowledgement of his achievement, that of having secured a lovely wife, Jonathan decided he would have little to do with this man. Lord Barclay would have to seek *him* if the man wished a better acquaintance.

To Jonathan's dismay, the opportunity to be aloof did not arise as the men retired after dinner to the Dancaster library for a smoke, for Lord Barclay elected not to join them, choosing instead the company of the women in the drawing room.

"Will you not partake?" Jonathan approached Lord Barclay as the party headed out of the dining room. "Lord Dancaster has an exquisite collection of glazed Aldermans."

"I am not much fond of the practice of smoking," Lord Barclay replied, stifling a yawn behind his fan.

"Indeed?"

"I find it hinders the body from performing to its full potential."

What the bloody hell did the man mean by that? Jonathan wondered. But Lord Barclay had moved on, following the women towards the drawing room. Jonathan looked with misgiving between the retreating backs of the ladies, their sloping shoulders made all the more slight when viewed with the broad shoulders of Lord Barclay. Then it seemed that Genevieve turned her head. Jonathan thought it was to look at him, but her gaze met that of Lord Barclay. A moment passed. A moment that was longer than a casual glance.

A cool, imaginary wind blew at the hairs on the back of Jonathan's neck, but he reluctantly followed the men into the library. The tobacco, late of the former Virginia colony, was a fine product, but Jonathan could not enjoy it. His mind dwelled on Lord Barclay. He was not alone, for the subject of conversation quickly turned to that dearest and only cousin of Lady Dancaster.

"Absurd," scoffed one of the older men. "What sort of man carries a fan?"

Jonathan agreed, but Lord Barclay did manage to carry it off with offsetting aplomb. If more of Phineas Barclay existed, Jonathan would not have been surprised if the fan became as common an article for men as the snuffbox.

"He disdains smoking," Jonathan contributed.

"I wonder at times if he is not a woman in man's clothing," Lord Dancaster offered as he poured himself a claret. "My wife will talk to him at length for hours. I could not survive half an hour with her, but Barclay seems adept at her tedious subjects."

It relieved Jonathan to picture Lord Barclay as a woman. He felt less intimidated. In truth, despite the man's elegance, Jonathan was convinced that Lord Barclay was not a man he would wish to cross swords with. He imagined those refined garments would melt away to reveal a most undeniable virility.

Jonathan felt warm. Why was he imagining Lord Barclay without a coat?

"A woman in man's clothing?" Mr. Smartwood grumbled. "You mean a wolf in sheep's clothing."

A murmur of agreement filled the room, then silence as they contemplated the fact that the wolf had been left with a room full of sheep.

"Perhaps we should see if the ladies are interested in a round of whist?" Lord Dancaster suggested.

Another chorus of agreement followed.

Half expecting to enter into a scene of a satyr chasing nymphs, Jonathan found the ladies sitting innocently about the harpsichord, being plied by Lord Barclay with long, swift fingers. His hands stretched firmly to reach impressive chords, then became gentle and controlled to successfully maneuver the trills. Jonathan shook himself from the reverie of watching Lord Barclay's hands. He could not remember ever being so engaged in the bodily part of another man.

The ladies applauded vigorously when Lord Barclay finished the sonata with a flourish. Jonathan went to stand beside Genevieve, staking his claim. The move drew Lord Barclay's attention and it seemed a smile tugged at the corner of his mouth. Jonathan found himself staring into a pair of eyes that were like deep pools of crushed sapphire. Like gems, the eyes possessed an inner fire. Jonathan felt it difficult to swallow and would have pulled at his cravat to relieve the constriction at his throat, but he did not wish to reveal the effect his lordship had had upon him.

Jonathan had had every intention of occupying the superior situation for he had youth, possessed a respectable countenance and form, and the most beautiful woman in the room was his. But when Lord Dancaster announced for the guests to seat themselves for a game of whist, Jonathan found himself at Barclay's side like a puppy seeking the attention of a greater canine.

"I find whist a more suitable game for the ladies," Jonathan stated. "Would you care to join me in Vingt-Un?"

Barclay would be less of a man if he dignified whist over Vingt-Un. Nonetheless, Jonathan felt his heartbeat quicken, for he did not trust that Barclay would indulge the challenge presented. A man who dared to carry a fan about him was not likely to care what others perceived of his manhood. It could also easily be explained that Barclay preferred not the game of whist over Vingt-Un but the company of women over men.

The gaze that his lordship fixed upon Jonathan made him squirm inside. Jonathan could not recall when he last felt such anxiety. Perhaps once. When he was a young lad, he had gone poaching with one of the servant boys, but his father had discovered him. That moment before the wrath and the castigation as he faced his father's smoldering stare was one that made the specter of death charming in comparison.

Instead of seeing anger, however, Jonathan saw a mixture of curiosity and amusement in the eyes before him. Without a word, Barclay inclined his head and, with fan in hand, made a sweeping gesture towards one of the card tables. Jonathan bristled, feeling as if Barclay was about to offer his arm next, as if Jonathan were one of his female prey.

They sat alone, the other men apparently preferring to stay near their wives.

"My wife, Genevieve, is often in the company of Lady Dancaster," Jonathan remarked, watching Lord Barclay shuffle the cards. The man wore an emerald set in gold and a signet bearing his seal. The jewelry, bold but austere compared to the man's garments, hinted at the different shades of character of its owner.

"I wonder that we have not made your acquaintance before," Jonathan added.

"Are you often in her company?" Barclay returned blandly as if he were asking after the weather.

"How am I not?" Jonathan blustered. "She is my wife."

Barclay dealt the cards. "I was referring to Lady Dancaster."

Jonathan colored, feeling foolish at the vehemence of his own reaction. "Yes, of course. I mean, no, I—my wife and Lady Dancaster delight in shopping together."

"You do not care to join them."

"I much prefer to observe a good pugilist. Do you follow the fights of Mendoza?"

"On occasion. But I am neither a stranger to the haberdasher or milliner. I make the time for both manner of pursuits."

Barclay glanced at Jonathan's cards, waiting for direction. Jonathan, whose facing card was a six, nodded. Barclay dealt him an ace.

"Ah, then you are not married," Jonathan said smugly.

"If I were, I should have less time for Mendoza."

With a disgruntled cough, Jonathan turned to look at his cards. They now totaled seven and ten. He nodded for another card before thinking. Barclay raised his brows. *Damn his patronization.* Jonathan nodded more vigorously.

A queen.

He threw up his cards. He took a sip of his sherry as Barclay dispassionately dealt another set of cards, and ventured to ask, "Is that why you choose to remain a bachelor?"

"Odds fish, m'dear. As talented as Mr. Mendoza may be,

I am not willing to have him govern any such important matters of my life."

Jonathan pressed his lips together but could not completely prevent them from forming a pout. The bloody debaucher was toying with his words, making him feel as if he were a boy barely out of the schoolroom.

"I meant . . ."

Was that a smile hovering over the man's lips? Did he mean to provoke with intention? Jonathan envisioned drawing swords with the man, but as he stole a glance at the man's physique, he determined that calling the man out, provided he had even a sound basis for it, would prove a hasty act. He felt an emasculating tug in his groin.

"Perhaps if I met a woman as beautiful as your wife, I would consider altering my state of bachelorhood."

It was the acknowledgement that Jonathan had been waiting for but, being tardy and upon the heels of his prior provocations, provided no satisfaction. It was a scrap thrown in pity to a tiresome mongrel.

"Perhaps," Barclay emphasized as he looked at his cards.

This time Jonathan opted to stay with his hand and fell short. Barclay turned over a card to reveal a pair of jacks.

By the time the evening drew to a close, Jonathan was down a good hundred guineas. Genevieve, who had been observing them from her table, gave him a reproachful shake of the head. Curbing his desire to sulk, Jonathan turned to Barclay.

"Well played, my lord," Jonathan praised and pulled out his purse.

Barclay shook his head and closed Jonathan's hand about the money. "Pray do not. I enjoyed the company far too much to require payment."

Jonathan stared at where Barclay's hand had rested briefly upon his own. He felt he ought to insist but could not find the words. The man's touch had him rattled.

"Odd fellow, this cousin of Lady Dancaster," Jonathan remarked to Genevieve later that night as they settled into their bed.

Genevieve made a noncommittal murmur and turned on her side, away from him. Jonathan pressed his lips together as he studied her, but her body betrayed no emotion.

He hesitated, wanting and loathing to ask the question of his mind. He was damned either way. As it appeared he was not likely to seduce his wife into granting him the favor of her attentions tonight, he decided to speak.

"Had you, er, ever met him before?"

"For what purpose do you ask?" she grumbled.

"He . . . he seemed to recognize you."

There was an agonizing pause. He was relieved when she responded with exasperation. "I am quite fatigued yet you persist in asking inane questions. Perhaps Lord Barclay has seen me before—or mistakes me for another. How am I to know what the man might be thinking?"

If he pursued the matter, he might place her in such a cross disposition for the duration of their stay that he would be unsuccessful securing even a kiss from her. Forcing himself to be satisfied with her response, he turned to extinguish the candle beside him. He slept fitfully as visions of Lord Barclay clouded his mind. He kept recalling the touch. When he awoke in the middle of the night, the bed felt less warm and more spacious.

Genevieve was gone.

The gurgle of laughter from behind closed doors was unmistakably hers. Standing in the hallway, alone but for the flickering shadows cast by the candle held in his trembling hand, Jonathan considered barreling through the door in righteous fury. But the devastation of confirming that he had been made a cuckold was tempered by his curiosity.

He had sensed the worst upon discovering Genevieve missing. *Sans* a robe to cover his nightshirt, he had hurried to the bed chamber of Lord Barclay. Kneeling, he put his eye to the keyhole but could see little in the dimly lit room. With his heart pounding in his head, he slowly turned the door handle and waited. From the sounds on the other side of the door, he surmised they were too engaged to notice. Holding his breath, he pushed the door slightly ajar. He waited for a gasp or cry, though he knew not why he should fear discovery as he was the innocent party.

Peering through the opening, he could see the four-post bed towards the corner of the chamber. Genevieve, her golden hair in disarray upon the bed, writhed beneath Lord Barclay, who had not donned his nightclothes and still wore his shirt and breeches. His cravat, however, had been tossed aside and Jonathan could see the upper ridges of the man's pectorals. Barclay lowered his head into the crook of her neck, making her gasp and moan.

The unfamiliar sounds reverberated in Jonathan's ears and made him flush. He blew out his candle and pushed the door open a little further.

Despite the blow to his pride, he felt a pronounced pulse in his groin as he watched Barclay moving atop his wife. With both her wrists captured in one hand above her head, Barclay began kissing the tops of her milky breasts. Genevieve squirmed in delight. After palming a breast through her corset, his free hand went down to unbutton his breeches. With abated breath, Jonathan stepped into the room. It seemed his heart beat strongest in his crotch. He needed to witness the organ that would make him a cuckold.

The light of the two lamps near the bed did not extend to where he stood. He had the advantage, albeit a bitter one, but he was afforded no glimpse of Lord Barclay's cock. Apparently it was swiftly buried in his wife's quim. Genevieve inhaled sharply, then began a steady moan as Barclay moved in and out of her while his mouth moved about her face and jaw. Jonathan marveled at how the man could continue the rhythmic thrusting of his hips while kissing her with purpose and precision. He took a step closer towards them.

The undulation of Lord Barclay's body was mesmerizing. As elegant as a swan unfurling her wings.

The movements slowed. Genevieve let out a haggard breath. She made an impatient sound, almost like the mewing of a cat. Jonathan had never heard or seen her so flush with desire. What was this strategy that Lord Barclay employed? Did he tease and torment his lovers? Is that what women desired? Genevieve attempted to encourage him by grinding her hips against his.

"Why do you stop?" she asked.

"We are not alone."

Jonathan started. His heart hammered against his ribs. The pair of sapphire eyes pierced through the shadows to find him.

Barclay resumed a languid thrust of his hips. Genevieve attempted to lift her head and follow his gaze, but he kept her body pinned beneath his.

Jonathan swallowed with difficulty, remaining motionless should he be mistaken that Barclay had seen him. Surely if they knew his presence they would be scrambling in shame to cover themselves?

"Not alone?" Genevieve inquired. "What mischief are you at, my lord?"

Her query quickly subsided into delighted murmur as Barclay continued his motions. Jonathan felt numb, trapped between a burning outrage and shame that he could not tear himself away. His blood simmered from an unmistakably prurient interest in what he saw. His cock stirred in evidence.

"Pray tell you do not intend to stand in the shadows the whole night."

Jonathan stiffened. Barclay was gazing down at Genevieve but the statement was directed at *him*. He felt his throat closing.

"Come," Barclay urged. This time he looked Jonathan square in the eyes.

"Hmm?" Genevieve murmured.

"I was speaking to your husband, m'dear."

It was Genevieve's turn to stiffen. She craned her head in his direction, but Jonathan did not move. He could only blink in disbelief. Despite the chill of wearing only his nightgown, he felt his palms begin to perspire.

"Come," Barclay said again.

This time it was less a beckon and more of a command. Jonathan obeyed and took a tentative step towards them. The flush in his body burned to the tips of his ears.

"Wh—" Genevieve gasped.

Was she mortified they had been discovered or indignant that Barclay had extended him an invitation? Jonathan found he did not care.

A faint smile hovered about Barclay's lips. Jonathan stepped into the light, his eyes fixated not on his wife, but his lordship.

Barclay eased off Genevieve and it was then that Jonathan glimpsed a glorious cock, its length stretching heavenward, beautifully proportioned between height and width, sleek and solid as a cannon. The bulbous head capping the shaft made Jonathan's mouth run dry.

Genevieve sat up in obvious panic, drawing her silken robe over her shoulders in fitting embarrassment. Lord Barclay, however, had no such modesty or humiliation. With his cock still protruding in the air as if its presence differed little from that of any other accessory that his lordship might carry—a fan, to wit—Barclay waited until Jonathan stood but an arm's length from the bed. Genevieve opened her mouth but no words came. She pinned an intense stare upon Barclay.

"Tsk, this is not a proper way to welcome your husband," he admonished, pulling Jonathan towards them.

Genevieve's eyes widened.

"Ever tasted of cock meat?"

She stared dumbly.

"Performed fellatio?" Barclay clarified. "I take it not."

"I am no strumpet, my lord," she responded between gritted teeth.

"'Tis a glorious act, not one to be ashamed of. Your husband will delight in it, I assure you."

Jonathan felt his mind reeling with excitement at the thought. And fear. What if Genevieve refused or made some comment sure to sink him further in Lord Barclay's esteem? But when Barclay pushed her head towards his crotch, she made no protest. Jonathan eagerly lifted his nightshirt before Genevieve could gather her wits about her. His own cock had retreated upon first being discovered and now hung in an unimpressive flaccid state. Even erect, it could not compare to the flagpole that Barclay boasted.

As Genevieve neared the wrinkled organ nestled in the patch of his dark brown hair, she hesitated, a look of pained doubt upon her pretty features. Barclay grabbed the penis—Jonathan nearly jumped out of his skin for *no one* had ever touched him there—and guided it into her mouth. His mind was on fire. From the feel of Barclay's hand upon him or the sensation of being enveloped in his wife's warm, wet mouth, he knew not.

"Suck," Barclay instructed, "like a babe at her mother's tit."

Like Jonathan, Genevieve was compelled to oblige his

lordship, albeit clumsily at first. Closing his eyes, Jonathan reveled in the thrilling new sensation. He had not had his cock serviced in such a manner since his first encounter with a naughty scullery maid at Eton. He later learned she had taken the cocks of many of his classmates down her throat. Nonetheless, he recalled her with fondness. To have his own wife encase his shaft in such a manner was beyond exhilarating, especially with Barclay looking on.

Creeping into his enjoyment was the memory of how it felt to have Barclay grasping him. His lordship had not hesitated. Had he been with other *men* before? The thought made his cock stretch. Genevieve made a muffling sound. Jonathan shivered as her tongue grazed his piss-hole. He opened his eyes and saw Barclay observing the two of them, idly stroking his own cock. The sight made Jonathan push himself deeper into Genevieve. She gagged and came off his cock.

They both looked to Barclay for direction.

"Lie down," Barclay instructed Genevieve. She did as he bade. He pulled her skirts above her waist, baring her cunnie, then pulled her knees apart and looked expectantly at Jonathan. "Will you not partake of her, Jonathan?"

His name uttered on that tongue of velvet made Jonathan weak in the knees. He had never heard his name caressed in such a manner. Pushing aside thoughts that Barclay meant to solidify his superiority to Genevieve by proving that Jonathan could not fill a hole enlarged by his lordship's cock, Jonathan knelt before her and cautiously placed his cock in her cunnie. He attempted to roll his hips in the manner of Lord Barclay, but he could tell from the frown upon her brow that he was not achieving the desired effect. He felt his indignation build. *Damn Lord Barclay*. The man meant to show him for a fool.

Circling a hand behind Jonathan's head, Barclay brought Jonathan's ear close to his lips. This time Jonathan felt his heart pounding in its proper place. His nostrils were filled with his lordship's scent. A pleasing scent of musk and charm, tinged with perspiration and arousal.

"Feel her with your cock," Barclay whispered. "Take her for yourself."

The breath sent tremors over the surface of Jonathan's body. The nearness of Barclay made the blood course powerfully through him. And yet he was not near enough. Jonathan dared not move, but his body yearned towards Barclay. His mind could not grasp how or why he had come to be here, a breath away from the man who had been fucking his wife. But he was disinclined to pursue such thoughts. He wanted only to drown in the moment, in the aura of Phineas Barclay.

Without touching him, Barclay's presence pressed against Jonathan like with the weight of a carriage and four. Jonathan felt a heady nervousness not unlike the first time he had lain with a woman. A sigh of equal parts relief and wistfulness escaped him as Barclay began to withdraw.

But Barclay, with fingers still entwined in Jonathan's hair, did not relinquish his hold. His jaw nearly grazed Jonathan, and before Jonathan could decide whether or not he could meet the other man's gaze, Barclay crushed Jonathan's mouth to his own. A blinding current shot through Jonathan, electrifying him to his extremities—his toes, fingertips, and cock. Barclay's mouth differed vastly from the soft yielding lips of a woman. Kissing Genevieve often reminded Jonathan of kissing barely formed gelatin. Barclay had substance and force.

Jonathan allowed himself to sink into the kiss, allowed Barclay's mouth to devour his own. Closing his eyes so he could better focus, he tasted of the burgundy that Barclay must have imbibed earlier. He wanted to melt into Barclay, their mouths forever locked to one another. Barclay's mouth moved over his with a ferocity that Genevieve had never exhibited, claiming his lips and stealing his breath. The blood surged in Jonathan's cock, and when Barclay probed into Jonathan with his tongue, Jonathan could have spent right then.

But Barclay pulled away. Jonathan would have preferred to have been deprived of air. When he opened his eyes, he saw Genevieve gazing up at him in wonder, a lustful blush upon her face. Barclay parted Jonathan from her, then grabbed Jonathan's cock. Jonathan groaned audibly as Barclay eased her wetness off the shaft. Barclay coated his own cock, then pressed a thumb to her clitoris, circling the nub of flesh. Genevieve immediately began to pant and moan. Without breaking his motion, he dipped two fingers into her cunnie and spread the glistening moisture upon his cock before guiding Jonathan's cock back into her folds.

Sufficiently aroused as not to care which cock was in her, Genevieve ground her hips against Jonathan. He wondered at her wanton display but was more curious to see what Barclay would do next. His lordship, who had positioned himself behind Jonathan, put a hand upon his arse, then a finger into his nether hole. Surprised, Jonathan attempted to buck his hips from the intrusion but his motion was hampered by Genevieve.

"Easy, m'dear," Barclay reassured him.

With a shaky breath, Jonathan settled back. Barclay inserted the digit once more. Instinctively, Jonathan clenched about the finger. Once he adjusted to the sensation of having a finger up his arse, he felt a second, stretching his rectum. He grunted, thankful to his wife for having provided the lubricant. The initial discomfort gone, Jonathan enjoyed the sensation of being filled. Barclay removed his fingers, and Jonathan felt the swell of Barclay's cock in their place. Though half terrified at the thought of such a pole stuck up his bum, he allowed Barclay to push into him.

A scream split the room. Jonathan realized he had produced the sound. Sweat broke across his brow at the sharp pain. Gasping, he forced himself to relax his muscles. When the pain subsided, he felt Barclay move and realized that only part of the cock had made its way in. He also realized he wanted all of it. He wanted to be filled with Barclay's thick meat.

Barclay obliged and eased his erection into Jonathan's arse. The sensation of fucking and being fucked was maddeningly glorious. When Barclay began to pump in and out of him, Jonathan found himself buffeted between two waves. His sack boiled. His abdomen clenched. Then his seed blew from his cock, streaming into the heat of his wife's cunnie. His release flowed with the vigor of a rushing river, causing his limbs to spasm. Even when he had spent himself, his thighs continued to quiver. Barclay grabbed him by the hips and rammed home his own climax. Jonathan felt hot liquid splashing into his rectum before he collapsed onto Genevieve.

When he opened his eyes, the dawn was peering in between the curtains. Jonathan sat up with a start upon realizing he was not in his own bed, though the body of his wife lay next to him in the tangled sheets. The memory of all that had happened came flooding into him. *By God, had he been buggered?* The soreness in his arse provided the answer.

"Coffee?"

Lord Barclay, dressed in a resplendent waistcoat and fresh linen, sat in a chair opposite. His hair was combed neatly behind him and his cravat sharply tied. Jonathan was aware of how disorderly he must have looked in comparison. He smoothed back his hair and rose from the bed, accepting the cup Barclay offered.

"Thank you," he mumbled as he took a seat on the other side of the small table.

Genevieve made a sound that resembled a snore.

Barclay smiled. "I have never known her to rise early."

The statement should have infuriated him, but Jonathan felt oddly calm.

"I see you are a lark," Jonathan said.

"I had not planned to stay beyond a night."

"Oh," Jonathan acknowledged, his disappointment palpable. "Lord Dancaster has fine grounds for hunting and a damn impressive breed of foxhounds. Shame to miss a good hunt."

As soon as he spoke, Jonathan realized Barclay most likely preferred a different sort of hunt altogether. He could feel his lordship's gaze upon him and decided to stare into his coffee.

"A shame, indeed," Barclay echoed. "Perhaps I could be persuaded to stay a while."

Jonathan glanced up, a shy smile tugging at his mouth. He no longer dreaded the days he was to spend at the Dancaster estate. And he would look with fondness towards the nights.

The Gentleman's Loving Spy

by K.T. Grant

Two naked men frolicked in the lake as Mrs. Abigail Barlow, the vicar's twenty-eight-year-old widowed daughter, watched with delight. She wasn't as shocked as she thought she would be.

Swimming *sans* clothes was not acceptable in polite society, but since this June of 1826 was warmer than most in English history, a short dip in a body of water to cool the overheated flesh was something Abigail would have enjoyed.

But she was a respected and proper woman, who most of Shobon's society admired, not only because of her role as a dutiful daughter to a well-respected man but because she was thought to be more worldly because of her age and once-married status. A British lady would never find herself in a situation where she would be naked in the great outdoors, unlike the two gentlemen who were doing just that without the slightest care for their reputations. Then again, a proper lady like Abigail should not be hiding behind a large group of shrubbery and spying on naked men, splashing and dunking one another under the clear blue water. It was only the second time she had secretly watched them. Now, she held back a gasp as the darker, more muscular of the two grabbed the paler one by the back of the neck and kissed him full on the lips with enthusiasm.

The last time Abigail had watched, the two men were lying on a blanket under an elm tree close to where she now stood. She was amazed as they took turns kissing and touching each other's cocks in such a way that made the gentlemen groan out loud and discharge a translucent liquid all over their stomachs and flanks.

Abigail's face had turned bright red and she had rushed back home and up into her bedroom, out of breath. It had been so long since she had seen a naked man or engaged in any sexual congress. If only her reform-minded husband had not gone to Manchester seven years ago, where he was killed during a military clash, better known as The Peterloo Massacre.

In the short time she was married, she had loved the press of a naked man on top of her and behind her, thrusting deeply into her womb, hoping a life would be created between them. But that was not the case, and so now she was full of longing for another man to fill her again as her impetuous husband once had.

That was until she had come across the two virile men at the lake.

Surprisingly, she was not disgusted by observing such a queer act, but rather intrigued. Her breasts tingled and the secret spot between her legs throbbed. She took matters into her own hands, lay on her bed and rubbed her woman's center until she found release, wondering what it would feel like to have the two men touch and kiss her, much like the two lovers did to one another at the lakeside.

Now, three days later, Abigail was back, hiding behind the same shrubbery and fanning her heated face as she witnessed another intimate act between the two men.

"Kneel down on the blanket and spread your legs wide," the darker-haired individual ordered as his upper lip curled and he stood with his hands on his hips. Abigail saw that his cock curved slightly to the right. She rested a palm over her heart and let out a small exhale.

"You are not in the mood for my mouth this time, Thom?" The blued-eyed, blond fellow said with a playful smile, and flicked the head of Thom's penis with his finger.

"Later, Halechester. I want to feel your asshole wrapped around my prick." Thom smacked him on the ass and Halechester got down on his hands and knees.

Abigail's eyes went wide at hearing the name Halechester.

No, it could not be!

Gabriel of Paschare, the Earl of Halechester, had passed away last month at the ripe old age of ninety. His grandson was said to inherit the Earl's immense hunting lodge. All of Shobon could not stop talking about the Halechester heir, who was rumored to have striking blue eyes, skin as pale as goat's milk, and a head full of curls much like an angel's.

Abigail's mind spun over the idea that Halechester was

a sodomite. If this was indeed the identity of the man into whose buttocks Thom was jabbing his cock, he would be ruined, regardless of his name and status.

As she moved back to leave, Abigail stepped on a fallen branch and stumbled, crying out loud as she fell to the ground on her rump.

"What the hell was that?" Thom ceased his buggering and pulled out of Halechester's tight ass.

He marched over to where he heard the noise and walked around the leafy shrubbery. He crossed his arms and stared down at Abigail, who was rubbing her ankle.

She looked up and covered her mouth at being discovered.

"Thom?" Halechester walked over and placed a hand on his arm. He looked down at Abigail and held back a smile. Her hair had a leaf or two tangled in her wavy auburn locks. She wiped the dirt from her hands and mumbled under her breath.

"Did anyone ever tell you that it is rude to spy?" Thom leaned down in front of Abigail and gently pulled the dried brown leaves away from her hair.

"I am rude? Spying? Last time I checked, it is rude to walk around naked where anyone can come upon you."

Abigail gave both men a disgusted look and held out her hand. "Please help me up."

Thom lifted an eyebrow and glanced over his shoulder at his friend. Halechester shrugged and walk back to the blanket to pull on his pants. Thom grabbed Abigail by the hand and she stood up and smoothed her peach muslin dress.

Because her eyes were elsewhere, she failed to notice Thom admiring the swell of her cleavage.

"You are a cheeky wench, aren't you?" Thom scratched his chin and before Abigail could respond, he walked back over to the dark plaid blanket where Halechester sat.

"Well, I never!" Abigail wiped any stray dirt away from her shoulders, fluffed out her hair made flat from the humidity, and walked over to the two men. Perhaps a shy and more bashful woman would have run away, but at Abigail's advanced age and life experience, she no longer blushed like some young girl entering society. She had enjoyed the marriage bed immensely and longed to know more. Because she was curious by nature and found herself bored to tears, she wanted to do something exciting and a bit scandalous, such as making conversation with half-dressed men who engaged in what some might consider to be abnormal sexual acts.

Abigail pouted as she noticed that both men had pulled on their pants and fawn-colored shirts. But the sight of Thom laying his head on Halechester's lap as Halechester ruffled his raven curls was not an unwelcome one.

"Why haven't you run away in horror . . . Miss, is it?" Thom turned his head, giving Abigail a bored look.

"I am a widow and not some naïve girl you may think me to be. I suppose a lady would have screamed and ran away to the nearest authority to report this incident. But honestly, I am not shocked or appalled by what I have witnessed here." Abigail pointed at Halechester. "Perhaps I am somewhat taken aback, since he is a very respected heir to an earldom. As for you, I am certain you are his servant or some employee of his lordship."

Halechester tilted his head back and let out a loud laugh. "This is rich. Thom, should I go ahead and tell her who you are?"

Thom patted Halechester's cheek. "Not just yet."

Abigail stomped her foot on a grassy bump and both men looked back at her. "It is very impolite for you to talk to one another and act as if I am not even here." She sat down on the edge of the blanket and spread out her skirt to cover her legs and held out a hand. "As for introductions, I will go first. My name is Abigail Barlow."

Thom sat up and leaned his arm on Halechester's shoulder. "I am Thom and you already know my friend here." He pointed a thumb at Halechester who smiled and took Abigail's hand in his.

"A pleasure, Abigail. My friends call me Gabe, although Thom doesn't." He kissed the top of her knuckles.

"It would not be right for me to call you by your Christian name." Abigail glanced out of the corner of her eye and noticed Thom's frown. She held back a smile at his reaction, somewhat pleased he was annoyed. She wasn't a wicked woman by nature, but the possibility that Thom was jealous because of her was exhilarating.

"I think we have gone way past that, don't you think, since you have seen us both in the buff?" Gabe lifted an eyebrow.

Thom snorted and Abigail gave him an offended look.

"Sir, Thom, or whoever you may be, I find you to be very boorish." Abigail lifted her chin and bestowed upon him a haughty stare.

"I find *you* to be a very saucy, yet blunt lady." Thom winked and lay back down on the blanket with his hands behind his head.

Gabe covered a laugh at Abigail's reaction to Thom's statement and squeezed the hand he still held. Delight was written all over his face. "Abigail, if I may be permitted to call you that, I must ask: why you were watching us behind a bush? Do you enjoy watching naked men swimming and loving one another as Thom and I do?"

Abigail looked down at her lap and shrugged. She knew she should leave and forget everything she had witnessed, but something deep inside of her was telling her to stay.

"Abby?" Gabe slid in closer and tilted her chin up to look at him.

"No one has ever called me Abby before." She blinked as she looked into Gabe's wonderful blue eyes. They were near hypnotic and she suddenly became very drowsy.

"Not even your husband?" Gabe asked softly.

"I was just Abigail to him," she responded and looked away.

"Would you mind if I did call you Abby? It suits you. And I expect you to do the same and call me Gabe and my friend over here, Thom."

"If it pleases you Gabe . . . and Thom." Abigail looked back at Gabe, smiled, and pulled her hand away.

"It will please us *very* much, Abby." Thom leaned up on his elbows and tilted his head to the side. He winked at Abigail again and she pressed a palm over her jumpy stomach.

Thom looked at her hand and his lips twitched as if he

knew how she was reacting to him. *She would be so easy for what he had in mind* . . .

Abigail gave a slight start when Gabe placed a hand on her shoulder. He looked at her, noticing her apprehension. "Forgive me, Abby, but your face is a bit pale, when only a moment ago your cheeks had a wonderful, bright pink color to them. This blasted heat can cause anyone to become faint. Why don't you lie down with us and take a rest? Or if you want, you can take a dip in the lake and we will keep watch so no unscrupulous men can come upon you and try to steal your virtue."

"You are too kind, but I have never swum in a lake to refresh myself, and doing so in front of both of you is a bit awkward since we have only just met. I hope you understand."

Thom sat up and leaned over and gently pushed back a stray piece of hair behind Abigail's ear. She watched silently as he tapped her chin. Her eyes met his and again she felt the pull of sleep tug at her as his brown eyes seemed to almost glow from the specks of gold in his irises. For some reason she could not explain, her nipples had hardened and her stomach clenched.

She dared not look down at her chest to see if her nipples were poking out in embarrassment. She covered a yawn with the back of her hand. "I really should be going." Abigail was interrupted as Gabe picked up her hand and linked his fingers with hers.

"Please stay. I know my request may seem a bit odd, but if you come to think of it, our meeting is a very strange one to begin with."

Abigail licked her lips and looked at both Thom and Gabe. Thom was staring at her in a way she couldn't describe—as if he was ready to take a nap, whereas Gabe gazed at her much like a puppy who whined at the dinner table for a slice of beef.

She lifted her shoulders, then relaxed. The shade under the tree looked inviting, as well as the two men who would keep her company. And since she wasn't expected back at home for another few hours, she could enjoy her time with these two very attractive men who were bound to make the time go by on an otherwise dull afternoon.

"Very well. I do find I need a rest during this time of day because of the heat." Abigail looked around for a spot to lie down when Gabe patted the empty place on the blanket between him and Thom.

"Why don't you lie here? We won't do anything too forward."

Thom lay back down and covered his eyes with his arm. His shirt gaped open. Abigail couldn't help but stare at his muscled chest, and the sprinkling of dark hair she saw through his shirt. His upper body was very different from Gabe's, which had no hair whatsoever.

Abigail climbed in between the two and lay on her back. She placed one hand on her stomach, and her other hand fell to her side. She turned and looked at Gabe, who grabbed hold of the hand closest to him, and rubbed his thumb across her fingers.

"Now we will all close our eyes and take a short rest. Afterward we can chat some more and perhaps take a swim in the lake?"

Abigail's eyes drooped as Gabe looked at her intently. She drifted off to sleep with his hand holding hers and heavy breathing in her ear on her other side from Thom, who watched her with undisguised hunger.

The screech of a bird woke Abigail from her slumber. She moved her head from side to side and opened her eyes when she felt something tickle her bodice. She glanced up and found Thom leaning over her as he drew circles over her chest.

"What are you doing?" she asked, in a hushed whisper. Before Thom responded, she turned to look at Gabe, who had placed his chin on her shoulder. His hand lay on her stomach under her own. He spread his palm out and flexed his fingers.

Abigail exhaled and her heart beat faster as her nerves set in. Thom continued to move his hand across the swell of her cleavage. Her legs shifted to the side. Gabe kissed her under her ear and moved his hand down further near her knee.

"Pl-lease . . ." She whispered again and bit her lip as Thom unlaced the front of her dress.

"Please what? Please stop or please continue?" Gabe asked and moved slightly down to lift up the hem of her skirt.

"Yes, Abby, what would you like us to do? We can stop and you can run along and hide in your bedroom aching for what we can give you, or allow us to make you feel wonderful." Thom placed a wet kiss on her cheek, reached his hand into her chemise, and squeezed her breast.

Abigail's eyes flickered. "We won't tell anyone. It can be our little secret, much like the secrets Gabe and I share," Thomas whispered, then licked her earlobe.

Thom placed more kisses on Abigail's cheek, near the corner of her mouth, but didn't kiss her fully on the lips. She glanced down at Gabe, who now sat near her feet, pulling off her slippers and stockings. She grabbed hold of his hand and permitted him to push her bare legs up until they were bent and the hem of her dress slid down.

"Say yes to the pleasures we can give you, Abby." Gabe placed a kiss on top of her knee and slid the palms of his hands down until his thumbs pressed in between her inner thighs. His eyes had grown bright by her lack of undergarments. She closed her eyes when he pushed her dress up higher until her rust-colored nether curls appeared.

She sobbed as Thom gave her a deep kiss that made her grab him by the back of his neck. She had never been kissed like this before, but Thom's skillful mouth made her push her tongue forward and touch his. He rubbed a thumb over her nipple and flicked it to and fro.

"You must say yes before we can continue," he said against her mouth and slid his face down to press kisses across her collarbone.

Gabe cupped her mound and Abigail bowed her back from the extreme indulgence of it all.

"Yes . . . oh yes." She moaned and turned her head as Thom licked the side of her neck. Gabe's head moved down, nibbling along the inside of her legs. Her hips lifted up as Gabe's warm breath drifted across her curls. When she felt his tongue slither in between her pussy lips, she cried out.

Thom lifted her up in and kissed her again, this time with more passion behind it. His tongue lapped over hers and Abigail grabbed his arms. Gabe positioned his head further against her pussy. She was mindless with yearning at the way Gabe's tongue and mouth seemed to swallow her whole. When his thumb thrust deep inside her, she sat up and broke away from Thom's masterful kissing.

"Come here." Thom growled and lifted Abigail until she sat in his lap, her legs spread open as Gabe continued with his tasting. Thom pulled apart her bodice and scraped his nails over her nipples. Gabe continued to lap away at the juices dripping down from her moist, oversensitive flesh. She spread her legs farther and shared more addicting kisses with Thom.

"Don't leave me!" Abigail shouted when Gabe moved away. She watched as he took off his shirt and stood as he pulled off his pants. His penis jutted out, and even though it wasn't as long as Thom's, it was very thick.

Thom grabbed hold of Abigail's arms and pulled them behind her back as Gabe knelt down and pressed himself against her torso. He shared a few kisses with her and as Abigail panted for breath, he moved his face away from her and reached up and kissed Thom hard.

Both men kissed each other as Abigail watched, unable to move because of the way Thom held her. Gabe gave Thom a deep lick with his tongue across his mouth and looked down at Abigail with heat in his eyes.

He cupped her cheek and placed a kiss on the tip of her

nose. "Will you let me love you further? I want nothing more to stick my prick into your pussy. Can I?"

Abigail was out of breath, panting from need. Thom granted her another open-mouth kiss. Gabe leaned down and sucked one of her breasts into his mouth.

Thom released Abigail's tender and very red mouth. "Will you let me lie behind you and rub my prick up and down your back and ass while Gabe fucks you?"

Abigail had never heard such appalling language before, but their scandalous words caused her to become wetter. All she wanted was more of the kisses and touches these two men were praising upon her person.

"Yes," was all Abigail could say in response. She shrieked when Gabe grabbed her around the waist. She fell forward and straddled his lap. His cock was hard and much like soft velvet against her stomach. When Thom let go of her arms, she reached down and grabbed onto Gabe's cock and stroked him.

Gabe's head fell back on his shoulder. Before he could even situate Abigail to his liking, she sat down on his cock and he slid in.

"Dear God, woman!" he said in a near yell as he landed on his back. He clutched Abigail's arms as she wiggled her hips, taking him in further, her pussy a tight clamp that almost caused him to come right then and there.

"Abby. Are you well?" he asked in concern, pushing away strands of hair that had fallen around her face.

"Yes . . . it has been way too long. Touch me." She panted and grabbed his hands and placed them over her breasts.

She bit her bottom lip and whimpered as Gabe shoved deep inside her. She recalled the mechanics of sexual intercourse, but never remembered feeling this full and breathtaking.

She was so lost in the sensation that she barely noticed Thom behind her. He tugged down the top of her dress and chemise, leaving him naked from the waist up, and moved her forward until her face met Gabe's chest. Thom rubbed his cock up and down her back, leaving a small wet trail on her skin. He licked away his come from her skin and when he and Gabe's eyes met, they both smiled.

Gabe turned until he and Abigail were lying on their sides. He lifted Abigail's leg over his hip and kissed her as he pumped slowly inside her. She wrapped her hands in his hair and kissed him back with abandon. She was so involved in matching Gabe's movements with her own, she didn't acknowledge Thom lying behind her. He pulled her ass cheeks apart and placed his cock there, where he wiggled deep into her crack. Abigail panted against Gabe's mouth as Thom pushed a hand in between them and grabbed hold of Gabe's dick as it slid in and out of Abigail's core.

"Thom, you sly dog." Gabe moaned. Abigail placed her face into the crook of Gabe's shoulder and bit down to stop from screaming,

All three rocked together until Gabe shouted and pulled out of Abigail. She cried out over the loss until Thom pressed her down on her stomach, lifted her flanks over his knees, and took her from behind. She hid her face in the blanket, not caring if the rough fabric left a mark.

Gabe's cries quieted as his release exploded over his stomach. He closed his eyes and his whole body went lax.

"Come for me." Thom slapped Abigail lightly on her ass. Her whole body trembled and, as her inner muscles squeezed his dick, Thom pulled out and came in deep spurts.

Abigail's release wasn't as loud as the men's, but tears fell down her cheek as she twitched and moaned. Her own come slid down the inside of her legs and she fell onto her back to take in some much needed air.

"Oh no." She moaned as Gabe climbed near her hip and dipped his head down to drink from her sweet nectar. She lifted a shaking hand and combed her fingers through his very damp hair as he made her come another time.

When Gabe's thirst has been sated, he laid his cheek on Abigail's hip, enjoying her fingers in his hair. Thom leaned up, wiping his mouth, and moved in between Gabe's legs. He wrapped his mouth around Gabe's cock. Gabe smiled and pumped his hips along with Thom's bobbing mouth.

Abigail could only watch and stare as Thom sucked down hard on Gabe's length. Every so often he would move his mouth and lick around Gabe's sacks that nested among a thatch of dirty blond hair.

Gabe grunted and exploded into Thom's mouth. Some of his come dripped down Thom's chin and he wiped it away. Both men held each other's face and shared a deep kiss. Thom then crawled over to Abigail and gave her a gentler kiss, sharing the taste of Gabe with her.

They broke away and Thom wrapped an arm around her waist and pushed his leg in between hers. Gabe placed his palm over Abigail's stomach and Thom reached out to grab it. As the three lay there panting, they closed their eyes and drifted off to sleep for another much-needed nap where they would regain their strength for more possible mid-afternoon fun.

"I expect you and your father for dinner tomorrow night, Abby. I will send a servant with a note to your house later this evening as an invitation." Gabe held her in an embrace as they waded in the lake. After their rest, Gabe wanted to take another dip, and was able to convince her to join him. She was so inclined when he threw her over his shoulder and dumped her in.

She kissed him sweetly as the lake water dripped down her hair and over her back. Thom remained silent behind her as he floated on his back, looking up at the late afternoon sky.

"If I come, will Thom tell me who he is?" she asked, looking over her shoulder and giving him a sly smile.

He laughed loudly and shook his head and stood upright. She almost reached out to rub her hands over his chest but stopped because of the way Gabe was massaging her own chest.

"Introductions will have to be made, after all, with your father joining his lordship and . . . well, you will find out soon enough." Thom flicked her nose and swam in circles around them.

"If our small dinner goes late into the night, as the host, I would expect you and your father to spend the night . . . for your own well being, that is. You never know when a group of unscrupulous men could come upon you as you ride home and try to steal your virtue."

Abigail swam back a bit and shook her head. "I think I found two such gentlemen who have stolen just that."

"I am only interested in your body for the moment, my lady. We can discuss what else we want from you at a later date." Thom wrapped his arms around Gabe and both men swayed back and forth much like a light breeze.

"What else could you mean? It is not like I have anything else to offer you." Abigail swam toward the shore to get dressed.

Thom looked down at Gabe and gave him a wide smile that showed his very white, but somewhat pointed teeth.

Gabe looked at Abigail as she donned her chemise. He leaned up to whisper into Thom's ear. "She doesn't realize we want her heart and soul as well as her body."

Thom pressed his lips to Gabe and his eyes gave off an almost unnatural twinkle.

"I knew the moment I saw her peeping on us she would be the only woman to satisfy our needs."

"And her father being a vicar is not lost on you?"

"Not at all. Makes her all the riper for the plucking."

"Rightly so, Lu . . . *Thom*." Gabe corrected himself and gave him a quick kiss. He swam away to join Abigail on the shore.

Thom spread out his arms and ran his fingers through the water. A small goldfish swam by him. When he looked down into its eye, the fish blinked, twisted, and floated up to the surface of the lake. Thom lifted his lips into a grin and looked out at Gabe and Abigail, who were holding one another and kissing.

"Gabe, my love, I took your heart and soul long ago and now it is time to steal another's." He chuckled, grabbed the dead fish, and threw it over his shoulder.

With a salute to the sky above, he swam to shore to meet his lover and their future bride.

The Encore

by J. Schrade

Isabella Morganstern pointed one lace-gloved finger. "Stop the wagon here, Aubrey. I'm hot, I'm covered with dust, and there's a beautiful waterfall over there with a pool just right for bathing."

Tired and dusty himself, Aubrey Snipes obediently clucked to the two tired horses, slapped them with the reins, and guided them toward a clump of mesquite trees. He jumped out of the wagon first and helped Bella off the high seat. "Where do you think the Colonel and the rest of the troupe are?"

"I haven't the slightest of ideas," Bella said. "That dust storm was so bad, it's possible they turned around and went right back to Santa Fe."

"Do you think we should go look for them?"

Bella shook her head. "It's getting late. We shall stay here for the night and decide what to do in the morning. Maybe they will find us."

"If they don't show up, we must try to get back to Santa Fe."

She stripped off her huge bonnet and shook out long blond curls. "Worry about that tomorrow, Aubrey. I am going for a swim."

"You really should wait until I take care of the horses. I should check to make sure there are no wild animals lurking in the bushes, and no Indians."

Isabella had joined Colonel James Maplethorpe's company of actors and entertainers a mere week ago, and Aubrey already had her measure. She would not wait for him, and would probably remove all or most of her clothing when she went swimming. Aubrey found her lack of propriety disturbing, her lack of manners disgusting, and her tendency to flirt with anything in cowboy boots annoying. She was nothing but a forward little tart.

Aubrey unhitched the team, pulled off their harnesses, and arranged them neatly on the wagon tongue. He brushed the animals quickly and led them to the creek running out of Bella's swimming pool to drink. Sure enough, the little tramp was already down to her knickers. She caught him staring and smiled. Embarrassed by her blatant display, Aubrey looked away.

"Come on in and swim with me, sweetie," she called. "You absolutely must wish to get rid of all that nasty dust."

Aubrey did want to wash, but not while Bella watched.

After he hobbled the team so they could graze, he gathered soap and a towel out of his trunk and walked back to the pool. Bella was splashing merrily in the water, stark naked. Aubrey took a peek, then turned away. He didn't find her lavish endowments alluring.

His mother had been very strict. He could still see

her iron gray hair pulled into a tight bun and her stern countenance as she lifted her cane and whacked him over and over. "Women are all whores, Aubrey. Don't ever let me catch you looking at one again."

The pool of water was cool and inviting. Aubrey unbuttoned his high-collared shirt, pulled it off, and laid it carefully on a nearby rock. He hunched low so Bella wouldn't see him and make fun of his modesty as he splashed cool water on his face and chest.

The water was refreshing after all the dust and dirt of the long wagon ride from Santa Fe. New Mexico was an inferno. Arizona would probably be worse. They were scheduled to do two shows at the Bird Cage Theatre in Tombstone in a week's time, if they ever found Colonel Maplethorpe and the rest of the troupe.

Suddenly, Bella rose out of the water in front of him. She was like some kind of ancient water nymph, her wet hair streamed down her body to her hips, her pink nipples pert and erect on round, white breasts. Aubrey goggled.

"Come on, Aubrey, don't be such a stick in the mud. Swim with me."

"Naked?"

She giggled. "You will ruin your good pants if you wear them into the water. And that white shirt will never be the same if it gets wet. I didn't bring an iron. Did you?"

No, Aubrey hadn't brought an iron. And he did want to swim. The water he'd splashed on his face had only given him a small taste. He wanted the whole experience. The deep, turquoise water beckoned. The tinkling waterfall was like a siren's call. "Turn around and close your eyes."

Bella was in water covering her hips. She stepped forward and Aubrey saw the curly blond triangle at the junction of her thighs. His face burned as she turned around.

Quickly, before she could turn around and spy on him—she was a capricious wench—he unlaced his half-boots, ripped off his wool pants, and dove into the water.

Bella was after him immediately. She grabbed his foot and pulled him toward her. "Come on, Aubrey, give me a little kiss."

Water streamed down his face from his thick mop of auburn hair. He slung it out of his eyes just as Bella pressed herself against him and pulled his head toward hers. This was not going as Aubrey planned. He wanted to run.

Her hand disappeared under the water. He felt it groping his shriveled manhood.

"Come on, love, what's wrong?" Bella complained. "Don't you like me?"

Buck Jerkins read the signs. A wagon had passed over this hill not too long ago. He stopped his horse, unhooked the canteen from the saddle D ring, took a long swig of lukewarm water, and wiped sweat out of his eyes.

He'd run into a dust storm on the way back to El Paso from his last cattle drive to Santa Fe. He'd lost the trail, was almost out of water, and he was whipped. He stood in the stirrups and stretched. His horse turned his head and stared at him.

"I know you're thirsty too, ole pard. We'll find us some water soon. Looks like a stream running up on those cliffs.

It's gotta make it down here eventually."

Buck spurred his tired horse over the hill. Suddenly, he heard the sound of splashing and female giggles. There must be a pond or a stream over that hill. Satan smelled the water. His ears went forward and he took off at a brisk trot.

When they crested the hill, Buck saw a small waterfall, a wagon, and two draft horses. The horses looked up as he urged Satan closer to the water. He rode right to the pool, stopped, and stared. A man and a woman were cavorting in the water naked.

Laughing, Buck urged Satan into the water. The two cavorters looked up startled. Buck dropped his reins and dove in. "Mind if I join you?"

He stripped off his filthy shirt, his chaps and his pants, and tossed them on the bank, along with his high-topped cowboy boots. Wearing only his hat, he turned to look at the two startled swimmers.

"My name's Buck. What's yours?"

When the cowboy rode right into the water, Bella squealed with delight. She'd given up on getting Aubrey interested. He must like guys, because she'd never had trouble seducing a man before.

The sight of Buck standing in the shallow water with a raging erection had her juices flowing. The cowboy was tall with narrow hips, a chest as wide as the prairie, and long legs. His face was rugged and tan with a square chin and a small nose. He had dark hair pulled back into a tail at his neck, and wore a big handlebar mustache.

She glanced over at Aubrey and gasped. Aubrey was staring at the cowboy like he was a prime cut of meat. His eyes were narrowed and his lips parted. Looking down, she saw Aubrey's shriveled little penis had leaped to attention. She'd guessed correctly. Aubrey liked men.

Buck waded into the water with his arms open. Bella threw herself into them. He picked her up and swung her around, stopped, and looked at Aubrey. "Come on over, young man, I'll take on both of you. Two's company, three's a sandwich, I always say."

The cowboy bent his head and kissed Bella. She opened her mouth, sucking at his tongue. He grabbed her breast and stroked the soft flesh, pulling on the nipple until Bella moaned into his mouth. Her sex was flaming hot and her whole body throbbing.

"What's your name, little girl?"

"Bella," she answered in a breathy voice.

"Mount up, Bella," Buck said. He grabbed her, lifted her out of the water and settled her on his huge organ.

When she felt it slide in, she screamed with delight, and wrapped her legs around Buck's waist. Her legs were instantly pulled away by Aubrey, who pushed close behind Buck to kiss the cowboy's muscular neck. Aubrey wrapped his arms around the cowboy's shoulders and glared at Bella.

When Aubrey saw the tall cowboy standing on the bank with his huge organ swollen and erect, his own bounced up, pulsing against his stomach. His head swam as all his blood rushed into his penis. He saw that trollop Bella leap into the man's arms and his heart plummeted to his feet. When the stranger invited him to participate, he didn't hesitate.

Diving in, Aubrey swam around behind Buck, stood up, and embraced him, his cock pressed against the cowboy's hard, round ass. He glared at Bella over Buck's shoulder and kissed the cowboy's ear, his neck, and throat.

Buck lifted Bella up and down on his dick. Aubrey ignored the tart's screams of delight, ran his hands over Buck's buttocks, and spread them, hunting for the treasure between. He found it and pushed his finger deep into the mouth of the cowboy's anus. Buck groaned and tilted his hips forward so Aubrey could get better access.

Aubrey towed the rutting pair closer to shore, found a good place to sit, and slowly pulled Buck onto his organ. The cowboy allowed Aubrey to penetrate him, even relaxing his anus like he'd done this a million times.

When Aubrey felt his penis slide into Buck's tight asshole, he pressed his face against the wide expanse of the cowboy's back to stifle his scream of pleasure. When he accidentally brushed Bella's breast, he caressed it. After all, they were in this together.

The shallow water sloshed around Aubrey's ass as he pushed Buck up and down on his rod. The cowboy was ramming his dick in and out of Bella faster and faster. Bella moaned rhythmically, a moan for each time Buck rammed his huge cock into her sex.

Aubrey knew he wasn't going to last long. He wrapped his arms around Buck's crotch and felt for his organ. It was slippery with Bella's juice. He touched her pussy when it came down on his hand, and rubbed her opening. He ended up shoving a finger into her just so he could touch Buck's erection. Apparently she liked it, because she screamed and collapsed on the cowboy.

Aubrey thrust three more times and shot his wad, the strength of his orgasm tearing a groan from his constricted throat.

Buck pulled himself away, turned around, and thrust his huge cock at Aubrey. "Suck."

Bella fell into the water beside Aubrey. Together they attacked the cowboy's penis with open mouths. Aubrey licked up one side and Bella the other. Their mouths met at the top and they kissed, Bella's tongue penetrating his mouth. Aubrey eagerly kissed her, then dropped his mouth over the top of Buck's dick. Bella licked the cowboy's stomach and ran her hands slowly up his body to his nipples. She pulled them, then dropped into the water, moving behind Aubrey.

She rubbed herself against his back while he shoved the entire length of Buck's organ in and out of his mouth. Bella squeezed his chest, stroking his nipples while she kissed his neck. Her hands on his nipples felt wonderful. She pulled on the nipples and he felt his cock rising again. She must have sensed it, because she dropped her hands into the water and caressed his erection.

"You have a woody," she whispered into his ear.

Buck held him by the hair and shoved his dick in and out of Aubrey's mouth. He felt the cowboy's organ swelling and knew he was going to shoot off soon.

"Fuck me, Aubrey," Bella whispered.

"Yeah, you have a go at her, boy," Buck said, as he pulled his penis out of Aubrey's mouth and shoved him on top of Bella.

His organ just seem to slide into her. He didn't have time to think about his mother because Buck quickly moved behind him, opened the cheeks of his ass, and thrust that huge cock into his asshole. Now Aubrey was the meat in the sandwich and he discovered he liked it a lot.

Bella was soft and yielding under him. Her breasts pressing against his chest felt incredible. He kissed her willingly for the first time, being the aggressor, he thrust his tongue into her mouth, enjoying the erotic sensations their twining tongues sent straight to his cock.

Buck's huge dick filled him, the lips of his anus stretched to the limit. The cowboy slowly pushed the big organ into him until Aubrey felt Buck's balls lying against his own.

"It's my turn to get some," Buck grunted. He slowly pulled his dick out to the very mouth of Aubrey's asshole, then pushed it back in. Each stroke stretched the tender mouth, giving Aubrey a rush of unbearable pleasure.

Bella's eyes were closed under him. Aubrey pounded into her, so stimulated and excited he could barely stand it. She reached around him, pulled the cheeks of his ass open and ran her hands over both sets of testicles. Buck yelled and shoved himself into Aubrey hard. The cowboy's cock bucked and pulsed deep inside Aubrey. At the same time, he felt Bella's sex grasp him in tiny convulsions. They had both reached their climax.

Aubrey took one more stroke into Bella's tight passage

and let loose with another load, his second in less than an hour.

The three of them lay there for a few minutes, enjoying the rush. Aubrey couldn't believe he'd had a woman. He'd done it. He'd become a man.

Buck groaned and clambered to his feet. "Well, that was fun. What do we do for an encore?"

Bella pushed Aubrey off, and used his body to haul herself upright. She slung her hair over her shoulder. "I usually sing a few bars of *Ta-Ra-Ra-Boom-De-Ay*."

The Loving Homecoming

by Janet Post

"Roy's coming home tomorrow," Jean Anne Touchton said to her best friend, Coral Fox.

Coral slid her hand under the front of Jeannie's chemise and lightly rubbed her nipples.

Jeannie sighed. "That feels so good, sweetie."

When Coral put her arm around Jeannie and drew her closer, they kissed, Jeannie enjoying the feel of Coral's full lips, so soft and tender under her own.

"Will you let me see him again?" Coral asked. "He's so handsome, I just want to look at him."

"Of course you can. We'll eat lunch at the hotel together."

Coral took her hand and stroked the palm with one finger. "I was thinkin' about a little more than lunch. When you're with him, can I be with him, too? You know, all of us together, in bed."

The thought of the three of them together in the same bed, her and Coral and Roy, made Jeannie shiver with delight. She loved Roy, but she and Coral were together every day while Roy was off with his band of outlaws. She'd heard his gang was wanted for bank robbery and murder. He was a dark and dangerous man, but he fascinated her.

"He's not a customer, Coral. He's special, but he's not easy. He's pretty rough around the edges. I don't know if he'd want to, you know, be with the both of us at the same time."

"I've never enjoyed being with a man, Jeannie. My brothers got me started early and they scared me. I might be more comfortable if you were there. I might even like it."

"I'll ask," Jeannie said.

Coral leaned over and pulled Jeannie's chemise down, revealing cone-shaped breasts with plump pink points. She ran her hands over them slowly, then pinched each nipple, tugging on them until they swelled in her fingers and tingled unbearably.

Jeannie opened and closed her legs. The rough horse-hair of the loveseat prickled her buttocks through the thin cotton of her white pantalets. Her mind was going numb as Coral's knowledgeable hands teased her. When her friend slid one hand under the waistband of her bloomers, she stood up. "Weather's stormin'. I think this evening's over."

As they walked through the house's parlor, dodging the many love seats, wing chairs, and small tables, Madame Francine, owner and operator of Francine's Sporting House, spotted them from her office. "You all finished for the night?"

Jeannie waved. "It's stormin' somethin' fierce out there, Frannie. Ain't a body with any sense gonna go out in that mess."

Frannie nodded. "Go ahead on, then. I'll see you girls in the morning." She winked. "Don't do nothing I wouldn't do."

Laughing gaily, the girls climbed the stairs arm in arm. When they got to Jeannie's room, they pushed through the door still giggling and fell into bed.

"Let me take off your stockings," Coral said.

"All right, darlin'." Jeannie lifted one leg and Coral tugged the black garter slowly off her thigh. She held it up for a moment, examining the tiny pink rosettes. Then she ran her hands up and down Jeannie's thighs, pushing her pantaloons higher so she could reach under them and brush her fingers across Jeannie's sex. Then she slowly rolled the black silk stocking down Jeannie's leg.

"You have the most beautiful legs," she said, holding the stocking up.

"Be careful with those. I only have two pair. Roy gave them to me."

"I wish I had silk. I have to wear these old cotton ones."

Coral picked up her other leg, removed the garter and slowly rolled the stocking down. She took Jeannie's foot and rubbed it. "Such lovely feet, nice high arches. I've got these big old clodhoppers."

Jeannie sat up and pulled Coral into a tight embrace. "Darlin', don't ever cut yourself down." She pushed Coral's robe off her wide shoulders and untied the ribbons of her chemise. "You have the most beautiful breasts I ever saw."

She lifted the creamy, white globes and kissed the succulent flesh. Coral's breasts heaved as she took a deep breath. Jeannie licked the left nipple, then sucked the delicate rose point into her mouth. Coral grabbed her hair and moaned.

Jeanie pushed Coral's pantalettes down and fell to the floor with her face buried in the woman-scented flesh. Penetrating the swelling lips with her tongue, she found Coral's ripe clitoris and sucked. Jeannie knew her friend's body. It only took a few minutes of sucking and driving two fingers into Coral's opening to bring her to a groaning climax.

"I'm getting into bed," Jeannie said after Coral tenderly kissed her. "I'm so tired and Roy will be here in the morning. I can hardly wait."

"Do you want me to sleep here with you like always, or go to my room?"

"I don't know, darlin'." Jeannie shrugged, then smiled. "Stay with me. I'd never get to sleep if you left."

They crawled into the big bed and snuggled close to each other. Coral was bigger, so she held Jeannie.

"You want me to pleasure you?" Coral whispered into her ear.

"No, darlin', I'm too tired. Just hold me."

Jeannie woke up about four hours later to sun streaming in the window of her bedroom and someone banging on the door.

"Jean Anne, let me in."

"It's Roy," Jeannie hissed into Coral's ear.

Coral's voice quivered. "What do I do?"

"Climb out the window." Jeannie raced to the window, threw it open, and helped Coral climb out on the balcony. "Knock on Maybelle's window. She'll let you in."

Jeannie shivered as she slid the window shut. The wind blowing down Main Street in Carson City was freezing. She ran to the door and flung it open. Roy picked her up in his strong arms and swung her around.

Spurs clanking, he carried her into the room and slammed the door shut with one kick. "I missed you," he said, rubbing his goatee on her chest.

"Stop, Roy, you'll give me a rug burn." Jeannie giggled.

"Get your ass into bed, girl, I been thinkin' bout you for forty miles."

Jeannie fell onto the bed, squirmed up to the top and propped herself up on a bank of pillows to watch Roy undress.

Roy hung his hat on the rack attached to the back of the door, then pulled his wool shirt off. He wore his black hair cut short. His chest was wide and his hips narrow. His arms were heavily muscled from a life working with horses. He clanked over to the bed and sat next to her.

"Boots."

She scrambled around and grabbed his left boot. He put his right boot on her rump and pushed. She yanked his high-topped riding boot off as she flew forward. When she grabbed his right boot, he put his stockinged foot on her butt and moved it between her legs. "That's what I'm waitin' for."

"Did you get caught in the rain?" she asked as she yanked off the other boot.

"Liked to drown. Me and Rocky were high-tailing it into Silver City when it started stormin'. The weather was so bad we couldn't find Brett and the boys. I decided to shitcan the whole operation and just come here. I been thinkin' bout quitting the life. I already bought me a little ranch in the mountains. I think I'd like to be a peeler."

"What's that?" Jeannie crawled back on the bed to wait for Roy to join her.

Roy flung his hat on the rack on the back of her door and climbed in with her, socks still on. "A peeler breaks horses. I can trap some wild ones up in the hills, break 'em and sell 'em to the army. Hard work, but honest. I got me a hundred acres in the hills north of Silver City."

"You gonna go straight?"

Roy grabbed her hips and yanked her pantalettes down in one move. He knelt over her, his huge erection bumping his stomach. Jeannie wanted to touch it, but sometimes Roy didn't like that.

"For you, sugar, for you."

"Oh, Roy." She sighed.

He lay down next to her and pulled her into his arms. "I love you, Jeannie. I'd do anything for you." He kissed her, gently probing her lips with his tongue. She opened her mouth and let him slide it in. They kissed while he rubbed her breasts. His hands were rough and calloused. Jeannie didn't mind. She arched her back, enjoying his caresses.

"Come into me," she whispered. "I'm ready."

"I been ready for two weeks," he said as he moved her legs open and slipped between them.

He filled her, stretching her opening wide with his huge penis. Groaning, he pushed inside her until his pubic hair rubbed her swollen clitoris. He held her tightly in his strong arms as he stroked.

When Roy made love to her she felt complete. He wrapped her in the cocoon of his love. She could feel it. She'd always hoped he loved her—now she knew for sure and it opened the lock on her heart and allowed it to soar.

His pace increased. She went with him. Holding his powerful buttocks, she squeezed them as she kept pace. Her heart raced as her excitement grew. The bed slammed rhythmically against the wall, the pounding in time with her heartbeat. Roy was nearing his climax. When she opened her eyes, she found him staring at her face. His nostrils were flared and his gaze hot. He bent and kissed her. Their tongues entwined as their bodies strained toward completion.

When her orgasm hit her, she screamed and opened her legs as wide as she could so she could feel him deep inside. He groaned and rammed his cock home twice, then froze. She could feel it pulsing as it spewed his seed.

They lay in each other's arms for a long time after they finished making love. Roy tenderly stroked her back. When she felt able to talk, she remembered Coral.

"Roy, do you remember my friend Coral?"

"The big old redhead?"

"Yeah, that's her. I introduced you the last time you were here."

"What about her?"

Jeannie hesitated. What if Roy got mad?

"What about her, darlin'? She need some help? I got a little extra money."

"No, she was just wondering, I mean she asked me if you'd like to sleep with both of us, you know, together at the same time."

Roy pushed her away and stared into her eyes. His gazed at her with that same hot look she'd seen only moments before. "You're talkin' all of us together in the same bed?"

Jeannie nodded. "Coral and I sleep together every night. We share everything. She said you were pretty and she wanted to be with you, too."

"Sugar, men ain't pretty. We're handsome, or rugged, or good lookin'."

"That's not true, Roy. You're beautiful." She ran her finger over his full lips. They were manly, but soft. He wore a short goatee and a mustache. His eyes were a startling bright blue. "Wanna do it?"

Roy rolled onto his back and folded his arms under his head. Jeannie lay across his chest, idly running her fingers through his happy trail.

He grinned, a lopsided smile that revealed the dimple in his left cheek. "What man wouldn't want two gorgeous women in his bed? You're blond, she's a redhead. What could be better?"

Jeannie leaped out of bed and shrugged on her wrapper. "I'll go get her."

Roy sat up and grabbed her hand. "You sure this ain't gonna make you mad or jealous?"

She flashed him a smile. "Oh no, Roy, I love you and I love Coral. We take care of each other. I'd be so proud to share you with her."

Jeannie ran out of the room and down the hallway. The floral wallpaper was illuminated by two small gaslights high on each side of the wall. She knocked on Coral's door. Her friend answered immediately.

Coral grabbed her hands, her eyes sparkling with excitement. "Did he say yes?"

"Oh Coral, he's going straight. He said he loved me."

"That's wonderful, dear one. Did he say I could join you two? Will he do it?"

Jeannie pulled Coral out of the room and into the hall. "Of course he did. Come on."

The two ran lightly down the hall arm in arm, giggling all the way. Jeannie threw open the door to her room and pulled Coral inside. "Here she is, Roy."

Roy lay on the bed naked. He leaned against the headboard, smoking a small cheroot. "Hey Coral, nice to see you again. Sure you want to romp in the bed with me and Jeannie?"

Coral froze the minute she entered the room. Roy was good looking in his chaps and cowboy hat. Naked, he took her breath away. His tan chest was smooth and hairless. His legs and arms heavily muscled. She could just imagine what they'd feel like wrapped around her body. She was tall, but Roy was taller. His feet reached the end of the bed.

"I'd love it more than anything."

"Jeannie," Roy called from the bed, his voice a husky rasp. "Take her clothes off for me."

Coral's heart raced as Jeannie pushed her satin wrapper off her shoulders. It fell to the floor around her feet. Jeannie untied the strings of her chemise and pushed the sleeves down. When she had it untied, she pulled it off, revealing her breasts. The creamy globes surged out of the white cotton, aching to be touched, the soft pink nipples tender and needy.

"Damn, woman, you got some beautiful tits," Roy said from the bed. "Get them drawers off, Jeannie. I wanna see her pussy. I ain't never seen the pussy of a redheaded *chica*."

Jeannie slid Coral's bloomers down. Coral's heart hammered in her chest, her sex hot and ready to explode. She saw Roy stroke his raging erection and gulped. He was huge. When her bloomers hit the floor, she stepped out of them. Jeannie slipped off her wrapper and they embraced, rubbing their naked bodies together.

Roy leaned forward to get a better look. "Get her on the bed, Jeannie. I got to grab me a handful of them titties."

Jeannie looked into Coral's eyes, tilted her head and smiled. "Ready?" she whispered.

Coral was more than ready. Her sex throbbed with need. She bent and kissed Jeannie. "Oh yeah," she whispered.

Jeannie climbed in bed beside Roy and drew Coral down with her. Coral snuggled up to one side of Roy and Jeannie lay on the other. Roy rolled toward Coral, lifted her breasts, and caressed the swelling flesh with rough hands. He rubbed his palms back and forth across her turgid nipples, sending waves of pleasure straight to her sex. She opened her legs and rubbed her aching flesh on his heavily muscled thigh. She pushed the lips opened so she could chafe her sensitive nub on his leg.

He pulled her on top of his body. As she squatted over Roy, Jeannie reached between her legs and opened her sex. "Isn't she beautiful, Roy?"

"Yes she is. Mount up, darlin'."

Coral knelt over Roy, her legs wide open. He took his cock and spread the lips of her sex with the swollen, red head. It slid back and forth, easily lubricated by her excitement. He moved the head back and forth across her clitoris, making her legs quiver and shake. Jeannie reached up and pulled on her nipples while Roy played with her pussy.

"Look at that red hair," he said, reaching down to grab a handful of her flaming pubic hair. "Her skin's like milk."

Roy grabbed the cheeks of her ass and pulled her onto his dick. Coral moaned with pleasure as his organ penetrated her. She'd never liked being with men before. She'd been too scared. Every day as a whore had been torture. The only thing that kept her going had been Jeannie. Having Jeannie here made her comfortable. She felt able to let go and allow the fear to dissipate and the pleasure to roll through her.

Jeannie climbed around behind her and shoved her body close to Coral's back. Reaching around, Jeannie held her breasts while Roy lifted her up and down on his cock. Jeannie lifted her hair and smothered her neck with sucking kisses while Roy hammered his cock into her.

Coral closed her eyes and floated, completely absorbed with pleasure. When her orgasm hit her, she released her breathe in a long sigh and opened her eyes.

"She's finished, Roy," Jeannie announced. "My turn."

Coral fell to the bed, lying back to watch her best friend in the world impale herself on Roy's cock.

Roy rolled Jeannie under him and flipped her over. "Eat Coral's pussy while I take you from behind," he ordered, his voice rough and thick with passion.

Obediently, Jeannie pushed Coral's legs open and buried her face in flesh already swollen and sensitive. Coral lifted her hips so Jeannie could thrust her tongue and fingers into her wet sex.

Roy knelt behind Jeannie watching. He spread Jeannie's buttocks and shoved his swollen cock into her from behind. Jeannie cried out and stiffened and Coral put her fingers in Jeannie's mouth. "Suck," she ordered.

Jeannie sucked Coral's fingers like a calf on a bottle. New excitement bloomed in Coral as Jeannie nursed on her fingers. Her friend dug stiff hands into her buttocks and arched her back as Roy pounded into her from behind.

The cowboy's nostrils flared and he closed his blue eyes. Coral could feel his arousal. It fueled her own. She was hot as a pistol. Grabbing Jeannie's head, she pulled it to her sex. "Do it," she gasped.

Jeannie licked and sucked her clit, making slurping noises. Roy groaned at each stroke. Jeannie panted and Coral urged her to suck harder. The three of them climaxed at once. Roy howled, Jeannie screamed, and

Coral fell back against the pillows moaning. The three of them collapsed onto the bed in a heap.

"Boy howdy," Roy said when he could talk.

"You're some cowboy," Coral said.

Jeannie was in the middle facing Roy, who held her in his arms. Coral wrapped her arms around Jeannie's back and stroked her breasts.

"Roy's got himself a ranch. He's gonna break wild horses for a livin'." Jeannie said.

"Me and Jeannie are gonna get married. Ain't we, sugar?"

"I don't know, Roy, you didn't ask me yet," Jeannie said. "How can I leave Coral here in this place without me to look after her? I couldn't do it, Roy. I love her as much as I love you."

Tears sprang into Jeannie's eyes. She touched Coral. "I do love you, darlin'."

"I love you, too," Coral said.

Roy lifted Jeannie's chin. "Don't cry, love. There's no need to leave her here. Bring her along. I'd love to have her. We'll make quite a threesome."

Jeannie sat up and pushed Roy's hands off her. "Don't play with me, Roy. Do you mean that?"

Roy pulled them both into his arms. "With all my heart."

"Coral, think you might want to be a rancher's woman?" Jeannie asked.

"As long as you're there with me, I'd love it."

Jeannie leaned over Roy and gave Coral a long, luscious kiss. Roy grabbed Jeannie and kissed her, then kissed

Coral. They fell back on the bed in Roy's strong embrace. Coral's heart sang with love for Jeannie. Her friend would have given up Roy and a normal life to look out for her.

"This is a dream come true," Coral said.

Roy burst out laughing. "You can say that again. Ain't a luckier man in Nevada."

Three on Twelfth

by Jo Atkinson

She had first spied him a few years before the events of 1920, on a stretch of beach in Camden, Maine. He had waded out into the water, his trousers rolled up to his knees, showing a length of leg, athletic and hairy. His shoes and stockings discarded on the beach at an appreciable distance from the crash of the waves, the man stood with arms folded, his dark hair swept out of its normal neatness, flat against his head, by the ocean breeze. Vincent never could tell if he was really there or simply a figment of her growing imagination. She did, however, remember him turning away from the vast blue traveling from the rocky coastline to the limit of the horizon and meeting her gaze. Though only for a matter of seconds, the connection was instant and more than enough to possess her.

His eyes, the richest gemstone shade of green, matched hers. The man smiled, or at least she believed he had, and something within her ignited. She smiled back before turning away and continuing on to the tiny rented house she shared with her mother and two sisters. Aware of every step and a kind of fire burning deep within her, she wondered if she'd been struck by madness, conveyed to her across the distance by the gentleman's eyes. When she turned back, he was gone, as were his shoes and socks, but a trail of footprints marked the ground in addition to her own.

She hastened back to the cottage, thinking her life depended upon reaching her room and, in particular, her clunky typewriter with its keys that routinely stuck and its lumbering carriage. The memory of the man on the beach made her pulse race and launched electric shivers through her core.

Vincent typed. Every clack of the keys heightened her discomfort. The poem's draft, her first since graduating Vassar, culminated with the arrival of the most powerful orgasm she'd ever experienced.

From that afternoon forward, whenever the poet Edna St. Vincent Millay invited another warm body to join her for a passionate tumble, there would be at least three bodies in the room: herself; whatever tasty distraction eager to know the brilliant young writer, whether man or woman; and him, the handsome brute with the gemstone-green eyes, who tended to trail her like a shadow.

She imagined that he, the muse, spoke with a properly austere British accent, and by the time of Vincent's relocation to New York City, so did she. Her sisters, already fuming over Vincent's sudden literary celebrity while they toiled at menial jobs, found this latest ruse particularly galling. The crowd at the party held in Hardwick Nevins' home in Greenwich Village, however, was bewitched by the magnificent creature newly arrived to the publishing world's capital.

It was nearly midnight when the young, crisply attired man spotted her across the room, and he was instantly smitten. The vision, with her bobbed red hair and vibrant emerald gaze, had arrived late to Hardwick's party. She reclined on the divan in a jaunty pose, wearing a flattering and colorful batik-print dress. A cigarette dangled from the long, thin fingers of one hand. The other held a glass filled with orange blossoms, the preferred drink of the night. The poet was beautiful, though not in the conventional manner. Her looks, thought the young man, bordered on the supernatural. She had cast her spell and captured his heart, he realized.

And not only he, if the look on his assistant's face was any indication.

The two men approached her, one trailing a step behind the other. The invisible fire that had burned within Vincent's core since that day on the beach in Camden surged sharply, its tongues licking at her most sensitive flesh. The party's host, one of the many Princeton Brahmins scattered about, had begged her to recite verse and the crowd, recognizing her new celebrity, had listened intently to every word, seemingly without daring to breathe. Vincent's euphoria at entertaining the room full of strangers with her long throat extended, her head cocked at a coquettish angle, and delivering the words, her lovely words, intensified. The looks on the two men's faces were impossible to misread.

"My name is Edmund Wilson," the first said, taking her elegant fingers in his. "My friends call me Bunny."

"Bunny," she parroted. "What a strange endearment!"

For a terrible instant, Bunny worried she was mocking him, that he appeared in those green eyes as something less of the man who had served proudly as an officer in the Great War. He drew in a breath before responding. The fragrance of magnolias reached him through the veil of cigarette smoke. Unlike the Chypre perfume that Mrs. Dorothy Parker seemed determined to drench herself in daily at the Condé Nast offices, the poet's scent was subtle, more intoxicating than the bathtub gin being swallowed everywhere one turned.

Lightning fast, he added to his introduction, "I am the editor of *Vanity Fair*."

Bunny. He was attractive enough, this man. So was his friend, who hovered with a ridiculous grin on his face and likely an erection in his trousers. The chemical lust igniting in Vincent's core, sending crackles of hunger into her blood, worsened at his revelation. He was the editor of a publication she desperately wanted to be showcased in. Now that was a thing!

Bunny introduced his friend as John Peale Bishop, his assistant at the magazine. He, too, interested her. Since that day on the beach, Vincent's sexual appetite had grown to voracious proportions. Rivaling her desire to bed the two men, perhaps even together, was her wish to get her latest masterpiece, "Dead Music—An Elegy," published in the July 1920 issue of *Vanity Fair*.

"Might you have the time for a drink?" Bunny asked.

"Or two?" This from John Bishop, the other Choirboy from Hell, that pet name she'd created on the spot for the lascivious Princeton graduates.

"A drink, and a fuck," she boldly answered, her British accent slipping along with her inhibitions. "Or two."

She saw Bunny's throat knot noticeably under the influence of a heavy swallow. A wicked little smile curled on John's lips. Then, as she imagined what those lips might be capable of, she caught sight of the man with the emerald eyes, hovering in a smoky corner of the room, arms folded, his green gaze locked disapprovingly upon her.

Embarrassment sliced through Vincent's joy. She glanced away, feeling her own grin flattening.

"About that drink," Bunny said, taking her elbow.

Vincent glanced back in the direction of her muse, only he had vanished into the wisps of cigarette smoke hanging wraithlike over the celebration.

Vincent loved men. Women as well on the not-rare occasion, those delightfully impressionable flappers, but most times it was the surety of a hard cock grinding in and out of her pussy that satisfied her needs best.

She led Bunny over to the bed, her moves as elegant and convincing as the fake accent that had enraptured all of the partygoers. Long fingers looped around his belt, Vincent heard Bunny choke down a dry swallow. The front of his trousers was a different matter completely: wetness crowned the tent at the front. With very little prompting, she knew she could make him erupt from mere teasing, if she wished to. Had the hour not been so late and her own aching wetness so needful, she would have toyed with her new thing, and enjoyed the act.

Square-jawed, with his hair parted neatly down the middle, it was easy to imagine him in his Army uniform, with all of its buttons and pockets, the trousers tight at the knees but slightly ballooning at both hips. Easy because, despite his ridiculous nickname, Bunny Wilson was a man with a body that was quite exquisitely, very male.

Vincent caressed the muscles of his legs while seated on the edge of the mattress. He growled a happy sound that seemed to start in his stomach. Bunny would soon roar like a lion, she knew, because Vincent was as excellent a lover as she was a writer. So her many readers and lovers routinely told her.

She unfastened his belt buckle and worked his trousers down. The raw, male scent of his excitement teased her next shallow breath. The editor's cock rose proudly before him, thickest at its middle, its lone Cyclops eye glistening with a single, pearly tear. The way his wetness caught in the candle's light briefly captured Vincent's attention, and the words flowed almost as freely as Bunny's excitement. The man obviously adored the poet and her verse, but she sensed it would show very poor manners if she suddenly extricated herself in order to feed a fresh sheet of paper into her typewriter to commit the words to the page.

This time, she resisted and cursed Bunny in silence.

Resigned to following through with this short play

she'd cast herself in, Vincent leaned forward and accepted him between her lips. Bunny's taste ignited on her tongue, pungent yet wonderful. A few deep suckles was all she dared; judging from Bunny's excitement, more and he would explode. Though she doubted there would be much trouble in coaxing his maleness back for a repeat performance, Vincent was already feeling the urge for privacy, because the typewriter was calling to her. It was the usual battle between arousal and aria, chemistry and creativity, that often left her dancing around lovers to satisfy one urge while seeking the privacy required to fulfill the other.

The man with the green eyes, she could almost see him near the window, growing impatient for her. He solidified from the ether, a ghost in the room only she was aware of. Had Bunny not seized her by the chin and leaned down for a kiss, she might not have finished. But the savagery in which he crushed his lips to hers, adding a flick of his tongue and not resenting his own taste, reignited the chemical spark. That a man would willingly enjoy his own musk was both narcissistic and debauched, and Vincent found that single act worthy of further exploration.

She stood long enough for her exquisite dress to fall. Bunny unhooked her stockings. Had he ripped the delicate silk, nothing would have salvaged the night. But they and then her undergarments slipped free with remarkable care, leaving her nude before him.

Vincent relaxed across the bed, assuming a seductive pose with one long leg laid against the other, and only her fluffy thatch of auburn curls exposed to him.

"You are lovely," he sighed, his eyes wide and unblinking.

Bunny licked his lips and set a hand upon her calf. Vincent felt him tremble and loved the authority she wielded over him. The icy-hot flicker inside her skipped through her flesh in concentric waves, much like the surface of the ocean after a stone has been tossed over it. His caresses launched a shiver down her bare skin. Then, using both hands, Bunny spread Vincent's legs.

"Yes," he growled.

Like so many past lovers, she allowed herself to love him, if only for this moment. Smiling, he moved closer, sniffed her public hair, licked at her seam, teasingly at first, and then he feasted.

She knew sleeping with Bunny was a mistake, but he was a mistake the poet often repeated. The same held true for John Bishop who, like Bunny, was convinced he was in love with her. Vincent loved the availability of decent coitus that this new arrangement offered—an arrangement that often had her scrambling to get one man out of her bed in order to freshen up for the other's arrival, not much later. But the only one she was truly, without question, *in* love with was the writing, the muse.

The man with the emerald gaze.

Since Maine, she'd come to think of this handsome hallucination as a male projection of herself. Her very own penis, after a fashion. After all, she did, as Bunny once remarked, take to the bed with all the promiscuity of a man. She was a woman who appreciated another woman's flesh in the carnal sense, which only added to Bunny's assertion.

Her muse was male, all male, filled with a man's possessiveness and drive, not some lithe Greek goddess of yore who pranced about in a flowing Hellenic frock. Her male muse could be a merciless taskmaster, and when she didn't heed his demand to write down the words, the guilt he unleashed was damning.

Not long after, desperate for privacy and a degree of freedom to create, Vincent rented an airy and spacious room in a brownstone on Twelfth Street, one city block away from the hospital she was named in honor of. The building frequently ran low on hot water, but Vincent didn't mind. In those instances when she needed to bathe, she visited Bunny's place, which he shared with numerous male roommates—an added thrill in that she often paraded shamelessly naked before one or more of his fellow Choirboys from Hell, loving the way she tortured them.

What did disturb her was the way the men in her orbit were increasingly falling in love with her, far too easily in her opinion, when all she wanted from them was the joy of a quick orgasm followed even more quickly by her suitors' departure so she could focus on her writing.

She attempted to court the muse at her new digs on Twelfth Street by decorating it with a comfortable daybed, a writing desk, and fresh flowers in the vase sitting beside her typewriter. After winning a prestigious poetry contest, she spent the prize money on elegant, tailored new clothes: an evening gown, shoes with straps, and silk stockings painstakingly embroidered up the front. She posed for him, and the muse rewarded her. Dressed only for him, she set to work and the fragrance of the tea roses on the desk and the cadence of the clacking keys soon worked her into a state of arousal.

Vincent imagined him leaning over her; the breeze spiriting in through the open window, caressing her throat, his breath. The warmth of the afternoon was the heat of his skin. She opened her mouth, unable to suppress a sigh, when an unexpected effulgence of light and energy teased her pussy. The hand gently rubbing her clitoris, opening her outer lips to exploration, was hers, having slipped off the keys. But in her mind it was his. How she loved him.

The poet stroked her sopping flesh. Drawing down the other hand, separating it from the keys, took Herculean effort. The sparks of imaginary electricity that crackled at rubbing the hard points of her nipples only surpassed the stab of fingertips against keys by a minimum of voltage.

Bringing herself pleasure at the typewriter was a routine indulgence. She only wished it would always be enough, and that she didn't need men, men with their cocks and their professing of love, love—true love was the harsh, loud clack of the keys as they struck against the ribbon, forging words and spinning sorcery.

The first flash of her approaching climax tickled Vincent from her throat to her toes. She bit back a moan. Eyes half closed, she thought of the man, the muse personified, standing alone against the crash of the waves on the beach then but now bringing them down upon her with his fingers, his tongue, his cock, his poetry.

Oh, Vincent thought, *the poetry of it all!*

The waves crashed and ebbed, and Vincent's howls burst past her lips. The temperature in her beloved brownstone room seemed to double before a cool breath of breeze stirred the curtains.

"I love you," she whispered.

She imagined him pledging the same in return. In all likelihood, the voice had originated from the street below, ascending to her window on an updraft of summer air. But she chose to believe otherwise, for the muse owned her heart.

Words flowed and so did Vincent's resentment of the men she took to her bed. The latest in a growing list of enamored suitors was Llewelyn Powys, a British writer known as 'Lulu' among his peers. Lulu, like Bunny, was convinced that Vincent and only Vincent was the woman for him, and he pursued her like a subservient puppy dog. This provided convenient opportunities to scratch that particular itch when she craved a quick tumble across the daybed, but when she wanted to be left alone to write, to court the muse, Lulu's clinging presence led to words shouted in a different sort of verse.

She, Bunny, and John Bishop were dining at the Algonquin—the 'Gonk', as it was known affectionately among the members of the Round Table—when she caught the muse's forlorn gaze from a corner of the dining room. She was distracted by Bunny's increasingly sexual advances from beneath the table, which had started with the tip of his shoe caressing her ankle but had grown to include his hand on her outer thigh. The brush of John's fingers across the opposite length of her leg when he pretended to drop his napkin worked her into a frenzied state.

They were both already there, judging by the swells in the fronts of their trousers, which she noticed with darting glances. Her pussy, she imagined, would be damp should she nonchalantly wander her touch between her legs. Wet, and growing wetter. Men and their cocks—she both loved and loathed them. Her stomach was full, thanks to the Gonk's blue plate special, but her hunger for other indulgences grew beyond maddening.

The muse, the writing, called to her, and Vincent knew that if she took one man home to satisfy her starvation, the other at the table would complain until she gave him an equal share of her precious and limited time. More time away from the muse. More distraction.

And then, in a moment of brilliance and *eureka*! the solution came to her. It would satisfy her sexual craving in a way no other tryst before had. In the aftermath, too, the nagging problem of having too many love-starved puppy dogs sniffing around her, demanding to rule her heart, would also be resolved, because they would be forced to reconsider their definitions of true love. At least, where she was concerned.

The best part of the bargain would be less distraction once the dust settled, and more time with her green-eyed ghost. They wouldn't want her heart after this night, only her pussy, and that suited Vincent.

Taking a discreet nip of the foul but potent bathtub gin from John's flask, she said, "Come with me, and make haste. The cool sheets of my bed on Twelfth Street need warming."

Bunny and John exchanged looks.

"Which of us—?" asked John.

"Who?" This from Bunny.

"Both of you. *Now*."

They staggered up the stairs behind her, silent save for the occasional boyish snicker. Though Bunny couldn't speak for his good friend and assistant, John, the hardness in his pants removed most of the urge to carry on like a schoolboy. With every step higher, his erection reminded him of its ache. It pulsed with strange energy, driven to its stiffest condition over the prospect of sexing Vincent with another man and his cock present in the room. At Princeton, he'd engaged in any number of daring adventures among his fellow Brahmins: skinny dipping and racing around the campus *au naturel*, usually after being plied with alcohol.

But knowing Vincent's debauched sexual appetite, catching her scent of flowers and, yes, he swore he could smell her arousal trailing in her wake, he was aware of John's closeness in a way he'd never considered the man. They would be rivals. They always had been for Vincent's affection, he supposed, only before the competition had always taken place in a disconnected style. Soon, they would be rivals in the same room. They would be two cocks, displayed clearly, stiffly, with no secrets left among the competitors.

He cast a glance toward John. The other man's handsomeness struck him more than it ever had before. Curiously, John's eyes were already upon him as though sizing him up in like, only to deflect guiltily a tense second after making contact. They were two cocks, sniffing the air, blindly in pursuit of the poet.

The hot, musky scent of her put a spell over Bunny, and he knew he'd do whatever she asked.

Bunny choked down a swallow, adjusted his erection, and followed Vincent to her front door, those last few steps feeling more like a hike of miles.

The teasing silk of her undergarments added to the thrill of the maneuver. The two men, she knew, would do anything for the chance to fuck her. *Anything*. The dance leading up to that moment was as intoxicating as orange blossom aperitifs and potent as bathtub gin.

If she thought too greatly of the plan, Vincent knew she might suffer the rare orgasm that would crash over her without the benefit of her so much as even touching herself. It had happened before, once in Ohio, during a reading. She'd gazed into the audience, saw Old Green Gaze, and there had been no stopping it from cascading through her. With the power in her voice increasing, the ripples and concentric waves crashed over her, her core igniting with the ever-maddening flickers of icy-hot arousal. The crescendo in her voice, timed perfectly with the final couplet of words, had sent the crowd to its feet in applause, her audience seeming to share in the raw emotion, driven wild by her climax.

The memory put a smile on her lips and, mercifully, tamped down some of her excitement. Enough that she was able to unlock the door, sweep in with a degree of flourish, and invite the two men over to her bed.

They followed, led by their cocks, a pair of erect, wooden entities aimed stiffly forward; divining rods in search of deep, purest water. When they were close enough, she cupped their crotches, one beneath each hand. John moaned. Bunny leaned down and nipped at her mouth with a kiss. This was almost too easy, she thought. Especially when, not to be left out, John lowered too, crushing his mouth over hers even before Bunny had removed his. She kissed back, removing both hands from their tented crotches in order to reach for faces. She guided their mouths together, and the two men found one another while seeking to possess her.

Vincent mewled around their lips. The first step had been effortless. The next might not be, unless she continued the dance as envisioned. She pushed Bunny away.

"You may have my lower half," she said to him, making clear who was in control. She licked her tongue across John's mouth, which elicited a breathless swear. "And you, dear heart, may have the upper."

They undressed her from both ends, Bunny removing her exquisite shoes with the straps, before lifting up her dress, exposing her undergarments. Vincent's crotch sopped with her wetness, source of that bewitching scent.

Bunny handed the dress higher to John, who took over, drawing it over Vincent's shoulders. John then worked at removing the poet's brassière; Bunny, her underpants. Soon, she was naked before them while they both remained clothed. Even so, her state of undress had empowered her. The two men studied her beauty, completely under her spell.

"Magnificent." John sighed.

Bunny's wandering thumb found the button of flesh above her seam and teased it with gentle, flicking revolutions. "None more," he said while dipping his face lower, his mouth replacing his thumb.

Vincent seized in place. Half closing her eyes, she imagined Bunny was her muse, the man with the green gemstones for eyes. It was *his* tongue circling her clitoris, his fingers working open her outer lips for his mouth to devour. When, quite unexpectedly, the wet warmth of a tongue invaded her ass, unleashing fresh chills across the whole of her body, it was his tongue, not Bunny's.

Equally exciting was the attention John showed her upper torso. He suckled the hard points of her breasts with alternating gentleness and savagery. Again, it wasn't John she saw but the muse. The two tongues focused upon stimulating her most sensitive pleasure zones, north and south, quickly brought Vincent to the verge of ecstasy.

Then Bunny ruined the fantasy with his giggling.

"Whatever do you find so amusing, old sport?" John asked.

"I rather suspect that in the case of annexing Vincent, I got the better share."

There's where you're wrong, thought Vincent. She closed her legs, cutting off access to her pussy, and folded her arms, shielding her breasts from John's greedy mouth. Her denial shocked the two men out of their cocky banter.

"I am not a territory, yours for the conquering," she said.

"Come on, Vincent," Bunny attempted.

In spite of her need for their cocks, she shot a frigid stare south and then north. "I find myself growing disinterested by the second," she said coldly.

"No, please," John pleaded. "Vincent, I beg of you."

"Unless, of course, you'd care to stoke my interest . . ."

Then she made it happen.

Getting the men to undress one another started awkwardly, ties and shirts and undershirts falling in piles onto the floor beside her daybed. But as Bunny reached for John's belt, his inhibitions seemed more at ease. He, at least, had resigned himself to the belief that tonight, if he wanted her badly enough, lines were going to be crossed.

He eased John's trousers fully down, leaving his Princeton brother dressed only in his undershorts and stockings. Those came off in the next pass, and John's endowment bobbed stiffly before his lips, its head glistening with excited wetness.

"Kiss it," Vincent commanded.

Bunny's eyebrows knitted together. For a tense moment, she half expected him to balk. But then he did as she wished, and Vincent's smile widened. She slid to her knees on the floor beside him, licked her way across Bunny's cheek and toward his mouth, that beautiful mouth where she tasted the tang of her own pussy and John's excitement. They then passed the standing man's cock back and forth, one sucking it down to the curls before loaning it to the other for a turn.

Reaching up, Vincent tickled John's balls, an action that sent him to the tops of his toes. John liked to be touched there, she already knew from their many past encounters, and his expression was one of utter bliss. But Vincent knew she needed to break him.

"And now," she said, standing.

Vincent guided Bunny onto the bed. She spread his muscular legs, gripped his cock by its base, and waved for John to join her.

"But—"

"Fair's fair," Vincent said.

Reluctantly, John joined her. They kissed once, deeply, before assuming position on either side of Bunny's erection. Every kiss after that was delivered through the excited pulse of the cock between them.

Seeing the two men lavish affection on one another without needing her to prompt them unleashed the last emotion Vincent expected: jealousy. Bunny and John lay on the daybed in a tangle of hair-covered limbs, arms and legs glistening with a patina of fresh perspiration. They faced each other, their eyes locked in a bottled gaze, knowing smiles fixed upon their lips.

She had lowered between their legs to fellate them and was rubbing their cocks together, one's underside against its rival's. But what seemed to be happening was a leap far beyond her intended goal to a place as yet unexplored and, for them, it was obviously an exciting new realm.

To Vincent, this idea of being invisible was far worse than being smothered and too visible.

"Oh, boys," she called in her most seductive voice.

The men broke eye contact and glanced down. Vincent

pressed both of their cocks against her lips and the spell she'd woven around their hearts re-exerted its pull, and it was again like that night in April at the party when they first laid eyes upon her and fell madly, deeply in love.

They took her, one man at either end. Vincent's excitement at getting them to willingly taste such forbidden fruit sustained her through two orgasms.

Later, as the men lay spent and sweating in her lovely daybed's tangled sheets, the robust smell of their male bodies in the warm night air overpowering all traces of perfume and flowers, Vincent slipped out of bed and over to her desk.

Sitting in the dark, she ran her fingertips over the keys and space bar, expecting the electric spark that normally resulted from contact, only it never came. She searched for the man with the green gaze, sweeping her eyes from one corner to the next, but the ghost had vanished.

John stretched in the daybed, settling one arm around Bunny's bare midriff, a surprisingly tender image. Her attempt to gain freedom from them had failed, because she found she craved their devotion for her more than she resented it.

They were still devoted to her, more so because of this night together on Twelfth Street.

Vincent's long, lithe fingers abandoned the typewriter's keys for the night. The poet stood and, feeling numb, she rejoined the two men in her bed.

Casting Couch

by Courtney Sheets

Hollywood, 1935

"You may go in now, Ms. Casey. They're ready for you."

Roxanne Casey nodded and let a faint smile grace her ruby-painted lips in acknowledgement of the receptionist's words. She stood and patted her perfectly bobbed and sleek blond hair to make sure everything was in place. Taking a calming breath, she skimmed her hands down the smooth fabric of her dress. The flapper-style dress was slightly out of style but fit her curvy body like a glove. When her landlady had offered to sell it to her for the audition, Roxanne had jumped at the chance. The shiny gold fabric was exactly what she needed to help make her a star. It had cost her the last of her savings and Roxanne desperately hoped her gamble paid off. She needed this part or she would be forced to crawl back to Kansas with her tail between her legs.

Roxanne came to Hollywood a few years ago, like so many other young women, to be a star on the silver screen. The newness of the motion picture industry had infected the land and Roxanne had been caught up in it, along with everyone else. Despite a depression crippling her hometown, her father had managed to squirrel away enough money to go the picture show once a month. Roxanne had spent hours, the silver light of the protector silhouetted across her face, soaking up the escapades of Douglas Fairbanks or Mary Pickford. She understood, in those stolen moments away from the drudgery of her life, that she was destined to be a star.

A few bit parts and a minor speaking role in a big-budget epic when she had still been under contract at RKO were all she had to show for it, though. Her scenes had ended up on the cutting room floor and her pay stub had included a pink slip that very week.

Cut loose from the studio and with a tiny taste of fame, Roxanne understood she wanted more from Tinsel Town. That was why this audition had to go well. She had to get this part and was willing to do anything necessary to finally see her name in lights.

When a friend who worked at Central Casting called last week about the audition, Roxanne had been ecstatic, if a little weary. The director, Michael St. John, a notorious womanizer and control freak, was casting for the newest creature feature in this booming new industry. It was whispered through the back lots and Hollywood hot spots that St. John could reduce the most hardened studio head to tears and rip the most seasoned actor apart with his poisoned tongue. Roxanne would willingly face St. John's demon reputation if it afforded her a chance to succeed in Hollywood.

If Michael St. John was a demon, Duncan Peters was the devil himself. Peters, known in Hollywood as the man with a million identities, was a brilliant if temperamental actor. His specialty was playing horror villains and scary monsters to absolute perfection. Employing unorthodox make-up techniques, Peters could change his face to suit any part. The man was a genius in creature make-up but there was always an air of mystery surrounding the man. His secretive nature fueled all sorts of wild rumors about that man. No director except St. John would work with him. And many had never seen Duncan Peters without the aid of movie make-up.

Roxanne stared at the white painted door to St. John's office, his name written in black on a plaque tacked to the wood. With one final calming breath, Roxanne knocked lightly. A muffled command sounding incredibly like "enter" answered her knock. Screwing what she hoped was a seductive smile on her crimson-colored lips, she pushed open the door.

"Roxanne, come in. We've been waiting for you." A voice as smooth as melted chocolate greeted her ears before she fully entered the room. Widening her bee-sting plump smile, Roxanne launched herself into the room full force, ready for anything. "Shut the door behind you."

The room was cast in semi-darkness. The large windows that looked out onto the studio back lot were shuttered, blocking out most of the warm California sunshine. Roxanne's kept a slight grip of the door handle as her eyes adjusted to the shift in light.

"Forgive the darkness, Roxanne, but you will be reading with Mr. Peters this afternoon and he prefers it this way," a tall man with wheat-colored hair said as he came to stand near her. She smiled up at him with just the right amount of teeth and vivacity. Roxanne felt the man's hand brush against hers as he shut the door behind them. He placed his palm on the small of her back, the heat from his touch searing through the thin satin of her dress.

"I'm Michael St. John. It's a pleasure to have you audition for us today." His voice was so rich, it ran down Roxanne's limbs like a caress. He was lean, but possessed corded, whiplike muscles. A strong jaw and patrician nose gave him a youthful air. Full lips curled into a half smile completed his features. She idly wondered why, with a voice like that and his boyish good looks, St. John wasn't in front of the camera instead of behind.

"I'm excited to be here," Roxanne said, letting Michael lead her farther into the room. "Is Mr. Peters running late?"

"Over here, my pretty ingénue." Another voice, this one gruff and harsh but no less enticing, filled the air. Roxanne felt her heart beat a little faster in her chest. Something about that voice sent her body on edge in an entirely too seductive a manner. She turned to seek out the voice's source and noticed the silhouette of a man lounging indolently on a large sofa against the far wall of the office. She could make out long lean legs stretched out from the torso and crossed lackadaisically at the ankles. A single arm was bent to allow the man to rest a lone finger against his temple. No matter how hard Roxanne squinted, she could not make out any of Duncan Peters's features in the dim light beyond general shadows and shapes.

"Forgive me, Mr. Peters. I didn't see you over there." Roxanne smiled, hoping to cover any gaffe she might have made with her previous comment.

"Never fear, no harm done. Please call me Duncan." He rose, a languid motion. Roxanne found herself drawn to the man, unable to tear her gaze away from his fluid shadow.

"Thank you, Mr. . . . Duncan." Roxanne felt Michael's hand slide away from her back, but not before his fingertips lightly brushed the rise of her bottom. Roxanne gasped, her shock more at her own suddenly dark desire than the director's roving hands.

"Come over here, my dear. Let's get started. I assume you have had time to peruse the sides we provided?"

Roxanne tore her attention from Duncan's concealed features and back to Michael, who now stood scant inches from the sofa. He held out a hand to her. In a daze, Roxanne crossed the distance and stopped between the two men. She looked down at her feet, not sure where else to look.

"Yes, I've read them," she said, finally looking up into the handsome face of Michael St. John. The director's gaze was heated, with creamy green eyes that resembled jade and drank in her curves hidden beneath her dress. Licking her lips, she turned her eyes to Duncan. This time she could see his features, highlighted by the scant bit of sun oozing through the shuttered blinds.

Where Michael was light, Duncan was dark. Thick, wavy black hair framed his sinfully handsome face, and eyes so dark they belonged on some Arabian prince bored though her. Those fathomless dark eyes devoured her every curve, every dip, every hollow. *Why would he choose to cover such a face under pounds of makeup and appliances?* she wondered. Roxanne inched to run her fingers through the silken strands, cut long in defiance to the standard.

Where Michael was long and lean, Duncan possessed the body of a circus strongman. Thick and heavily muscled, the man looked capable of massive feats of strength. Roxanne licked her lips, her breath coming shallow pants. She fought to control the raging emotions these two men managed to stir up in her.

"Relax, Roxanne. We won't bite you," Duncan said in his gravelly demon's voice.

"Yet." Michael's voice came so close to her ear, she felt his hot breath on her neck. Her gaze flew to the director's face and in that instant when their eyes met, she knew this was not to be any ordinary audition.

And she didn't care. Her body was suddenly on fire for these men. Her blood ran deep through her veins. Moisture, hot and thick, pooled at the juncture of her thighs. Their combined seductive pull drew her closer and she was powerless to stop it.

Michael crossed to the bank of windows lining the office and opened the blinds slightly. A sliver of light filtered through, casting intriguing shadows along the walls of the room, and the occupants.

"Shall we begin?" Duncan asked.

"What do you want me to do?" she asked, her own voice coming out whiskey-soaked and full of promise.

Sinful thoughts attacked her fevered brain. Duncan reached out and snaked an arm around her waist, pulling her lightly against him. She felt Michael's hand touch her shoulder and run a soft path down her back to finally rest near Duncan's hand. The heat from both men's bodies swirled around the trio, caressing up her nerve endings and setting the blood roaring in her ears.

"Kiss me, my pretty ingénue." Duncan brushed a feather-soft kiss to her lips, testing her response to this game. Roxanne let out a tiny gasp. Michael dipped his hand lower until he came in contact with on firm globe of her bottom. He kneaded her flesh and pressed kisses on her bare shoulders. Duncan slanted his lips more fully against her mouth, wetting the seam with his tongue, begging entry. This time she groaned low in her throat, losing herself to the exquisite feel of both men's lips on her body. With his free hand, Duncan skimmed along her front, stopping to cup her breasts and squeeze the lush mound.

"Like that?" Michael purred in her ear, running his tongue along the delicate shell of her ear. He pressed himself more fully against her back, gently grinding his growing erection along the seam of her bottom. Roxanne whimpered as Duncan flicked the pad of his thumb around her tightening nipple. Moisture pooled in the juncture of her thighs, wetting her panties. She had never been so aroused in her life, and by two men. Roxanne knew she should be shocked by her wanton reaction but the prospect of both these men wanting her, using her, only added fuel to the building desires in her.

"Have you ever been fucked by two men, my pretty ingénue?" Duncan asked, breaking free from the kiss. He slid his free hand up her body to cup her other breast, drawing lazy circles around her hardening nipples.

"No." She sighed out her answer, her thoughts too consumed with Michael's hand working its way up her skirt and Duncan's thumb on her nipple. She moaned when Michael's fingers began to caress the bare flesh of her thigh above her stockings. Michael dropped to his knees and pressed kisses to the exposed skin. Duncan bent his head and captured a single nipple between his teeth, sucking the hardened bud through the satin of her dress. Roxanne cried out with uncontrollable pleasure. She felt the cool air of the office lick her skin as Michael slowly began to raise her hemline higher up her body.

"Do you want us to fuck you? How badly do you want this part?" Michael asked, running his tongue under the top of her stocking. The snapping sound of her garter being released brought her back to reality. She did want this part, but more importantly she found she wanted these men and the wicked things they could do to her. Shrugging away from them, she stepped out of their collective embraces.

She took a few steps away and turned back to face them. Michael remained on his knees before the couch, his expression confused. Duncan's sinful face looked amused, with a touch of irony. She met both of their gazes, looking from devil to angel and back again. Wordlessly she reached a hand to the long metal zipper at her back. With a naughty smile on her lips, she tugged it down, the rasping sound echoing through the air. Michael rose from his knees to stand next to Duncan. She pulled the straps of her dress down her arms and freed her shoulders. Before she completely bared her ample breasts to their hungry gazes, a wicked idea took hold of her fevered mind. She kicked off her black peep-toe pumps.

"Before I let you have me, there is something I want you to do for me," Roxanne said, holding the bodice of her dress against her chest like a shield. The two men eyed each other and from the look that passed between them, Roxanne understood she was probably one of the first women to not simply go along with their game.

"What do you want?" Michael asked wearily.

"Kiss each other," Roxanne said, her eyes dancing with unappeased desire. "It will turn me on."

Michael turned to Duncan. The other man's lips curled in amusement. Duncan snaked a hand out and cupped the back of the other man's head. He pulled Michael close and claimed his lips in a crushing kiss. Roxanne's felt heat race though her veins, thick and sweet, pooling at the juncture of her thighs. She watched enraptured as the two men kissed, their groans mixing in the air, sending blood pounding in her ears. The two men ran their hands along each other's bodies, for their own enjoyment as well as Roxanne's. Their tongues parried and Roxanne drank it all in. Duncan rubbed his palm down the placard of Michael's pants, cupping the other man's erection.

She let the dress fall down the length of her body until she stood clad only in her garters, panties, bra, and stockings.

"Very nice. Is it my turn?" Roxanne asked. The two men broke apart and turned glazed expressions to her. Heat flared in Duncan's eyes and Michael's gaze devoured her nearly naked flesh.

"Come here," Duncan demanded. He began fumbling with the buttons on his trousers. Seductively, Roxanne crossed the distance and pushed his hands away. Placing a hand on each hip, she guided him to the sofa. Understanding what she was doing, Duncan knelt on the couch and rocked back on his feet. Roxanne crawled up next to him. Glancing over her shoulder, she sent Michael a come-hither look. His handsome face broke into a knowing smile. He came to kneel behind her on the sofa.

Arching her back, she offered Michael a view of her silk-encased bottom. The loose material of her drawers barely covered her already soaking pussy. While Michael fumbled with the fly of his trousers, Roxanne set to work freeing Duncan's impressive erection from his pants. She slid the zipper down and pushed the garment over his hips. His erection strained against the material of his boxers. Gliding her hand inside the silk, she boldly cupped his hardened cock in her hand. She relished the feel of him against her palm, so thick and hard. Her mouth went dry with the desire to suck him, taste him.

Impatiently she shoved the boxers down, eager to see all of him. Duncan's erection sprang free from the confines and filled her palm to overflowing. She licked the head, enjoying the salty sweet taste of him. Roxanne groaned as Michael ran his hands along the planes of her body, dipping down to cup her breasts in his palms and squeeze her nipples. He pressed his erection against the seam of her bottom, rubbing slightly. She arched back, grinding her against his swollen cock.

"Suck me, my pretty ingénue, while Michael fucks that sweet little pussy from behind," Duncan whispered from above her. Roxanne felt Michael peel her silk drawers down off her bottom. He teased a finger along her opening, slick with desire.

Roxanne's tongue darted out and licked at Duncan's cock again. She moved closer, swirling her tongue around the head. He groaned, a low rumble that told Roxanne he liked that very much. She mewed her own pleasure as Michael worked a finger into her tight channel.

"You're so hot and wet. I can't wait to put my cock inside you." Michael leaned down and gently bit her shoulder. Roxanne cried out against Duncan's cock, her muscles clinching around Michael's finger. She heard Duncan groan with pleasure as she continued to lick his long shaft.

Scooting closer still, Roxanne licked along the base of Duncan's shaft, cupping his balls in one hand. She squeezed, and a moan torn from Duncan's lips was her reward. She fucked Duncan's cock with her mouth while Michael continued to finger her from behind.

"That's a good girl. Climb up here," Duncan said, the moan tearing from his lips. Looking up with confused eyes, she met Duncan's gaze. "I want that pretty pink pussy on my cock while Michael gets your sweet little ass." Understanding dawned on her and forbidden longing snaked through her, making her even wetter.

Michael pulled his fingers from her pussy and worked them over the tight button of her ass, lubricating her with her own juices. Duncan placed his hands on her shoulders and gently pushed her back toward Michael. He slid his lower body down farther on the sofa and reached for her. She crawled up his body with measured care, wanting to draw out the pleasure these men seemed intent on giving her.

When she stradded Duncan's lean hips, Roxanne bent over slightly at the waist, offering her ass to Michael, letting him lubricate her with her own juices. The seduction sensation of his large finger sliding around and in her tight rosebud made her pussy run hot with anticipation. Bracing herself on Duncan's shoulders with both hands, she began to lower herself inch by tantalizing inch down on his cock. They both groaned as his thick length stretched her. Michael took that moment to nudge the tip of his cock into her opening. She cried out, unable to stop herself from doing so at the dual invasion taking control of her body. The intense sensation of fullness was devastating, all encompassing was something she'd never before felt. She met the eyes of Duncan as Michael slid further into her ass.

She started to gyrate back and forth slowly, testing the feel of both men buried deep inside her. The men groaned.

"That's it, Roxanne. Come hard for us." Duncan grunted, slipping his palm down their joined bodies to finger her clit. She threw her head back with a deep moan of pleasure as she swiveled her hips to create the most erotic sensations she had ever experienced in her pussy and her ass. For brief moments only the sounds of their collective moans and labored breathing filled the office as they took their pleasure from each other. Passion flooded through Roxanne's mind and body, sending her closer and closer toward her peak. She closed her eyes and concentrated on the sensations racing through her veins: the feel of Michael's cock, so hard and unyielding; Duncan's erection and her vagina, soft as velvet, wrapped around him.

Whimpering with the building excitement she began to thrust her hips up to meet him, keeping perfect time with the men. Michael slid his hands around her torso to cup her breasts, pinching the nipples slightly. Michael pumped in and out of her tight hole as she continued to ride Duncan's thick cock. The rocking of her hips became more frenzied, meeting Duncan stroke for stroke. She clawed at his shoulders, desperate to hold on to something solid as her orgasm overtook her. Pinpricks of light burst behind her eyes. Her body vibrated with pleasure. Their groans of pleasure mixed with hers as they reached their peak together. Duncan drove deep into her final last time, her muscles milking every last ounce of pleasure from him. Michael came in a hot rush inside her, a guttural cry ripping from his lips before he collapsed spent onto her back.

The three lay tangled in a pile of limbs and sex-dampened bodies for a few moments as they tried to catch their collective breaths.

"Well done, my pretty ingénue," Duncan said in a whisper, his breath teasing the strands of hair against her temple. Michael lifted himself from her body and gently pulled his penis free from her ass. Roxanne sighed and stretched like a contented cat. Languidly she got up from the couch and reached for her dress.

"I must admit that was the most fun at an audition I have ever had," she said, scooping up the dress and stepping into it. Roxanne smiled as she watched Duncan move himself into a seat position and zip up his fly. She licked her lips, thinking of his delicious cock. She slid her arms into the sleeves of her dress. Michael reached over to help her zip up her dress.

"Miss Casey, it is my distinct pleasure to offer you the role," Michael said, wrapping his arms around her waist and pulling her back flush against him. He pressed a soft kiss to the juncture of her neck.

"I accept," she said with a sly giggle. Slowly she untangled herself from Michael's arms and headed toward the door. Reaching for the knob, she turned back and glanced over her shoulder at the two men who had so thoroughly had their way with her. Michael stood by his desk, a satisfied smile painting his lips. Duncan still sat stoic and silent on the couch, but a teasing gleam twinkled in his dark eyes. With one final glance at the two men, Roxanne turned back to the door, ready to make her exit.

"Roxanne." Duncan's voice drew her attention. She turned face and met his gaze, her hand still at the ready on the doorknob.

"Be prepared for lots of research as my leading lady. You will need to spend inordinate amounts of time under my . . . tutelage," Duncan said, a wicked smile pulling his face into a grin. Roxanne felt her breath quicken. She knew exactly what kind of research they would be doing together.

"Looking forward to it," she said with a wink and threw open the door. She was staying in Hollywood after all.

French Kiss

by Cathleen Ross

Paris 1938

Sophie Weston, now undercover as Sophie Vallat, unlocked the door of her Parisian apartment, slipped out of her fitted army jacket, and flicked her beret on the hall stand. With her short black curls, chocolate-colored eyes, and ruby mouth, she looked every inch the French woman she was supposed to be and not the first of the American undercover multilingual code breakers. Living in Paris was everything her French mother had told her it would be, especially the handsome men and in particular her French boyfriend, Henri.

Slipping off her high heels, she froze.

Groans and sighs, followed by phrases in German met her ears. Storming down the corridor, she shoved open her bedroom door. A blond woman licked and touched Henri, who lay on their large bed, his hand stroking her breasts.

"Henri!"

"Sophie, you're early." Henri pushed his black fringe behind his ear.

"What are you doing?"

"Waiting for you. I have a surprise for you. *Ménage a trois*."

A cold shiver ran through her, not only from the shock of seeing her boyfriend with another woman, but it dawned on her that she'd heard Henri speak German, a language he professed not to know.

"Come and learn to please me, Sophie," he urged.

"One man for two women? You think too highly of yourself."

"This is the best sex you can ever have," Henri said. "You don't know what you are missing."

Sophie tuned on her heels and ran.

Massaging her brows, Sophie forced herself to knock on the office door of her commander, Major Philippe Benoit. Fluent in four languages, she had rare skills which were highly prized by her superiors. Was Henri a spy? What had she discussed with him? She struggled to remember their conversations. Would she be in trouble?

"*Entrez.*"

Sophie opened the door, stood to attention, and saluted.

"At ease, Sophie," Major Benoit said.

Major Benoit had dark, short cropped hair and startlingly green eyes. With a hooked nose and wide mouth, he was more sensuous looking than handsome, but there was something about him that attracted her from the moment she had signed on at the base. He looked sensational in his crisp army uniform, but she could barely look him in the eyes. Guilt never sat well on her heart.

She dropped her hand but her shoulders ached with tension as she took in the Major's office and the handsome officer standing next to him. Like her boss, he was dark, with well formed musculature and penetrating eyes that suggested he missed nothing. Every woman in the office had noticed Christian because although handsome, he spoke little and never flirted, unlike the other officers. Some of the ladies even went so far as to suggest he enjoyed men.

Major Benoit extended his arm. "Let me introduce you to Major Christian Du Pres."

Major Du Pres nodded to her.

Sophie nodded in return before turning to Major Beniot. "Sir, I need to report something. A situation . . ." She glanced at Major Du Pres.

"It's fine to talk in front of Christian. He is my eyes and ears."

For some reason the skin around Christian's throat tightened, as if he were embarrassed.

"It's a situation brought on by my own foolishness," she added.

"Sophie?"

"I have done a terrible thing," Sophie confessed, glancing at the wall where cuffs were attached to a metal bar.

Philippe raised his eyebrows, walked around, and stood behind his desk. "I find it hard to imagine you could do something terrible, but I fear we are on the brink of entering a war and that changes a person's character."

She watched as he unbuttoned his jacket and slid it

off, enjoying the breadth of his shoulders and the way his body tapered down to a slim waist and long, sturdy legs. Many times he had offered to show her the sights of Paris, but she'd been involved with Henri, so she had refused.

Fear made her shiver. How often had she discussed the possibility of war with Henri, dropped in little bits of information, news from what she had deciphered?

"I am so ashamed."

Philippe walked in front of the desk and leaned against it. Not for the first time did she think how attractive he was, how strong, how dedicated to his job, yet so stern.

"Are you referring to your friendship with Henri Broissant?"

Major Du Pres colored, folded his arms and turned from her.

Oh, good God in heaven, had they been watching her? "I believe he could be a spy. I heard him speak German. This afternoon I found him ... with a German woman. I ..."

Philippe marched towards her so that when he stopped, he towered over her. "I have watched your pain, Sophie and wished I could take it away from you. We have long suspected Henri Broissant of working for the Germans, which is why we installed peepholes in your apartment."

Sophie gasped. "You spied on Henri and me?"

Philippe nodded, his dark eyes full of desire. "It was necessary."

Christian raised his eyes and met her gaze. For the first time he seemed to be looking at her as if she had her clothes off.

She didn't want to say it and the words left her lips in a whisper. "In my bedroom?"

"You're a very beautiful woman," Philippe said.

"You both watched me?"

The temperature in the room increased. "I sleep naked," she said. "Henri likes me that way."

"He is wasted on a stunning woman like you," Christian said.

Sophie raised her hands to her lips. Christian had the most magical deep voice. He was staring at her with a hunger that raised her blood pressure.

"I've wanted you from the moment you joined this company," Philippe said, his tone husky.

"We've both wanted you," Christian added.

Henri had often urged her to try another woman with him, and she had never seen the appeal of sharing her lover with another woman, but two men . . . especially these two handsome, sexy soldiers at the peak of their fitness.

Philippe tucked his fingers under her chin. His gaze dropped to her lips. "I have arrested that bastard and I intend to make him pay for every humiliation and for every betrayal."

Just then, there was a knock on the door. "*Entrez*," Philippe said.

A soldier walked in, his arm clenching Broissant's. "Strip Broissant and handcuff him to the wall." Philippe indicated a rail which ran along the wall. "He does not deserve the honor of wearing the French uniform."

"Sophie, do something," Henri implored, struggling.

Christian shrugged off his military jacket, strode over,

grabbed Henri, and helped strip him and pin him to the wall so he was soon shackled by the handcuffs. When Broissant was chained to the railing, the soldier saluted and left the room, closing the door behind him.

"I have done more than enough for you, Henri," Sophie said. Soon she became aware of her whole body trembling, until Philippe did something unusual. He took her in his arms and pulled her in close.

"Hush, Sophie, there is nothing to fear. You were not to know he was a traitor. I will see to it that he does not cause you any more pain. Instead, I intend to give you such pleasure you never dreamed of."

She wasn't sure if it was the anger or the protective intensity of Major Philippe, but she knew she wanted him, and she wanted Christian too.

Philippe strode over to Henri and seized him by the throat. "You are aware, Broissant, that we had peepholes in your apartment. I saw you make love to Sophie. On many nights, I observed you did not look to her pleasure. I have decided that part of your punishment will be to see how it is to have me and Major Du Pres pleasure her."

Henri's mouth gaped. "She's beautiful," he said, hungrily eyeing her, "but she doesn't like sex."

"That, I don't believe," Philippe said. He led Sophie to his desk and cleared it. He leaned forward and kissed Sophie, unbuttoning her shirt and loosening her skirt.

Christian knelt and pulled down her long, tight skirt and nylons, flicking them in Henri's direction as if to taunt him.

A ripple of pleasure passed through Sophie at the feel

of two men's hands on her body, kissing her, caressing her, touching her in the most intimate places. When her gaze darted up into Philippe's face, she saw his eyes were gleaming with lust.

Philippe unclipped her bra and slid the straps over her shoulders and down her arms, freeing her breasts. "So beautiful," he said, cupping her breasts. He leaned forward and licked her nipples.

Chained to the wall, Henri groaned.

A short, sharp thrill zinged through her body. Philippe's control of the situation excited her. She wanted him to take her and she wanted Henri to watch. The air bathed her skin so that her nipples, wet from Philippe's tongue, peaked.

Philippe picked her up and sat her on his desk. Spreading her legs wide so Henri could see what he was doing to her, the Major dropped to his knees and buried his face between her legs. He rubbed his cheeks, his lips, his face across her as if he couldn't get enough of her. When his tongue darted between her delicate folds, Sophie gasped.

Christian struggled out of his shirt and trousers, pulled off his boxers and shoes. He rushed over and cupped her breasts, kissing them, first one and then the other.

While Philippe's tongue plundered her sex, she could feel his hands clasping the cheeks of her bottom, drawing her close, tilting her hips forward so she opened up to him. Sophie leaned back onto her elbows and looked at Henri. Already he had an urgent erection but there was no way he could free his hands to satisfy himself.

She rolled her hips and groaned as Philippe's tongue

teased over the bud of her clitoris. Soon her breath came in gasps and her hip movements became jerky. Philippe inserted his fingers deeply into her. She writhed, but Philippe gripped her hips holding tightly, trapping her, licking her until she thought she would die from the pleasure. Never had Henri done this to her with such enthusiasm.

Reaching over, she felt for Christian's cock while he kissed her. It was thick and hard and the thought that this could go on forever, two men pleasuring her, tipped her over the edge. Her body became rigid, her back arched, and her lungs gave out short, sharp gasps of desperation. Her cries rose loud in the space around her until, spent, she slumped, her hands on his shoulders, seeking support.

Philippe unzipped his trousers, pulled out his cock, and guided it into her, thrusting hard until his penis met the top of her womb, and she swore she could feel every ridge, every movement, he filled her so tightly. She'd never experienced a man so big and while it was the most erotic feeling, vulnerability shook her to her very core.

"I can't . . . I can't take this. You are so large," she moaned. She'd never given herself over to lust like this.

"You were meant for me," Philippe said. "Not that fool over there."

"Bastard," Henri moaned. "You took my promotion and you wanted my woman. That is why I worked against you."

"One more word from you and I will cut out your tongue," Philippe said to him.

Pushing her down on the desk, Philippe continued to thrust deeply.

Christian rubbed his cock over her nipples and she turned and licked the sweet pre-come from the head of his penis.

She could feel herself swell as Philippe's cock slid in and out of her, again and again. Her fingernails dug into his shoulders until they left moon-like marks on his crisp shirt. He looked so commanding in his uniform. In the distance she heard Henri moan in misery, but she didn't care.

"Harder," she groaned, thrusting up to get maximum penetration from Philippe until she cried out as waves upon wave of pleasure had her gripping his shoulders and rising to meet his every thrust. She felt him shudder his release and finally he stilled. Kissing her tenderly on the lips, Philippe pushed himself off her.

"*Madamoiselle?*" Christian asked, his face suffused with blood, his eyes desperate with desire.

"More. I want more," she begged. Never had she done anything as exciting as this.

Christian slid into her entrance, filling her, stretching her, and she thought she'd gone to heaven. He grunted and thrust deep, like a man with an urgent need.

Sophie met his rhythm and when Philippe pinched her nipples and suckled on the tender lobes of her ears, she came with a screaming rush until she slumped. Christian followed her with a roar that filled the room. She lay on the desk, languid, exposed, and satisfied in the knowledge that Henri had seen everything.

Walking over and picking up her clothes, Philippe handed them to her.

Sophie reached out and took them, thanking him and smiling at Christian. Inside she felt inexplicably happy. She sat and looked over at Henri only to see tears of frustration roll down his eyes. Lowering her gaze, she saw his cock remained hard and unsatisfied, but she had no sympathy for his crocodile tears.

When she was dressed, she stood on her tiptoes and kissed Philippe full on the mouth, then Christian. She turned to Henri. "*Merci*, Henri. You're right. A threesome is the best sex. Thank you for your advice."

Henri cried out in misery.

Sophie left the room, her head held high.

Tea Time

by Rebecca Leigh

1955

"Did you hear what Betty did?" Carol whispered through the phone line.

"No, what?" June said, breathless with anticipation. Betty was a divorcée who was rumored to have had an affair with a married banker in downtown Mayfield. June had also seen Betty reading medical romance novels while getting her hair done at Zuzu's Salon.

"She flirted with Kathy Johnson's teenage son, right in front of Kathy!" Carol giggled with excitement at telling the naughty nibble to someone who hadn't already heard.

"No."

"Yes. The boy had been working on the lawn and Betty touched his bare chest."

"Scandalous. What did Kathy do?"

"Well, I heard she kicked the harlot out of the house and told her never to come back."

"Amen to that," June agreed. "Are you coming over for

tea later?" June and Carol got together every Wednesday for tea and gossip.

"Yes, and I made fresh chocolate-chip cookies."

"Fabulous."

"Do you mind if I bring a new friend? Her name is Harriet. I met her a couple of days ago at the supermarket."

"Sure, Carol. The more the merrier. See you at two o'clock." June hung up the phone, her ears still buzzing from the latest Pine Street rumor.

June had two hours to finish her daily chores before the girls arrived. Her husband refused to buy her a dishwasher, saying it was a novelty he didn't believe would last, so June washed the morning dishes by hand. She also dusted, vacuumed, and mopped the floors.

She took her job as housewife very seriously. No one could ever come into her home and say it was anything other than spotless and picture perfect. The inside was as immaculate as the outside. Like all the cookie-cutter houses on Pine Street, June's yellow-trimmed home was surrounded by a perfectly manicured green lawn and a white picket fence.

She dressed the cherry dining room table with an antique lace cloth her mother had given her when she was a child. She'd kept it in her hope chest until she'd married Eddie. Now she used it only for her weekly luncheons with Carol and special occasions like Thanksgiving and Christmas.

She reached into her hutch and pulled out three sets of her best china teacups and saucers. Usually she and Carol made do with the everyday china, but June wanted to make a good impression on Harriet. The little red roses on the teacups were complemented by the deep maroon color of the table.

At precisely two o'clock, the doorbell rang. June opened the door with a warm smile.

"Carol, so nice to see you," she said, giving her friend a hug and a peck on the cheek.

"June, you look wonderful." Carol turned and motioned to the woman next to her. "This is the friend I told you about, Harriet."

"Hello." Harriet smiled and reached out to shake June's hand.

"Oh, none of that, we are sisters here." June grabbed the woman's hand and pulled her into a tight hug. Harriet's body melted into June's welcoming arms.

"I brought a cherry pie and some whipped cream," Harriet said.

"Thank you, dear." June took the dessert from her and led the two women into the dining room. "Carol, why don't you set your cookies down on the table?"

"Harriet just moved to Mayfield," Carol said.

"Where are you from?" June asked.

"California," Harriet answered.

"What brings you to Ohio?"

"My husband's accounting firm is doing some work for the local bank. We'll be here a couple of years."

"How wonderful." June glanced at Carol and winked. "Carol and I are so glad you agreed to join us for tea. It's always nice to make new friends."

"Yes," Carol agreed.

"Carol told me what fun you two have every Wednesday." Harriet's smile reached all the way to her green eyes as she slowly unwound the green scarf she wore around her neck. Her long brown hair settled over her milk-white shoulders.

"Yes, we do." A whistle sounded from the kitchen. "Tea's ready. I'll be back in a jiffy."

While she was away, Carol and Harriet made themselves at home. June returned a few minutes later, carrying a teakettle. She had made herself more comfortable too.

June's yellow sundress lay neatly folded on the kitchen workshop. She was now naked except for a blue floral print apron that barely covered her voluptuous bosom and ended mid-thigh. The color of the apron accentuated the deep blue of her eyes. She had taken her blond hair out of the bun she'd worn it in to clean, and now her hair fell halfway down her back.

Carol and Harriet both sat on the high-backed cherrywood chairs wearing nothing but their Maidenforms and panties.

"Tea time," June announced and set the kettle on the table. Carol and Harriet both giggled.

June filled all three women's china cups with hot tea.

"May I have some honey?" Harriet asked.

"Certainly." Carol poured a spoonful of the sweet nectar into Harriet's cup but a few drops dribbled onto Harriet's hand. "Oh dear," said Carol.

"Here, let me help." June reached over and cupped Harriet's hand in hers. She lowered her head and gently licked the honey from the side of Harriet's thumb. Harriet shuddered.

"Do you mind?" June asked.

"No." The word left Harriet's mouth with a soft puff of air.

"What if I did this?" Carol said and dripped honey over Harriet's shoulders. Carol used her fingers to smooth the topaz liquid over her new friend's skin. It warmed under the friction and tasted heavenly in Carol's mouth when she licked it up greedily.

"I never knew there were so many uses for honey." Harriet said, her breasts heaving each time Carol stroked her shoulder with her tongue.

"Carol and I have found many uses for honey. This, too," June said, picking up the whipped cream.

June stood up and walked behind Carol. Lifting up the woman's short brown hair, she squeezed the tip of the pressurized can until white foam covered Carol's nape. "Would you like to try some?"

Harriet nodded and leaned over to Carol. She stuck her tongue out and laved up the cream. June joined her, each woman licking Carol's neck until Carol whimpered in pleasure.

"Are you sure you've never done anything like this before?" June asked when her face was barely an inch from Harriet's.

Harriet giggled. "Maybe a little, at camp when I was a teenager."

As Harriet and June lapped the last of the cream, their tongues met. June let out a sigh when Harriet gently jutted her tongue into June's mouth. Harriet's mouth was hot, wet, and sweet. The sensation sent a jolt of desire down June's spine.

Harriet reached one arm around June's head and pulled the woman closer. With the other hand, Harriet deftly untied the bows that held the floral apron around June's neck and waist. The apron fell into a crumpled pile at June's feet.

The tickle of Harriet's fingertips against her skin made June shiver with pleasure. The flames that ignited in her stomach were as powerful as they had ever been with only Carol. June quickly realized that although Harriet may be new to tea time, she was nevertheless a mistress of seduction.

"What's going on back there?" Carol twisted around to find her old friend and her new friend locked in a passionate embrace. "Ooo, don't leave me out."

Carol reached between their bodies and grasped one of June's breasts and one of Harriet's. She rubbed the women's nipples until the soft, pink nubs peaked under her touch.

June's arms wrapped around Harriet's thin waist and she trailed her fingertips down past the small of Harriet's back until they glided over her butt cheeks. Harriet responded by lowering her fingers until they tangled in the nest of blond hair that covered June's pussy. With her other hand, she did the same with Carol's brown bush.

Both Carol and June cried out when Harriet flicked their clits in slow, circular motions. Carol's head fell back and she groaned. "Oh, Harriet. I'm so glad I invited you."

"Me too," Harriet said. She rubbed Carol's labia, then slipped her index finger inside Carol's pussy. "Do you like that?"

"Yes." Carol's face and chest flushed with a light red glow.

Harriet pumped Carol with one finger until Carol's cunt was soaked in her own juices. Carol moved her hips up and down in rhythm with Harriet's hand and her pussy tightened around the manicured finger. When an orgasm finally rippled through her body, Carol's strangled screams filled the dining room.

Feeling June humping the air just above her own pussy, Harriet wasted no time switching from Carol to June. Carol's nectar still coated Harriet's finger when she inserted it into June. June's pussy was tight and gripped firmly around Harriet's finger. Harriet thrust in and out until June's cunt loosed enough to allow Harriet to add a second finger.

June moaned and closed her eyes. She'd never felt pleasure with her husband the way she did at tea time—and she never wanted it to end. Even better than a finger fuck was bringing pleasure to her partner. Normally that partner was Carol. Today it was Harriet.

Her hands splayed over Harriet's buttocks, she gently parted each cheek. Harriet gasped as June's fingertips pressed against her crack. Harriet's tight hole puckered under the pressure.

"Oh God," Harriet said with a hard puff as June gently slowly pushed her finger inside Harriet's anus.

June thrust into Harriet in the same rhythm of Harriet's

finger in her own pussy. The women moaned and their breath pitched. Their thrusts became more urgent and their thighs slapped against each other as a ravenous hunger overwhelmed them.

Still buzzing from her own orgasm, Carol wrapped her mouth first around one of June's breasts, then around Harriet's. She laved her tongue over their soft mounds, lapping up the glistening sweat covering their bodies. Carol nipped each woman's nipples and sucked them like they were cherries from Harriet's cherry pie.

Even though June was on the verge of absolute rapture, she managed to maintain enough control to use the hand that wasn't butt fucking Harriet to caress one of Carol's boobs. Carol's chest was only a size A Maidenform, but her breast fit nicely into the palm of June's hand. She rubbed her thumb over her best friend's nipple and delighted in the feel of the hard kernel between her fingertips.

Surrounded by precious rose-covered china, thin white lace, and cherrywood, June and Harriet brought each other to simultaneous orgasm. That was something else June never experienced with her husband. Even Carol enjoyed a second spasm of pleasure brought on as much by June's and Harriet's screams as June's massage of Carol's breast.

When the afterglow finally subsided, June pulled her hair back into a bun and wrapped the floral apron around her waist.

"Would you ladies like a piece of pie or a cookie?" she said in her sweetest hostess voice.

"Both, please," said Carol, slipping back into her party dress.

"Me too," said Harriet already fully clothed in her capris and angora cardigan.

"Carol, has Harriet met Betty yet? You must tell her about the scandalous thing she did with Kathy's son." June's statement was filled with the same excitement that Carol had experienced earlier in the day at having revealed the rumor to another who had not yet heard.

Carol retold the story while June reheated the kettle and served dessert. The three friends sipped tea and enjoyed each other's company long into the afternoon.

"Same time next week?" June called from her door as Carol and Harriet walked down the stone path that led to the driveway.

"Yes, two o'clock next Wednesday." Carol said.

"May I join you again?" Harriet asked.

"Of course," said June. "You are always welcome."

Carol and Harriet climbed back into Carol's Plymouth and drove away down Pine Street. June smiled to herself, admiring the perfect row of matching houses to each side of her own. Kathy Johnson was walking her dog on the opposite side of the street, and June waved politely before closing her door.

It was four o'clock and her children and husband would be home soon. An hour was just enough time to clean the dishes from tea time and start supper. And long enough to daydream about next week's tea time get-together.

Purple Haze

by Melanie Thompson

Dan and I hadn't seen each other since we graduated from Lee High School in 1964. My name is Jan. Yup, that was us, Dan and Jan all through our senior year of high school. Five years later we bumped into each other unexpectedly at the brand new McDonald's in Springfield. We discovered we'd both applied for and been accepted by the FBI. We were due to report in September for in the same classes. Go figure. We'd been high-school sweethearts and now, after a five-year separation, we'd chosen the same career.

After that first shocking meeting, we dated for a month, and in the face of my mother's stringent objections, moved into a small apartment together. Dan was working for his dad's furniture company and I was working for Ma Bell as a telephone operator under my mother, who was supervisor. I made $2.28 an hour and Dan made three bucks. It was barely enough to pay the rent and feed ourselves, but it didn't matter—we'd taken care of our future.

One night after making love, I was enjoying a few moments of post-coital bliss when Dan reached into the drawer of the bedside table and pulled out what I immediately recognized as a doobie.

I bolted into a sitting position. "What are you thinking? That's marijuana, the killer weed."

"Relax, Jan, it's just grass. It won't hurt you."

He lit it and inhaled a huge lungful of smoke. The pungent aroma filled the bedroom. "Take a hit, babe. You'll like it if you try it."

"We're FBI agents, Dan. You're crazy."

"Know your enemy, I always say. How can we understand the people we're hunting if we haven't experienced what makes them tick?"

He took another drag off the bulging joint and handed it to me. "Come on, it'll loosen you up."

I didn't want to smoke pot but I loved Dan and if he said it was a good thing to do, all of my mother's years of training told me I should listen. Mom believed my father was a god and if he said jump, she asked how high.

"Okay." I took the joint, looked at it for a moment, stuck it in my mouth, and inhaled my first lungful of the killer weed. "Harsh," I gasped.

For the next few minutes the only noise in the bedroom was inhaling and an occasional barking cough. Before long a bubble of happiness lodged in my chest and I was incredibly horny.

Dan ginned at me. "You look so cute. I love your long hair. The agency's gonna make you cut it off." He grabbed a long blond length and held it above my nose. "Jan's got a mustache."

We started giggling and couldn't stop. He pulled me

into his strong embrace and tickled me. I thought I was going to pee myself. When he went for the really sensitive spots on the inside of my thighs, I begged him to stop.

"Dan, you'll make me pee," I gasped, then I farted. Couldn't stop it. We'd eaten burgers for dinner.

The fart set him off into hysterics. He blew some raspberries on my boobs then pushed them together and motor-boated them.

I felt his erection against my legs and grabbed it. He moved above me and we were joined. It was the most fun I'd ever had in bed. We rolled around, making love, tickling each other and laughing for an hour. When we climaxed, I saw stars and screamed with the intensity of my orgasm.

"Shhhhhh, Jan, we'll wake the neighbors."

"I couldn't help it. That was wonderful. Where'd you get that stuff?"

"Brother John's contact. It came straight from 'Nam. I heard Mexican weed's not as strong."

"How's he doing out in California?" Dan's brother joined a commune six months ago. He was a member of the Hog Farm.

"He said he and his family are coming to New York for a big rock concert, the Woodstock Music Festival. They're gonna set up a tent and feed the masses organic, vegetarian food."

He propped himself against the headboard and fished in his drawer again, this time pulling out a pair of tickets. "I bought us some tickets. One last fling before we become 'The Man.'"

"You wanna go to a rock concert? I don't know, Dan. Should we? I mean we're the feds."

"Not yet, we aren't. Besides, I wanna see John. We'll drive up in my little sister's VW van. Sherie said I could borrow it. I'll swap her the Fairlane for the weekend."

"That hippie thing? Dan, we'll be stopped by every cop from Virginia to New York."

"We'll be fine and we'll have fun. What could go wrong?"

August fourteenth found us puttering north through Pennsylvania in Sherie's green and white van. She'd bought it already converted into a camper with a small stove, a built-in cooler, and a bed. Dan's Shepherd/Doberman mix hung over the front seat, panting softly. I had the map out, plotting our way along every back road we could find.

The drive was beautiful. We sat close together on the bench seat, the stick shift between my legs. The little engine chugged up the inclines and flew down the other side. I'd never felt so free. When Dan pulled out the hash pipe and crumbled some golden Lebanese hashish into the bowl, I watched him light it with a match, eager to take a hit.

The hash was a lot stronger than marijuana. Before long I was flying high, sailing down the road enjoying the sunny day. But the weather turned dreary when we crossed the New York border.

"Jan, look, some girl's hitchhiking. I'm gonna pick her up. It's about to rain cats and dogs."

"Do you really think we should?"

"You always take the safe road, don't you? Let loose, live a little, let your hair down."

He pulled the van over and I saw the girl was about eighteen and a hippie. She wore a long skirt and a white Mexican tunic covered by a serape. Her hair was tucked under a red French beret. Dan bounced out of the van and ran to help the girl with her pack. He slid the back door open and shoved Duke aside. "Don't mind him, he's a sweetheart," Dan said.

"Far out, dude. I love dogs. Like, you know dog is god spelled backwards."

Dan tossed her pack in and closed the van door behind her.

The hitchhiker settled in the seat with one arm around Duke. "Hi, my name's Rosemary Kravitz, but all my friends call me Sissy." She stuck her hand over the seat and I shook it.

"This is the coolest van. You're so lucky to have it."

Don started the van and pulled out on the road. "Where're you headed?"

"I'm going to the big rock concert in Woodstock, man. There's supposed to be half a million people there. I heard traffic on the roads from New York City is bumper to bumper."

"Half a million, no way," I said. "Dan, that's bigger than most cities."

Dan grinned. "Well, Sissy, you lucked out. We're going to Woodstock, too. You already got your ticket?"

"They're saying nobody's gotta pay. The fences are down and it's free."

"I can't believe the promoters are allowing that to happen," Dan said.

"I know, ain't it groovy?"

Sissy took off the beret and shook out her long black hair. It fell in a wild mane down her back. I could see Dan staring at her in the rearview mirror. She had ivory skin with soft pink highlights and rosebud lips. When she took off the serape, loose double-Ds swayed back and forth under the tunic, nipples high and pointed pressed against the fabric. I gritted my teeth. Sissy was gorgeous.

We smoked some of Dan's golden Lebanese, passing the pipe back and forth across the seat. When Sissy's hand touched mine, she managed to turn every accidental touch into a caress. The higher I got, the more I yearned for her to brush my hand. I kept turning around in my seat to catch a look at her breasts and those nipples. I licked my lips, my mouth dry.

"So, Sissy," Dan asked. "Where you from?"

"Pittsburgh. My dad works in the steel factories and my mother watches soap operas all day. I graduated from high school last year. There's nothing happening in Pittsburgh, dude, nothing. It's a bummer town full of nowhere people. I split last week. After Woodstock, I think I'll hitch a ride to San Francisco and hang with Jefferson Airplane or maybe the Grateful Dead. I'm beautiful, you know." Sissy tossed her hair. "Men want me."

Dan nodded. "I just bet they do."

We pulled over about thirty miles from Bethel, where the dairy farm hosting this monster festival was located. Dan said he was too tired to drive anymore, so we found a deserted dirt road and set up camp for the night. He got a campfire started and I pulled packages of hot dogs out of the cooler. We stuck sticks in them, roasted them over the fire, slathered them with mustard and relish, and scarfed them up, tossing Duke the burnt ones.

The three of us sat on camp stools watching the stars overhead and the flames. As night fell, the temperature dropped. I couldn't stop staring at Sissy. I'd never seen a real person that beautiful. Dan looked, too. I knew he'd notice how gorgeous she was.

Dan got up and began pulling sleeping bags out. Sissy stood with her hands on her hips watching. She crooked her finger at me. "Let's go find the ladies' room."

Giggling, we hiked into the bushes. It was typical August, hot and steamy. "Watch out for snakes," I said.

She grabbed my hand, pulled me behind a bush, and kissed me. My first lesbian kiss. I couldn't believe how soft her lips were, so unlike a man's mouth. Stoned to my eyeballs, I melted against her body. She was taller than me, but slim as a reed. When she wrapped her arms around me, my hands went right for those double-Ds.

The feel and weight of them in my hands was like nothing I'd ever known. I rubbed Sissy's pointed nipples and felt immediate heat flood my groin. This was wrong.

Sadly, I broke the embrace. "I can't. Dan wouldn't like it. We live together, you know."

"We could ask him to join us."

That was a facer. Suddenly, I had to think about Dan in Sissy's hot embrace. After a moment of consideration and another kiss from Sissy, I realized, I couldn't. The whole idea was immoral. My mother would freak.

"I can't. It's wrong, Sissy. Dan and I are a couple. We might get married. Just because we live together and smoke a little grass, doesn't make us into all that free love and sex stuff."

"Whatever you say."

We walked deeper into the bushes, pulled down our panties, and squatted. I almost couldn't go. All I could think about was Sissy's naked sex. I peeked at her and caught a glimpse of her round ass. It was just as beautiful as the rest of her.

We climbed into the van and nestled together in our sleeping bags. The night was cool. When I woke up I was the meat in a Dan-and-Sissy sandwich. Sissy's breasts were pressed against my arm and Dan's leg thrown over mine. I took a deep breath and told myself no.

The ride to Woodstock went fast, it was only thirty miles. As it turned out, we took the right route in. There was no traffic. But the festival was already so packed we had to park in a field with hundreds of other vehicles across the main road from the farm and about a mile from the concert.

I was so excited. The atmosphere was electric, like one huge party. Hippies and straight people blended in a huge crowd, all walking toward the music. Sissy stopped us about a half mile down the dirt track. She opened her crocheted bag and took out a piece of white paper with three purple dots on it. She tore the paper into three pieces and handed me and Dan one.

"Swallow this. It'll make the concert so much better."

I looked up at Dan. He nodded and grinned. All three of us swallowed our scrap of paper with the purple dot.

"What was that?" I asked as we continued the walk.

"Purple Haze," Sissy said. "Acid. You're embarking on the trip of a lifetime. Hang on for the ride."

"Dan, we just took acid. We're screwed," I screamed at him. "You let me take acid!"

He grabbed my shoulders. "Stop it, Jan. You'll be fine. I told you, you need to relax. Maybe this'll help. You're so uptight."

Sissy took my hand. "Come on. We'll have fun."

Her hand in mine filled me with indescribable excitement. We skipped down the road, weaving between long-haired hippies, short-haired guys in plaid shirts, pretty girls in bellbottoms and families with children. It was a bizarre blend of Americans hanging out together, enjoying a weekend of peace, love, freedom, and happiness.

When we arrived at the festival grounds, the first thing I saw was the Hog Farm's tent. "Look, Dan. Maybe John's there."

Dan stood in the center of a group of hippie women wearing no bras, sporting long hair, long skirts, bellbottoms, and semi-transparent blouses. He slowly rotated and stared. A tingle crept up my spine into my neck and my stomach rolled. I figured it was the acid. I grabbed Dan's hand. "Come on, Dan. Let's look for your brother."

"Sissy," I said. "I think Dan's tripping."

When she looked at me, I groaned. Her eyes were like

saucers, completely dilated. She gazed at me blankly. I pulled both of them toward the Hog Farm tent. It was ten in the morning and they were passing out plates of oatmeal and honey. A line quickly formed at the plywood counter. Dan's brother, dressed in ragged bellbottom jeans and a flannel shirt, doled out scoops of oatmeal from a huge cauldron.

He'd grown a beard since I last saw him and his hair was tied back. "John," I called. He looked up, saw me and Dan, and dropped the scoop.

He vaulted the counter in one leap and grabbed Dan. Dan did not respond so John shook him. "Dan, it's me John."

On a platform across from the Hog Farm's tent, a band set up and started tuning their instruments. The discordant sounds hurt my ears.

Dan finally recognized his brother. He pulled the beard and mumbled, "Hardly know you."

"What'd you give him?" John demanded.

I pointed at Sissy. "It was her. She gave us Purple Haze acid."

"Fucking A, Dan, you should know better than to take that shit," John said. He pulled his brother around to the back where cots and seats were set up. He shoved Dan into a folding chair. "Sit here. I'll get you some coffee."

Outside, it started to drizzle. Sissy grabbed my hand again. "Leave him here. I wanna hear Jimi."

"Jimi who?" I asked, following her out into the rain.

"Jimi Hendrix, stupid."

We left Dan and wandered around the site finally

locating the huge natural bowl filled with people. At the bottom, music blared from a stage. Loudspeakers set in the trees carried Arlo Guthrie's voice singing about arriving in L.A. on a plane with keys of marijuana. I'd never heard it.

Hundreds of people listened from the top of the hill, some danced. Sissy pulled me close as Country Joe and the Fish took the stage and began playing the Fish Cheer, which I had heard. We danced as Country Joe sang *Porpoise Mouth* and light flickered in through the trees becoming a kaleidoscope of color. Sissy stripped off her shirt, revealing those huge breasts. Mesmerized, I watched them sway in time to the music.

"Come on, Jan, take off your shirt."

I allowed her to pull it over my head. We embraced, her breasts pressed against my bra. When we fell to the ground, we got covered with mud. I wallowed in the slick, brown goop like a pig, the feel of the mud on my skin indescribably delicious as Sissy unsnapped my bra.

"You don't need this," she said.

A hand roughly jerked me to my feet. "Jan, how could you wander off and leave Dan? Where the hell is your shirt?"

It was John. What a bummer he'd become. "I don't know. I was following her."

I pointed to Sissy.

"Are you with them?"

Sissy grabbed John and kissed him, covering his clean flannel shirt with mud. "Yes, I guess so."

John pushed her off. "Not interested," he told her. "I have a family now. Get your shirts."

He grabbed us both by an elbow and towed us to the
tent. Dan sat hunched over, drinking something steaming
from a paper cup. John pushed Sissy into a chair and
manhandled me into another. He handed us hot cups of
coffee. We started giggling and couldn't stop. John threw
up his hands. "I have to get started on lunch. I don't have
time for this shit."

The rest of the day passed in a blur. I remember
music, dancing, and Sissy. Later, the lights still haloed and
twinkling, we stumbled back to the camper. Dan followed
us, stopping every few minutes to pick up a leaf or a rock
and stare at it. When we finally reached the van, Duke was
happy to see us and Dan had come down enough to build
a fire.

We sat staring into the flames for an hour. Sissy got
up, poured some water into a plastic tub, and fished a
washcloth out of the camper. "Jan, help me get this mud
off."

She pulled her clothes off, all of them. I tried not to
feel the electricity between us. She lifted her arms and I
washed her breasts and her belly, my brain freezing when
I thought of what lay beneath her belly button.

"Go on, wash me."

"Yeah," Dan said. "Wash her."

I spun around to find Dan, eyes glassy, staring at us.
"Really?"

"Oh yeah," he croaked.

I knelt in front of Sissy. Her legs were slender and
muscled. I ran the soapy cloth up and down her thighs
and calves, removing the mud. She even had mud in her

black public hair. I guessed she wasn't wearing panties or a bra. Taking a deep breath, I rinsed the cloth and pushed her legs apart. Sissy opened them. I washed her public hair, ran the soapy cloth between her legs and washed her sex. She grabbed my hand and pressed it to her mound. When I looked up at her, those blue eyes were hot.

She turned around. "Now the back."

I washed the globes of her ass. She pulled the cheeks apart and bent. I saw the tiny pink mouth of her anus and heard Dan groan. I was completely absorbed. I washed between her cheeks and even boldly shoved my finger into the pink hole. Then I ran the wet cloth between her legs from behind, spread the lips of her sex with one hand and stroked her. I was ready to explode.

She turned around and pulled me to my feet. "Your turn," she said, her voice husky and deep.

I didn't protest when she pulled my shirt off. My bra was somewhere back at the festival deep in the mud. "Take off your shoes."

"I unlaced my hiking boots with shaking fingers and kicked them off. She unfastened my hip-huggers and pulled them down. I stepped out of them. For the first time in my life, I was naked in public. Camp fires blazed across the field as people returned to their vehicles. I didn't care. All my resistance was gone. I felt freed of a terrible burden.

Sissy filled her tub with clean water and rinsed the cloth. She moved close to me. Her black hair was a silky cloud around her shoulders and down her back. When she kissed me, I opened my lips and allowed her tongue to rape my mouth.

She stepped back and ran her cloth over my breasts. They immediately swelled and the nipples hardened into aching points. I stifled a groan.

When they were clean, she leaned down to suck each one. My sex sang. Every part of my body felt alive and tingled. Sissy washed my arms and belly, kneeling to clean my legs. Then she opened my sex with one finger and ran the rough cloth between the lips, back and forth, she chafed me until I was weeping with need.

"Turn around," she ordered.

Reluctantly, I did. She washed my back and my legs, the cold water giving me goosebumps. Then she placed one hand on my back and pushed me down at the waist. I bent over and she ran her hands between my legs, spreading my butt cheeks. Holding them open, she turned to Dan.

"This is what you want, isn't it?"

"Yes," Dan breathed, and I realized he was as close as Sissy.

"Get in the van," Sissy said to me.

I scrambled to obey. Dan and Sissy were in with me in seconds.

"Lie on your face," Sissy ordered. Every word she said to me made me hotter. I'd discovered I liked being ordered around by her. She sensed this and took advantage.

I buried my head in the pillows, then lifted it to see what was going on. Sissy and Dan were locked in a hot embrace. I could see his huge erection. It had never been that big before. Dan grabbed Sissy's breasts and squeezed them while they kissed. When they broke apart, Sissy fell on top of my legs, pushed them apart and thrust her fingers inside my dripping wet sex. She pumped two fingers in and out, bringing me to a rapid climax. I lay gasping when she opened my buttocks and held them apart. Her two fingers entered another hole.

I tried to protest, but she laid next to me and kissed me. "No, baby," she crooned. "You want this as much as Dan. I know you do.

"Fuck her, Dan," Sissy snapped then. "Stick it in her ass."

Dan prodded my virgin anus with his dick. I tried to squirm away but Sissy held me. "Relax," she whispered into my ear as her fingers expertly stroked my sex.

Groaning, Dan shoved his huge erection into my butt. Sissy's clever fingers had me buzzing again. I relaxed and after the initial burst of pain, his dick in my ass started to feel incredible. It stretched the pink mouth of my anus which tingled with each stroke. Sissy's hands on me and his dick in my ass had me more excited than I'd ever been in my life.

He grabbed my butt and squeezed as he pumped. His breathing grew ragged and he panted like a dog. Sissy panted with him. Her hand moved faster and faster on my aching sex. I lifted my ass so she could get to it easier and felt Dan stiffen. He froze on top of me, pulled out, and fell on the bed.

Sissy rolled me over and shoved her dripping pussy on my face while she buried hers in mine.

I'd never even dreamed of eating out another woman. The smell of her excitement, the taste of her juice, all added to my arousal. I found her ripe clit. It was huge and swollen. I sucked it into my mouth and Sissy moaned into my open flesh.

Dan came to life. He shoved his hand between us, pulling on my nipples, fondling Sissy's breasts. When she climaxed, I felt her opening clamp down on my tongue. She arched her back and squealed. Her orgasm brought me to orgasm. I rushed with pleasure, my face still buried in her flesh.

We lay in a heap long after we were finished. I was exhausted. The long day, the drugs, then the sex had me wasted. Dan tossed the sleeping blankets over us and we crashed. Duke laid outside the van, guarding our sleep. He woke us up in the morning, barking and growling. Two guys were sneaking around the back of the van. They picked the wrong group of people to mess with.

Dan pulled on his pants, snagged the pistol he kept hidden under the seat, then went to talk to them. Stark naked, Sissy climbed out of the van and stood beside Dan. "Put the gun away," she said. "This is a new age of peace and love. They won't hurt us. Will you, guys?" I looked out the van windows. The two guys both had long hair and beards, but they wore leather. I scrambled around to the other side and saw four big Harley choppers parked in the grass. Bikers.

The guys were just getting over the shock of seeing Sissy naked when I jumped out of the van, also naked. I grabbed Sissy, kissed her on the mouth, then whispered in her ear, "They're bikers."

"Hell no, we won't hurt you," a big man in his early thirties said. He was covered in tattoos and his long greasy black hair fell over his eyes. "We just want to join your party. Looks like you got more than enough to share, dude. Put down the gun."

The other two bikers suddenly appeared behind us. Duke went crazy barking and growling. "Drop the gun, mister," a big biker behind me said.

I watched Dan taking in the situation. He slowly rotated, his eyes clear and focused. A massive, red-headed biker weighing over three hundred pounds stood behind me slapping a tire iron slowly into the palm of his meaty hand. His pal held a Louisville Slugger. The two original bikers pulled knives and we were surrounded.

"Drop," I yelled to Sissy, put my hand on her back and shoved her to the ground.

"Duke, kill," Dan pointed to the red head and the dog leaped on him, carrying him backwards to the ground. I jumped to my feet, whirled, and dropped the biker holding the bat with a combination jumping front kick followed by a roundhouse kick to the head. A set of hard toes under the chin, followed by a whack from the top of the foot along the side of the head, will do that.

Dan fell to the ground and swept the other two off their feet with one leg. When they were in the dirt, he flipped his pistol over and smashed the butt into the biggest one's forehead, turned fast enough to avoid being stabbed, disarmed that biker, took the knife, flipped it over and climbed to his feet, barely breathing heavy, pistol and knife pointed at all of them.

"Jan, show these men the door." He called Duke off. The big dog released the red-headed biker and sat next to Dan's feet.

"If you four mangy hounds want out of here in one piece on bikes that still function, I suggest you get on them now and take off," I said.

The four slowly climbed to their feet, brushing mud and clumps of sod out of their hair and off their leather vests and jackets. Grumbling and growling, they mounted up, gunned their engines, I guess to show us how bad they were, and took off, tires throwing chunks of mud everywhere.

We stood together and watched them leave. When they were gone, Sissy nodded her head. "Totally awesome. You guys are intense."

"We're FBI agents," Dan said. "Well, we will be in September."

"No way."

"For real," I said.

"What about the Purple Haze? You guys dropped acid. Don't you want to be part of the peace and love movement?"

"Oh, we are, aren't we, Jan?" He grabbed me and kissed me hard. I felt his love for me stronger than ever before. Our experiences had opened our minds and cemented a bond between us that would never break.

"Groovy, baby," I said, and shot Sissy a peace sign.

After we dropped Sissy at the bus station we went

home to Springfield, and in September started our FBI training. The years passed quickly. We saw a lot, and had many experiences, some good some bad. But we never forgot Sissy and the Purple Haze. Peace.

Woodstock

by Garland

Moon Flower was sandwiched between Ronnie and Ariel. Cock in her ass. Cock in her pussy. The mattress springs squeaked out the rhythm of their fucking. The headboard beat against the wall like a tom-tom. Ronnie and Ariel pounded into her in perfect synchronicity. They could feel each other's cock and that turned them on even more.

Gritting her teeth, Moon Flower squeezed her pussy and ass. The boys' balls tightened and their cocks throbbed as they shot their loads within seconds of each other letting out long low grunts.

"Ahhhhhh," Moon Flower breathed out, back arching. "Groovy, guys. Groovy."

Ronnie and Ariel were still buried deep inside her. Smiling, her and Ronnie kissed deeply. Their tongues danced together as Ariel planted little kisses along the back of her neck, making her body tingle.

Ariel rolled off her and she rolled off Ronnie. The two boys kissed her as their hands explored each other. Ronnie and Ariel gently squeezed each other's dicks as they bit

Moon Flower's hard nipples, the color of a virgin girl's first blush.

Moon Flower smiled contentedly. She had met the two hippies four days ago. They were the most sexual guys she had ever met. Four days of straight fucking. She would have to remember to thank her mom for making her visit Gran. Ronnie and Ariel had shown her a whole new side of life and passion she didn't even think was possible. They had welcomed her into their world. Given her a hippie name. She loved it. If only her mom could she her now. She would have a heart attack. Her mom said all hippies were deviants.

"So are you going with us?" Ariel asked in between kisses.

"I don't think I can," she responded breathlessly.

"Come on, man," Ariel continued. "Don't let your ancestors bum your trip."

"You gotta come with us, man," Ronnie added. "You're our soul fire."

"And you two are mine," Moon Flower promised. "But what am I supposed to tell Gran? She'll never let me go."

"So sneak out," Ronnie suggested. "That's what we're doing. You're eighteen. We're nineteen. Adults."

"Yeah. Don't be a . . ." Ariel finished his thought by outlining a square with his fingers.

She thought about it for a few moments. She wanted to go with them. It was supposed to be the music event of all time. Everyone was going to be there. She didn't want to be left out.

"All right," she finally declared. "Let's do it."

"Groovy," the boys ejaculated.

Ronnie took out a celebratory joint and the three partook of its sweetness. They swayed to the psychedelic music that filled the room, lazily caressing each other. The three hippies were in a complete state of euphoria until—

"Lisa Marie," Gran's ancient voice jovially called as she opened the door.

"Shit." Moon Flower gasped, eyes wide.

Quick as lightning, Ronnie and Ariel rolled off the bed. The two boys giggled as they tried to be silent as a whisper. The sweet smell of pot was still strong in the room.

"Hi, Gran," she smiled innocently trying to act as normal as possible, though she was still naked.

Gran looked at her, head turned quizzically. "Dear, why are you naked?"

"I got hot," Moon Flower answered quickly, wondering if she could smell the pot or the come on her pussy and in her ass.

Gran continued to stare at her making her feel even more vulnerable. She prepared for the wrath of Gran but surprisingly the old woman smiled and said, "I do that all the time. Especially in August."

Moon Flower smiled and, trying to remember how to breath evenly, wished Gran would leave.

"Well," Gran continued. "I just came up to tell you I'm baking some fresh chocolate-chip peanut butter cookies. Your favorite."

"Groovy." Moon Flower smiled. After that marathon fuck session, she was starving.

Gran sniffed the air and got a queer look on her face. "What is that wonderful aroma?"

"New perfume," Moon Flower lied.

"Very nice. I'm going to have to borrow it some time. A few whiffs of that and your grandpa will be all over me." Gran laughed crudely, then quickly blushed. "I'm so sorry, dear. I don't know what made me say that. I'll go check those cookies. I'm suddenly so hungry."

Moon Flower had to fight to maintain her composure. Gran had no sooner shut the door when Ronnie and Ariel leapt back onto the bed. The three looked at each other silently for a second, before bursting into great belly laughs.

"Contact high," Ronnie announced puffing on the joint. "Groovy."

"You know," Ariel said, contemplating deeply. "I got really hungry down there too."

He kissed her, lightly flicking her clit with his fingers.

"Me too," Ronnie agreed. "But I'm not hungry for cookies." He winked at her.

"Oh yeah?" she teased, spreading her legs wide and casually rubbing her swollen lips. "So what do you boys feel like eating?"

The boys raised their eyebrows, and like starving men they descended. Her back arched. Her eyes bugged out of her head. Her toes curled as they feasted on her pussy. She still hadn't gotten use to their tongue skills, especially Ronnie's. What that boy could do with his tongue should be illegal.

Crying out, her fingers got lost in their long, thick,

luscious hair when they shoved their tongues deep inside her. Deeper than she thought possible. Their thick tongues tickled every g-spot her pussy walls possessed and even found a few. They flicked against each other in an erotic battle to see who could give her the most pleasure.

Moon Flower's stomach tingled. She was so close. She . . . was . . . right . . . there . . . when . . .

"Cookies!" Gran's voice announced cheerfully as she walked in.

Ronnie and Ariel barely missed discovery.

"Enjoy," Gran said, taking a generous helping for herself. "I wish I knew why I'm so hungry all of a sudden," she asked no one in particular as she left.

"If she comes in again, she's joining in," Ronnie declared.

Moon Flower laughed as she slowly picked up four cookies and placed them on her body. Her lips. Her tits. Her pussy. The warmness and gooeyness of the chocolate and peanut butter made her pussy wet and her nipples hard enough to cut diamonds. Slowly the boys ate the cookies off her body. No crumbs were left. Any rogue chocolate or peanut butter was licked up. There were no interruptions from Gran as they feasted on flesh and cookies.

That night, Moon Flower snuck out and the three hippies hitchhiked to Woodstock. Her heart was pounding the whole time they were in the back of that semi, scrunched in between livestock on their way to slaughter in New York.

As soon as they got to the grounds it was like they had entered another world. A Neverland for the free spirited.

The psychedelic air filled their lungs, feeding them. All around them glorious hippies smoked, fucked and frolicked. Most were nude and before long Ariel, Ronnie and Moon Flower had shed their suffocating garments and proudly displayed their bodies in all their natural beauty. No judgment. No squares. The music of Jefferson Airplane. The Who. The Rolling Stones. Moon Flower never wanted to leave. She longed to have the power to freeze time so they could stay like this forever.

A cool summer rain fell from the still pale blue sky. The sun was bright and warm. A brilliant multi-colored rainbow was already smeared across the sky.

Little wet beads hugged their skin. Gooey mud squished between their toes, tickling them. Moon Flower felt like she was floating. This was the greatest high she had ever experienced.

Grabbing hold of her boys she pulled them to her and kissed them. Long. Deep. Passionately. Their hands explored each other. She was wet. They were hard. It didn't matter that they were in the middle of thousands of people.

"Fuck me," she told them.

Slowly the three sank to the ground. Ronnie and Ariel's hard cocks throbbed against her smooth creamy skin. Her pussy lips pulsated with lustful blood as the boys kissed her all over.

"You two kiss," she moaned, almost begging.

Moon Flower rubbed herself as she watched Ronnie and Ariel, best friends since childhood, kiss with a tenderness she didn't think possible for two men to have for one another. Their tongues darted in and out of the other's mouth as their hands left no inch of flesh unexplored.

Kneeling between them, Moon Flower sucked their dicks. The boys groaned into each other's mouth and gently bucked their hips back and forth. Moon Flower squeezed their balls and played with their asses as they fucked her mouth.

Lying on her back with her legs spread wide, Ronnie fucked her. Ariel straddled her face, feeding her his cock. Ronnie was caressing him and they kissed.

As Ronnie continued to fuck her, Ariel moved behind him and slowly entered his virgin ass. Ronnie grunted out as his tight hole was stretched by Ariel's thick cock.

"You're so tight," Ariel whispered, kissing his friend's neck.

"You like that tight ass?" Ronnie asked, not missing a rhythm of his fucking.

"Mmmmmm . . ." was all Ariel could say as he found his own rhythm.

Ariel's weight pushed Ronnie deeper into Moon Flower. Gasping, she clutched his back and kissed his shoulders. Her body shuddered. Her eyes rolled back in her head. He was deeper than he had ever been before. She couldn't speak. She couldn't even moan. It felt like he would split her open.

"You want a piece of her?" Ronnie asked Ariel after a while. "'Cause I want a piece of you."

Ronnie winked at his friend and they kissed.

Ronnie lay on the ground. Ariel slowly lowered himself on his friend's cock before Moon Flower impaled herself on Ariel's. The three were still as statues enjoying the cool rain drenching their bodies.

Slowly they began to fuck. As they found their rhythm, their moans and cries became more and more passionate. People stopped to watch the three hippies fuck to the music that was vibrating the grounds.

The crowd began cheering them on. "Free love. Free love. Free love."

The chant fueled them. They felt like warriors. Advocates. Activists. Moon Flower's chest swelled with pride as she watched people stop and fuck in the mud.

Looking up to the sky, face drenched, Moon Flower smiled as she ground her hips against Ariel's balls and squeezed Ronnie's. This was the greatest feeling she had ever experienced.

"You want both of us inside your pussy?" Ariel asked, squeezing her tits.

"Yes. Oh God, yes," Moon Flower screamed out as an orgasm ripped through her.

She got on her hands and knees. Ariel was underneath her. They smiled at each other and kissed. His cock throbbed against her pussy. Moaning into Ariel's mouth she felt Ronnie's cock enter her pussy, stretching her out even more. She couldn't believe both would fit inside her.

The two boys fucked her slowly. Their moans were loud and long. She never wanted it to end. She wished they could fuck her until the end of time. Screaming out, she felt a massive orgasm overtake her and her pussy squirted as Ronnie and Ariel filled her to overflowing with their come as the music swelled into its own orgasmic finish.

The crowd cheered. For them and the band.

Moon Flower smiled as the three made their way to the lake to wash up. Ronnie and Ariel's arms were around her, fingers gently brushing her wet, muddy skin. She was so glad she had decided to go with her new friends on this journey. She knew this would be an experience she would never forget.

Snap Decision

by Elizabeth Coldwell

She was late. Morgan looked at his watch and decided he would give her another five minutes before writing her off as a complete loss. Not that she would be the first girl who had agreed to come to his studio for a test session, only to get cold feet at the last minute.

Still, it would be a pity if this one did let him down. She had a potential he so rarely saw in the would-be models who came to him. He had found her in one of his favourite haunts, Medusa on Carnaby Street. The brainchild of the free-spirited Julia Cardoza, the daughter of a wealthy Spanish aristocrat who had fled to England to escape his country's Civil War, the boutique had become the only place to see and be seen. It had been described in the *Evening Standard* as "not so much a shop, more a happening." Morgan would wander through on Saturday afternoons, when its three floors were crammed with the young and fashion-conscious, searching for the latest threads or simply lounging on the beanbags and oversized cushions which were scattered throughout the shop, stoned out of their minds and enjoying the passing parade.

Some of the sights he had witnessed were burnt vividly in his memory. Hardly anyone bothered to use the admittedly cramped changing rooms, and girls would simply strip in the middle of the shop floor, not caring who saw their bare breasts as they shimmied into a little crocheted mini-dress or diaphanous cheesecloth top. On one never-to-be-forgotten occasion, two blondes had posed in the shop window in nothing but bras and panties, trying to convince passers-by they were just another couple of display mannequins.

Medusa was also the boutique of choice for many of Swinging London's up-and-coming rock musicians and actors, and they were no more well-behaved than anyone else who shopped there. Morgan had not been in the shop on the afternoon when a girl had apparently been caught giving a blow job to one of the Rolling Stones behind a jewelry display cabinet, but reports of the incident did not surprise him in the least. A sexually charged atmosphere pervaded Medusa, obvious as soon as you walked through the shop door. How could it be any other way, with hundreds of young and beautiful women on the premises, all of whom were infected with the spirit of sexual permissiveness which seemed set to define the era?

Perhaps that was why so many girls changed their mind after initially agreeing to model for him, Morgan reflected. They suspected he was simply trying to lure them to his studio in one of the little alleyways off Wardour Street so he could fuck their brains out. He wouldn't be the first so-called photographer who had used that tactic, he knew. But Morgan was nothing if not professional. For him it was always business first, then pleasure.

Though it looked as though there wasn't going to be any business this afternoon. He'd given her as long as he was prepared to—now he ought to go and start taking down his lights. It was her missed opportunity, he told himself, not his. As much as she intrigued him, she was far from the only pretty girl in the West End.

Wrapped up in his thoughts, Morgan almost missed the knock at the door. He strained his ears, wondering if he had really heard it. There it was again, more insistent this time. He flung open the window and yelled into the street, "I'll be down in a second." He dashed down the stairs, almost missing his footing in his haste. He found her standing on the doorstep, every bit as beautiful as he remembered her. Poker-straight, ash-blond hair framed a face dominated by huge brown doe eyes, almost impossibly long-lashed. Her coltish legs, clad in the new fashionable nylon tights, emerged from a tiny pelmet of a skirt. Shyly, she smiled at him. "I'm so sorry we're late."

It took him a moment to register she wasn't alone. The man who stood by her side was almost as striking as she was: a good six feet tall, with fashionably shaggy dark hair and piercing blue eyes. His body tapered from broad shoulders to lean, lithe hips hugged by bellbottom jeans. Clearly the boyfriend, come to offer whatever support might be needed. Or, more likely, stop the photographer from getting his grubby hands on his girl.

He moved to usher the two of them inside. "Come on in. It's Joan, isn't it, and—?"

"Ah, yeah, about that," the man said, as he followed Morgan up the stairs to his pad. "We were talking about this on the way over."

"I'm sorry," Morgan replied as politely as he could, "but I don't believe we've been introduced."

"Of course. How rude of me. I'm Anton de Beauvoir, Joan's manager."

I'm sure you are, Morgan thought. *I'll bet anything that before I approached your girlfriend in Medusa, you were plain old Tony Beevers.* But this was the Sixties: anyone could, and did, reinvent themselves in pursuit of an opportunity.

"Anyway," de Beauvoir continued, "we were thinking Joan Berry maybe isn't the most exciting name for an internationally famous model, so we were trying to come up with something a bit more striking."

"And did you?" Morgan asked, smiling at de Beauvoir's presumption.

The other man shook his head. "Not yet. But we will."

Morgan watched the girl as she hung up her afghan coat and brushed out her hair with her fingers. She had the innate grace and slight nervousness of a woodland animal, he decided. It set her apart from some of the brasher, more knowing girls he saw browsing in Medusa, and perhaps it was what he had first noticed about her. The name came to him without prompting. "Fawn," he said.

The girl turned, as though trying the suggestion on for size. "Fawn," she repeated. "I like it. What do you think?"

Her boyfriend—manager, whatever he chose to call

himself—thought about it for a moment before replying, "Nice. Just Fawn. No surname. It'll have that element of mystery."

"Of course," Morgan cautioned, "a lot will depend on how these test shots come out. Would you like to come this way?"

The couple followed him through to what had originally been the flat's second bedroom, before he had converted it to his photographic studio. Draped white sheets acted as a simple backdrop, and he asked Fawn to stand in front of them. He liked to have music in the background while he worked, and he slipped one of his favourite LPs, the Beatles' *Revolver*, on to his turntable. Anton made himself comfortable on a wicker chair as Morgan went to work.

Reaching for his trusty Leica, he guided her through a series of poses. It only took a couple of shots to realize the girl was a natural. She seemed to know instinctively how to use her hands to frame her face in a close-up, or how to stand so her body was presented at the most flattering angle. Morgan found himself having to give her only the briefest of instructions, and almost without noticing it he used up a whole roll of film.

"Let's take a few more," he decided, feeling a mood had been created between himself and his model which he needed to make the most of. "I've got a few outfits hanging on that rail over there. Why don't you find something you like and go change in the bathroom?"

Fawn quickly rifled through the hangers and selected a couple of items. As Morgan bent over to pick a fresh roll of film from his bag, he had the strangest sensation, as though Anton was staring at his arse. He glanced over his shoulder to see the other man smiling at him. Was it possible he swung both ways? The establishment might frown on such couplings—indeed, gay sex had been illegal until very recently, and men had gone to prison for daring to indulge their passions—but everyone knew they took place. So what if Anton was into men as well as women? If he was honest, he quite liked the idea of being an object of admiration for this louche stranger. With his auburn head of corkscrew curls, sleepy brown eyes and androgynous good looks, it shouldn't surprise him if guys found him just as attractive as girls did. A sudden strut in his step, he slotted the film into his camera and waited for Fawn to reappear.

When she did, she almost took his breath away. She had found the most daring outfit on the whole rail: a lime green see-through dress. It was intended to be worn with a thin slip beneath it, but Fawn hadn't bothered with that. Hadn't bothered with underwear, either. Morgan could clearly see the twin pink points of her nipples and the soft fluff of hair on her mound. He felt his cock stiffening at the sight. Summoning every scrap of his professionalism, he asked her to assume a pose which felt comfortable for her. He knew that with the light behind her, every detail of her breathtaking body would be visible in his photographs. He couldn't believe she had not realized that, and he glanced over at Anton again, wondering what kind of game the couple were playing with him. Did it excite them to have other men looking at Fawn in a state of near-nakedness? Was this a fantasy they had always wanted to act out, or were they simply as wild and uninhibited as the customers in Medusa, forever looking for a new kind of thrill?

His mind churning, he worked his way through another roll of film in minutes. Fawn was exuding a combination of innocence and raw sexuality, making it almost impossible for him to concentrate on what he was doing. His balls were tight and aching, and he longed to throw the camera to one side and plunge his cock into her sweet little pussy.

When he looked over to Anton, he saw the man was almost absent-mindedly rubbing himself through the crotch of his bellbottoms. Fawn had noticed what he was doing, too, for she suddenly said, "Get it out for me, baby. Let me see that big, hard dick of yours." To Morgan, she added, "You don't have any objections, do you?"

He hardly knew how to respond, but he didn't have to say a word. Fawn glanced down at his groin and almost burst out laughing. Morgan followed her gaze. The tight-fitting velveteen trousers he wore revealed the outline of his cock in almost indecent detail, leaving him unable to deny how turned on he was.

"Why don't you get yours out, too?" Fawn said, husky. "It looks far too nice to keep trapped in those trousers. Come on, let's party."

As she spoke, she pulled her dress over her head and threw it aside. Morgan didn't object as she reached for the buttons on his fly and quickly popped them open. Her cool fingers circled his shaft, her eyes widening as she realized just how big he was. Must be bigger than her boyfriend, he thought smugly, as he saw her look over at Anton, making the comparison. Not that size was everything, of course; it helped if you knew what to do with what you had, but he'd never had any complaints in that regard.

Fawn urged Anton to come and join them. On her knees, she took both men in hand, stroking and rubbing. From the expression on her face, she clearly couldn't believe her luck. She wrapped her lips round her boyfriend's cock, slowly swallowing as much as she could. Beside him, Morgan heard Anton's breathing quicken slightly in response. Somewhere in the background, the LP had come to an end and the needle was circling unattended in its groove. No one moved to turn it over and play the other side. What was happening now didn't need a musical accompaniment.

For a minute or so, Fawn laved Anton's length, then turned her attention to Morgan. Lips stretched widely round his girth, she flicked her tongue over his helmet, lapping up the salty drops which were forming there. Like Anton, he was soon panting shallowly. He hadn't expected the photo session to end with such a delicious blowjob, but he still fought to stop the spunk rising in his balls. Luscious as Fawn's mouth was, he was loath to come there. Not when he knew he had the possibility of sampling her pussy.

Fawn let Morgan's dick slip from her lips. Mischievously, she pressed it and Anton's close together, so she could run her tongue over both of them. The contact was unexpected but not unpleasant: Morgan could feel a pulse beating in Anton's shaft, almost in time with his own, and he found himself struck with the urge to touch and even taste the other man's cock.

Anton smiled at him, and Morgan suspected he was feeling a similar urge. He sensed Anton was much more experienced when it came to these matters, but that wasn't a problem. The mood he was in, he was more than willing to experiment.

"You know," Fawn said, "you two are a bit overdressed. Why don't you strip off, get more comfortable?"

Morgan needed no more prompting. He and Anton quickly shucked out of their clothing, throwing each item haphazardly on the floor as they took it off. It enabled him to admire Anton's smooth, almost hairless body. The man had a firm arse, and Morgan suddenly found himself wondering what it might be like to bury his cock in the dark valley between those tight cheeks.

The thought caused his cock to surge upwards even more powerfully than before, and he expected Fawn to resume sucking him. Instead, it was Anton who reached out and took his hard shaft into his fist.

"You're okay with this?" Anton asked as he wanked Morgan with slow, assured strokes.

Morgan could only nod. He couldn't believe how much he was enjoying the feel of Anton's hand shuttling back and forth, gliding on the velvet sleeve of skin that covered the hard inner core of his dick.

"You want me to use my mouth?" Anton's tone was husky, impossible to resist.

Morgan nodded again. Fawn was sitting on the wicker chair Anton had occupied for the photo shoot, legs splayed carelessly. Her fingers were between her legs, a couple of them pushing up into her glistening pussy.

To watch her frig herself while her boyfriend sucked him off would add another dimension to his pleasure. He no longer cared whether this was an orchestrated game, or simply something which was happening on the spur of the moment. All he wanted was for this gorgeously wanton couple to use him in whatever way they wished.

"Let's go somewhere more comfortable," he suggested.

"Lead the way, man," Anton replied.

Morgan's bedroom was just next door. It smelled strongly of incense, since Morgan liked to burn a spicy joss stick or two to help him relax. The bedcovers were crumpled, just as he had left them when he got out of bed this morning. He swept them to the floor and climbed onto the bed, inviting Anton to join him. Fawn made herself a nest on the floor out of the discarded bedding. She sat, legs crossed, in what would have been a beautifully contemplative pose if it hadn't been for the fact that once again she was cramming as many fingers as she could into her pussy, while diddling her clit at the same time.

Morgan lay back, cock rigid and anxious for the feel of Anton's mouth. He didn't have to wait long, as the other man's lips closed around his plum cockhead. Almost unbelievably, Anton had the ability to take him right down into his throat. God knew where he had learned this particular technique, and how he could take quite so much of Morgan's considerable length without discomfort, but he was certainly adept at it. Morgan felt Anton's dark hair tickling the inside of his thigh as he was swallowed almost to the root.

"Yeah, suck him down, baby," he heard Fawn urging. "You look so good with your mouth full of cock . . ."

Morgan had never known anything like this girl. She had the face of an angel and the mouth of a Mersey docker, and she was turning him on like mad. Her filthy exhortations, coupled with the gripping suction of her boyfriend's throat, brought him almost to the brink of climax, which was when Fawn gave her next instruction.

"Stop now, baby," she said as she pulled her fingers, shining with her nectar, out of her cunt. "I want him to lick me while you fuck his arse."

It was the most perverse request Morgan had ever heard. He'd never had anything in his back passage before, and the thought simultaneously alarmed and thrilled him. "Don't worry," Anton whispered in his ear. "I'll take it slowly."

Among the clutter on Morgan's bedside table was a bottle of baby lotion which he often used to add lubrication to his solitary wanking sessions. Anton squeezed a generous amount into his palm and greased his cock with it. Then he turned his attention to Morgan's virgin arse, aiming a jet of lotion into Morgan's crack. Morgan shivered as he felt it dripping down slowly, coating his hole. Anton rubbed him there for a moment then, as Morgan relaxed into the sensation, he gently eased his fingertip inside. Morgan fought the urge to tense up, knowing instinctively that if he bore down it would make the penetration easier. As Fawn encouraged him, Anton pushed deeper, opening Morgan up to the point where he could take a second finger, then a third.

He felt stretched wide open by the time Anton decided he was ready to take his cock.

"Oh, my—" Morgan lost the ability to speak as Anton ploughed into his arse. There was a little pain at first, but then Anton seemed to hit some hidden spot inside him which was the seat of dark, delicious pleasure. *I can take this*, Morgan thought, *and I like it*.

That was the point at which Fawn could no longer stay out of the action. She slithered down the bed, coming to rest so that the apex of her thighs was beneath Morgan's face as he crouched on all fours, still firmly plugged with Anton's cock. Morgan bent his head, enticed by the rich aroma of her love juices. When he tasted her, honey and brine mingled on his tongue. He couldn't help but want to lap up every last drop.

Other girls he had been with had complained that, all too often, men were reluctant to go down on them. Morgan was the opposite. He considered himself to be a connoisseur of cunt. He liked nothing better to lick a woman to the point where she was exhausted from coming, enjoying the way each of his lovers had their own unique taste and smell and their own way of announcing orgasm, from shrieks to curses to heaving sobs. Admittedly, he had never given a woman head while his arse was being fucked at the same time, but he was more than willing to try it.

At first it was awkward. He had to brace himself by holding tight on to Fawn's thighs, and every thrust from Anton pushed him hard and deep into her matted blond pussy. Gradually, though, he grew used to the rhythm, and as Anton fucked him relentlessly he used all the tricks he knew to have Fawn writhing beneath him and begging to have his tongue deeper inside her.

It was Fawn whose pleasure crested first, grabbing Morgan's tousled curls and holding his head to her wet slit as she moaned and thrashed in orgasm. Skewered on a hot cock at one end, smothered by soft girl-flesh at the other, Morgan was truly in heaven. *If this is the sexual revolution, he thought, bring it on!*

He could feel Anton's thrusts growing faster and more erratic, and knew the man was moments away from coming. One last, hard push and Anton's spunk was flooding Morgan's arse, while Fawn rode out the waves of a second orgasm.

He felt Anton grasp his shaft once more, pumping his fist rapidly. Morgan's balls tightened, his back arched, and long ropes of pearly seed shot from the end of his cock. Panting, heaving, he rolled on to his side. It had been good, almost too good, but he knew there was more to come. A shot of whiskey from the bottle he kept in the kitchen cupboard, a shared cigarette, and they would all be ready to go once more.

As Morgan walked naked to the kitchen, limp cock already reviving as his mind toyed with the possibilities of what two men and one woman could do with each other, he blessed his fortune in spotting Fawn in Medusa. Not only had he discovered the woman who he was sure would become the iconic model of her generation, he had enjoyed the first of what he hoped would be many, many threesomes with her and her hunk of a boyfriend.

Tomorrow, he would develop those photos. One look,

and every magazine editor in London would be fighting to put Fawn on their cover. As for the shots in that see-through dress, they would be his private secret, something to bring back memories on cold winter nights. Though who needed photos when the real thing was lying on his bed, anxious for him to return and impale her on his length? Whiskey bottle in hand, he went back into the bedroom to start the party all over again.

Center Part

by Hobart Glasse

Long, slender fingers squeeze the trigger of the hose's nozzle, sending jets of liquid steam into the dark brown mane that fills the basin of the sink.

"How's that, Nat . . . too hot?"

"You know me, Hil. Never too hot."

Natalie watched Hillary bite a plump lower lip to nip a sudden laugh in the bud. It was the go-to method of most high-end hair salon professionals and something she'd shared with her almost two years ago during their first sit together. It was back when she was still a stranger at the mercy of new scissors, and Hillary had been quick to set her at ease. "A hairdresser is like her customer's best friend," she'd revealed, touching up a few streaks of gray under a heat lamp, "only better. We're the only one who knows the ugly truth and we can't betray that trust."

Best friends are forever, she'd gone on to explain, but they're still the competition. "Your hairdresser wants you to look better than she does," she'd said.

But as far as Natalie was concerned, that was impossible.

Despite having recently achieved official "cougar" status, Natalie knew her fair, freckled skin—stripped of paint, of course—and Eastern European bone structure could turn heads even in her khaki work uniform. Hillary, on the other hand, was biracial perfection, with touchable, wild hair kept sun-kissed and curly, and she had the largest, most expressive emerald eyes Natalie had ever seen (since coming face to face with an adult tiger at feeding time). Having worked as a zoologist in the Bronx before taking over as exhibit curator for New York's Central Park Zoo, she'd never studied as exotically beautiful a creature as Hillary Jane Devore.

Not since *her*, anyway.

Two years this June, she counted.

Two years since her Safi disappeared.

Natalie shook the memory from her mind and blew a long sigh. Occupying the slightly more handsome side of womanhood in comparison to Hillary's more effeminate physiognomy, her "better-than-best-friend" was right about the cherished intimacy between the two of them. A woman never revealed her beauty secrets to a solitary soul unless she was getting paid to do it. Your hair person—the one covering your flaws and helping you edge ahead of the pack—was as precious as your lady in waiting. Only, this one didn't know the *whole* truth. Or did she?

"Yeah, I do know you," replied Hillary after a curious amount of hesitation. "You're tough . . . but not *too* tough. You know what I mean?"

She shut off the water and added a two-second squeeze of shampoo, working it in until the suds sounded to Natalie like an orgy of cumulous clouds. Then she began collecting large fistfuls of hair from close to the roots and squeezing the soap along the entire length to the tips. *That tugging feels glorious*, thought Natalie, especially when it forced Hillary to lean closer. She had tenderly weighted breasts that swung elegantly forward, widening the opening of her loose sweater. The skin showing around her neck and down her shirt—every inch, Natalie imagined, the same shade of stirred macchiato—was visible to her navel. She'd dreamt of slowly gliding the back of her hand over it, turning her palm down when the opportunity to gently cup a soft mound presented itself.

She dreamt of that and more.

Once Hillary was through lathering, she used her fingertips to scrub Natalie's scalp. Her breasts exposed deep views of cleavage as she brought her forearms together for better leverage. The vision—dipping now and again below Natalie's sight—acted like a feather on a string in front of one of the big cats she used to observe. She could actually sense her mouth opening to bare her teeth, and eye soreness from straining to see forced her hands between her thighs to keep from reaching out.

Natalie wondered if her lustful thoughts could somehow be transmitted out through her scalp and into Hillary's strong hands, and she had to bite down on her own lip to keep from asking. She was, she realized, never fond of censoring herself. So with her pinky fingers now pressing firmly against her covered labia, she had no choice but to try and release the pressure verbally.

"Hillary, you're . . . amazing."

"Feels good, doesn't it? I love it, too."

"Oh, honey . . . you have no idea what I'm talking about, do you?"

Hillary stopped for a moment, then resumed.

"Hmm," she said, working a close-mouthed smile that produced two adorable dimples. "Maybe you should explain."

Natalie felt her lips go dry and licked them back to life. "Hil, I . . . oh, shit, what am I doing?"

Hilary continued scrubbing for a few more moments, then stopped and looked Natalie in the eyes. "Just say what you have to say, " she said, and turned the hose on her once more. "There's nobody here but us."

Natalie relaxed a little and rubbed her eyes. The heat caused by Hillary's closeness was distracting now, and her eye ache was now replaced by an ache of another kind.

"Her name was Safiya. Safi, if you were close to her. And I was. Very. In fact . . . we were lovers."

Hillary continued to rinse, repeatedly closing her hand around generous portions of Natalie's hair and letting the thick, matted pieces slide dexterously through her fingers. The familiarity of the sensation—suggesting to her that nothing had yet changed between them—relaxed her even more.

"We met at work. I was a married woman enjoying a zoology career I was passionate about, and she was a biology student from Nigeria studying abroad."

"You never told me you worked at the zoo."

"Didn't I?"

"I think I'd remember if you did."

Natalie nodded in deference. "Yeah, I guess so."

"Go on."

Hillary switched off the water and began patting down the tangle of hair with a large white towel. An edge drifted over Natalie's eyes, and another layer of reticence shook from her psyche like an errant feather.

"Anyway . . . it was my job to explain everything I was doing—thinking out loud, that sort of thing—and hers to tail me as closely as possible. We spent hours and hours together." She worked to swallow the image of Safi following her.

Hillary filled the pause. "Sounds like you two got close pretty fast."

"Oh, we did. She was extremely bright for her age . . . for *any* age. And stunningly beautiful. She looked a bit like you, actually."

Hillary put her hands behind Natalie's head and gently lifted her into an upright, seated position. There, she resumed drying her hair, only this time Natalie could sense something new in her technique; whereas before the task seemed somewhat heedless, this time it felt purposeful and—if her perception hadn't been totally washed away with the bubbles—reassuring.

"Aww . . . what a sweet thing to say," cooed Hillary. Natalie could feel her hips pressing into her shoulder as she continued to dry. She wanted so badly to wrap an arm around them and lean into her, rubbing her cheek across her stomach with a feline grace. But as natural as it seemed to do so, she resisted.

Natalie regained her focus and said, "It's true. Your

skin's much lighter than hers, though. Safi would have been a starless night against your clear, bronze morning."

The image brought a shudder that straightened her back, followed by a sudden urge to flee. Not to go far, but somewhere to hide and watch. She was falling in love with Hillary through the memories of a woman whose sudden absence from her life had brought about an inordinate amount of pain, and she was just now realizing she'd put herself in harm's way. Her confessions were quickly closing the distance to her desires, and her instincts were now telling her to retreat, circle, and wait.

But it was too late. With trembling lips, she began, "Hillary, I think—"

Hillary finished. "I know." She placed the towel inside the sink and stood in front of the chair. With both hands she combed back through Natalie's hair, working out the remaining tangles and presenting her neck in the process.

Natalie nestled her chin just above the softly pronounced clavicle that waited there, closed her eyes and inhaled. She felt Hillary's knee wedge a spot on the seat against her thigh, and exhaled slowly as a hand cradled the back of her head. *How many ways can this woman stimulate me?* she wondered. And she imagined that, like her beloved Safi, the entire history of language could be revealed in the subtle modifications of her touch.

"Our skin says more about how we feel than we do," said Hillary. "Yours never seems to want to let go." She pulled away but remained leaning on the seat, using her hand to tilt Natalie's face upward. "What happened?"

"To Safi?" responded Natalie.

"Mm-hmm."

Natalie took Hillary's hand away from her face and gathered her fingers as if to protect them.

"No one really knows. She returned home because her mother had taken ill, and her village came under attack by a neighboring militia. I tried to phone, write . . . I even hired someone to look for her, but the situation was too volatile and chaotic to penetrate."

Hillary stroked Natalie's hair as she listened. Her face showed a quiet concern, with a tiny cleft suspended like a dark sliver of moon between her gracefully arched eyebrows.

"Tell you what, Nat . . . there's no one booked for another hour or so. And since we're only cleaning you up today, I've got an idea. Game on, sister?"

Natalie nodded and smiled. Even though Hillary was about the same age as Safi—or Safi would be, *perish the thought*—she shared the same sagacious soul. And looking out of those crystalline eyes was a spirit born of an ancient earth that belied her youth. It was as if she were both goddess and god, or given the fresh blush of her beauty, the blessed progeny of such a union.

Hillary squeezed Natalie's hand and slowly helped her to her feet. Together they walked out of the shampoo room and into the revealing light of the cutting room. Natalie knew she would have felt embarrassed in this well-lit, open space were it not for Hillary's reassuring grip.

The interior design of Her Secrets Salon reminded Natalie of an ad-hoc campsite tucked safely above an arid expanse of the Serengeti plains. She said the colors to herself—sunset clay, river slate, insouciant creams over virile greens—and it was this earthen combination that had first caught her eye. Hillary, naturally, had been the second thing. She appeared born here, and raised among the mocha styling chairs and ghost-lit walls that stretched all the way to the mottled drop ceiling.

When they'd first spoke, Natalie found herself terrified. At first she didn't know why. She was sure she'd blushed nakedly, but her learned fear of being discovered as a lover of women hadn't been the reason, or so she surmised on her drive back into the city. It wasn't until she returned a half-dozen more times that it finally came to her: the personal style of a bisexual zoologist didn't *need* such a place as Her Secrets Salon.

She had only ever asked to have her hair kept long, dark and cut straight across the bottom, echoed by a shiny curtain of bangs over her eyes. It was the same request every time, and Hillary had never suggested anything new. She'd complimented the texture and apparent health of her hair but the cut itself—center part, a few even snips—required approximately five minutes, including drying. *She must know*, thought Natalie, over and over until she began to imagine her returning—every two weeks, without fail—as a private joke between them. However, now, as Hillary led her along the polished hardwood floors past their favored chair and into the inviting darkness of a back room, Natalie was both nervous and relieved that the joke was, at long last, a thing of the past.

But was Safi?

Hillary pulled her in and closed the door so that only a

narrow ribbon of light was permitted to join them. With her hand on Natalie's lower back, she escorted her to the rear of the room, her arm outstretched until it found the smooth sound of vinyl.

"What is it?" asked Natalie, understanding that it must be some kind of table.

"It's our monolith massage system," she whispered, "which is just a fancy name for an adjustable massage table. But it's very nice and *very* comfortable."

"You've tried it?"

"Not really. I'm the only one that can give them and I haven't booked a single client."

"Why not?"

"The thing's so damned expensive, I've been waiting for someone worthy of getting it dirty."

They laughed like hidden conspirators and it reminded Natalie of the Safi she knew before their first kiss: Safi, the biology student; Safi, the girl; Safi, the friend.

"So you want to try it?" she asked.

"Me? Are you sure?"

"Go on," she said, rubbing Natalie's back. "Take off your smock and clothes and I'll go warm up some oil."

Natalie pulled the smock away from her body and felt her nipples rise from their sleep—as they were wont to do when the thrilling conflict between propriety and passion began raging within her body. She realized long ago that her heart had made a choice that many would find objectionable, and yet, for the past twenty-two months, it was that rub alone that kept her libido going.

But would Safi approve? It was silly to hold onto her,

but there had never been the closure Natalie needed to move on. In fact, in many ways she still considered them a couple. Luckily, as she undid the front buttons of her blouse, each pinch brought with it Safi's approving breath on her quivering muscles. And as she turned to the larger button of her jeans and started on the zipper, she thought she heard the door of a large birdcage swing open.

By the time Hillary returned, Natalie was lying on her stomach, feeling the chill of the air-conditioning on her buttocks. She wondered if it was the danger of being discovered or the anticipation of Hillary's touch that raised tiny goose bumps from her yielding but well-exercised flesh.

"Okay, here we go," said Hillary, and Natalie felt the first drops of buttery sun drizzle along her spine. "I'm not even going to ask if that's too hot."

Natalie laughed, and said, "Finally, after two years, you're learning."

"And you're finally telling."

Natalie hoped their previous conversation would once again find its bearings. Having done so in such a natural way made it that much better.

"Are you saying you had no idea? Really?"

"Maybe." Hillary dug her fingers into the base of Natalie's neck, careful to keep the pressure even. Then she drove her thumbs along either side of her spine, rocking them a little to work out the tension. Her movement downward towards Natalie's butt, only an inch or two at a time, inspired a fantastic suspense at each interval.

"Maybe, huh?"

"Well . . ." she paused to add more oil, "I could feel something during our shampoos . . . but I try not to judge. And what am I supposed to say, 'Hey, you checking me out, girl?'"

"I wish you had," said Natalie, some of the words wrenching out under pressure.

Hillary reached the small of her back and stopped, resting her hands there. "I might've if you pinged at all," she said, her voice rising in mild disbelief.

"If I what?" asked Natalie.

Natalie resumed massaging. "You know, sent out *that vibe*. Some people do it and don't even know they're doing it. Hell, sometimes they're the last to know they're gay."

"Oh, I'm not gay."

"No?"

"I mean . . . I was married for six years, dated men all through high school and college . . . I even melt every time Clive Owen does that thing with his mouth."

Hillary laughed, and said, "So, what do you call yourself?"

For the first time since lying on the table, Natalie thought of Safi and how she had asked the very same question. In fact, they'd asked it of each other in a full, topless embrace after spending all night tasting each other's lips and tongues. Then, like magic, they'd answered at exactly the same time.

"In love."

Without saying a word, Hillary lifted her hands from Natalie's body and—for all Natalie could tell—stood frozen and agape. The suspense in Natalie's spine was of an entirely different sort now. Each second added to her unease like another cube of ice and she was painfully reminded that she was a good fifteen years older than Hillary and should have assumed the young beauty might not be interested in someone her age—if she was interested in "love" at all. She opened her mouth to apologize and felt Hillary's hands return, this time finding her ass.

All ten of Hillary's warm, slippery fingers squeezed at once and held, allowing Natalie to free them at her discretion by tensing her gluteus muscles. This delightful collaboration lasted a few, blissful minutes before Hillary said, "Too hot?"

"You know me," said Natalie, her voice throaty and raw.

Hillary kept a light grip on Natalie's far buttock and leaned in close to her face, using her free hand to move a few damp hairs behind her ear.

"I'm not trying to be Safi," she said quietly, "but we can bring her back, if you like."

Natalie felt her entire body tingle and her face grow hot.

"How?"

Hillary closed the tip of Natalie's ear between her teeth and gently slid her bite around the curvature of the ridge. Then she laid her cheek on the back of Natalie's head and said, "Just think of her . . . call to her. I'll know what to do."

Hillary slid her middle finger along the bifurcating crevice of Natalie's bottom, riding the oily globules collected there until she reached the sweltering folds of her moistening slit.

"It's okay . . . I promise," she said, her voice pitched with innocence.

Natalie hadn't wanted to dream of Safi. She'd wanted to enjoy the massage and escape from the torment that had been hounding her for the better part of two years if only for a few minutes. But now that matters had turned a sexual corner, she realized Safi had been there all along. She'd been watching, admiring, and looking on Hillary with those huge, grateful eyes. Hillary had simply *known*. Natalie wasn't sure how, but at the same time, wasn't the least bit surprised. Hil, her "b-t-b-f", had learned of it through touch—through those brilliant antennae at the caring end of her lithe and powerful arms—just as she'd been made to know of Natalie's affection. Still, not once had she mentioned nor done anything to discourage it, or at the very least, dissipate the tension. *Why?*

"Not everyone pings, Nat," she purred, her finger finding entry inside Natalie's velvety walls. "But love, if it's real, finds a way. Sometimes it just takes time to define."

Natalie moaned with appreciation. "A long time?" she said.

"The time it takes for one love to became two," said Hillary, adding to her finger another and opening her wider. "You don't have to let Safi go, Nat. I can see her, feel her . . . and there's more than enough room for us all."

As if something snapped into place, Natalie felt both her body and mind realign, and the subsequent release of an oppressive weight had her floating. She didn't need to hold out hope for love; she only needed to allow it to help her heal. Hillary had tapped into her heart and set all of them, now and together, transcendentally free.

At that moment, Natalie felt the two fingers penetrate her in full, twisting as they went, and she shuddered with an unexpected orgasm. A moan escaped from her in stages that sounded like weeping, and in many ways she was: with release, then relief and finally, joy.

Hillary slid her fingers out of Natalie and rubbed a sticky drop of her wetness into the shallow depression of her anus. Any last bit of residual tension hiding among the tall grass decamped through her pores via a final, violent tremble. Then Hillary said, "Turn over, baby."

Natalie rotated using her arms and hips, and Hillary's lips were there waiting. She probed the tip of her tongue into Natalie's belly button and traced it up her front until she reached the glistening shoals of her modest cleavage. From there, Hillary brushed her lips from one breast to the other until she had visited each nipple at least three times; stopping to suck in the entire bud and lifting her head until the roseate ovals of tightening flesh slipped away on their own.

Then she continued up Natalie's breastbone, further along the pulsing jugular at the side of her neck, and onward to her strong jaw before finishing at her ear. "Close your eyes," she said, her whisper crackling like the rustle of leaves, "and ask her to kiss us."

Natalie pressed her eyelids tightly together and Safi appeared—more vividly than she had in months. Natalie could see her high, broad cheekbones and wide-set, almond-shaped eyes. Her nose, slender and pleasantly rounded at the tip, ran in a straight line down to her shapely lips that created an opulent bow for her dainty, narrow chin. As instructed, she said aloud, "Kiss me, Safiya. Kiss *we*."

Safi parted her lips only just and laid them against Natalie's waiting pout. Her tongue found its partner and Natalie closed her lips around and drew it in deeper. With that, a finger found her clitoris and began rubbing, coaxing it from under its hood. Natalie's clit was on the larger side—much larger than Safi's (who, she was told, had seen her share)—and it was now fully awake. Only, it wasn't Safi's hand she was feeling. There was no mistaking to whom it belonged and who was reading her mind.

Safi kissed her harder now, her tongue finding every waiting hollow in Natalie's willing mouth. At the same time, Hillary's hand began rubbing more vigorously: it, too, exploring the range of intimacy in that warmest of spaces. It felt to Natalie as if both of her lovers were in sync, communicating simultaneously, knowing exactly when to probe and when to lessen so she would remain on the brink of ultimate satisfaction. No longer content to keep her arms by her sides, Natalie reached out and found a clothed breast. She recognized the shape and size of the nipple and the way it fit like a petal in her hand. It belonged to Safi, and she held on roughly in desperation.

How could it be?

No, I don't want to know.

Just, please . . . don't stop.

As if her prayer was to go unanswered, Safi pulled away. Then, in place of her lips, came a soaked set of fingers that found their way inside Natalie's mouth. She loved the taste of her own juices and was reminded of how hot that made Safi, who would insist on bringing them to her partner's waiting lips for the better part of their lovemaking—often climaxing as Natalie cleaned and suckled them. Sometimes they suckled them together. Often, it was Safi's lips that held the taste she so craved.

As if by decree, Safi's hungry mouth found her eager pussy. She placed kiss after kiss on every part within reach—*gods, those lips*—and with a hoist of Natalie's knees, a few just beyond. There, Safi's tongue went stiff and breeched her snugness. At the same time, her fingers left Natalie's mouth and returned back inside her pussy, gathering more honey for the feast. True to fabulous form, just as an orgasm appeared on the horizon, Safi withdrew and Natalie was once again savoring the flavorful fluid she'd made.

"Oh gods, Safi," moaned Natalie, just as the fingers left her mouth for another round, "please, please, *please*."

Hillary's voice answered. "What do you want, Natalie? What do you want her to do?"

"You know," replied Natalie. "You must know."

At that, fingers became intertwined in both hands and Natalie saw in her mind the most beautiful vision she could ever hope to see: her former lover, Safiya, stretching her lovely neck over Natalie's nude body to meet her new lover, Hillary, in a passionate kiss. Night met morning, and around them birds let fly, sending clarion calls of lust into the warm, misted ether. As she watched them trade soft, wet tongues, Natalie exploded with the fiercest, most intense climax of her life. Just when she thought it would ebb, it surged again, mirroring the vehemence with which they sought each other's souls.

At last, the shaking subsided and Natalie felt a rush of cool air between her legs as they were lowered to the table. A final kiss on her soaked patch of hair opened her eyes, and there, in the dusk of the room, she saw both women. A single blink and there was only Hillary, a single hand in hers, and a lone voice.

"How do you feel?"

Natalie drew Hillary to her by their clasp and kissed her. It was a sweet kiss that felt like a promise returned.

"I feel wonderful," said Natalie. "But—?"

"Shhh . . ." said Hillary, resting a delicate finger on Natalie's lips. Natalie thought she might have broken some sort of trust, but the scuffing of feet in the distance cleared her head.

They giggled, and Hillary whispered, "I'll get the door while you get dressed. And then maybe we do something about your hair. I've got a couple of ideas."

Natalie nodded and released her grip on Hillary's hand. As she watched her leave, her delicious curves silhouetted by the light from the open door, she thought she might be ready to say goodbye to her center part, if that's what Hillary had in mind.

Just Friends

by Cynthia Gentry

Back when Matt and I were trying to be lovers, he used to talk dirty to me on the phone, teasing me slowly into orgasms over the course of many long-distance phone calls. Eventually, being lovers didn't work, especially over a distance of two thousand miles. I finally gave him an excuse to become angry with me and stop returning my phone calls. We made up after a year of silence and now I think of him as a friend. An odd one, maybe. But I think about him and all I think about is how I'd like to be enfolded into his arms.

I'm in New York on business, staying at the Doubletree. I am amazed when I walk into my room. It has a separate bedroom, with a door, and a sitting area with a long, low chaise longue and an ottoman. I laugh when I see the bed. It's an iron bed with patina grillwork on the frame. I laugh because one of the fantasies that Matt used to torment me with was a scenario where he would tie me to a bed and have his way with me. "That pussy's mine," he'd whisper over the phone, as I masturbated to orgasm after orgasm, hundreds of miles away.

Now here I am in Manhattan, alone again. I'm meeting Matt for dinner but since he and I are just friends now, this lovely bed will go to waste. Oh well. I shower off the airplane grime and change my clothes. I think about how Matt used to talk about waiting for me in a hotel room while I was at a party; how he'd describe undressing me, peeling off my black cocktail dress, sliding my black thong panties over my hips and down my legs. But now, because we are just friends, I throw on a pair of jeans and a blackT-shirt. How times have changed.

Twenty minutes later, I arrive at a Mexican restaurant on the lower West Side. He's already sitting at a table, drinking a margarita. He gives me a big grin when he sees me. He's cut his hair, for which I'm glad. I hated the ponytail and moustache he sported for a while. But now here he is, clean-shaven with short blond hair falling over his blue eyes. He stands up and hugs me. I'm tall, but still I have to go up on my toes. I like this. I like men being taller than me. It makes me feel, for a moment, like I'm not a large clumsy Amazon—an image of myself I picked up in junior high when I was two feet taller than everyone else.

"I'm sorry I'm late," I say. "The plane was delayed."

"That's okay, babe," he replies. "Can I get you a margarita?"

At the word "babe," a tingle runs through my body. He used to call me "babe" when we were more than just friends. I loved it because it let me pretend for a moment that I wasn't a supercharged, professional, got-everything-together kind of woman. It let me feel that I was, well, a "babe." I know, it's politically incorrect to admit that.

"A mineral water," I tell him, then, when he raises an eyebrow, "I don't drink anymore. I thought I told you."

This is true. I drank a lot when Matt and I were more than just friends. Entire bottles of wine by myself. When I thought he had dumped me, I decided it would be romantic if I drank myself to death. Thankfully, I changed my mind and joined AA instead.

"That's right," he said. "You told me that. I'm sorry."

"No need to apologize."

"Do you mind if I drink?"

"Why would I? You're not the one with the drinking problem."

I feel very positive and magnanimous in my sobriety. It's what got me to re-establish contact with Matt in the first place. I heard about the possibility of him losing his job because his division was being closed down. I sent him an e-mail saying I was sorry and was thinking about him and he wrote back. We made up and now we're friends.

And now he's doing what friends do: asking me about my job, which is boring, although I should be thankful I have it; my relationship with my boyfriend, whom I love but to whom I am no longer attracted; my writing. Then I take the focus off me and ask him about his love life. I play counselor. This is what I'm good at, especially with men. Sometimes it ends up being a way for me to worm myself into their beds, but with Matt, I really want to know. He's involved in a hopeless romance with some woman fifteen years his junior. Instead of being threatened, I laugh and tease him. I tell him what I think. I begin to get a reaction from him and switch over to flirting mode. I can feel myself doing it. Lowering my head to look up at him mischievously, I smirk, pout, and punch his arm lightly. It's fun. I feel alive.

"How's your sex life?" he asks me suddenly.

I find myself entranced with a piñata hanging from the ceiling. I don't want to talk about myself anymore.

"My, this flan is good," I say with exaggerated enthusiasm. We both laugh.

"That bad, huh?"

I relent. "No, it's fine." Then I blurt out, "As long as I fantasize."

It's as though I've been the one drinking margaritas.

"About what?" He grins at me.

I'm not going to play. "Oh, you know. The usual."

"No, I don't know. Tell me."

"Matt," I say primly. "That's private."

He laughs. "Okay, babe."

Oh, so he's going to drop it that easily? "You should know what my fantasies are, Matt. You gave them to me. Over the phone. Remember?" I've just crossed the line. Now let's see how he'll react.

He doesn't. He sits back, smiling. For some reason, I think he's relieved. But why? I'm not sure I want to play this game anymore.

"Let's get a coffee somewhere," I say. There. Back on safe ground.

Outside the restaurant, he puts his arm around my shoulders. I look up at him.

"Thanks for dinner," I say, and lean up to give him a quick kiss. It's a test. He passes. He didn't try to stretch it out.

We turn back to the street and almost run straight into a young man with dark hair and cheekbones that could cut ice. He's dressed in jeans and carries a gym bag, like he just came from working out.

"Hey, Rich," Matt says. "What's happening?"

I feel a twinge of adrenaline. Rich? My fantasies, the ones Matt gave me, include a Rich. I didn't realize he actually knew one. Matt introduces me. Pleasantries are exchanged. It's decided that Rich will join us for coffee.

Over cappuccinos, Rich surprises me. I'm shy with him at first, as I usually am with handsome men. Guys with his looks aren't usually so funny, so smart. Matt pretends to be bored while we discuss movies. But he's sitting close to me on the couch. I sink into it and rub up against him.

"Poor Matt, left out of the discussion," I say. "What would you like to talk about?"

"I'm just teasing you."

"What else is new?"

"You seem to like hanging out with guys," Rich says.

"I get more attention that way."

"You don't seem like you need a lot of attention," he says. "You seem extremely self-sufficient, actually."

I'm pleased but instead I make a face of displeasure. "Oh Rich, I thought you'd see through my facade. I need lots of attention. Lots. I'm insatiable, in fact."

Our coffees are finished. But none of us seems to want to separate. Then Matt makes his suggestion.

"Let's go hang out at this giant hotel room you keep telling us about."

I feel another shot of adrenaline, of pure fear, like I'm

about to do something very bad. "Only if you boys behave yourselves."

"Scout's honor," says Rich.

I lead them in. Matt, of course, pokes his head into the bedroom and grins. I feel my face getting warm as I reach past him to pull the door shut.

"The mini-bar is that way," I tell him. Drinks are poured. They sip tequila. I'm suddenly very thirsty. Rich, ever the gentleman, goes to get ice. While he's gone, Matt sits down in the chaise longue and stretches his legs out on the ottoman.

"Come here," he says, and suddenly I have no will of my own. I squeeze into the chair with him. He looks into my eyes. "It's good to see you. Every time I do, you become more and more of a babe. Don't make that face. You are."

There's a long pause. My mind is suddenly blank.

"Do you mind if I kiss you, for old time's sake?" he asks. My heart begins pounding.

"No tongue."

"Sure. No tongue." I tilt my head up and let him. At first he keeps his lips closed. Then his tongue slips between my lips. The heady fumes of tequila fill my mouth.

"You said no tongue," I say, but I don't pull my head away.

"I lied," he answers, and keeps going.

"Is this going to ruin our friendship?" I whisper.

"No. It will make it better."

I would like to believe him, but my experience with him and others tells me he's wrong. No matter. I keep kissing him. Then I'm conscious of someone else in the room. Rich.

I pull away from Matt, embarrassed. "Sorry, Rich. Your friend grabbed me." But Matt doesn't let me go and Rich only smiles.

"Don't worry about it. It looked like fun." He pours me a glass of water, which he sets on the coffee table. He sits down on the ottoman, near our feet.

"It is fun," Matt says. "She's a good kisser." He turns to me. "Rich broke up with his girlfriend recently." If this is calculated to get my sympathies, it works.

"Oh God," I say. "Then you don't need to watch us kissing." I try again to pull away, but Matt doesn't break his grip.

"Yes, I do," Rich says.

At times like these, there comes a moment when we make decisions: to decide whether to stay with what is familiar and tell ourselves that we are being good, or to go with the unknown. And though I don't consciously know it, it's at this moment that I've chosen the latter.

"There's only one problem," I hear Rich say. Matt and I are kissing deeply now. He has pulled me closer to him. I'm letting him stroke my back, my ass. At Rich's words, we stop and look at him.

"I'm sitting here thinking how much I'd like to be kissing those beautiful lips myself."

His words were catnip to me. I'm already wet between my legs, now I feel my cunt lips fill with warmth, soften and open. My heart thuds in my chest. Can't they hear it? I pull away from Matt and sit at the edge of the chair. I picture myself as supremely benevolent, the Queen of Kisses, bestowing them out of charity and goodwill. I take his face between my hands and lean forward. My lips meet Rich's and I've made another decision.

I start to French kiss him, but he says, "Wait. Slow down." He puts a hand on my cheek and kisses me gently with his lips closed, and then again. With each new kiss, he begins to slip his tongue a little further between my lips. We begin kissing deeply, his tongue playing with mine. Finally, I pull away.

"There," I say. "How was that? Do you feel more included now?"

He smiles. "Matt is right. You are a good kisser. I'd like to kiss you again."

"Don't stop on my account," Matt says. We both shift our positions so that I'm sitting on the edge of the chair with my back toward him, his legs on either side of me. He puts his hands on my hips.

"One more," I say to Rich, telling myself that will be the end of it, but I know I'm wrong. As I kiss Rich, Matt leans forward and slides his hands under my shirt, playing with my breasts. I feel him nuzzle my neck, my ear. He unhooks my bra and gently rubs my nipples. Then he slides one hand down my stomach into my pants. I freeze.

"Is this okay, babe?" He whispers in my ear.

I stare into Rich's eyes. They are warm and earnest.

For a split second no one moves. Then I put my lips to Rich's again. Matt's hand continues its explorations down my pants, under the waistband of my underwear.

But because of the jeans it can't get much farther than that. I shift my hips almost involuntarily, trying to give him access. His other hand leaves my breast and unfastens the buttons of my jeans. He slides his hand back down and discovers the wetness between my legs. I hear his intake of breath and I moan as he caresses my clit. Meanwhile, Rich continues kissing me. My mind is so full of sensations that I can't think.

Again, I pull away from Rich and lean back into Matt, whose hand is deep inside my wetness. Rich takes off my shoes. He reaches for my jeans.

"We should stop," I say, but have no will to make that happen. They have to decide.

"Is that what you want?" Rich asks me.

"I don't know."

"It's okay, babe," Matt says. "Let's go into the bedroom. Let Rich give you a massage. Then you can decide."

In the bedroom, I turn and stand before them. Matt stands behind me and pulls my T-shirt over my head. I let him ease my bra off my shoulders. Rich slides my jeans over my hips and down to the floor, kneeling as he does so. I step out of them. He hooks his fingers into the elastic band of my panties. He smiles at me as he slides them off. I'm completely exposed to both of them. I want to cover myself. He begins stroking my legs. His hands move up the back of my thighs, then around to the front, and he traces the V of my pubic hair with his thumb. If Matt weren't holding me up, my knees would have given way by now. I wait for him to put his mouth where his hands are, but he rises instead.

"I've got some massage oil in my gym bag," he says and leaves the room.

Matt turns me around to face him. "Nothing will happen that you don't want to happen," he says.

"I know."

He pulls the comforter, blanket, and sheet back from the bed. "Lie down." He takes off his shirt.

I stretch out on my stomach. Matt stretches out next to me and we kiss. Rich returns to the room with his bag. I turn my head and see that he has also taken off his shirt.

"I'm going to take off my pants," he says, "so they don't cut into you." He does, and I see the huge bulge under his briefs. I turn away and wonder why. To preserve *his* modesty? A moment later I feel him straddle me lightly and begin to stroke his hands over my body. Slippery with oil, they glide over my skin and his strong fingers knead my muscles. I sigh with pleasure. "You're tense," he tells me. "Relax."

"Matt, are you bored yet?" I ask, trying to make a joke.

"Not at all," he answers, smiling. "You have such a beautiful body. Such beautiful skin."

By now, Rich is finished with my back. He massages my buttocks. He slips a finger between my legs and lets it stop at the opening to my cunt. I groan.

"You're so wet," he whispers.

I don't want him to stop, but he keeps moving down my legs to my feet.

"I'll go to sleep if you work on my feet," I tell him. I'm not lying.

"We wouldn't want that," he says, but he massages

them nonetheless. All tension melts out of my body. "Turn over," he says, finally, and he continues to work on my feet.

Eyes closed, I hear Matt shift on the bed. He takes my wrists in one hand. I open my eyes and see that in his other hand, he is holding a long velvet scarf. He smiles and begins to slowly wrap it around my wrists.

"Let me do this," Matt says. "I won't hurt you."

"I know, but . . ." He covers my mouth with a kiss even while he loops the other end of the velvet through the grillwork of the headboard. It holds my arms above my head, firmly, but not too tightly.

"I want to make your fantasies come true," he says, smiling at me. I look down to see Rich's reaction. His eyes gleam.

"Nothing is going to happen that you don't want to happen," he says again, reaching down into his bag to pull out more velvet ropes. He hands one to Matt. They part my legs gently and tie one ankle loosely to one bedpost and one to the other. There is enough slack so I can bend my knees. I begin to twist. I feel too exposed.

"Matt, I don't know about this."

He slips his jeans off. His erection is huge. He climbs on the bed and stretches out next to me. He kisses me and plays with my nipples.

"Let yourself go," he says. "You can't help it."

He is right. I know they would stop if I became frightened. My heart is pounding in my chest, indeed. But whether it is from fear or excitement, I have no idea. Matt has remembered my fantasy of being tied down. He has remembered the fantasy about Rich. But there's something more about the fantasy that Matt gave me about Rich. How could I not have realized this sooner? Was it because I didn't want to? I can hardly breathe.

"Matt, is Rich . . . is Rich a . . . ?"

Matt laughs. Rich smiles. He has climbed onto the bed and between my legs.

"Yeah, babe. Rich's from an escort service."

I remember lying on the bed with the phone pressed to my ear while I masturbated furiously, as Matt described sharing me with a male prostitute. A male prostitute named Rich.

And now, I am at their mercy. Matt has made the fantasy real.

"Oh Matt, I can't believe you did this."

"We can stop any time you want. This is all up to you."

"Do you want me to go?" Rich asks, kissing my knees, the inside of my thighs, my belly.

There is a long silence. There is a voice in my head saying, *Good girls don't do this. This is beyond the pale. This will come back to haunt you.*

I look at Matt. "What if this doesn't work?"

I hear Rich laugh. "It will work," he says.

I look at him. Suddenly, practical thoughts enter my head. I have to ask.

"Are you . . . Is this going to be . . . ?"

It's as if he has read my mind. "I'm straight. I only do women. And it will all be safe sex. Don't worry."

They are both looking at me. Neither man has stopped touching me. Their hands are everywhere—stroking my nipples, my ass, my legs. I look up at Matt. I can't say the words. But he understands. He knows my answer. He smiles, but then his face becomes quite serious.

"Rich will do anything I tell him to," Matt says. "And I'm going to tell him to do a lot to you. I hope you're ready."

I look back at Rich, who is still rubbing his hands up and down my legs, brushing my pubic hair lightly. He smiles at me, that same smile, warm and implacable.

"Yes," I say, my voice hardly above a whisper.

Matt continues. "First, I think I'd like Rich to lick your pussy."

Rich obeys, but he doesn't dive right in. No. He kisses my pussy gently, like he kissed my other lips earlier. Then I feel his tongue slip between my cunt lips and barely touch my clitoris. I moan and arch my back, straining against the rope that holds my hands.

"Yeah, that's right," Matt says. His fingers are playing with my nipples.

"You taste beautiful," Rich says. He reaches down into his gym bag and pulls out a square of latex. I've never seen a dental dam before. I know that we must do this, yet I'm afraid that it will numb the feeling I've just had, the feeling of his tongue on me. But he manages to make this act erotic, spreading my cunt lips apart and stroking the latex into place. He puts his tongue back between my legs and I feel its soft, insistent pressure as strong as a finger, flicking back and forth across my clit.

"Do you like that?" Matt asks me.

"Oh God, yes."

"Good. Rich, put a finger into her. I want to see you fill her up."

Rich obeys. He slides the index finger of his right hand into my already sopping cunt and moves it in and out slowly.

"I think you should put another finger into her. Into her ass, though."

I moan. There is something about having a man touch my asshole that seems taboo, which only makes it even more exciting.

Rich puts his middle finger into my cunt. At first, I think he's misunderstood Matt. But when he pulls it out, I realize that he has just been wetting it with my juices. He then slides it down to the entrance of my asshole. I think I'm going to come right then.

"Not so fast," he says, taking his mouth from my cunt. "I think she needs something bigger in her," he tells Matt. "A big cock."

"Do it," Matt says. "Get her ready for yours."

Rich reaches into his bag again and pulls out a large, pink, lifelike dildo. He puts his hands back on me, touching my ass, but he puts the dildo at the entrance of my cunt. He looks to Matt.

"Do you want it?" Matt asks me. "Do you want that big dildo in you?" I can only nod. "Of course you do."

He nods to Rich, who very slowly slides the dildo into me. He lowers his head back to my cunt and resumes licking as he fucks me with the dildo. With each push of the dildo, he slides his finger a little deeper into my ass. Matt begins to gently suck on my nipples and I hear my own moans grow louder. As if in response, Matt covers my mouth with his lips. My arms strain against the velvet ropes.

"I'm going to come," I say, pulling my mouth away. I can't believe it's happening this fast. Sometimes it takes as much as an hour before I can climax.

"That's good," Matt says. "I want to see you. I missed out on that before."

Before. Yes, when we almost became lovers. A memory flashes through my mind: of me on a different hotel bed and of Matt parting my legs. I stare at him and then I come. I throw my head back and cry out as the waves course through my body. I forget about the ropes holding my hands. As the orgasm subsides, Rich slows his licking. Then he pulls the dildo out of my cunt and his finger out of my ass. They are both grinning at me.

"We're not done with you," Matt says. Rich is untying my ankles from the bedpost. Almost instinctively, I close my legs. I think I see him smirk. Matt positions himself on his left side so that his cock is level with my face. Gently, he puts his hand on my cheek and turns my head. He presses the tip of his penis against my lips. I part them and take his cock into my mouth. I know that if my hands were free I could do more, but as it is, I just lick the tip and then begin sucking.

"Oh God," he says, moaning. "I forgot how good those lips were." I look up and see that his eyes are closed in pleasure. I want my hands free so that I can stroke his ass, his balls. Then almost reluctantly, he pulls himself out of my mouth. He flips himself so that he is lying on his right side, his face even with my hips and his cock again at my mouth. "Keep sucking it, babe," he says, and I comply. I'm afraid that my arms are going to cramp. Then I feel his hand caress my stomach.

"Are you ready to be fucked good and hard?" he asks me.

I forget about the ropes and the numbness in my arms. "Oh, God, yes. Fuck me."

"Not yet. I'm going to let this male hooker fuck you first. I'm going to share you with him."

I pull away from his cock and look down. Rich has a condom wrapper in his hand. Another adrenaline rush hits me. I watch, my heart racing, as he opens the wrapper. To me, the moment when a man puts a condom on is one of the most exciting moments in sex. It means that the sex is about to happen; that I'm about to be fucked. But by this stranger?

Rich spreads my legs and puts his knees between them. He positions his cock where I can feel it at the entrance of my cunt. It's wet from the recent orgasm and getting wetter. Rich places his hands on either side of me and braces himself above me.

"Put it in just a little," Matt says.

Rich does, and I moan. My pelvis moves against him involuntarily but he pulls back.

"Do you like that?" Matt asks me. "Do you like being fucked by a stranger?"

"Yes," I say. "Yes."

"Do you want him to do it more?"

"Yes."

Then Matt begins rubbing my clit. For a moment I think, *No, it will be too sensitive.* I'm surprised to feel sensations of pleasure once again.

"Put it in a little more," Matt orders Rich and he complies. I know Matt can see everything from his vantage point. It makes me feel even more exposed, more powerless, and at the same time, more turned on.

Rich begins to slowly fuck me. We stare into each other's eyes. I wonder how many women he's looked down on like this. My ego rises up inside me. I tighten my vagina around his cock. His eyes widen and his face contorts momentarily in ecstasy before he composes himself. I want to put my hands on his ass and pull him to me.

"She's good," he tells Matt. "I'm going to have to do her slow."

"I want to do her mouth," Matt answers. He moves up the bed, stroking my side with his stiff cock. Softly, he brushes my cheeks with it. Rich lifts one hand from the bed and again turns my cheek to Matt's erection, which I take between my lips.

"Oh God, she's sucking you really good," Rich tells him. I'm pleased and overwhelmed by sensations as Matt begins rubbing me harder.

"You're going to come with his cock in you," he says.

Rich's thrusts become more even, slow and hard, as Matt's finger rubs faster and faster. Even though Matt's penis fills my mouth, I've stopped sucking and have started moaning.

I come again, slamming my pelvis against Rich. I open my eyes in time to see the look of surprise on his face and

I know he is coming, too. Matt pulls his hand away so that Rich can collapse on top of me. We are both sweating.

He rolls off, panting hard. "That doesn't usually happen," he says to the ceiling.

Matt laughs. "I'd better see what all the fuss is about." He shifts position and gets a condom. I look at him in surprise. "I said we were going to share you," he reminds me.

I realize again that my arms are aching. "Untie me," I say. Matt begins to reach for the rope but Rich is there first. I lower my freed arms and Rich rubs them while Matt slips his condom on.

Once suited up, he spreads my legs again. I gasp as I feel his still-hard cock slide into my wetness. Then he's looking down on me. "You're so wet," he says. "You're so, so wet."

"I didn't think this was ever going to happen," I say. Indeed, I didn't. A few years before, it was all I could think about. But Matt had been the one who wanted to wait to consummate our relationship. We'd taken it right up to the edge before he pulled back, perhaps sensing the intensity of my neediness. The further he pulled back, the faster I came at him, until I no doubt drove him away. Now—when I least expected it, when I had completely embraced the idea of us just being friends—it happens.

Now while Rich watches, Matt fucks me slowly, hard. "I knew this would feel good. I knew it." He turns me over and pulls me onto my elbows and knees. I feel him enter me from behind. He grabs my ass cheeks hard and the pace of his thrusts quicken. "You have such a great ass," I hear him say.

"I want to see you come," I tell him. He flips me over and enters me again.

"That's it," he moans. "Fuck me, fuck me, fuck me." Then he comes, his body shuddering, his face even more contorted then Rich's.

Later that night, I wake up. Matt sleeps beside me, breathing quietly. I hear the toilet flush. Rich enters the room and begins to collect his things. I watch him dress. He glances over at the bed and sees me.

"Hi," he whispers.

"Hi."

He finishes dressing and comes over to my side of the bed. He kisses me on the lips. "Bye," he says. "Take care of yourself."

"Do I need to . . . ?" I can't believe I'm about to offer to pay him.

"Nope. All taken care of." He heads for the door.

"Wait," I don't know quite what I'm doing, but I get out of bed and follow him out of the bedroom to the door of the suite. He looks at me questioningly. I put my arms around his neck and kiss him deeply.

"What was that for?" he asks.

"For making one of my wildest fantasies come true."

"Matt made it come true. Not me."

I hear the voice in my head ask, *So this was just another job to you?* I mentally kick myself. Surely he's heard that question before. And I'm sure he tells them all they were special. So I take a step back. "Thanks anyway," I say.

"Any time."

"Really?" I say teasingly.

He gives me a strange look. Suddenly, he drops his bag and grabs me. We begin kissing madly, almost as though we were trying to devour each other. He picks me up and I wrap my legs around his waist. He takes me back into the sitting room and together we fall onto the armchair. He fumbles with his pants, then fumbles with a condom, and then he is in me again. Our sex is even more intense this time because we have made a silent agreement to be quiet. This is no performance. He never takes his eyes from mine. Finally he comes, and lies against me.

"That was on the house," he whispers in my ear. "That was for me."

A tremor goes through me. "How do I know that?"

"Because. Because I want to see you again."

Rich is gone. I crawl back into bed beside Matt, who stirs in his sleep and reaches over to me. "How are you?" he asks groggily, pulling me to him. Here is another fantasy come true: me enfolded in his arms, safe.

"I'm fine," I say, despite the other fantasy's unexpected turn. Can one cheat with a male prostitute on someone who is just a friend? Why do I want so badly for him to leave, to not be there when I wake up in the morning? And then the feeling subsides. "Thanks for tonight."

"What are friends for?" Matt says, and goes back to sleep.

When in Rome

by Mercy Loomis

Suzi unpacked the bags, humming softly under her breath and stealing occasional glances out the window. Not that the view was very good—mostly she could just see the Flamingo Casino across the street—but that wasn't the point. They were here.

Finally.

The "Girls Gone Vegas" vacation they'd always said they would do.

Suzi danced back over to the dresser, her arms full of clothes. Myriah laughed at her antics from where she lounged on the generous sofa, flipping through the channels on the TV.

"Keep shaking that booty, girl, and I'll have to put it to a better use than ferrying my wardrobe," Myriah teased.

Suzi grinned, bouncing on her toes as she refolded several shirts. "Promise?"

Myriah got up, crossing to stand just behind her lover. Grabbing Suzi by the hips, she jerked her backwards, pressing their bodies tight together, and gave Suzi's earlobe a playful bite. Suzi moaned, one hand reaching up to touch Myriah's face.

Myriah stepped back, giving her sub a resounding smack on the ass. "Later," she said with a smile, and went back to the couch.

"Yes, ma'am!" With a happy sigh, Suzi turned to make another trip to the dresser.

The door that connected their room to Kimbra's opened, as usual, with no warning. Kimbra poked her head in, tossing her red curls out of her face.

"I'm all settled in. You guys gonna be a while? I was thinking of taking a look around before dinner."

"I'm just about . . ." Suzi frowned as she took a look at the outfit Kimbra had changed into. "That's my miniskirt, isn't it?" she asked flatly.

"Yeah, I borrowed it. Doesn't it look great with this shirt?" Kimbra smoothed her hands over the emerald green halter top.

"Kimbra, we've talked about this. Stop going through my closet!"

"I know, I know. I will. Have you seen the how many shops they have here?" Kimbra's look was hardly apologetic.

Myriah appeared at Suzi's elbow before she could do more than clench her fists. "I think we're going to hang out in the room for a bit. Why don't you go on ahead?"

Kimbra shrugged. "Okay, I'll see you back here around five?" Without waiting for a reply, she turned and left.

Suzi stared murderously at the closed door. "I've had it. I have so had it with her."

Myriah stroked Suzi's long brown hair. "I know, love. Relax. You're supposed to be relaxing, remember?"

"I can't help it. She makes me insane." Suzi rested her head on Myriah's shoulder, leaning into the caress. "She knows I hate it when she goes through my things, but she keeps on doing it. I'm tempted to start gaining weight so we won't be the same size anymore."

Myriah tugged sharply at Suzi's hair, forcing her head back. "Now that's just not allowed. You are not ruining that perfect ass because of one obnoxious roommate." Myriah kissed her hard, until she felt Suzi melt against her. "That's better," she purred, breaking away. She tested the door thoughtfully, and it swung open. "Why don't you finish unpacking, love? I have an idea."

Kimbra returned to her room flushed from walking and more than ready to get some dinner. She hadn't even made it a fraction of the way through the shops in the Forum, and she was already drooling over a half dozen items.

Suzi is so going to dig this place, she thought, wishing the rooms reflected the Roman themes that were the hallmark of the public spaces downstairs. With a thrill of voyeuristic anticipation, she reached for the door to Suzi and Myriah's room, more than half hoping to catch her lovely roomies *in flagrante delicto*.

To her surprise, the door was locked.

Kimbra paused. They rarely locked the doors at home even with Kimbra's manufactured habit of not knocking, which had bolstered her hope that one day, if she could work up the courage, her overtures might not be unwelcome. Biting her lip, she tapped on the door.

"Hey guys, I'm back."

There was a muffled rustling sound. "We'll be a few minutes," Myriah called. "Why don't you hop in the shower?"

"Sure."

Kimbra retreated to her sumptuous bathroom, unable to stop the flood of images that raced through her mind. Glimpses stolen from other times when she'd walked in on the two women, sounds that crept through the walls at night. Kimbra felt her skin flush with heat, and turned the shower on cold.

Get a grip, she scolded herself as she stripped, tossing her clothes into a pile on the bed. Twisting her hair into an unruly knot to keep it out of the spray, she walked into the shower. She gasped, the freezing water making her skin pebble and her nipples tighten almost painfully. Almost.

The first time had been an accident. She'd thought the girls were out, and had been looking for one of the CDs Myriah liked to borrow from the stack in the living room. Kimbra had thought her face would light on fire when she walked in on the two. Suzi had been bound and gagged—which explained the quiet—spread-eagled on the bed, ass in the air, while Myriah stood behind her, black leather gleaming against her chocolate skin, three fingers buried in Suzi's pussy.

It was the look on Myriah's face that haunted her, though. Pure impatience. *Well, in or out?* her expression had seemed to say.

Stammering apologies, Kimbra had gotten out.

Now, even under the cold needles of the shower, she felt fresh heat pool between her thighs at the memory of that look.

"Dammit," she said, sighed, and turned off the shower.

They were so *happy*, that was the worst of it. Kimbra had always thought of herself as straight, or at least she had until then and the hot nights that followed, where she could hardly close her eyes without her imagination providing a different ending to that encounter. She loved Suzi and Myriah like sisters, and maybe more, but how did you intrude on people who were so obviously well matched and content with each other? Especially when your own feelings were so frighteningly, maddeningly new?

Cold, frustrated, and horny, Kimbra stepped onto the tiles and looked around for a towel. Frowning, she realized that the racks only held hand towels, and the shelves were bare.

"Lovely," she muttered, and dried off with a hand towel, rubbing hard enough to leave pink streaks against her fair skin. Tossing the towel into the corner, she stormed naked into the bedroom. And stopped dead.

Suzi lay spread-eagled on her bed, ass in the air. Her face was turned to Kimbra, but her eyes were closed, her expression that mask of blissful submission that always made Kimbra burn with envy and longing.

Myriah stood at the end of the bed, every line of her body infused with regal expectation, but gowned in leather instead of brocade, crowned with nothing but her own stylishly short hair, every inch the ruler of the room. In one hand she held a riding crop, which she tapped lightly, rhythmically, against Suzi's raised behind.

Kimbra stared, frozen with hope and terror.

Myriah stalked toward her on her stiletto-heeled boots, hips swaying, tapping the crop against the palm of her hand. Kimbra felt her insides turn to Jell-O under that commanding gaze and had to fight not to fall to her knees.

"Stand up straight," Myriah snapped, and Kimbra shot to attention. Her cheeks flamed as the leggy dominatrix walked slowly around her, the crop trailing a teasing line across her hip, tracing the swell of her buttocks, and over the other hip as Myriah completed her perusal.

"Nice," Myriah commented, and Kimbra's heart leapt. The other woman walked around her again, this time stopping directly behind her. Slender fingers unwound the knot of Kimbra's hair, combed through it with gentle— and not so gentle—tugs until it fell like cornsilk down her back. Spectral hands traced the shape of her curls against her skin, finally coming to rest one on each hip.

"Better," Myriah said. A little squeeze, then the heat of another body pressing against her, the smell of leather. "Someone has been making my sub very sad lately," Myriah murmured in Kimbra's ear.

A hard pinch on the meat of her right butt cheek made Kimbra jump with a squeal.

"I don't like it when Suzi is sad. And I don't like the disrespectful way you behave." Another pinch, on the other side this time. Kimbra managed not to squeal, though she still jumped. "Maybe you need some training."

The crop touched her back, the leather tracing a line from her shoulder blade to the cleft of her ass.

Kimbra shivered.

"Do you think you would benefit from some training?" The crop tapped one cheek lightly, then the other. "Would you like that, Kimbra?"

Kimbra's head was spinning. So much, so fast. Did she want this—them—like this? Right now?

"Yes," she whispered before she could overthink it.

"Yes, what?"

"Yes, ma'am?" Kimbra asked, tensing.

"Very good." There was real warmth in her voice now, a purring approval that Kimbra already knew she'd be chasing with just as much devotion as Suzi. "But first," Myriah continued, guiding her forward with a hand at her waist, stopping her directly behind Suzi, "I think you owe someone an apology."

Kimbra turned to look at her in a panic.

Myriah only arched an eyebrow. "Kneel. Unless you don't want to play after all?"

Kimbra licked her lips. "I, uh . . . I don't know what to do," she said helplessly, gesturing toward the bed.

Suzi giggled.

The crop landed with a resounding smack. Suzi hissed, arching her back. Her butt wriggled.

"Behave," Myriah told her, then turned back to Kimbra. "Kneel," she said again, with surprising gentleness.

Kimbra knelt.

Myriah tapped Suzi's knee with the crop. "Wider." Obediently, the little brunette spread her legs until her stomach was almost flat against the mattress, her nether lips face level to where Kimbra knelt behind her.

Kimbra stared into the nest of folded skin, mortified by her own inexperience. "What do I do?"

The crop touched her knee. "Wider," Myriah said.

Kimbra spread her knees, tensing as Myriah knelt behind her.

"All I want you to do," Myriah whispered in her ear, "is put her pleasure before yours. Focus everything you have on pleasing her."

A fingertip touched the inside of her thigh, and Kimbra quaked in reaction. She hadn't realized how wet she was until she felt the juices trickling down her legs.

"And if you run out of ideas, just do to her what I do to you, only with your tongue," Myriah purred. "If something makes you uncomfortable, say 'stop.'"

Myriah began to play with her labia. Kimbra let out a shuddering breath and leaned forward. "Okay," she said.

Everything seemed totally foreign at first. She'd always loved oral sex, but with Suzi the taste, the texture, the smell, not to mention the mechanics, were completely new. But that first hesitating flick of her tongue had made the other woman moan, and that was one similarity she could hold on to. With growing confidence she traced the folds of Suzi's lips with her tongue, following the path that Myriah's fingers made between her own legs. It felt so good to be touched, but it distracted her from what she was doing. She had to put Suzi first. Kimbra tried to push those wandering fingers from her mind, burying her face against Suzi's soft body. Her world narrowed down to the quivering flesh beneath her mouth and the sounds, disembodied and directionless, that accompanied each desperate motion.

From behind her came Myriah's voice, demanding, insistent. "Come, Suzi."

Kimbra latched onto Suzi's clit and sucked for all she was worth, and the little brunette shook as if she'd grabbed hold of a live wire, screaming her release into the mattress.

A hand twined through her hair, pulled her hard against Myriah's body. Kimbra shuddered, suddenly overwhelmed by the stimulation she'd been trying to ignore.

"That was very good, Kimbra," Myriah said menacingly. She let go of Kimbra's hair to pinch one nipple between her fingers, her other hand still playing between her legs. "Maybe you deserve a little reward. What do you think, Suzi?"

From the bed came a muffled, "Oh, yeah."

"Do you want to come, Kimbra?"

"Yes, ma'am!"

Another pinch, fiercer now, a pain that shot straight to her groin and drove her higher. "Beg me."

"Please," Kimbra whimpered, the words tumbling out, almost meaningless. "Please, ma'am, please let me come, please . . ."

A chuckle. "Since you ask so nicely." The hand left her nipple, slipped around behind her. A jolt of gratification as Myriah shoved her fingers up inside her, rubbing her clit hard, squeezing it. "Come for me, Kimbra."

The orgasm seemed to explode from her, ripping shrieks from her lips, her back arching against Myriah, her hips grinding, shuddering, all control absolutely shattered by that simple command.

Kimbra collapsed, wrung out and sated, in Myriah's arms. She looked up to see Suzi, twisted around on the bed to face her, grinning like the Cheshire Cat. With an exhausted laugh, Kimbra smiled back at her.

"That," said Myriah, "was very good indeed. Now, you hop back in the shower and clean up. And if you behave yourself at dinner, I'll let Suzi dress you up when we get back." Myriah helped Kimbra get to her feet. "Suzi, love, come help me get out of this gear and then you can finish me off in the shower."

Suzi winked at Kimbra, who wrinkled her nose playfully. "Yes, ma'am," they chorused.

House of Treasures

by Laura Neilsen

Savannah eased the car up to valet parking in front of the mansion. I had been under the impression we were attending a small cocktail party in a humble setting, but the house was a staggering French-styled mansion, sprawling over numerous acres of land. Surprised, I said, "Is that a house or a gated community? You could shelter an entire town in some parts of the world in that."

I folded the visor down and applied a coat of lip gloss, "I thought you said this was an intimate get together with a few old friends."

"It is," Savannah said. Then four more cars pulled up. "But with a few hundred others as well." She half laughed, then combed a few strands of hair away from my eyes and said, "You look wonderful. Just make yourself at home. You're going to have a great time."

Savannah is a power broker at the law firm I started working at a couple of months ago and, from what I've heard, a deadly adversary. She can chew up and spit out almost any opponent for breakfast, but with extremely good looks, I think most people find her distracting, as do most of the men around the office. They can hardly take their eyes off her. But at the first moment I saw her, I sensed there was something different about her. I couldn't quite put my finger on it, but I knew the long-sleeved turtlenecks and white frilly blouses didn't even begin to hide who she really was.

When she invited me to the party, I couldn't have been happier. "Absolutely," I said. "I'd love to go." It was exactly what I needed—a good evening out. I'd been working long hours and bringing my work home most nights. I was new in town and didn't know a soul. I was suffering from loneliness and edging on claustrophobia, spending night after night for more than a month alone inside an incredibly small, one-bedroom apartment, thanks to the firm.

A butler greeted us at the door. "Good evening, Savannah."

Apparently, he knew her. *She must be a regular around here*, I thought. He directed his attention to me. "Would the young lady care for a tour, or prefer to get acquainted with guests in the ballroom?"

Savannah jumped in. "The ballroom will be fine." She sounded apprehensive. I didn't know why then, but I do now. She wanted to ease me into the experience ahead, and she wanted to do it on her own terms. She had a plan.

We walked down a lengthy sandstone corridor decorated with French tapestries of couples frolicking in the countryside, and Regency paintings of women wearing pantaloons. Then hordes of voices could be heard, as well the sounds of an orchestra, which pulled us towards a dance floor. Banquet tables of food were scattered around, and waiters dashed about with an assortment of champagnes, wines, and liquors. About half the people were dressed in costume: bewigged as George Washington, Prince, or Elvira. And many guests wore Venetian decorative masks, or seductively held them by handles to their faces, offering flirtatious glimpses.

An obvious close friend approached Savannah and whisked her off to the dance floor. I was on my second martini when I noticed them locked together, arm and arm, walking upstairs with the predetermined destination of the closest bedroom, I presumed. I decided then that if I didn't meet someone interesting by the time I finished my third martini, I was calling it a night.

Then he walked into the room—no, correction—he floated into the room, like blocks of time drifting in fog. Fascinated wouldn't even begin to describe the effect he had on me. He was dressed in a black suit, cloak, and black leather mask—and when he stared into my eyes from across the room, I was trapped.

"Allow me to show you the view," he said, taking my hand and guiding me through the estate down a long staircase leading outside to a patio, nestled within the canyon. Side by side we stood along a wrought iron fence, talking and sipping champagne, overlooking a panoramic view of the ocean. A chilling wind began to blow and he wrapped his cape around my shoulders. Then, with one hand behind my head, he guided my mouth onto his, breathing into my lungs, filling me more with each exhalation, wreaking heavenly havoc on any good sense I might have had about behaving myself that evening.

Time vanished and I lost myself, forgetting all that was and was not, as the internal flames of human combustion erupted. Our embrace grew tighter, our lips pressed harder, and my eyes, weighed heavy with passion, closed. His lips roamed up and down my neck, and across my chest bones to the most sensitive part of a breast.

Then, lacking in all reason, I felt the presence of someone. My eyes opened and I looked to the side, discovering an extremely beautiful woman watching us. She waved a hand, motioning me to come over. I remained speechless, and for reasons I'm not sure of, I held her stare for a few passing minutes, as he lowered my dress below my shoulders, exposing my naked breasts and laving each tight nipple, causing my head to rear back giving into sensitivity.

Her expression told me she understood my desire, but when the sensation became too overpowering and my breath labored inside my throat, she turned and scurried off.

"What is it?" He paused.

"A woman was out here. I think she wanted us to come with her." I described the appearance of the demi-goddess and asked, "Do you know her? Because I sure don't."

"No. I don't know who that can be. Look, I hate to let go of you." His hands squeezed around my waist. "But I can see you're concerned."

We went back inside the house, entering a game room offside the pool.

"Is that her?" He said, seeing a woman disappear around a door jam.

"Yes."

We trailed after her around a corner, and down a long hallway. The woman looked back at us a few times. Then, oddly, she picked up the hem of her gown and ran at full speed.

"She wants us to follow her," he said, rushing after her.

"I think she wants to get away from us." I grimaced.

"Let's just take a look for a moment at where she was going."

He opened a concealed door that lead to a long passageway that ended with an enormously large room. My high heels instantly put on the brakes, and I covered my mouth with my hands in shock, saying, "Oh my God. What kind of place is this?"

Stale air hung heavy in the room with the stench of sweat and what I dared to think foul bodily fluids. The room was dimly lit by one hanging chandelier. Dark furnishings stamped out any additional light. Purple and black velvet couches and chaises were carelessly scattered, and oversized pillows were tossed on the floor with blankets concealing throes of thrashing bodies. And in dark corners, shadows painted bodies intertwined in motion crawling over walls. Soft music played, and undertones of a woman giggling could be heard, as well as a woman whimpering. And another woman whispered breathlessly, as a man groaned and moaned, huffing and puffing, hollering louder, met by the high-pitched, lilting sounds of a woman's "ohhh's" and "oooo's" until together harmonizing in one lengthily, strident scream.

I ran out of the room and down the passageway. I needed to get out of that place. I felt like I was going to start retching. I reached a hand out, searching for a wall to lean on. Then there he was, my masked man. His arms wrapped around my waist, steadying me on my feet.

"I bet you can use some fresh air," he said, guiding me outside onto a balcony. "I can see this is your first time here. Would you like to go someplace more private?"

"Yes, that'd be great." I said without thinking, feeling utterly comfortable and safe with a complete stranger in a house of freaks. The lawyer side of my brain knew it made no sense, but the woman inside me resigned herself to being overpoweringly drawn to the enigmatic man behind the mask.

We walked down a stone corridor. Torches on walls lit the way, drawing attention to dungeons, and torture chambers, and dingy rooms with barred doors. I glanced inside a room where a man was pinned to a brick wall, held by black iron cuffs around his wrists and ankles. A black rubber dildo was in his mouth, while at once a man deep-throated his cock. I gasped with shock and quickened my step, passing another room with a female dominatrix wearing a black leather mask, four-inch black leather boots, and a black leather bustier with the breasts cut out with diamond studded nipples. She shouted, "On your hands and knees! Lick my feet, slave!" and cracked a leather whip that burned red marks against a man's naked buttocks. His balls tightened and so did his cock ring, and he groaned at her feet, pleading for more humiliation and merciless agony.

I hurried up a flight of stairs to a security door. He swiped a card through magnetic sensors and a green light flashed—Open Sesame. I began to think this was some sort of membership place, that people actually joined a club to get their wildest freak on. It was absolutely mind-blowing.

We followed a path entangled with trees and lush vegetation to a private beach. Couples lay naked in hammocks tied to palm trees, while stone rock fireplaces burned. Then there were tents: amazing, lavish, canvas tents. I counted ten, situated a good private distance from one another. I felt like I just walked onto the set of *Lawrence of Arabia*.

A couple of could-be college women greeted us. Both women were topless with firm, small breasts, and thin bodies, each wearing the same exact sarong and sandals. I gathered this was the preferred uniform for this sexual Disneyland.

"A tent for you, sir?" a receptionist inquired.

"Yes, the Classic Concierge."

"We have the Classic available this evening with a king-sized featherbed. Would that be acceptable?"

"It would be perfect."

I noticed he took his shoes off, so I did the same. A girl zipped behind a counter and returned with a couple of pairs of straw-soled beach sandals for us.

Then a young man brought a couple of saddled horses out from a barn. One of the girls said, "Your tent is ready.

If you'll climb up, will be happy to show you the way." I was completely flabbergasted. It was like I'd walked into an adult simulation of Fantasy Island, and Tattoo was going to pop out at any minute.

We walked the horses down a sandy beach with whitewash rolling in and out. The horses sped to a trot and suddenly I couldn't tear my eyes away from the naked breasts of the girl riding the buckskin next to me. They bounced up and down like a bowl of Jell-O. I thought how sexy they were, and how they must turn all the men on that come there. She caught me staring once, twice, thrice, but I couldn't veer my eyes away. I don't know what came over me. I'd never had such an inclination. However, I'd never experienced anything remotely like this place. Not even in my wildest dreams.

Further down the beach, men with long, dark hair stood guard at each occupied tent, clad in only a loincloth and black leather, military boots. They all seemed to have bronzed skin with streamlined rippling muscle. And each man folded his arms across his sculpted chest, staring sternly straight ahead.

Our guard might as well have been a Greek god. He was burly, formidable, having all the omnipotence of a gladiator. I almost said, "*Good evening, Apollo,*" as I nodded, entering the tent.

It was stunning, decorated entirely in a Moroccan theme. A hand-woven rug lay over the canvas floor, and an exotic four-poster canopied bed took up most of the space with sheer, white silk curtains around it. In the corner sat a hand-painted chair. Aside the bed was a mosaic table with an old-fashioned basin and pitcher of water for washing. The girls showed us a display of body oils, lotions, and condoms inside the table, and handed us a stack of hot moistened face towels to clean our hands and presumably other various parts. Then with the usual finesse of a superlative hotel staff, the girls said, "Can I get you anything else?"

"A bottle of Champagne," he said.

A girl clapped her hands twice, and shouted, "Champagne!" A loin-clothed male jogged over in seconds flat, carrying a bucket of ice, champagne, and two crystal flutes.

Then the girls closed their hands together in a Buddhist salutation, nodded, and said, "Enjoy," and respectfully left the tent.

We sat down on the bed together. "Feeling better?" he asked.

"Very much, thank you. But I feel I must be dreaming. As sure as I know I'm sitting here, this can't be real."

"Well, this is the sort of place where dreams come true."

I nodded, seeing how that apparently seemed to be true no matter how freaking bizarre one's fantasies were. His fingers slid under my chin. "I thought you'd be more comfortable out here—that this suited you better."

"It's paradise." And in that moment, I was hit with the knowledge that this gorgeous man had every intention of having a love fest with me. I was overwhelmed and had to restrain myself from going headfirst, straight for the dick.

He handed me a glass of champagne, toasting, "To us."

I took a long sip and said, "To you. None of this would have happened if it wasn't for you."

Then it was on. I took a deep breath, pressed my mouth against his, slid my hands under his shirt, feeling soft, smooth skin, and the next thing I knew, I was feeling the shape of full, supple breasts, and inquisitive, hard nipples. "What the hell is this?" I pinched a nipple hard, shocked out of my mind, hoping the perky boobs weren't real—that this was some kind of a joke.

She screeched; then smiled mischievously with insisting breath. Nope, they were real.

I stared into the eyes of the mask—how could this be a woman? How could I not know? Could this be both man and woman? Then boldly I reached my hand into the crotch of her trousers, brusquely searching for any sign of a dick—none, nothing, but the curve of a female vulva provocatively motioning up and down.

"Okay, who are you?"

She smiled back at me—beautiful lips, beautiful teeth, soft, feminine features. How could I have not known? But her voice, her walk, her touch, was similar to that of almost any man's.

"You've gone to a lot of trouble here. Is this some sort of a joke, a test? Did someone put you up to this?"

She shook her head from side to side. Then took my hand, raising it to her lips, kissing the palm, and then my fingers, while staring seductively into my eyes through the holes in her mask.

"Don't you think it's time you took that mask off? The jig is up."

She ignored what I said completely, and slid my hand inside the front of her slacks, forcing two fingers pushing inside her. She was slickly wet, and my fingers went deep—and she pressed hard, wildly thrusting her hips up and down, as salacious whimpers emerged from her throat.

I'd never been with a woman before. The thought of it before today never occurred to me. Now, the sexual urge overpowered me. I wanted to do to her what I liked done to me. It defied everything I thought and I knew about myself, but it was uncontrollable. I desperately wanted to see between her thighs, taste her, drink the weeping core of her sex, and I wanted to excite her, and watch her explode and release.

I kneeled on the floor between her legs, and began undressing her. Her skin was smooth and tan, and her body was firm and graceful. I took her shoes and socks off, unzipped her slacks—pulling them off with her black, silk panties. I unbuttoned her shirt, and caressed her round breasts, and rolled each of her erect nipples on my fingertips. Then I spread her legs wide apart, and she was saturated—slick heat stretched from lip to lip. I slid my nose through her short, black pubes, and dragged my lips from front to back through her well-groomed garden, and up and down her feminine folds, embracing the unknown. I licked long, savoring strokes from one end of her beautiful, copper vulva to the other. I slid a finger inside her, exploring, looking into the brown eyes peering through the mask, then paused, licking her perfect nature off my fingers. Then she slid her hands over my dress, squeezing my breasts saying, "It's my turn."

She watched me undress and climb onto the bed. I straddled my legs around her neck, squatting—same as I would with any man.

"Turn around," she said.

I did, kneeling apprehensively like a virgin on all fours.

"Lie down." She slid a hand down the length of my spine, causing my flesh to shiver electric tingles.

I was flat on my stomach. We fit perfectly together. My face fell right between her thighs, and my center, settled on her tongue. I imbibed her slick ambrosia, and she from me. Her hands held each of my buttock cheeks firmly, licking from one end to the other. Next, her tongue slid in and out of my sex, and a finger pushed, simultaneously delving inside me.

I did the same to her, penetrating each of her tiny openings, exploring her, joining our flesh together in the most personal way, and without warning, I'd worked myself into a violent climax. As my body recovered, she gently licked the soft, velvety flesh of my vagina. And when I was ready, her hips in earnest swayed up and down, and her mouth copulated me again, repeating the same words: "Come again."

I withstood the culmination by my sheer desire to satisfy her. I inserted a finger, sliding across the roof of her vagina, stimulating the G spot, as I repetitiously slid a finger probing inside the other, while at once my tongue battered her clit. Her hands fisted my hair, her voice wailed wild pleas gasping for air; then her pelvis visibly flexed. I slid my finger out from her vagina and to my surprise a delectable excretion pulsated in a jet-like emission.

She pulled me lying down next to her, and in wonder I stared at the roof of the tent—breathless and shocked by what I'd just done.

Then a bell rang outside the tent, startling us. We looked to the entrance, and our guard was peering his head inside. His eyes fixated on her perfect body. "Everything okay?"

I was mortified, wondering just how long he might have been there. But opportunity had knocked, and she wrapped a leg around my hips, lifted one of my nipples into her mouth staring at him all the while, not saying a word, fluttering her tongue in titillating strokes. Then her fingers reached to my clit circling, followed by mine doing the same to her.

We lay on our sides, with our hips rocking back and forth with all the force of a cock driving deep inside us. She looked at him watching, then at me. We read each other's expression. We knew what each other wanted. Then we looked at him—gazing at his loincloth. At least eight inches of hard cock stood handlebar hard.

She motioned me onto my back. I wrapped my legs around her hips. Our vaginas met one on top of the other. I understood the position, and why. She swayed her slickly wet center back and forth, across my clit as if she was fucking me. Then, sticking her ass out, kneeling on all fours—looking over her shoulder—she invited the gladiator to make a move, a move inside us. He simply stared—beautiful face, dark features, dark hair, perfect, muscular body, and lusty, hard cock too. She stuck a finger inside herself from behind, gliding in and out, riding her hips up and down, and said, "Don't just stand there. Come and get it."

He untied his loincloth, dropping it to the floor. We both licked our lips in anticipation, as he hustled with rolling on a condom. My legs cinched tighter around her waist, raising my ass high, as if he'd make an approach inside me. He slid two fingers inside her, held a large bicep-rippling arm around her waist, and claimed her mouth with primal passion, as he raised against her backside—sliding one deep stoke, all the way inside her.

His passion raced through her blood with a fiery sting, rousing a vehement savage. Ferociously, she squeezed my breasts together into one mound, seizing both nipples at once. Then he hoisted her knees out from under her, standing her onto her feet—and she was swept away by the strength of his erection. With each stroke he came fuller and deeper, and her hips met his with a thrust that edged on violence. He pumped a feverish pace, knowing that was what she wanted; slapping his flanks against her ass, incinerating a heady spot until it shot through her entire body in a long, tight orgasm.

He pulled his cock out, and swiftly replaced the condom with a new one, then without impeding his stride, smoothly invaded my slick center in one potent thrust.

She crawled to the head of my body on all fours laving each of my turgid nipples, then worked her way down to my clit—as I licked the vestiges of her orgasm.

My hands unconsciously ran through her dark mane, causing her mask to move slightly to the side—and my mind flashed, recognizing, *Savannah*? Wow! I never would have imagined, and with that, I loved the thought of it even more, realizing the entire escapade had been a set-up from the get go.

I inserted a finger, then two, invading her as I ravaged her clit. Her hips rotated in tiny axels, met by my hips swaying on the gladiator's lusty pleasure. He gazed an intoxicating stare into my eyes—and the effect it had on me was more potent than his penetration—and not only did it extend, it didn't break. Searing heat filled and fulfilled me as I ached beneath her. My fingers raked her hair, my hot desire throbbed in her lips, and I couldn't resist—I was there, right there, and she beckoned me to the apex, repeating, "Come again. Come again."

The gladiator heard my body's pleas and pumped a cadence of stiff bliss, pushing me through waves of orgasms coursing through my body. Simultaneously, thick wetness streamed against my tongue. And on queue the gladiator made a guttural groan, pulled his cock out and the condom off, and sprayed his pleasure, collapsing on top of her.

Her mask thoroughly fell to the side of her face. No longer was it any question; it was Savannah. She saw my expression. How easily in such a short amount of time we had learned to read each other—even with masks, even without words, we knew each other's thoughts and desires, and understood each of them. She winked at me. She didn't have to ask me, not to speak of it to anyone. We didn't have to say a word about it. We knew our secrets were safe with each other, and we never spoke of that night again.

*

Several months had passed by, and I often thought about returning back to that house to visit the gladiator, but never found the nerve. But I think Savannah sensed my desire for him, seeing how on my thirtieth birthday, she sent a very special gift to my home. Yes, it was the gladiator, clad in a rice paper loincloth with a red bow tied around his hips. Needless to say, it quickly came undone: not by any physical means of my own, but by a steely erection, rising to attention, after capturing the desire in my eyes, that still holds me night after night to this very day.

Vince and Vi's
Caribbean Adventure

by Reno Lark

The engines roared as the plane hurtled down the runway. I felt the adrenalin rush I always do just before takeoff. The sheer power of these machines is awesome.

I glanced over at Violet sitting beside me, but she had already closed her eyes. She had on a nice fresh white blouse, and it was unbuttoned enough so I could see the swell of her breast being pushed up by her bra. She likes to show her cleavage, and I certainly don't object. She has a pretty nice rack and knows it's one of her main assets.

We were on our way to the Caribbean for a winter break, as we always were this time of year. I was looking forward to it, and was hoping we would get along a little better than we had in the recent past. I couldn't remember the last time we'd had sex. We had just been too busy lately, and the cold weather sure hadn't helped.

Closing my eyes after takeoff, I could already picture the sandy beach and the crystal clear water at our destination. Then I remembered that our friends, John and Julie, were coming down later in the week to spend some time in an apartment next to ours. We had become close over the past few years. John is a handsome guy. He's well built and keeps in shape with his part-time landscaping work. Julie is a really sweet lady too, a real thinker, and a few years older than John.

Recently we had invited them to our house for dinner, and later in the evening, after quite a few drinks, had ended up nude in the hot tub with them. Violet and I had lived in Europe for awhile, and always went in naked the way Europeans would. As we had learned since meeting them, John was known in his family circle for naked antics and was eager to join us. He finally managed to convince Julie to go in nude as well. Judging by the glimpses of her I got as she was climbing in and out of the tub, she has some small, but nice, assets.

It was a fun evening, as was the weekend we had spent at their cottage on a pristine northern lake, with lots of wine, good food, laughs, and sexual innuendo. I realized now how glad I was they were coming down: Vi and I always seemed to get along better when they were around. There were definitely some sparks flying between John and Vi whenever the four of us got together. He was clearly in lust with her.

Since it was a red-eye flight, I thought I had better get some shut-eye, so I put on my blindfold, blew up my neck pillow, stuffed the hearing protectors in my ears, and fell asleep. Before I knew it, we were getting ready to land.

The hot Caribbean air hit me like a huge wave as I stepped out of the plane onto the tarmac. It felt wonderful!

After taking a taxi to our apartment, we registered, dumped our suitcases, jumped into our bathing suits and were soon floating in the delicious blue-green water.

Over the next couple of days we eased right back into our southern routine of snoozing, reading, swimming, eating, and lazing, with more than our usual quota of sex. It was the tenth time we had come to this place. I was happy that things between Vi and I were on the mend, and it was not long before we picked up John and Julie at the local airport.

It was great to have them join us down here. We saw a lot of each other, sharing some dinners and playing a few games of strip poker. But no matter how hard John and I tried, we had no luck getting the girls out of the few pieces of clothing they were wearing, and ended up sitting buck naked every time. The girls just giggled at our misfortune.

During the second week of our stay, everyone at the resort was invited to an evening garden party. There are two things in particular I love about this place: one is the community of which we had become a part over the years; and the other is that you can sit outside at ten in the evening in shorts and a T-shirt, listening to waves crashing, and not have to worry about bugs. Even in summer, we can rarely sit outside in the evening up north without a light sweater or being pestered by critters.

As the party got under way, we had fun with all of our local acquaintances, eating good food and drinking copious amounts of rum and beer. I poured everyone shots from a bottle of Metaxa I had bought at the duty-free shop on our way down. Julie seemed to be tuckered out though, probably from the hot Caribbean sun and all the swimming she had done during the day. She decided to call it a night before the rest of us and, after apologizing to everyone, retired to her apartment. John, Vi, and I stayed with the others until there was almost no one left, then headed upstairs to our respective quarters.

"Come in for a nightcap," said Vi to John when we reached our door. "Julie won't miss you. She's probably already fast asleep."

We were feeling pretty fine from the bottle of Metaxa we had emptied, and the tropical breezes and heavenly warmth had already contributed to our horniness earlier that evening. The atmosphere was extremely charged. Caribbean rhythms played in the background.

John accepted her invitation eagerly. We went inside and turned on the lights; then the three of us sat down at the island in the kitchen. The patio door on our second-floor apartment was still open when we arrived and the room was fairly warm. Vi and I hate turning on the air conditioning, preferring to be hot, since that was why we come down in the first place.

After Vi had poured us all a shot of fifteen-year-old rum, she said, "I'm hot. I think I'm going to shed some clothes and get more comfortable. Back in a minute."

John's ears perked up when he heard the part about shedding some clothes, and a big grin appeared on his face. Vi disappeared into the bedroom, and on her way back went into the bathroom to pee. After I heard her flush the toilet, she ran the water for quite some time. I wondered what she was doing. Then I realized she must be washing herself after peeing to make sure she was fresh. She does that a lot when we are down here. Sometimes she takes so long, I know she's not just washing.

When she reappeared, she had changed into her "nightie." I had asked her a few days earlier to try on my athletic undershirt and we had both felt turned on when she had modeled it. I like the type with the opening cut really low at the side. I guess she had decided to give John and me a thrill. Her generous breasts undulated under the cloth and bulged out of the shirt at the sides as she strolled naughtily back to the kitchen. Her large brown areolas where clearly visible through the white fabric and her perky nipples strained against it. The fact that they were semi-erect in this heat confirmed my suspicion that she had rubbed herself a little longer than necessary when she had washed in the bathroom. John's eyes were nearly popping out of his head as he savored the eye-candy.

"Cheers!" said Vi flirtatiously, as she held up her glass and plunked down on the chair beside John, who was seated at the end of the narrow kitchen island.

"Nice looking little package, eh?" I said.

"I'll say," agreed John.

"Would you like to have a little peek at what's underneath the shirt?" I asked.

Vi protested loudly, but didn't seem too sincere.

"You bet," he replied.

"Okay, honey, why don't you change into this right here and show us what it looks like on you?" I asked.

I pulled off my sleeveless T-shirt, which was a lot shorter than the A-shirt she had on, and threw it over to her. I could see her thoughts racing as she stood up. It looked like she was getting ready to go back into the bedroom to put it on, but then she suddenly changed her mind. Shyly, she pulled the A-shirt over her head, put on the sleeveless T-shirt, and sat back down again. I noticed she had not bothered to put on any panties when she had changed, and this shorter shirt covered less down below. But since she was sitting with her legs crossed, our view had definitely not improved. In fact, the T-shirt covered more of her up top. The shirt switch was all over in a flash, but John had gotten his promised peek. She looked a wee bit embarrassed as she reached for her rum and took a large gulp. I took a drink too and asked John, "Well, what did you think?"

Taking a long sip, he thought for a moment, then grinned. "It was nice, but it sure was a short peek!" We all laughed at that. It was easy to tell he was hoping for more.

"I guess you're right," I said. "And now we can see less of her than we did before! I'm surprised by how much of your beautiful assets that sleeveless T-shirt hides," I complimented her. "I think I like the A-shirt better. Can you put it back on, please, honey?" I held my hands in prayer to show her we would be appreciative.

After the praises we had sung, she appeared to feel more confident and peeled off the T-shirt, very slowly this time. She put it in her lap and still totally naked, reached for another sip of her rum. As she raised the glass to her lips, she straightened up and pulled back her shoulders to flaunt her titties. They were just gorgeous!

"I have never seen anything like this!" John said, as he

reached over and boldly but gently grabbed one of her areolas. She was a bit taken aback by his audacity, and feeling self-conscious, put down the rum, slapped his hand, and quickly put the A-shirt back on.

"Bad boy," she said. "You are only supposed to look! Do you want a refill?" she asked, trying to change the subject.

"Well, okay," said John. "But what I was really hoping for was to get a longer look."

Appearing to ignore him, she got up and went over to the kitchen counter to get the rum. As she stood up, she dropped the T-shirt that had been resting on her lap. John and I were following her every move as she got up in the flimsy, short A-shirt that barely covered her bum, and when she bent over to pick up the T-shirt, her backside emerged from underneath the material. You could see everything: buns, anus, and a rear view of her pussy. John took in a sharp breath as he stared.

When she heard him, she looked around, still bent over, and asked, "Can you see something?" with an elfish grin, before reaching back and pulling the A-shirt back over her bum cheeks as she straightened up. Then she tossed the T-shirt aside, picked up the rum bottle, sashayed back and liberally topped up our three glasses. She was smiling as she teased us.

After a few more sips of rum and grooving to the music, John suddenly proclaimed, "Wouldn't it be cool to do a three-way!"

We were all feeling pretty good, and you could feel the erotic tension, but Vi countered, "I could never do that to my husband!" Deep down, she was fairly conservative, and had had a strict upbringing. When I met her, she had never had any sex other than the missionary variety.

"Yes, I agree," I said. "I don't think that's a good idea. Vi and I really value our friendship with you and Julie, and it would never be the same afterward." I was certainly not conservative when it came to sex, and my upbringing had not been all that strict, but I admit I couldn't predict how I would feel after another man had done my wife. Nakedness, showing off her body and so on is one thing, but when it comes to the ultimate act, I am not really sure I want to share her. Of course, I admit I do lust for some of her female friends, and have fantasies about doing two women, but that's another story.

"Yeah, I see what you mean," said John. "I'm sorry I mentioned it."

"No need to apologize," said Vi.

"I must admit, it's a nice fantasy," I added. In fact, he had given me an idea.

"For now, maybe you can just help me get Vi ready so she and I can have some hot sex later on . . . maybe she will let us look at her assets again?" I ventured, peering at her with a question in my voice.

"Well, we'll see," she replied. She didn't know what to do next, so she took another sip of her rum.

But I knew what I wanted! Thinking about showing her off was really starting to turn me on.

"Aw honey, we just want to have a long, close look!" I pleaded again.

"Please," John added, still seated at the end of the island. I looked over at Vi to see if she would approve. I could tell she was feeling a little bashful. She didn't say yes, but then, she didn't say no either, so I took the initiative.

"Okay, honey," I said. "I know it's warm in here, but let's see if we can raise the temperature another notch. I think I know how I can help you with your shyness."

Leaving the two of them sipping their drinks while they listened to the music, I closed the patio door to get more privacy. "You'd better take your shirt off too," I said to John. "It could be getting warmer in here." The double entendre was not entirely unintended.

I then went to my briefcase in the bedroom. When I came back into the kitchen, they were sipping their rums and playing footsies. I turned off the overhead light to set the mood. The lighting was now fairly low, with only a lamp in the far corner still on.

"That's better," she said. "I was feeling like I was under a spotlight."

"Here, let's put this on you first," I said and brought out the blindfold I had used on the plane. She put up a mild protest, but I suspected she wasn't serious.

"I want you to sit down on the island, Vi. Let me help you up," I said. I asked John to help me. He stood up and we each held onto one of her hands while she climbed up on his chair, then turned and sat down on the end of the counter, facing the chair. She kept her legs tightly pressed together since the A-shirt just barely covered her crotch.

"Now let's lose these," I said, removing her specs. Then I placed the blindfold over her eyes so she was completely in the dark. My theory was she probably wouldn't feel so shy if she no longer had to watch while John and I ogled her. John sat back down on the chair at the end of the island. He now had a full frontal view of Vi seated on the counter and stared at her breasts straining against the almost diaphanous fabric.

"Here we go," I said. "Raise your arms over your head."

She pretended to be reluctant when she complied, but I could tell by how fast she lifted her arms up that it was just an act. Her boobs tightened and elevated underneath the fabric as she stretched. It was now so warm in the apartment, she was perspiring a little and the material was becoming more and more see-through around her tits. Her nipples were still semi-erect despite the heat. I gently tied her arms together above her head using one of our rubber exercise bands that had been hanging over a chair. When it was snug, I told her that she was now our plaything and no longer had any say.

"Oh," she replied meekly.

With that, I very slowly started rolling the A-shirt up, one inch at a time. I paused to tease John as I approached the middle of her boobs, just below the nipples. She was sitting very still. I took another sip of rum, then rolled up the cloth until it was under her armpits. Her luscious knockers popped out as I rolled the fabric past the widest point of her chest. They were now fully exposed to John's stare. Since she is short and he is tall, her boobs were just below his eye level, about twelve inches away from his face. His eyes popped as he took in the marvelous sight of her jugs, and I noticed that his cock was starting to bulge under his shorts. So was mine. Vi was still trying to keep her legs together, but they were slowly parting despite her best intentions. I could sense she was starting to let go of her inhibitions. Lowering his gaze from her tits, John looked at her pussy. I was amazed at how quickly our eyes had adjusted to the dim light.

He and I took another sip of rum and savored the heavenly view for a few minutes without saying anything. She was completely helpless and fully exposed to our stares. She had started to sway her upper body in time with the music. I stood up to give her a little sip of her rum while John watched. She managed to find the glass in her blindfolded state, but a little bit poured out the sides of her mouth when I lifted the glass too fast, and it dribbled down onto her chest. I was now really getting turned on.

"Okay, you can have a little feel," I encouraged John and sat down to watch.

She protested meekly, but I reminded her, "Tied up wenches have no say!"

John was very eager and, reaching forward from his seated position, placed one of his rough gardener's hands on each of her breasts and gently massaged them. She seemed to be enjoying it, judging by the expression on her face. That encouraged him. He grabbed a nipple between each thumb and forefinger and gently tugged. He lifted her tits up. He twirled them a bit. He seemed to be having a lot of fun, and all three of us laughed at his antics. Vi seemed to be getting comfortable with the situation, but then said her back was really getting tired, and I could tell she was serious. We were just getting into it though, and I hated to stop.

"Why don't you just lie back on the island?" I asked.

"I can't," she said, but she hadn't refused, so I put one arm around her back and gently lowered her until she was lying prone, her legs bent at the knee and swinging over the edge at the end of the island, her back arched. She had easily complied, so I knew she was still into it too. Her soft tits changed shape as gravity acted on them, and her legs spread a little further as she lay back on the counter. I went to get a pillow to put under her head and make her comfortable. By the time I came back, John had stood up to get a better look. The cool counter on her back had made her nipples more erect.

"Why don't you move over to the other chair?" I suggested to John. He complied, but not before taking another peek at her virtually hairless pussy from his frontal vantage point. It had become even more exposed now that she was lying flat.

When he sat down in the other chair, we were seated opposite one another, one on each side of my wife stretched out on the counter. Her nipples were hard as pencil erasers. My mind was racing.

"This counter is hard," she suddenly complained.

I thought fast. I needed to get her comfortable. Luckily, it occurred to me that we had an exercise mat nearby that I could use for her to lie on. I went to get it, wondering how I was going to get it under her without breaking the rhythm of what was happening. Then I had it. "Can you lift her up so I can get this underneath her?" I asked John.

He grinned at me. "Of course!" With that, he swept her up easily in his brawny arms and lifted her. She is petite and you could tell he was thrilled with having this naked creature in his arms. She was cradled as if she were about to cross the threshold on her wedding day, but of course you normally don't do that with your arms tied over your head and an A-shirt rolled up under you armpits. But I could tell she was loving it, pressed against his solid pecs. I placed the exercise mat on the table and folded it over to make it softer. Meanwhile, I was planning my next moves.

"Okay, put her down now, please," I said to John.

He gently lowered her back down onto the mat on the countertop and reluctantly let her go.

"Is that better?" I asked.

"Mmmm," was all she answered. I took that as my signal I could continue our adventure.

"Do you like ice cream?" I asked John.

"Um, yes . . ." he said, wondering what I was getting at.

I got up and went to the freezer to get a tub of ice cream we had bought earlier, and took a small spoon from the drawer behind me. I scooped out a bit of the cold treat and dabbed it on her right breast. She gasped as the ice cream touched her erect nipple. I then put some on her other breast. The ice cream immediately started to melt.

"Help me lick it up," I said to John, and started to suck the ice cream off of her right tit. John did the same to her left boob, and continued sucking on it even though there was no ice cream left.

"Oh, that feels delicious," she moaned, and her legs involuntarily parted a little further. The dew on her pussy was glistening in the dim light.

"Don't stop!" she said. I starting sucking again on her other nipple and soon she was moaning with pleasure.

A man on each breast! A completely new sensation after twenty-five years of monogamy.

"I think I need to get fucked," she moaned, still blind-folded, but turning her head towards me. That gave me another idea.

"Not yet," I said. "It's too early for John to retire. I know you like rum," I said to our friend.

"You betcha," he confirmed.

I put the ice cream back in the freezer, then got out a baster from the kitchen drawer. While I was doing this, I motioned to John to go around to the other side of the table. He tiptoed over in his bare feet and I went to where he had been standing. Now we were in opposite positions from when I had blindfolded her. I drew a little rum from one of the glasses into the baster, then proceeded to dribble some between her tits. John knew what to do and started to lick up the rum.

"Oh, that feels good, honey," she said, thinking it was me doing the licking.

When he had finished licking it up, I remembered she had washed earlier and decided to see if he would suck on her pussy while I watched. I dribbled some more of the rum on her outstretched body, first on her nipples, then between the breasts. I traced a path down her belly, across her belly button, which I filled, then continued down to her clit and into her pussy. Her lips were really swollen now. She was still trying to keep her legs together whenever she remembered, but they kept on spreading further and further apart as she got more and more relaxed and turned on.

I pointed at her pussy and looked at John. Wagging my tongue in a licking motion, I raised my eyebrows at him. He nodded as he got the message. His eyes had nearly popped out of his head, and his stiff cock was starting to protrude from his shorts.

He slurped up the fine nectar, starting at her tits, moving slowly down to her belly button, where he stayed for a while, then on down to her clit, which he eagerly sucked on for what seemed like ages. Then he scooped what he could out of her pussy with his tongue from his position beside her. She writhed in pleasure. I could feel my cock pulsating as I watched him slurping my wife's pussy.

"I need to get fucked!" she pleaded. I turned around to make sure the patio door was tightly closed. She was getting louder now.

"Not yet," I said. "You're not ready." She seemed confused by where my voice was now coming from, and lifted one side of the blindfold with the side of her arm stretched over her head. She blushed when she saw John and I had changed places.

"Oh my, oh my," she said. "I didn't know it was you doing that to me, John! I thought it felt different than usual."

"Don't peek," I said, "or we will have to give you a spanking." I quickly replaced the blindfold and filed that thought for another time.

"Now," I said, "Let's get you really ready."

With one hand, I raised one of her legs, grasping her ankle and bending her knee toward her chest so that her lower leg was parallel to the island top. Then I pulled it slightly toward me with my other hand. It was shapely and silky smooth. She is one of those fortunate few ladies who doesn't have to shave her legs. I lightly stroked the inside of her thigh to keep her primed.

"Do the same on your side," I said to John.

He did, and now her almost bare cunt was gaping. I hadn't seen it so wet in a long time. She was protesting and tried to counter our pulling by attempting to close her legs, but we were too strong for her.

"It's pink inside, you know," I said. I wrapped my arm around her leg to keep it in place, then reached down with my free hand and parted her engorged pussy lips even further with two fingers to reveal the pink oyster inside.

"Isn't it gorgeous?" I said. "I can't understand how her doctor doesn't get a hard-on when she is in this position in his office." She had stopped protesting and was now moaning, louder and louder. I pointed to her pussy and John went to the end of the counter, leaned down, put the leg he had been holding over his shoulder and drove his long tongue deep inside her tunnel. In and out it went, and she squirmed with pleasure. She no longer resisted having her legs spread so far apart; all modesty had vanished.

"OK, hang on, let's try something else," I said, but he kept on tonguing her, going so deep that I thought he was going to push his nose inside. She must have tasted really sweet.

I reached over to the kitchen counter behind me to a fruit bowl and pulled out a banana about the size of a six-inch cock.

"Okay, take a break," I repeated to our friend. He finally stopped and went back to holding up her leg, Vi's pussy juices all over his face.

"This should fit," I said. After satisfying myself there were no sharp edges at the end, I started to slowly insert the fruit into her slippery opening. It slid in easily; she was so soaked.

"Now we are going to pretend to fuck you," I said. "And we are going to take turns." She gently rocked her hips up and down in agreement. Zero protest. The banana went in deeper and deeper. John was pulling her raised leg toward him again and I was doing the same on my side. Her cunt was spread quite wide. I let John have a turn at sliding the banana in and out.

"Oh, fuck me, fuck me," she cried out.

But I could see that the banana was not cutting it. I had another idea. Letting John continue banana-fucking my wife, I lowered her leg, went to the fridge and took out a cucumber. It was longer than the banana, and fatter. I picked her leg back up, motioned to John to pull out the banana, and placed the cucumber against her slippery pussy lips. She gasped as the cold veggie touched the opening to her tunnel. Slowly I began pushing the cucumber inside. It was spreading her much more than the banana had, and her breathing was getting heavier and faster. I shoved it gently in and out as far as it would easily go, but always pushing it until I encountered resistance. Every time I gave the final shove, she pushed back with her hips and made a loud noise in her throat. As her pussy stretched wider and wider, the cucumber went in further and further, until finally it was past its widest point, about four inches in. John was watching intently, awestruck. She was now again writhing in pleasure, and pleaded, "Deeper, deeper! Make it go deeper!" I did as she ordered and plunged it in as far as I could.

"Massage her tits and kiss her," I ordered John. But before he could comply, she started to heave. She was breathing very fast. "Oh, oh, oh, I'm coming, I'm coming," she managed to say.

And did she ever come! Wave after wave shook her body. I had never seen her climax like that. John just stared in amazement. After a while, I slowly withdrew the cucumber and put it in the trash can.

Her breathing finally started to settle down. John and I had picked up our glasses and clinked them in a toast. We were very pleased with ourselves.

"How was it?" I asked Vi when she had started to breathe normally again. She had crossed her legs now, with her feet on the countertop, her knees up and her legs swinging slowly to and fro.

"That was marvelous, boys," she said. "You both deserve a reward. And I'm ready to go again! We ladies are never quite satisfied with a one-shot deal . . . untie me so I can take off this blindfold." She was now clearly taking charge, as she is wont to do.

And Damien Makes Four

by Em Brown

"Why don't you come on in and have a glass of zin?" Jeremy offered to the tall, hunky man standing in the doorway. Damien Rohnert was six feet, three inches of taut muscle, nicely revealed by a tight short-sleeved shirt, and it was all Jeremy could do to keep from drooling.

A glass of zin. It had all started with a glass of zin.

"We have a nice bottle of Dasche Cellars," Margaret added as she stepped over the threshold and dropped her purse. It had only been six months since Margaret officially moved in, but she was now as much a part of the household as the first set of chairs that Jeremy and Brad had picked out together after getting married.

"Sure," Damien replied, but the frown indicated he wasn't very sure at all.

Jeremy wondered if it was the zinfandel or Madge that had persuaded Damien. Probably Madge. But Jeremy didn't care. It wasn't often that one got to have such delectable eye candy. He raked his eyes appreciatively from Damien's sculpted biceps to the leather chaps encasing a pair of muscular legs. He glimpsed Damien's silver BMW motorbike in the driveway before closing the door. Damn. He had always had a thing for a biker man, though he wasn't a rider himself. All that horsepower rumbling under one's balls . . .

"Damien!" Brad hailed, entering the living room with the bottle and three wine glasses. Jeremy noticed right away how his partner's eyes lit up. After nearly eight years of marriage, there wasn't a whole lot Brad could hide from Jeremy.

Brad was one of those guys who would always look ten years younger than his true age. Right now he could have passed for a college student. With soft brown hair falling over sparkling blue eyes and a slender build, Brad was the physical opposite of Damien. Brad had a more winning smile, but Jeremy found Damien's harder edges equally attractive. He idly wondered what would have happened if he had met a gay equivalent of someone like Damien. The sex would have been raw. Hard. Powerful. But marriage wouldn't have happened.

Although Brad had thrown his own curve ball, Jeremy recalled wryly as his gaze fell on the petite brunette settling into the sofa with her pouch of chocolate-covered blueberries. There had never been much in the way of sweets in the house until Margaret arrived. Now the freezer had three different pints of ice cream, the pantry had boxes of Girl Scout cookies, and there was chocolate to be had at every turn.

Damien greeted Brad after shedding all his bike paraphernalia. "How'd the movie shoot in L.A. go?"

"Great," Brad replied. "We just need a distributor now. I'll go get another glass."

"Thanks for giving Madge a lift," Jeremy said to Damien, who glanced over at Margaret with suspicious frequency. Jeremy went to sit down next to her on the sofa—out of possessiveness or to place himself in Damien's line of sight, he wasn't sure. He put an arm around her and casually kissed her on the top of the head. A muscle seemed to ripple along Damien's jaw.

"How were rehearsals?" Jeremy asked Margaret.

"Good," Margaret replied cheerfully, "though Mr. Director here made us repeat Act II, Scene Three, *twelve* times."

"Get it right next time and you won't have to do it so often," Damien said as he settled into an armchair and took the glass of wine that Brad held out for him.

Margaret wrinkled her nose, but it was a sign of her respect for Damien as a director that she made no retort. Jeremy remembered the day Margaret had returned home from the first day of rehearsals of the new play she was in, fuming over the tactics of the new director. Brad had still been filming in L.A. at the time, and it had seemed to Jeremy that Margaret had been more vigorous in her lovemaking with him that night. He had thought it was because she missed Brad. But now he wondered if it had more to do with Damien. She had disliked Damien with a tad too much vehemence for nothing to be going on.

But did Damien have a thing for Margaret? That was harder to believe. Jeremy had known Damien for some time. He met him at a cast party for a play that Brad had been in years ago. The women that gravitated to Damien, and whom he flirted back with, were not like sweet little Margaret. Not that Margaret was a hundred percent wholesome—Brad had caught her masturbating on their bed—but she was more gentle and tame. With her long dark hair, lithe body, and rosebud lips, Margaret was attractive enough. She had a sense of style and was quietly sexy, but she wasn't the big-busted blond bombshells that Jeremy figured were more Damien's type. An accountant by day, Margaret was more Minnie Driver than Kim Basinger.

"So what have you been up to these days, Damien?" Brad asked, choosing to sit on the floor near Margaret. "I thought you'd be in New York directing the latest hit from off Broadway."

"I didn't want to make the move," Damien answered. "Too far from my daughter."

"Oh, right. How is Miranda—?"

"Marissa."

"How is Marissa? She's in middle school now?"

"Seventh grade."

"The middle school years are tough."

"For the kid or the parent?" Margaret asked.

"Both, I guess. I hated my teen years—what are they calling it now? Tween years? I can't imagine what it would be like now. There's so much more pressure around sex. Have you seen what the girls today are wearing? They look like they all shop at Sluts-R-Us."

Margaret's cheeks reddened and she exchanged a glance with Damien. Jeremy wondered what that was about. He also wondered if Damien had ever experimented with another man. Had Damien ever thought about it? He had to have thought about it. All men do. Even straight ones. Hell, the guy worked in theater. He was surrounded by gay men. Maybe he had to kiss another man in rehearsals. Or maybe in an impromptu scene. Damien seemed pretty confident in his sex. He'd have the balls to kiss another man.

"I wasn't crazy about the tween years either," Damien agreed, "but as bad as they were, I'd much rather be the kid going through them than the parent. I'm not a fan of firearms for civilians—I don't believe in that Second Amendment crap, but when Marissa brings home those boys from school, I swear I wish I had a shotgun."

Jeremy pictured Damien holding a rifle. A long rifle. Naked. No. Naked except for the leather chaps. Jeremy pulled at his shirt collar, his cock stirring at the visions.

"Those boys are probably no worse than you were at that age," Margaret said.

"That's why I wish I had a shotgun, Missy."

She let out an exasperated breath. "The name's *Margaret*."

A faint smile floated on Damien's lips before he took another sip of his wine. The epithet clearly irked Margaret, but Jeremy could tell Damien knew full well it would get a rise out of her. In fact, Jeremy rather suspected "Missy" was more a term of endearment than a put-down.

Noticing that Margaret was rubbing her back below her shoulder, Jeremy offered, "Let me get that knot for you."

She angled her back towards him, and he kneaded his

thumb into her sore spot. He glanced over at Damien, whose gaze rested on them for only a few seconds, but the intensity of that gaze made Jeremy shiver. He placed both hands on her.

"Ohhh, that feels great, Jer," she purred.

The first time Margaret had stayed over at their place, because she lived more than an hour's drive away at the time and was rehearsing a play with Brad, Jeremy had been massaging her feet after they had all had a glass of zin. He liked Margaret, had dated women off and on before deciding his preference was for men, but he had been furious with her when he discovered her in bed with Brad. He had suspected for some time that his spouse might have been venturing a little outside their marital vows, and poor Margaret had borne the brunt of all his pent-up anger.

He had expected her to cower and slink away in guilt, but when she made some offhand remark about him not being man enough, something in him had snapped. He had fucked her like he had never fucked a woman before, and the heat in Brad's eyes as he witnessed it all was what made Jeremy extend another invitation to Margaret even though he had been prepared to throw the minx out. The addition of Margaret took their sex to a place it had never been, renewing their passion for one another and opening the door to exciting new possibilities.

After conversing about the play, Brad's movie, Jeremy's work, their favorite vintners, and even the state of the country, Brad opened a third bottle of wine. "Another glass?"

"I *love* this wine," Margaret responded, holding up her glass with a wobble. "I knew next to *nothing* about wines until I moved up here. I mean, I couldn't tell ya if Pinot Noir was a red, a white, or even a pink—excuse me, *rosé*. But it's hard *not* to become an oenophile living here in Sonoma County."

As she pulled the wine glass back towards herself, some of it spilled out onto her hand. Brad licked the errant drops off her before turning to Damien with the bottle.

"Thanks. I'm going to get a glass of water first," Damien replied stiffly as he stood up and turned towards the kitchen.

"I'll show you where the glasses are," Jeremy said.

In their Tuscan-styled kitchen, Jeremy opened a cabinet to retrieve a glass and filled it with water. He gave it to Damien, who was leaning against the kitchen counter, one ankle crossed over the other. Jeremy couldn't help but do a sweep of those long legs. Damien's jeans weren't meant to be that fitted—Jeremy and Brad both preferred a pair that molded the lower body—but he looked hot anyway. Meeting Damien's eyes, Jeremy realized he had been caught ogling.

"So what's the deal with you two and Margaret?" Damien asked.

"What do you mean?"

Damien folded his arms. "This *ménage a trois* that you guys have going on."

"Why do you ask?" Jeremy returned, glad Damien was interested. What he wanted to say was, *do you want to join us?*

"I don't want to see Margaret hurt."

That wasn't the response Jeremy had expected. "Who says Margaret's going to get hurt?"

Damien raised his brows. "You telling me she's not just a plaything for you and Brad?"

Jeremy bristled. "We like Madge. We care about her."

"Come on, Jeremy. I know you guys. Brad may be a little naïve, but you're not. Margaret deserves better."

"Better? You mean someone like you? I know about you, too, Rohnert. You don't exactly have a stellar track record." He looked down at Damien's empty ring finger.

"Fuck you. My ex had the affair."

Jeremy winced inside, wishing he could have taken that part back. He *had* assumed, given the broken hearts that Damien had in his wake, that Damien had been the reason behind the divorce. Still, who the hell did Damien think he was?

"Don't knock our relationship just because you don't understand it," Jeremy said instead and walked out of the kitchen, more rankled than he wanted to be, a seed of guilt sprouting deep within him.

When they walked back into the living room, they found Brad nibbling at Margaret's neck. Jeremy sensed Damien stiffen beside him. So the guy did have a thing for Madge.

"Let's go upstairs," Brad growled into her ear, pulling her up off the sofa.

"Wait! We have a guest," she objected, but in her current state of inebriation, she wouldn't be protesting for long.

Brad looked over at Damien. "Damien can come, too."

Margaret grabbed Damien by the hand and gazed up at him with those wide almond eyes of hers. "Do you want to?"

Jeremy held his breath. He hoped—what did he hope for? A part of him would be relieved if Damien just grabbed his stuff and left. The other—he was almost too afraid to go there.

Though he held his alcohol well, Damien had consumed his fair share of wine. To Jeremy's surprise, he allowed Margaret to lead him up the stairs to the master bedroom. Jeremy followed silently, not wanting to shatter the moment. His heart was beating rapidly, and even though he was wearing a loose linen shirt, he felt extremely warm.

Up in their bedroom, Brad threw himself onto the king-sized bed and pulled Margaret on top of him. The two began kissing. Jeremy glanced over at Damien and his crotch. There was a definite bulge there. But there was still a chance that Damien would decide to storm out.

Brad had never really gone all the way with a woman until Margaret, but he had been in enough make-out scenes with women that he soon had Margaret panting and writhing her hips against him. It was a different Brad that made love to Margaret. He held back, and it satisfied Jeremy that Brad saved his vigor for him. When the three of them fucked, Brad or Margaret usually did the watching, and though Jeremy found the voyeurism of watching his partner arousing, he was more engrossed with watching Damien's reaction.

The nostrils flared slightly but Damien, standing two feet from the bed, was otherwise motionless. Jeremy stared at the mouth, wondering what it would be like to have those lips pressed to his own. Was Damien a good kisser? Jeremy imagined the guy was. His own cock hardened at the thought, at the vision of trailing his mouth down Damien's sculpted abs, to his crotch, of breathing in the scent of his pubic hairs.

Margaret rolled onto her back and shimmied her cropped pants and panties down her legs. Brad pulled her tank top and bra straps down past her shoulders and began sucking on a nipple. Margaret had small breasts, the kind that didn't get in the way. Jeremy doubted Brad would have gone for a big-busted woman, of which there were many in the film and theater business.

Again, Jeremy looked from Margaret and Brad, who were immersed in each other, to Damien, whose chest rose and fell with deep, hard breaths. Was Damien seething with jealousy? Was he titillated? Did he find that jealousy fueled his arousal? Jeremy had found that to be the case for himself. For a while, he had found himself pounding Brad extra hard in the ass because of all the anger and jealousy he felt about Brad's cheating. He was willing to forgive Brad's curiosity about a woman, but it enraged him to think that Brad might have been intimate with another man. Maybe that was why he had been willing to allow Margaret into their lives; if it could keep Brad from straying.

Looking at Damien, however, Jeremy could understand why Brad might be tempted. And it wasn't as if Jeremy hadn't fantasized about someone other than Brad. He simply hadn't had much time to consider an affair between running his own company and supporting his partner's desire to be an actor. And he, at least, had been satisfied with the sex they were having. But here he stood, next to a walking wet dream, wanting . . .

Wouldn't it be cool if the threesome was between him, Brad, and Damien? He imagined Damien standing with his hands against the bed, his cock projecting out like a flagpole, being deep-throated by Brad while Jeremy sucked on his sack. Jeremy felt pre-come dampening his khakis.

Now it was Margaret who had unbuttoned part of Brad's shirt and was nibbling on his nipple. Jeremy admired his partner's lean body. They both worked out on a regular basis. Brad could use a little more flesh in the ass, but other than that, the guy had a beautiful and toned body. And he sucked cock like no one else.

Margaret unbuttoned Brad's jeans and pulled out his cock, aiming it at her pussy. Jeremy heard Damien inhale sharply.

"You guys don't use condoms?" Damien grumbled.

"She's on the pill, and we've all been tested," Jeremy answered, his voice coming out more husky than he intended. "At Madge's request. We got tested for her."

So you see, we do care about her, Jeremy wanted to add. Damien didn't look particularly satisfied, but to Jeremy's surprise, Damien took off his shirt.

So I'm not the only one feeling the heat, Jeremy thought as his gaze rippled over the chest and down the six-pack.

He would have been content to masturbate to that vision alone, but he felt like a predator in hiding, not wanting to move a muscle lest its prey should decide to bolt.

Brad was sawing steadily in and out of Margaret, who was angling her hips and grinding her crotch against his. The wine had dulled her senses, and Jeremy imagined it would take a little longer than usual to get her to climax. He and Damien stood in the shadows watching the two on the bed, the room illuminated only by the moonlight coming in through the window. Brad and Margaret alternated grunts, their bodies united in a common goal as they strained, thrust, and arched into each other. Over and over again until little beads of perspiration dotted their foreheads.

Damien unbuckled his belt and whipped off his pants. He took a hold of Brad's shoulder.

"Let me show you how it's done."

Surprised, Brad backed away and off the bed, allowing Damien to take his place. Jeremy saw Margaret's eyes widen. She hadn't expected this and wasn't sure what to do. But the lust in her eyes did not diminish. Her legs remained parted for him.

Jeremy wasn't able to get a good look at Damien's cock before it entered Margaret, but by her loud gasp, he surmised it had a good girth to it. He watched as Damien gently pushed the rest of his cock into her until his pubic hair was tangled with hers. Margaret grabbed the sheets of the bed beneath her as she adjusted to him. From where he stood, he had a nice view of Damien's rock-hard ass. He couldn't wait any longer and reached down his pants for his own cock. It felt like lava was pulsing through it.

Slowly, Damien withdrew his cock and languidly he pushed it back in. Margaret shivered. He laced his fingers with hers and pulled her hands above her head. His beautiful back, with its perfect V-shape from the tapered hips to the broad shoulders, was arched so that he could achieve the right angle for his cock to graze the bottom of her extended pleasure bud. His body loomed so large over her that Jeremy could barely make her out in the darkness.

Margaret released a sound best described as a shaky wail. She sounded both terrified and delighted. Damien didn't piston as much as he *rolled* in and out of her, and it was working havoc on Madge. She trembled, and her ecstatic cries filled the room. Jeremy looked to Brad, who was working his cock, well lubed already by Madge's juices. Jeremy thought about walking over to Brad to either aid him in his masturbation or to drive his own cock into Brad's ass, but he was too mesmerized by Damien. There was something elegant to his motions. Like a dancer. Like the heave and fall of ocean waves.

Sensing Margaret's climax looming, Damien quickened his thrusts, with force enough to cause her boobs to bounce and the bed to sway. Brad came first, shooting his load mostly into his hand, but a few drops hit the bed and dripped onto the carpet. Usually it bugged Jeremy that Brad couldn't aim his load better and keep his stuff off the expensive new carpet that had been installed recently, but Jeremy chose not to say anything. Unzipping his fly, he pulled out his own cock and stroked it more vigorously.

Margaret's body jerked violently against Damien as her

orgasm bowled through her. It was like she was overtaken by dozens of spasms surging from head to toe. An agonizing cry tore from her throat, but Jeremy knew she was experiencing the orgasm of her life. Little aftershocks, cringing, and a satisfied moan followed. Her eyes opened briefly, rolled upwards, and closed again as she settled back towards earth. Her breath, ragged, gradually returned to a more even pace. She looked to have fallen asleep.

Jeremy inhaled deeply, breathed in the scent of sex around him. Brad had collapsed on the floor and was leaning his head against the wall, eyes closed.

Nothing to do but jack himself off, Jeremy supposed. But then his eyes met Damien's, and in that instant, Jeremy knew. He knew something different was going to happen. Something new. And he wasn't sure how he was going to feel about it afterwards, but he wasn't going to pass up this opportunity.

Damien pulled out of Madge, his cock still hard. Climbing off the bed, he advanced towards Jeremy.

"Turn around," Damien said.

Barely able to swallow, Jeremy took his gaze off Damien's beautiful rod—it curved slightly from the body and had a nice-sized knob—to pull down his pants. He braced himself against the foot of the bed while Damien positioned himself behind and popped his cock, lubricated from Madge, into Jeremy's anus.

Fucking amazing.

The feel of that hot throbbing member buried inside his ass was every bit as marvelous as Jeremy had imagined it to be. He was thankful that Damien had done Madge first. Without the lubrication, it would have been painful. Damien was thicker than Brad, and Jeremy felt his asshole stretched. His lower body was on fire. He couldn't remember wanting to come so badly since losing his virginity.

Damien pulled his cock out until only the tip was still buried, then slammed all nine inches back inside. Grunting, Jeremy gripped the bed harder and braced himself for another stabbing. He knew he wasn't going to get fucked the way Madge had been fucked. There wasn't going to be any tenderness. Any lovemaking. Just raw, hard power.

Jeremy's legs quivered as waves of pleasure rippled through his body, reveling in the way his ass was getting pummeled by Damien. The forceful pounding made it feel like they would become one. Over and over Damien's hips shoved at Jeremy. That delicious, tingling ache simmering in his belly engulfed his loins, boiled his balls, and shot up his penis. There was no stopping it now. A stream of white cream erupted from his cock before he could catch it. A few drops landed on Margaret. The rest puddled on the bed cover and dripped down his pulsing cock.

He groaned through his clenched jaw as one more spurt of come pushed itself out his piss hole. Behind him, he heard Damien howl, then felt hot liquid filling his ass. After driving home the last of his climax, Damien pulled out and stumbled back, leaning against the dresser. Jeremy glanced at Margaret, who was staring agog at Damien, then at Brad. Had Brad seen it all? Was he okay with it?

But Jeremy felt too tired to answer how Brad might be

feeling. He wanted to relish the glow of his orgasm before having to deal with the aftermath. Sliding around the edge of the bed, he collapsed down next to Margaret. The room was silent except for his panting—his and Damien's.

When his breath had returned to normal, Damien reached for his shirt and pants. He headed for the door.

"Wait!" Pulling her bra and tank up, Margaret bounded off the bed. "You, uh, you want another glass of zin? Glass of water?"

In the light of the doorway, Jeremy saw the look Damien fixed on Margaret. The eagerness with which she had leaped off the bed hadn't escaped his notice either. Suddenly, Jeremy felt jealous. Of both of them.

"Sure," Damien responded.

The pair headed downstairs. It was unlikely Damien would find himself up in this room again. Jeremy felt sure of it. And that made him both wistful and relieved. He stared at the ceiling, not sure which emotion was supposed to prevail.

Brad climbed onto the bed next to him. "You lucky bastard. How am I going to compete with that fucking?"

Jeremy put his arm around Brad, glad there was no anger or hurt in Brad's tone.

"The great thing about being married, Brad, is you don't have to," he said.

The statement was perhaps a little naïve—it wasn't like he was going to forget the ass-pounding he got from Damien any time soon—but he wouldn't trade Brad for Damien even if Damien was available. And Brad knew that.

"I love you, Jer," Brad said as he nestled his body next to Jeremy.

They locked lips.

"Back at you," Jeremy replied, pulling Brad closer to him. He sensed a change in the air. Something was going to be different. For better or worse, he didn't know. Maybe just different. For now, he was content to take in the smell of Brad's cologne, feel the heat of Brad's body, and taste the wine on Brad's mouth. A full, rich zinfandel.

Two Men and a Lady Prequel

by Brit M.

In the dark the throb of the music felt like a great cat rubbing its furred body across her skin; her pulse was the beat's pulse. The old concrete floor was chipped but smooth and her feet slid across it while her fingers wove heavy glowing patterns in the air. She caught the DJ's eye, watched him mouth a kiss at her. Jason threw the best raves. He knew the music she wanted and how to push a crowd to new heights. He knew what she wanted from the evening, what would happen as soon as Nadia took over to spin her own set.

To pass the time until then, she danced, touched and brushed the half-nude men and women around her. Every contact felt like a brand on her sweat-slick skin. The song fell into a breakdown and she slowed as well, stretching her arms above her head. The tattoo-boy, as she'd thought of the other raver all night, also swirled to a stop in front of her. His eyes were pale blue and his skin was just a little tanned, but the part of him that had caught her eye was the ink. His chest, his back, his upper arms were all thickly lined with black designs, tribal sun and moon and stars.

She flicked her eyes up to Jason. He was watching, his fingers caressing the soundboard. He quirked his lips in a grin and winked. Approval given. To the slow buildup of the next lyric, she slid her hands down her chest, glow sticks clasped between her slender fingers. Tattoo-boy tracked the motion while she touched her own hips, outlining the swell. She took one step toward him and smiled, ducking her head to peer up at him through her bangs. Daring him.

She closed her eyes and licked her lips.

His fingers were a hot, smooth contrast to the hard plastic glow sticks in between them on her bare arms. He touched the crook of her elbow, felt her pulse, and stepped closer while his hands slid up to her shoulders. His breath ghosted over her throat, his lips following like wet silk.

"I'm Luke," he said against her neck. His body swayed against hers to the music as if he couldn't control it.

"Eve," she said.

She licked the silver hoops in his earlobe and felt a pulse of delight. His skin was soft and salty under her tongue. He clutched her closer and the dance turned into an undulation. His thigh between her legs, hers between his, pressing against intimate areas. The weight of him hard against her nearly made her shiver. His bare chest pressed her breasts between them, a wall of heat. Sweat mingled around the lines of her cut-off tank top.

He dropped the glow sticks to wrap his fingers in the short hair at the base of her neck and pull her head back, gently. A curtain of dishwater-blond hair fell around them while he brushed their mouths together. His tongue traced the fullness of her bottom lip, faintly ticklish. Her skin burned with heat. Between the humidity in the old warehouse and the man kissing her slow and deep, she was almost overwhelmed.

She felt him stiffen a moment before he made a noise into her mouth and familiar hands clasped her waist. Jason was smiling, his chin resting on the tattooed man's shoulder. He was just a little taller.

"This is Jason," she said to Luke. "Do you mind?"

He craned his head to look over his shoulder and Jason kissed his cheek.

"You're the DJ," Luke said.

"Yeah. Eve has special tastes."

She pressed her hands to Luke's chest, tracing the lines of the sun tattoo. He smiled; a slow, easy expression. It made him look wicked. She stared up at them, the black wisps of Jason's hair sticking to the other man's face.

"I can do that," Luke said, turning his head a fraction. She watched the men's mouths hover so close that they nearly touched. Jason closed his eyes and licked the full roundness of Luke's lips. A burst of pleasure spread out from her core at the sight of them kissing, slowly at first, just lips sliding and pressing. One of Luke's hands left her waist to cup Jason's chin, deepening the kiss. She could hear the wet noises of their tongues slipping against each other.

She shifted, rubbing her legs together. Her panties clung to her skin, damp with sweat and desire. Luke's free hand found its way to her buttocks, kneading forcefully. Jason reared back from their kiss with a small gasp, his cheeks red. He blushed so easily. She wondered if he was pushing his erection against Luke's backside and could imagine intimately how it felt.

"Do you have a place somewhere?" her stranger murmured, his mouth glistening with shared saliva. "I came with a friend. No car to take home."

"Yes," she said. "But I usually like to have the first course here."

He grinned, palmed her groin in the tight shorts and bent down a little to whisper in her ear, "What's on the menu?"

His thumb pressed surely against her clit through the thin material and he rubbed a slow circle, sending sparks of pleasure up her spine. She moaned and grabbed a handful of his hair to pull his mouth to hers. Jason's hands wormed in between them, tracing the hard outline of Luke's cock. "She wants this," he said. "But don't give it to her yet."

Luke brought his hand up and smelled it, one deep inhale.

"Don't talk about me like I'm not here," Eve said. She wriggled her fingers between Jason's over the tattooed man's erection and squeezed it gently. "I'm the one who wants to suck your dick in the car."

"Who says I don't?" Jason smiled at her.

"Oh, hell," she said. "Let's go ahead and leave."

"Nadia, am I clear to go?" Jason yelled, waving a hand at the other DJ. She gave him a thumbs-up. She'd only worn two little crosses of electrical tape over her nipples and her breasts bounced with the motion. Dancers hooted at her and she grinned out at the crowd, Jason forgotten already.

Eve laced her fingers with Luke's and turned to lead them out of the warehouse, her pulse throbbing between her legs. They only did this once every few months, and her tattoo-boy was a real treat for the eyes. Jason hadn't reacted so strongly to any of the men she'd picked in a long time. She shivered at the burst of cold night air that enveloped them when the door opened; sweat drying instantly on her skin. It did nothing to quell her desire. *Who would do what?* she thought. Luke on top of her, fucking her while he sucked Jason off, letting her watch his pink lips sliding back and forth? She nearly moaned.

"Maybe you two should just get in the back," Jason said.

He hit the unlock button on his key ring. Eve led their guest to the compact sedan, catching a quick kiss on the cheek from her lover before climbing into the back on all fours. Luke whistled from behind her, and before she could turn to lie on her back he pressed himself up against her backside. She took in a startled, pleased breath at the rush of fire that spread up her spine from his point of contact, his hips ground firmly against her round butt.

"I think even your shorts are wet, honey," Luke murmured.

"House is fifteen minutes away," Jason chimed in, revving the engine. "That's plenty of time."

"Sure is," the other man said.

Eve turned her head to look at him. His hair cascaded across his bare shoulders like a waterfall, sticking to the sweat on his toned body. The contrast of his black ink next to the dusky pink of his nipples made her mouth water.

"Hold on to the seat," Luke said, his thumb teasing the dip of her spine where the shorts clung tight. "And don't let go of it, not unless I tell you to."

She hadn't expected him to order her, but the tone of authority in his voice made her shiver harder. She clasped her fingers around the soft edge of the seat and bowed her head. He used that single thumb to peel her shorts up away from her buttocks and down her thighs, dragging them sensuously. The smell of her musk was so strong that even Jason made a little noise from the front seat. Luke stroked a finger across the soaked, skimpy lace thong Eve was wearing. She breathed steadily, trying to calm herself, make the pleasure last a little longer. He pulled up on the back of her thong lightly, letting it slip between her full outer lips.

"Now, that looks nice," he murmured.

She jumped at the first touch of his tongue, a little ticklish flicker right at the joint of butt and thigh that slid inwards, so slowly. A shaky gasp slid from between her teeth when he buried his face between her legs and licked a long, hot stripe from her clit to where the lace disappeared between her ass cheeks. He moaned, licking her again, and again, over the panties. It was maddening. The contact wasn't quite enough, though the rough, sopping wet lace felt so good against her pussy.

"Please," she said. "God, please, do it for real."

He laughed against her and she twitched, gripping the seat harder.

"You'll get it when I feel like it."

"Ten minutes," Jason said, and she peered up long enough to see him staring intently at them in the rearview mirror. She ducked her head again.

Luke's hand found its way under her shirt and up to her breasts, kneading and squeezing gently, each one in turn. His rough palms against her nipples sent sharp bolts of pleasure through her body, just as much as the thorough massaging he gave them. The fingertips of his other hand spread the outer lips of her pussy and he bent to work again. He flicked his tongue in quick strokes over her clit, still covered in thin lace. She tensed up, willing herself closer to orgasm, each touch building upon itself. She moaned, low and long, and leaned back into him.

Luke backed up and teased his tongue instead around the rim of the entrance to her body, laving it with short, soft licks. She wanted him inside so badly it almost hurt; she felt empty, wanted desperately to simply plunge her own fingers in and come. She lifted one hand from the seat.

Instantly, he grabbed her wrist and twisted the arm up her back. She gasped and shuddered, the slight pain pushing her so close to the edge she felt like she could come at the slightest breeze, anything, if he would just give it to her.

"Driveway coming up," Jason said, covering the sound of a zipper opening. She moaned into the upholstery, weakly, wishing for relief. The car came to a stop. There was a small sound, and she perked up, moving to turn her head.

Luke plunged inside of her, suddenly, as far as he could go. She screamed, one short, abrupt sound, and his second shove pushed so deep that it held an edge of pain. The climax hit her on the third thrust, bowing her spine and tightening every muscle in her body. She cried out, jerking in Luke's hold, clawing the seat. His balls slapped against her and he rode out a few more short lunges before the contractions stopped and she went limp under him, groaning with the pleasure of it, her hips already working backward for more.

"Help her inside," Jason said, sounding husky and pleased.

Luke pulled out slowly, letting her feel every magnificent inch, before he slipped free. He couldn't resist running his hand over her slippery cunt, watching her shudder again. He peeled the condom off and tossed it on the floorboard.

"Come on, honey," he said, rolling her onto her back with a gentle push.

"Wow," she sighed, closing her eyes for one brief moment to savor the languor that had taken her over, the bone-melting goodness of such a sudden, intense orgasm. Luke pulled her shorts up as best he could, and she shifted to put them on completely.

"More to come." He grinned at her and zipped up his pants, careful of his erection, then climbed out of the car. She followed on unsteady legs.

Luke held the front door open for her and locked it behind them. The simple care in that action brought a smile to her face. A clinking noise from the kitchen drew her attention, and she took Luke's hand to guide him.

It was warm and still a little sticky. She blushed and he laughed, rich and open. The sound of it made her heart flutter.

"I thought we might enjoy a drink," Jason said from the counter. He'd sat out three glasses. "Wine or Schnapps?"

"Wine," Luke said. "Are we going to talk about the arrangement?"

"Yeah," Eve said. She went to the cabinet and pulled down a small bottle of wildberry Schnapps for herself. "I know it seems a little impersonal, but it's good to have everything out in the air beforehand."

"Nah," Luke said. He took the full glass Jason offered him, leaning against the counter next to the couple. He looked faintly ridiculous without a shirt in the domestic setting, his hair wild and tangled over the tattoos. "I don't want to cause any trouble, just have fun. You are two very lovely people."

"Thanks," Jason said, sipping from his own glass.

Eve poured herself a small shot. "First, we're both clean, but we obviously use condoms." The memory of it tightened things low in her belly. Luke grinned. "Second, this should only be a one-time thing. If we see each other again, let's just be friends. Jason and I are committed to each other."

"No objections. I'm not attached to anyone," Luke said. He looked to Jason. "Do you have any special rules?"

"Only that you treat us both with respect, and we will you. Oh," he added, raising a hand to clasp around the back of Luke's neck. He pulled the other man close, letting their noses bump. Goose bumps broke out on Eve's arms watching them hover at the line of a kiss. Luke flexed against the grip, but Jason held him fast. They sat down their glasses almost in synchrony. "You can boss her, but I'm in charge."

"Yeah?" Luke said and tangled his fist in Jason's hair. He yanked the other man's head back, straining against his grip to lay the very edge of teeth on his throat, just below the ear. He bit, gently, and Jason exhaled. The muscles in their arms bunched and flexed.

Suddenly Jason wrapped a fistful of blond ponytail around his fingers and jerked. Luke grunted, staggering momentarily, fighting the downward pull. Jason had the advantage. After a long, tense moment, he acceded with a growl, sinking to his knees. Eve slipped her hand into her shorts, brushing the hard nub of her clit softly at first.

"Open up," Jason said, voice rough. Luke actually moaned, let his jaw drop. Jason kept his grip on the ponytail like a leash and unzipped his pants. He didn't have to say anything more; the other man went forward without prompting to nuzzle his cock. Eve said nothing, even though the view wasn't perfect. She didn't want to disrupt the masculine power struggle.

Jason took a deep breath and let it rush out through his nose, dropping his head back. His hips began to pump. The wet, smacking sounds of his dick sliding in and out of Luke's mouth were obscene, gorgeous. She began to work her fingers in steady circles, stimulating herself. Her breath came in quick gulps, and she closed her eyes to better imagine the picture. The noises stopped, and she blinked, peering around Jason's back.

Luke knelt on the floor with his hands open, lax on his thighs in utter submission. His lips were swollen and red, his chin slick with spit and his eyes half-lidded. He panted for breath.

"Bedroom," Jason said, stripping out of his pants rather than trying to zip them back up. He laid them over a dining room chair and threw his shirt on top of them, striding nude down the hall. His tanned buttocks flexed enticingly with every step until the shadows concealed him.

Eve held a hand down to Luke, who snagged it and pulled himself up to full height. She kissed him, hard, searching out the taste of male musk on his tongue. He cupped her ass in his hands and squeezed, gently at first, then harder, until she made a sound into his mouth.

"I want to fuck you," he said, raw and honest. Her whole body seemed to throb in response.

"Bedroom," she repeated breathily.

They stumbled down the hall, still embracing, mouths sliding against one another in messy, slippery kisses. Jason was waiting for them, sprawled out on the bed like a sculpture, the fine trail of black hair on his belly leading to the somewhat formidable sight of his erection, still glistening with spit, standing at attention. He broke the tension with a grin, patting the sheets next to him.

Eve started to climb up onto the bed; Luke grabbed her hips from behind and Jason got hold of the back of her neck. He knelt up on the bed, his cock bumping against her cheek. She stuck her tongue out to lick it, enjoying the heat and velvety texture. Luke stripped her shorts and panties off in one smooth jerk, leaving them pooled

on the floor for her to step out of. His pants made a soft
susurration as they dropped.

"First like this," Luke said, smoothing his hands up her
back.

"Then he'll be inside you while I fuck him," Jason
said, locking eyes with Luke over top of her head. "Sound
good?"

"Yeah," she said, feeling as though she hadn't come all
night. The need was back already, every inch of her skin
tingling with the desire for touch. "Come on, let's do it."

"You don't need a lot of warm-up, do you?" Luke
murmured.

"I got that watching you dance," she said. He chuckled.

"Wait," Jason said. "We should switch."

"Why?" Eve said.

"Because every man should have you suck his cock at
least once." Jason ran a hand through her hair, smoothing
it away from her face. She grinned up at him. "Luke, get
up here."

"What's so good about it?"

"You'll see," he said, patting her once on the cheek
before sliding off of the bed to kneel behind her.

Luke settled on the edge of the mattress, his legs spread
around her. His hair, in intricate loops and strands, stuck
to his chest, gold outlining his artwork. The tribal designs
flowed from ankle up, not just on his chest. She bent her
head and nuzzled the crease of his thigh and groin, darting
her tongue out to taste the salty sweat gathering there.
The tattoos did continue, a little curl of black ink on each
side swirling out to touch the very base of his member.

She brushed her lips across them, imagining she could feel the difference. The smell of his musk was strong and heady, undeniably masculine. She inhaled deeply, almost dizzy with lust. There was a fine bead of pre-come at the tip of his dick, and she ran her closed lips up the shaft, reveling in the velvety texture. Luke's hand slid into her hair and he tugged her up a little further, pushing his hips forward in obvious invitation.

Jason's warm, broad hands stoked her sides, rubbing up and down from her shoulders to her hips. She wriggled under the touch and ran the flat of her tongue over the slick head of the cock in front of her, tasting pleasantly bitter fluid.

"Go for it, baby," Jason murmured, and she slipped the first inch into her mouth, licking thoroughly, getting it wet.

Slowly, she worked down the length, delighting in the way the unfamiliar ridges felt on her palate. There was something almost transcendental about giving head. She pulled back to the tip, flicked her tongue hard at the frenulum. Luke jerked and hissed, thrusting shallowly. She pressed her thumbs into the curves of his hips and took a deep breath before sliding her lips down the length again. Heat spread in her belly, through her center. She loved this. The weight, the warmth, and the slick smooth texture excited her intensely.

Instead of stopping when he bumped the back of her throat, she angled her head up and relaxed. A sharp thrill ran through her at the strangled sound Luke made while his dick slid centimeter by centimeter down her throat.

The stretch was pleasant; he wasn't quite as big around as Jason. She kept going until her lips touched the blond curls on his belly, then held him there, swallowing around the bulk in her throat rhythmically to keep from gagging. She felt her own wetness dripping down her thighs. Luke grabbed at her frantically, his head thrown back, squeezing first her shoulder, than running a hand through her hair and finally grasping the back of her head, his breath coming in short wheezes.

"Oh, my God," he moaned, pushing his hips up against her mouth. "This is so fucking good."

"Gets better," Jason murmured, still stroking her back, helping her stay relaxed.

She moved back, a mouthful of thick saliva dripping down his shaft while she heaved in a deep breath. Immediately, she sucked him back in until there was no more to take. Then she began to bob her head, slow enough to keep control of the motion. Luke made a sound like a whimper, legs trembling while she fucked her throat with him.

"You can move now," Jason said, and grabbed a handful of her hair to hold her still. "If she smacks your leg, stop."

Luke groaned, low and long, thrusting shallowly at first. If she'd had the time to take a deeper breath she would have moaned as well. Jason held her perfectly still, removing her control, letting Luke truly have her. He began to push harder, then a little faster. She drifted in her head, saliva running down her chin to wet the sheets while they took her. Transcendental was a perfect word.

"I'm going to come if I don't stop," Luke gasped, ragged-voiced.

"Can you get it up again?" Jason said.

"For you guys? Fuck, yeah."

"Do you want to swallow his come, baby?" Jason said, pushing two of his fingers into her pussy and twisting them. She squealed, concentration suddenly shattered. It felt so good. "Then go ahead and do it."

"Yeah," Luke said, throwing his head back and clenching his jaw around a yell. He yanked her head forward and thrust in again, so far down her throat that she couldn't taste him, but she felt the pulsing on her tongue, against her lips. Jason's fingers twisted again, working her, and she came as well, her cries silenced. When Luke pulled out to flop back on the bed, she gasped for air, still writhing and whimpering with climax. The pleasure went on and on, sweet and heady, not as powerful as the orgasm in the car, but better. When she calmed, Jason stopped fingering her.

"You made a big mess," he said, and she could hear the grin in his tone. "You've come all over the carpet and the sheets are going to have to be washed."

"Wow," Luke said, lying on his back. "Never done that before."

"Took her years," Jason said, helping his girl up onto the bed as well. She curled up against Luke's side, pressing herself to him.

"I like doing it," she said, her voice rough. "I have to give up my control, you know? I like it a lot."

"Well, thank God," Luke said with a laugh. "Give me a few minutes and I'll be ready again."

"I'm going to go get some water," Eve said, prying

herself away from the warmth of her lovers. Her first few steps wobbled. "Be right back."

She couldn't wipe the silly smile off of her face. She hadn't been so satisfied in a long time. Not that Jason wasn't enough for her, but he was having so much fun, too. Sometimes the men or women they brought home weren't his type; they didn't get along well enough. Luke seemed to fit perfectly with them. She felt a little twinge at the thought of him leaving in the morning forever, then shrugged it aside.

The chill of the freezer was wonderful on her overheated skin. She stood in front of the open door for a long moment, letting the tacky dampness of sweat and sweet fluids dry on her legs, then poured herself a glass of water. There was a faint soreness, but otherwise her throat felt fine. Sometimes it would hurt if she and Jason did it too long.

After a few sips, she filled the cup back up to the rim and padded back down the hall. She felt languid and absolutely luxurious. The evening wasn't over yet, though. She pushed the door open and froze.

Jason had Luke held down on his stomach, one hand fisted in that gorgeous ponytail, the other between his ass cheeks. The bottle of lubricant was open on the nightstand. The blond man let out a low groan, his toes digging into the covers. Jason withdrew glistening fingers and then pushed them back inside, torturously slow.

The sleepy pleasure of a moment before flared to life, a sudden need and ache between her legs. She took a shallow breath, her fingers numb around the glass, and leaned against the wall. Jason bent forward to bite at the thick, ink-lined muscle of the other man's back. Luke yelped, straining for a moment, his head pulled back from the pillows by the grip in his hair. His eyes were half closed; his mouth was open, lips slick and reddened. Jason began to move his hand.

"God," Luke gasped, gripping the headboard white-knuckled. "Oh, yeah."

"Want me to fuck you now?" Jason rasped, still bent over his arched back, and bit him again.

"Yes!"

"Please," Eve murmured, striding over to put the glass down on the end table. "I want to see it."

Jason slipped his fingers free and let go of the other man's ponytail to grasp his hips and pull him up onto his knees. The muscles in his arms bulged with the effort. Eve squeezed herself onto the bed next to the pair, entranced with them. They were nearly ignoring her, so caught up in their own struggle and passion, but it was somehow all the more arousing. They weren't doing this for her; they wanted each other.

She watched with a dry mouth while Jason slid his dick back and forth against the crack of Luke's ass, teasing him. The tattoos didn't cover his tanned buttocks; they framed the cheeks like two commas, wisping around the backs of his thighs.

"Now," Jason said, using his thumb to guide himself into position.

There was a moment of strain, finding the right angle, and Luke bared his teeth around a snarl when Jason finally snapped his hips forward and buried himself deep. She almost had to close her eyes at the sight of Jason holding himself still, his broad hands sliding up Luke's sweaty, muscled back, across the red marks his teeth had left, to hold the man's shoulders.

He pulled out slow, letting Luke adjust and letting Eve look her fill at the sight of him on top of another man. Then he used the grip on his shoulders to yank him back at the same time as he thrust forward, bottoming out on the first stroke. Luke howled, a primal cry, but it was a sound of pleasure. They moved fast after that. Every thrust was almost a slam, both men grinding their teeth around shouts and grunts.

She could only resist for so long before she let her hand go between her legs, finding herself drenched again. Luke rose up on his arms, throwing his head back against Jason's shoulder to catch his mouth in a ravenous kiss. His golden hair flew with the movement, sticking to them both in a beautiful curtain. It was like watching gods fuck.

"Please," she said. "Let me get under you."

Luke turned his head to her and hissed, "Yes."

He grabbed her by the leg before she could move herself and reared back. Jason altered his grip, locking his arms around the other man's chest. His teeth sank into Luke's neck while he dragged her into position. She gasped, a flash of heat racing through her veins. Jason shoved Luke back down onto her, holding him there with a hand on the back of his neck. Luke panted against her throat, his hands squeezing her buttocks. He lifted her hips, forcing her to wrap her legs around his waist. Jason rubbed her calf with his free hand.

"Fuck her," he growled.

Luke fumbled for a condom and she snatched it from him, rolling it onto his hard cock. She was as frantic for it as he was, the sound of her lovers' flesh slapping together with each thrust, the smell of their sweat, the sight of them, muscled and straining against each other with barely contained violence.

She screamed when he shoved inside her, clutching at his arms. Her nails dug in and he groaned, letting Jason's quick pace drive his own movement. She lay helpless beneath the onslaught of pleasure, the awkward way he held her off of the mattress preventing her from gaining any leverage. She cried out sharply, raking her nails down his arms.

"I want to come inside you," Jason hissed into Luke's ear. "I want you to feel that while she squeezes you with her gorgeous pussy. Feel me, in you."

Luke made an inarticulate sound, yanking her onto every hard thrust. Her eyes rolled back a little with the intensity of the sensation. He struck that spot inside her with every thrust, and each magnificent inch felt like more sliding in and out. She worked one hand between their bodies and began to circle her fingers around her throbbing clit, sweetening the feeling of lightning racing through her nerves.

"Almost there," she gasped, staring up at her men.

"Quick tonight," Jason panted, still fucking Luke hard. "You like watching this that much, huh?"

"I want to watch his face," she groaned. "When you make him come."

"God," Luke snapped out, breaking rhythm to suddenly speed his shoves into her, stealing her words and breath. She rubbed harder, faster, and grit her teeth while another climax built.

"Not yet," Jason said, pulling Luke back and off balance. He slid out of her, denying her release, and she made a startled, almost hurt noise. "I want you to really watch."

He knelt back on his heels, Luke shifting to sit astride his lap. Luke stretched one arm back to steady himself against Jason's back. He stroked that beautiful cock, slick with her juices, without moving. Luke's chest heaved with exertion, every breath a struggle. His face was an enticing shade of red. Then Jason reached down and lifted his balls even closer to his body, revealing to her the sight of them joined. She moaned.

"Move," Jason said.

Luke lifted himself a short distance and dropped back down. He swallowed a groan and did it again, faster. His strong thighs worked hard while he rode Jason's lap, a look of concentration and ecstasy on his face.

"Goes real deep this way," he managed to whisper. "That's so fucking good."

"Then you'll really like this," Jason whispered back, holding him still a moment to pull out. Luke moaned with the loss. "On your back. Eve, ride him."

He rolled as instructed, still panting for breath, and opened his arms to her. She crawled on top of him, her breasts heavy and nipples tight with desire. He nuzzled between them briefly, massaging them while she straddled his lap. They'd done this before. She sat a little farther forward than usual, waiting for Jason to arrange a pillow under the small of Luke's back.

"I'm dying here," Luke said, his eyes fevered and bright with lust. "One of you needs to start this up again before I explode."

"No problem," Jason said. She glanced back at him. He also had a look of intense concentration, but she knew that to be his general attitude toward arousal. He wanted it to be perfect for everyone involved, always the most pleasure, always the best way.

He lifted both of Luke's legs over his shoulders, putting his hips at an angle. Eve wriggled and reached back to lift his cock away from his stomach. She could tell the moment Jason pushed back inside because Luke's eyes went wide, then closed tight, within the flash of a second. He groaned, rolling his head on the pillow as if it was too much to handle. She slid down onto his shaft, glorying in the stretch and fulfillment, and watched him bite his full bottom lip.

"With you like this," Jason said, massaging Luke's thighs and Eve's buttocks where they touched. "I can hit that spot straight on." He accentuated his words with a hard push up, and Luke's mouth fell open, his eyelids fluttering.

"Yeah, that's it," Eve murmured, intimately feeling his dick twitch inside her. It was a lovely sensation. "Let us take you."

As if her words had been the key, Luke let himself

go lax under their attentions, his arms lying loose on the bed. He surrendered to the pleasure. She shuddered above him, leaning back to feel Jason's hot skin against her own. This was for her pleasure. She moved her hips in tiny increments; ground them in a circular pattern against Luke's pelvis. The direct stimulation to the spot inside her that felt almost swollen with so many shallow orgasms was nearly too intense. It trod the line of perfect pain, but she kept moving, gasping for air. Her fingers worked quickly on her clit, stroking, rubbing. She used him like a favorite toy while he moaned continuously underneath her.

"Soon," she said.

"Good." Jason sounded strained. "He's squeezing me so hard, I think I could shoot off right now."

"Then do it."

He began to really move again, short, almost brutal thrusts that drove him against Luke's prostate unerringly. Eve watched with fascination while Luke grimaced with the feeling first, then his jaw slowly dropped and his hips began to pump slightly, but not with her. No, he was working back onto Jason's pounding, speeding the rhythm. She kept her eyes on his face. It was so beautiful. She bounced on him, pushing herself closer to the edge with each motion.

"That's right," Jason suddenly said. "God, that's just about . . ."

He pushed hard against Luke's thighs to get a better angle and truly rode his ass. She felt Luke's cock pulse inside her, hard, then again and again. He was coming so much that she wished for a moment there was no condom, that she could feel all that heat pouring into her and dripping back out while she kept riding him. She grit her teeth around a yell and came, colors behind her eyelids and every muscle locking up.

Luke did shout, at the end, when Jason slammed into him hard and fucked him in tight, short thrusts to work out his own orgasm. She saw the whites of his eyes, felt him jerk under her hands.

"God!" Luke yelled, then Jason bit her shoulder while he eased down from his high of pleasure and pulled out of their lover.

Luke was trembling, she noticed, gingerly rolling off of him. Jason stripped them both of their condoms and threw them in the trash. He had a tender look in his eyes, watching Luke shiver with aftershocks. He combed a hand through the hopelessly tangled mane of golden locks and picked it up like a large snake to lay it across the top of the bed, out of the way.

"Ssh," he whispered to Luke, nudging him onto his side. "I know."

"Just intense," he murmured, still hoarse.

"Rest for a minute. I'll get you two cleaned up."

He rose from the bed, stiff with the overexertion of a moment before. Luke wrapped his arms around Eve and snuggled against her back. His hand rested gently on her stomach. She felt a little sore inside, but it was a pleasant ache, a reminder of some truly fantastic sex. Jason returned with two damp cloths and wiped them both free of lubricant and fluids.

"I'll hold you," he said, flipping the lamp switch. The

room plunged into darkness. There was only the warmth of their bodies, their breath. Eve listened to her men kiss, a slow, wet sound, before Luke settled between them. Jason's hand wedged between them, touching her back and Luke's stomach. She heard a sigh and murmured words, felt lips on her neck, and drifted to sleep with a smile on her face.

Later Days, Saints

by Kilt Kilpatrick

I know, I know, this is the part where I go straight to hell. But honestly, can you blame me? Are you trying to tell me you wouldn't have done the same thing in my place? Bitch, you're such a liar!

So listen, there I am, minding my own business in the Swinging Bachelorette Pad. I should have been working on my term paper, but I was still collating my data and letting the outline marinate a while. Get off my case already, that's my process, and you have to respect that, right? So anyway, I'm at home, just back from my last class of the day, kicking back on the couch grooving to Katy Perry in my sweet new iPod speaker dock and reading *The Straight Girl's Guide to Sleeping With Chicks*, which is such a totally fucking awesome book, especially for a closeted tight-ass like you. So I'm laughing my tits off and plotting who I'm going to nail using this newfound knowledge. Yeah, that's right! So better watch out, little Miss Sexypants!

The doorbell rings and of course I think it's you or Nanda or Akiko-chan, so I just up and throw the door open wide, all set to yell, "Where my bitches?" in my hilarious pimp voice. But instead, it's these two Mormon boys, and I have to do this complete one-eighty—Ehrrrrrrrrrk!—to rein in the crazy act and not terrify these guys. "Oh! Hi!" I say while I recover my balance, trying not to giggle and just smile like a non-crazy person.

Now you gotta understand, on any other day I would've just told them, *no, thank you* and to fuck off, but in a nice way. But timing is everything, isn't it? I was still pissed about the LDS church pumping all those millions of dollars for that fascist proposition H8 and felt it was my duty to do what I could to undermine theocratic fundamentalism in some small way, or at the very least confront them with the inherent contradictions of their dogmatic paradigm— and well, they were just so damn cute. Shut up.

You know what I mean; most of them have this creepy white-bread-Children-of-the-Corn-Stepford-Wives thing going on. I'm just saying. But these two . . . damn, girl! They're both clean-cut and so polite. And they're just so nerdy cute in their starched short-sleeved shirts and ties and little name badges. One says "Elder Steward" and the other "Elder Harper." And of course the whole "Elder" thing cracks me up, because they can't be more than their early twenties and seem younger. I'm maybe three years older than them, if even that, and I already felt like a worldly wise urban sophisticate of a woman by comparison.

Even in their preacher drag I can see that both of them are fit little hard bodies underneath. They're both so lean and sculpted, I'm sure they both have to be swimmers or dancers or karate experts, something like that. Mmmm, yum. And so good looking! I keep picturing them as underwear models. But best of all, they seem totally unaware of their inordinate hunkiness—so shy and sweet. Just adorable.

Elder Stewart is Amerasian; you could tell he had gotten the best parts of both parents. He's got black-brown hair, a great smile and these soft dreamy eyes you wouldn't believe. I just know he has to have a Japanese or Hawaiian first name. Elder Harper triggers all my geek girl buttons—he's so Elvish-looking, but not too Orlando Bloomy; just these nice cheekbones and something in the ears and eyebrows that's otherworldly and enticing. His dark brown hair is cut really short, all business, and he has this, I dunno, sharp look to his eyes, like I could see him being an archer, or a young district attorney. And is it my imagination, or does he have a faint Australian accent? Yumska!

So they do the whole Hi, we're from The Church of Jesus Christ of Latter Day Saints and we're in your neighborhood today to share with you blah blah blah spiel, and I say, "Hey, I'm Sabrina," and I'm all, "Wow, that's great, come on in," like I never heard of such an amazing undertaking before. "Really? Another testament of Jesus Christ?" While the whole time I'm already concocting my evil plan to jump their bones.

I've never attempted such a crazy combo maneuver—The High Level Religious De-pantsing and the Simultaneous Double Seduction? It's unheard of, never been done! I feel like an Olympic athlete. I focus accordingly.

First hurdle: I'm still holding *The Straight Girl's Guide to Sleeping With Chicks* in my hand; gotta lose that, so I use my ninja skills to stash it under a throw pillow fast, like a reverse pickpocket. Score!

It's a good thing I'm just back from class with a professor I want to impress, because I'm not dressed in anything too riot grrl or hippie chic and not loafing around in my über-comfy Cal-Berkeley sweatshirt/nightie and grizzly bear slippers. In fact, I'm totally rocking the smart, studious co-ed look; my hair is in a kicky ponytail, and I'm wearing my naughty librarian glasses and a super cute pink short-sleeve, button-up blouse that hides the Celtic triple-spiral tattoo on my shoulder. I'm in the jeans that make my legs look long and my butt irresistible without being slutty about it. I'm not even wearing my lucky thong, just unpretentious fuchsia panties from JC Penney's.

I snap open the top button on my blouse on the sly and turn down Katy Perry before she starts in about kissing a girl and liking it; the whole time I'm quickly scanning the room for anything else potentially incriminating. Luckily I straightened up recently—wow, timing really is everything!—so there's no sex toys, porn or uppity feminist/godless/science reading material in sight. The only potential giveaway of my dangerous inner nature—a small poster of Eleanor Roosevelt with her (and my) motto, "Do one thing every day that scares you." Can do, Eleanor baby.

Okay, so now I'm thinking, where to hold our uplifting chat? Bedroom is right out, couch is tempting but too forward, so the wobbly little table in the dining room it is. Dreamy Elder Stewart takes the lead, walking me through the intro of his little blue *Book of Mormon*. I nod and make polite interested noises while he tells me how in 1830-something upstate New York, the prophet Joseph Smith—who I swear looks just like a young James Spader in a cravat—got the scoop from the angel Moroni that all other religions were bullshit (I'm paraphrasing) and really displeasing to the Lord. Tell me why angels of the Lord always appear to prophets in remote, secluded locales instead of God just telling everybody? Or why a god would wait until the friggin' 1830s to get it right, but whatever. Bite your tongue and stick to the plan already, Sabrina!

So the boys take turns telling me how Joseph Smith translated golden plates using the magical Uma Thurman stones or something; it all sounded very Harry Potter, to be honest. I'm plotting while they go on about Aaronic and Melchizedek Priesthoods, Celestial, Terrestrial, and Telestial Heavens, the three witnesses who vouched for all this, and eight other witnesses who vouched for them, and that if we prayerfully sought answers from our heavenly Father, he would give us a burning in our bosom so that we might know The Truth.™

My eyes are glazing over a little, so I review my options. I've never been one for the In-Your-Face-Wanton-Sex-Goddess approach: *Screw all this made-up bullshit, boys! Let's fuck!* and I'm fairly sure they'd both bolt in terror if I tried. And I'm not nearly glam enough to pull off the Femme Fatale, simply-staring-them-into-drooling-lustful-submission, Marlene Dietrich style. So I'm half-

listening to their talk of lost Israelite tribes escaping the
Tower of Babel (!), sailing to the New World, and, because
of their sin (!!), turning into American Indians. (I know,
right?!?!) But really I'm in my default Nice Girl seduction
mode: leaning in close, feigning rapt interest, laughing
at anything remotely resembling a joke, and taking any
opportunity for innocent, accidental bumping elbows or
touching hands.

But damn my inner anthropology major! Even while
my panties were calling the shots, my spoilsport brain still
couldn't keep from butting in with its stupid questions
and nearly nixing the whole deal. Though in my defense,
there was a lot of snickering to suppress: all the pictures of
the Nephites and Lamanites were pretty lame; the models
all looked like Conan the Barbarian and ancient America
looked like a Dungeons & Dragons convention. So I
decided to drop the Innocent Seeker approach and shift
to a different strategy: the Saucy Challenging Opponent.

"Wait, it really says these guys had steel swords and
silk togas and chariots and elephants in America over
two thousand years ago? And that millions of them were
killed . . . in upstate New York?" I'm genuinely puzzled.
Oh yes, they nod. My appalled inner archeologist comes
out swinging. "But has anyone ever found any of these
battlefield sites? Or steel artifacts? Or elephant bones?
And you realize there were no horses to pull their chariots,
or silkworms outside of China in 600 B.C. right?" They
squirm a little and promise to locate a good book on
Mormon archeology for me that will clear up the matter.

Believe me, this back and forth goes on for *fucking*

ever, and every two minutes I'm sure I've overplayed my
hand and they're going to storm out all offended any
second now, but they stick it out. Oh! So finally I say,
"Hey, if Joseph Smith translated it, why is it in King James
English?" They smile kind of nervously, and say something
about it being a very accurate translation from "reformed
Egyptian," whatever the hell that is, but by now I think
even they are feeling a little shaky about their answers.
Honestly, I tried not to be too harsh, but hey, after all, they
were the ones who came knocking on my door, right? I
swear I wasn't a total bee-yotch about it, though. I don't
bring up polygamy even once (seems like a cheap shot)
and I'm completely set to cheerfully grit my teeth through
any talk of how many babies good Mormon women would
be expected to pop out.

And all good-natured sparring aside, I've got my diplo-
mat hat on. I keep things super-friendly and take careful
track of any encouraging signs—and signs are good. Both
guys seem to like the closeness when we occasionally bump
up against each other by accident. I'm very scrupulous to
accidentally touch both of them equally. And I totally love
that both are being so careful not to be caught staring
down my top, even though their eyes keep getting drawn
to my forbidden goodies within. Ex-cell-ent . . .

When I accidentally contemplate out loud that it
would be easy enough to check if American Indians and
Jews were related with DNA evidence, they turn a little
pale, and that's when I think: Okay, cool it, Brainiac. Time
to switch from Bad Cop to Good Cop, pronto.

"Hey, can I get you guys something to drink?" Oh,

just water's fine, thank you. "Coming right up." I adjust
my jeans ever so slightly as I head off to the kitchen, just
to give them something to think about. So get this . . . I
pop out again with two glasses of orange juice, and then
I stop and make a *d'oh!* face. "Oh shoot, you guys said
water, didn't you? What was I thinking? Are you guys even
allowed to drink Sunny D?" Oh sure, they assure me.

Where was I? Right, so I drop the Xena, Scholastic
Warrior Princess act and switch to Florence Nightingale
mode. They're weary from their hard travels and their
defense of the faith, so let's make nice now, right? Let me
comfort you and tend to your wounds. So I go, "Hey, can
I ask you . . . what're your names?"

Dreamy eyes Amerasian Elder Stewart smiles and says,
"My name's Cameron," and Elvish Elder Harper says in
that sexy, is-it-Australian? accent, "I'm Aidan." Aidan! I
could have jumped him right there. I say, so it must be
tough being on your mission and all, and they say, yeah, it
can be tough; you're far from home, you're on your feet
all day, there's a lot to do, and you get lots of rejection.
And . . . did you know this? They aren't allowed to listen
to music or the radio—not even the news! And they can't
read anything except missionary lessons and scripture.
Whoa. I had no idea. I really felt for them, you know?

I ask them where they're from, and it turns out Cameron
is from just outside Honolulu. So I tell Cameron I was so
sure he'd have a Japanese or Hawaiian name, and get this
— he says his middle name is Kavika, which is Hawaiian
for David! How funny is that? And yes, he's a swimmer; in
fact, they both play water polo.

Then I ask Aidan if he's from Australia, and he looks surprised and says no, but you're close, I'm from New Zealand; he says that most people think he's Irish or English, so good on you, and I was really proud of myself.

We talk some more, just about small stuff, nothing churchy or deep; they wanted to know how I liked U.C. Berkeley and what I was studying, what I liked to do, stuff like that. And it's really nice, but the whole time I'm getting so fucking horny that I'm sure they can hear my pussy growling, and I start visualizing the next phase of Operation Double Horndog. I flirt with the Damsel-in-Distress tactic: I'd fake a massive groin pull, see, and then they would have to carry me over to the couch. I'd lie down and have them elevate my leg. Here, Aidan, could you stand over there and massage my thigh? It really hurts! Yeah, just cradle my leg in your crotch just like that, yes . . . And Cameron, can you lean over and rub my neck and shoulders? No wait, I guess it's really my ribs and pecs that hurt. Just lean over and, yes . . . that's it . . . Oh Aidan, I don't mean for my foot to be kneading your privates like that, it's just an involuntary muscle reflex. Cameron, your tie is in my face; here, let me get that for you . . .

We're still chatting and I just about have this whole Damsel thing mapped out and wonder can I really pull this off, when I suddenly have this ultra-mind-boggling triple epiphany. It starts when they said something about having to go visit so many houses in a day, and I start to make up some total bullshit like, oh I wouldn't bother worrying about the rest of the neighborhood, they're all Baptists and Hare Krishnas, no need to waste your time hunting there, and then whammo, I realize, hey, these guys have been here for over two hours already—they've totally blown their day's schedule. And then it hits me, wait a sec, they've gotta have strict rules against male missionaries visiting unmarried young girls unchaperoned or something. I realize these guys are already totally breaking their rules. And once I realize all that, I get this incredible bright shining beautiful burst of transcendent certainty—I can totally do this. These two gorgeous man-children *want* to be seduced. I know it with a deep, divine burning in my bosom: I am so going to nail both of these Mormon boys.

But you know, I gotta say, for all my plotting and conniving, it was humbling, downright miraculous really, how simple it was. At this perfect pause in the conversation I just suddenly know, zenlike, it's time. I stand up, pull my glasses off and my scrunchie out, letting my hair go wild and free. Voilà! Schoolgirl to Sex Goddess, just like that. I give them a look and a smile, then reach over and take them both by their neckties. "Come on," I say, leading my captives back towards the couch. And amazingly, they do.

I sink into the couch and pull them down after me. For a sec they just look at me, all nervous and excited, not quite sure what to do next. I keep a firm grip on their neckties and look from one to the other. "Eeney meeney miney moe . . ." I finish on Cameron and draw him in for a long, big wet kiss; it's everything I had hoped for from that luscious mouth. Then I turn to Aidan and reel him in for his chance. Oh, yes. Two for two.

Mmm . . . happy Sabrina . . . I lounge between them

like this, taking turns pulling them in for deep, yummy tongue kisses, back and forth. I'm so impressed with how well the boys share. They stroke my legs and arms while they wait their turn. It feels so good, I think it'd be just dandy if this could go on for a few more hours. But then they start nuzzling my neck from both sides and that feels so amazing I totally lose my grip on their ties. I give them a little free range and wrap my arms around them. I grab big handfuls of their hair and they each start rubbing a breast. I enjoy that for a minute, then I let go and work my way out from under and tell them to let me stand up a sec.

I was going to give them a strip tease, but I feel a little dizzy and decide it will be more fun to have them do the work anyway. I have them unbutton my blouse; I make Aidan start at the top and Cameron at the bottom, then I do the honors of unhooking my bra. The look on their faces is priceless. I lower myself towards them and wind up sitting on my knees on the couch and hanging on to them so they can each get at my boobs. Damn, I feel just like a mother goddess with the two of them having a mouthful of me. I know I had to stay in charge and not give any puritanical Mormon-y impulses a chance to raise their ugly heads.

I push them off for a sec, unsnap the fly and slither out of my jeans as sexy as I can manage. My panties are soaked, but it feels exhilarating as hell to stand there for a moment with my thumbs tucked in the elastic and my hips cocked, while they sit there all dazed in their Geek Squad shirts and ties, looking up at me worshipfully. I peel off my panties and kick them away, then give my adoring congregation a little twirl to show off my ass.

Since I started with Cam last time, it seems only fair to give Aidan first crack this round. I flop down on the couch and order him to get on his knees in front of me. Then I reach down between my legs to grab his tie like a dog leash again and pull him face first into my wet little love trap. "Go on, get busy," I growl. Then I look over at Cameron and say, "C'mere, Pretty Boy." I snatch his tie too and pull him down for some more Frenching. I have to break it off after a little bit to give Aidan a few pointers; it really was his first time going down on a girl. He has good instincts, though, and picks it right up. God, yes! I shudder out my first orgasm right there; it's been a long time coming, but fuck me, so worth the wait! It's unreal having Cam snog me and caress the girls while Aidan is partying it up downtown. I keep my right hand buried in Aidan's hair and reach over to the front of Cam's slacks with the left. I ran my palm down the stiff bulge there (Mm . . . nice!) and slip it down and hook around to totally cop a feel of that sweet little butt of his. Another minute of that, then I make them switch places. Tough, but fair.

Cam doesn't disappoint on his oral exam either, and I'm all over Aidan's junk like it was a Braille book. It feels high time to raise the nudity quotient in the house. So I take my tongue out of Aidan's mouth and bring Cam up for air. I get them in close so I can let them in on a little secret: "Listen up. I put vodka in your orange drink. Can you feel all that alcohol working in your bloodstream, making you drunk and reckless? You're in trouble now, aren't you? You've totally fallen into my sinful trap."

Their eyes get wider, but it looks like everything thus far has overwhelmed the verbal half of their male brains as well as their moral centers. I snake my hands down to caress their cocks through their trousers.

"And tonight you're going to do what I tell you, aren't you?"

They shoot anxious looks at each other. "Don't look at him, look at me! I want to hear you say it." First Cameron, then Aidan croak out, "Yes."

"Yes, what?" I glare.

"We're . . . going . . . to do what you say." God, they even stammer in unison.

Girl, I played it cool, but I gotta tell you, on the inside I came a little just hearing that. You know I hate cigarettes, but fuck if I didn't want to make them light up and smoke a whole pack. Corrupting the innocent is a total turn-on! Mostly I figured to get the most mileage out of them I would have to take all the responsibility for their downfall and become the authority figure. I also want to give them an easy out for later. Their tender psyches can blame it all on the evil temptress and her wicked will-sapping potions tomorrow, and no doubt would. But tonight, it's time to give yourselves over to sin and buckle up, boys! "That's what I wanted to hear. Now, both of you get over here and kiss me so I can taste myself on you."

My hunky little slaves obey instantly, then I get up and take them by the neckties again and lead them off into the bedroom. Yes, by the neckties again! Don't judge me, bee-yotch; you try it just once and then we'll talk. I'm loving it, and they aren't complaining either. I sit down in the corner papasan chair where stuffy bear sits and make them stand in front of the bed.

"Now, I wanna get a good look at the two of you. So start by taking off your shoes and socks. Good. Now your pants. Toss them over there." I was going to strip off their shirts and ties myself, but I just sat down and now I'm feeling lazy and well, to be honest, more than a little drunk with power. "Okay, now take off your ties and shirts." Then I'm struck by inspiration: "No wait. I want you to take off each other's." That gives them pause, but they swallow, look nervously at each other, and at last (bingo!) reach over to the other's collar and start unbuttoning. Ohhh yeah . . . I touch myself while watching them undress each other. Honest, I really don't have a fetish, but when they tugged each other's neckties off, I think I peed myself a little. That was so hot.

And oh my God . . . I almost forgot. I'm getting ready to order them to finish the job and strip off their T-shirts and boxers already, when I realize that's not it . . . Holy *crap*, they're wearing that sacred Mormon underwear! I hadn't really thought that shit was for real, just some urban legend, but there it is, right in front of my eyes. They've got the little holy symbols stitched in and everything. For a moment I'm tempted to fuck them with it on, just for the blasphemy factor, but honestly, they're just too goofy looking, like Victorian bathing suits or something Olive Oyl would wear. I order them to peel off and throw them to me. Now we're talking.

"Inspection time. Turn around and face the bed." Did I mention they did water polo? Their butts are to die for! I come over and stand between them—the better to grope them with, my dear. I simultaneously give them both loving caresses and run my fingernails up their backs and over their shoulders before brushing my palms down their chests and tight stomachs, then down to grasp their cocks. I can't play favorites; they're both so perfect. "Ready, boys?"

I leap onto the bed with a giggly little happy-shriek, and they bound after and start grabbing and tickling me. Where did that come from? I go, "Hey, hey, hey!" and re-assert my authority with my death-stare, holding them at bay with my pointy finger while I fish around in the nightstand for the string of emergency condoms and my trusty bottle of Astroglide. Then I sit back up and take their dicks in my hands. So tough to pick. I look up at them, smiling from one to the other. "You first," I tell Cameron.

I rub a little lube in my hands and start slathering up boy toy number one. I don't want number two to get jealous, so I reach a hand around his neck and whisper in his ear, "Aidan, it would turn me on so much if you watch Cam fuck me." He nods. I tear off a Trojan and roll it on Cam. "Then I want him to watch while you fuck me, okay?" Aidan's down with it. "Good boy." He cradles me while I lie back and take Cam by his hips. I pull him down between my thighs and guide his glistening cock into me. He looks so beautiful there on top of me, scared and horny and blissed out all at the same time.

He lays his hands on Aidan's shoulders for support—wow, they are a good team—and I wrap my legs around

Cam and link my ankles tight. I reach back around to hang onto Aidan too. God, I'm in fucking heaven (no pun intended, I swear). The three of us sweat it out for what seems like ages; but then I'm bucking like a bronco, and Cam is breathing hard, his eyes closed tight and his head keeps dropping and rising almost like he's in a trance. Then he throws his head back with a gasp, and I can feel him coming. I'm not quite there yet, but I forgive him. Besides, I gotta pace myself. I hold his sweet face in my hands for some congratulatory kisses and a few quick words letting him know how hot that was.

Then it's Chinese Fire Drill time; Cam collapses happily next to me and Aidan takes his place. He's raring to go and so am I, so we work together. I get him good and lubed, and he rips open the condom packet, works it down and saddles up. Surprise! He grabs my ankles and hikes them up on his shoulders, sinking his rod into me, with no hands! Whoa! Fuck, he's hitting me so deep, and the angle is dead-on; he's nailing me right on my G-spot, wham-wham-wham. I brace myself with both hands on the wall behind me and push back while he fucks the bejeezus out of me. Cam is helping hold me down, and enjoying the show, all wide-eyed. Aidan starts lifting me, bouncing my butt up and down in time to the rhythm, which gets me goggly-eyed as a Muppet. I'm coming all over the place with a gaggle of quaking, moaning orgasms, all toppling over each other in their rush to come out of me. Aidan comes fast and hard, with several sharp huffing grunts. Damn, what an animal!

Well, we're all three just sweaty, quivering piles of

Jell-O now. The boys make a Sabrina sandwich of me, lying there panting softly with their arms and legs over me. I gaze down at them and play with their hair and stroke their cheeks while they rest their weary heads on my bosom. They look so innocent, you know? I feel very maternal. We don't say anything, but after a long while I notice they're looking up at me, as if waiting for something more. It's a very surreal moment, and I can't even tell you why, but I take them each by the back of the neck, and softly tell them, "Now I want you two to kiss." I gently but insistently push their faces together, and damn if they don't do it without a fuss. Their mouths are open and everything, and I wonder how long their repressed little Mormon hearts have been subconsciously jonesing for this. They sit up, and I see Cameron's hand come up to touch Aidan's chest. Aidan's are sliding over to Cam's hips. I'm getting all hot and bothered again.

While they're distracted in Bi-Curious Land, I sneak off to the bathroom for a wet washcloth. I slip back into bed before they even realize I've been gone. I get back in director mode and tell Aidan to stand up and lean back against the wall. This puts his penis at convenient face level, and I take it in my hands, trash the dead Trojan and clean him up with the warm washcloth. He smiles and groans as I get him nice and hard again, which makes me smile; I take pride in my work. Then I turn to Cameron, who's just watching all this, and say, "You know what's next." His look tells me he really doesn't, but too bad for him. I hold up Aidan's cock with my left hand, and take hold of Cam's chin. It's just like feeding a two-year-old, except I resist doing the here-comes-the-airplane-zoom thing. "Open wide, Baby," I coo to him. "I want you to take it all for me now."

About now I consider telling them the truth—that I didn't really put any vodka in their drinks—but decide that would be truly evil. Besides, the high fructose corn syrup is doing the job just fine.

Cam leans forward, keeping his hands on the bed, relying on me to guide his mouth onto his teammate's shaft. He has a little trouble at first, so I murmur encouragement. "That's it, Sugar. Careful with the teeth, ooh yeah, that's so good. Mmm, so nice . . ." It doesn't take much, and then he's all over it, sucking the head while I work the shaft for him, kissing the balls, and yes, earning major bonus points for making eye contact with Aidan. He even tries to deep throat him, bless his heart. That'll take some practice, Honey. I let him experiment for a minute while I strip off his condom and wash him down, too. Just in time, as it so happens; Aidan's getting antsy up there, writhing against the wall and finally reaching down to stroke Cam's head, so I let Aidan come down and wow! Aidan pushes Cameron on his back, and they arrange themselves into perfect sixty-nine formation without a lick of coaching from me.

I gotta say, I'm so loving the front row seat here, watching these handsome specimens taking each other in their mouths, stroking legs and flanks, grabbing asses. The wet, lusty sounds of their smacking and slurping are just killing me. It's so fucking hot, steamy and unexpectedly . . . quite touching. I'm so proud I could cry.

Then uh-oh, there's trouble: Cameron surfaces, breathing hard, tries to get Aidan to stop. Is he crying? I look hard for tears or other signals of a freak-out, but that's not it. He pulls Aidan around, suddenly grabs his face and gives him this huge lip lock. Then he breaks it, still holding Aidan's face in his hands and fixes him with the most intense stare. "I want you in me," he says in this low, totally earnest, totally sexy, voice. "I want your cock in me." Aidan is so choked up he can't talk at first, just nods numbly.

They both turn and look at me, and now it's my turn to be all flabbergasted, but my good hostess genes kick in, and I grab the lube and start facilitating. They're trembling like stallions before a race. I give Aidan's tool a liberal squirt of Astroglide, and he preps his shaft while I do Cam. I take a big dollop in my hand and massage the entrance to his little butt, working the goo all around and in with first one well-lubed fingertip, then a whole finger, then two. When I judge he's ready, I get out of the way. Cam takes hold of his own thighs and lifts his legs; Aidan takes hold of his new boyfriend's ankles and spreads them wide apart in a V formation. I can't resist butting in, but they don't mind. I lift Cam's balls and help guide Aidan in. It's a community effort, like an Amish barn raising. I tell them to go slow and give short clips of advice and encouragement, and then the boys are flying.

I wished I had my camera phone handy, but I don't dare miss a second, and it all gets permanently etched onto my brain anyway. Aidan grunting, muscles taut and flexing as he keeps hold of Cam's ankles, easing his hips oh-so-slowly in, inch by inch. Cam looks like he's in labor, his face keeps twisting in exquisite agony. When Aidan starts making slow, careful thrusts back and forth into him, Cam's head goes back, his mouth quavers open, and he starts making this unreal keening sound. Did I mention I'm wildly rubbing one out myself throughout this whole display? Appropriately enough, Aidan has his eyes screwed tight as he screws Cameron tight, and he starts making those animal, coming-soon growls. Next thing I know, Cam is giving these loud, sharp, sudden gasps, and then . . . there she blows. He sends flying a few quick, jiggity arches of come. He comes. Aidan comes. We all come. It's the Fourth of July.

Maybe I overthink things, but when our little escapade began, I had a variety of exit strategies cooking on the back burner, depending on how well things went. They ranged from Best Case: planning our new lives together over breakfast in bed; to Worst Case: blackmailing them into silence by telling them I had a Nannycam hidden in the teddy bear. But it was quite anticlimactic, really. We all lay piled on each other for ages like Abercrombie & Fitch models, not saying anything, just luxuriating and lightly touching each other.

Then one of them pops up and goes, "Shoot!" (guess I should have taught them how to cuss, too). They realize it's dark outside, and they're way overdue—there'll be hell to pay back at Mormon HQ. I hate to let them go in such a delicate state, but what can you do? They grab their clothes and their sacred long johns, kiss me, frantically get dressed and run out the door, promising to call.

Ain't that just like a guy? But I can't get mad at them.

So yeah, now I'm waiting to hear back, and I'm just dying to know what's happened to my boys. Are they busted by the LDS cops? Will they go back to the fold and marry Molly Mormon, breeding another generation of closeted *Brokeback Mountain* types? Seems like the smart money is on biology trumping theology, but I know it isn't always that easy. Maybe they'll return to me, or maybe I'll bump into the two of them doing the Lambada at a sex party in the City.

Hey, speaking of sex parties, did you hear Kiki is planning a Cuddle Party? I don't know either, I guess that's like a PG-13 orgy, but anyway, I'm down. What can I say? I study anthropology—I'm a people person.

Oops, hey, I gotta run. No, yeah, look, it's just that see, there's two Jehovah's Witnesses at the door right now, and well, I'm just thinking . . . Shut up!

Web Swingers

by Tony Wards

I'm not going to lie: I absolutely love Halloween. Ever since I was a little kid, I remember getting excited about dressing up in a cool costume and going door to door, trying to get as much candy as possible. Even now, the thought of dressing up and going out still seems exciting. Of course now it is for entirely different reasons.

I'm thirty years old and my wife, Beth, is twenty-nine, but we still go to costume parties every year. In the past, we've gone to events hosted by online friend groups, relatives, and co-workers. This year, however, we were invited to a party by someone I hardly knew. I recently joined one of those fantasy football groups on the Internet and became friends with a guy named George. He lived in New York City, not far from us. We've e-mailed a few times, but we weren't really friends, so this made my wife uncomfortable. I can't say I blame her for how she felt, but I figured what harm could come from a party invite?

George sent me all the information I needed for the party. It turns out it was some club in the Village. Beth was skeptical about the online stranger aspect but trusted me enough to go along with the idea.

I decided to go dressed as my favorite web-slinging superhero, while Beth would be his redheaded girlfriend. We went to our favorite costume store in the Times Square area to buy the costumes we needed. My wife looked so damn hot; I wanted to jump on her as soon as she came out of the dressing room. She had on the long red wig, which was a new look by itself. Beth has long brown hair, so the red wig really threw me for a loop. She wore a tight, black, one-piece Spandex cat suit. She was supposed to be the girlfriend, but looked like she could be a comic book heroine herself. I wasn't complaining and for two reasons. First, Beth liked the outfit. Secondly, she looked damn hot in it.

Beth has 38 C-cup breasts, which are still doing a pretty good job of defying gravity. I can see the difference from ten years ago, when we first met, but I have to say they're looking pretty nice. She has narrow hips and a small ass. I keep telling her we should have children to help fill her out. I'm sure that day will come, but for now she says she's not ready.

The day before the party I e-mailed George to tell him about our costumes. He asked about a million times and even after I gave him the info, he kept confirming. It's not like I was going to change my mind. We had our costumes and that was that. He never did tell me what he was going to dress up as, since he said he would look out for us.

On the night of the party, Beth and I took the subway down to the Village in our costumes. We live in upper

Manhattan, but figured we would blend right in with all the other nuts that came out on Halloween. We arrived at the club, aptly named Sohomosexuals, probably after the neighborhood, I thought to myself. Beth seemed nervous and I didn't blame her, since I felt the same way. We entered and immediately a hostess, dressed in a Cat Woman costume, handed us each a condom, then guided us to a big room. The room looked like an open dance floor, with the music pumping. There was a bar located in the center, but something was different. I surveyed the area, and realized what it was that struck me as odd. There were no walls, per se. Rather, the perimeter was lined with doors. I couldn't tell if the doors were just decorative or actually functional, since nobody was approaching them. Also, if they were real doors, then I wondered what was behind them. Beth and I stood beside the bar in this great big room, as I stared at these mysterious doors, all of them with different signs on them. Finally, curiosity got the best of me.

"What is this place?" I asked Beth.

"I don't know. I was just going to ask you. It kind of looks like a swingers club."

"You think? What are we supposed to do? I mean, we've never done anything like this before."

I looked at Beth and hoped she would agree to stay. On the other hand, the thought of another man fucking my wife made my blood boil.

"Why else would they hand us a condom on the way in? Ever think of that? And what is behind those doors? Huh? Probably rooms to fuck yourself silly in."

I laughed at how excited Beth was getting. "You're too funny. I'll tell you what, let's go around and check out the signs on the doors. That's what is getting me curious."

Beth and I held hands, mostly because we didn't want to get separated in the crowd that was growing in the room. We started in one corner and read the signs on the doors: Batman and Cat Woman. The next sign read Batman and Robin. Interesting. Another one said Superman and Lois Lane. My favorite read Archie and Edith. I had to laugh at that one. Josie & the Pussycats was the label on another door. The next one was meant for us. I was sure of it. It had our character names written clearly on the sign that covered the door. I checked the next couple of doors, but no, this must be for us.

"This is the place, Beth," I said.

"Are we going in there?" she asked.

"I suppose we should. Let's take a look first." I hesitantly opened the door just a crack. I peeked through the crevice to see a dark, almost empty room. The dimensions were probably about ten by ten, tops. There was a single uncovered red light bulb burning dimly from the ceiling. Against the far wall was a twin-sized bed and nothing else. That was the whole room, so I guessed Beth was right. These rooms were here for sex play.

"So is the coast clear, web-head?"

"Yep. Let's go inside," I ordered.

We went inside the room and sat on the edge of the bed. "Are we going to stay and fuck for a while?" asked Beth, catching me completely off guard.

"Yeah? You want to? Cool!"

"Might as well. We're here. It might be kind of hot to have sex knowing all these people are outside the room, maybe listening . . ."

"Or maybe they'll walk in on us," I stated.

"I'm pretty sure people are following the rules," Beth rebutted. "I think it'll be fun. Besides, it could just be a quickie and then we'll get out of here."

"Okay. Sounds like a plan. Do you want me to go get us a drink?"

"I'm okay, Pete. Go get your drink and when you come back, I promise to be a Peter eater."

"Oooh, baby. I like the sound of that. I'll be right back."

I weaved through the expanding crowd until I got to the bar. I bought a couple of shots of Jack Daniels before heading back to the room. I usually don't drink, but this place made me a little nervous, so I wanted to take the edge off. I breathed a huge sigh and entered the room again, feeling like all eyes were upon me.

"Holy shit!" I entered the room to find Beth with her legs spread a mile apart with some dude dressed in the same costume as me, eating out her pussy like a wild cannibal. The room was dark, but I could see Beth's eyes open in surprise when I entered the room. She looked at me, then looked at her costumed lover, then back at me.

"Peter?"

"Yes, Beth. I'm the guy not eating your pussy. Who are you?" We both looked at him, and waited for an answer.

"It's me. Your favorite web-slinger," said the stranger, obviously using a fake superhero voice. The voice was artificially deepened, making me think this wasn't a guy at all.

I walked up to wife's mystery lover and, in one swift move, pulled open his pants with one hand and reached down to his crotch with the other. *Just as I thought.* My culprit didn't move, actually seemed to like the attention.

"Guess what, Beth? Your mystery pussy eater is a woman. Here, see for yourself."

Beth got up off the bed, naked, with her pussy trickling her delectable love juices slowly down her inner thighs. I held the fake web-slinger's pants open and my wife dipped her hand in. She fumbled around our mystery woman's pussy, until a finger was inserted into her wet vagina. "Mmmm. Looks like you've been enjoying yourself. Why don't you tell us your name and then get out of these clothes?"

"Georgette. My name is Georgette. I know your husband."

"Is this true?" Beth asked.

"I don't know you. I never . . . oh . . . OH! I get it now. You're George, aren't you? Why didn't you tell me before?"

"I go by George so the guys in the fantasy league won't get all bunged up after finding out they're losing to a woman."

"I understand," said Beth. "Guess what? This, now, is not fantasy. This is real."

Beth planted a huge, wet kiss on George's mouth, even though she still was wearing her mask. I lifted her legs one at a time to take off her boots. I made a mental note that they were much cooler than the ones I had bought. I slowly pulled off her tight Spandex pants while Beth pulled off her mask. She was actually kind of pretty, I thought. I didn't know what to expect, but I was pleasantly surprised. George had short, curly blond hair, green eyes, and pale skin. As for her body, after I took her pants off, I made a full inspection.

First of all, I was immediately turned on by the fact that she wore no underwear. She probably figured the pants were so tight, how could she? She had a neatly trimmed blond pussy and nice wide hips. She was average build, which to me means that you couldn't bounce quarters off her stomach, but you could definitely hold onto her tight while fucking her from behind or while munching on her pussy.

Beth removed George's top to reveal her small, firm breasts. I'd say they were probably B-cups with long, hard nipples which I absolutely love. I was ready to feast on my fantasy friend, but it seems that Beth was quicker than me. Beth sucked long and hard on each nipple, treating them like miniature cocks. Her lips slid up and down slowly over each hardened nipple, giving both equal attention. Then Beth painted George's areola with her soft, pink tongue.

"Mmm," purred George. "That is so hot. My pussy is drooling. I need this mess cleaned up quickly."

I volunteered for "mop up" duty in a heartbeat. I stripped down to my birthday suit, dropped to my knees, and started licking all the nectar escaping from George's pussy. Her lips were glistening, even in the dim light of the room, and a constant flow poured out of her into my waiting mouth. Beth continued to suck off George's nipples, as I took two fingers and placed them up into my wife. I held George around her hips with one hand, forcing her wetness onto my face. With my other hand, I reached up into my wife's love nest, and rubbed her G-spot. Before I knew it, both women were panting and moaning, while their leg muscles slowly gave way.

"Come on, Pete. Lay me across this bed and fuck me now. Hurry, I want you," ordered my wife. I pulled my fingers out of her sopping wet pussy and helped her onto the bed. She lay there, on her back, with her legs opened waiting for me.

"What about me?" George sounded upset, since I had to stop licking her soaked snatch in order to accommodate Beth. "I want some too, unless you guys aren't into that."

"Hey, don't worry. There's plenty to go around. Right, Beth?"

"Lie down on top of me," suggested Beth. "That way I can play with you while my husband fucks you."

George loved that idea and so did I. I remembered the condom I was given on the way in and I wasted no time slipping it on. I wasn't used to using them, since I only have sex with my wife, but the timing was perfect. Meanwhile, George lowered herself on top of Beth and my wife quickly went to work.

Beth reached around and played with George's nipples with one hand while she spread her pussy lips with the other. She rubbed George's swollen clit with two fingers. I was about ready to explode from watching the show. Instead, I put my hard cock into George, as she reached back with both arms and grabbed Beth's face. She turned her head to kiss and lick my wife's face, as I pumped her pussy harder and harder.

"Oh, fuck me. Fuck me," George cried out, as she continued kissing Beth passionately.

"Come on, Pete. Fuck her good." My wife cheered me on and I rocked my hips faster than before. "Take that thing off and come inside my pussy."

I gave George a few more thrusts, but I knew my time was short. I couldn't hold out any longer. The reality of having two women was too much for me and my will power. After my last entry into George's drenched hole, I pulled my cock out, quickly removed my condom, and inserted myself into my wife. Beth was open and ready for me, grabbing me with her muscles. George was having an orgasm of her own, under the constant care of Beth's busy fingers.

"Oh, I'm gonna come, baby. Oh!" I flooded my wife's pussy instantly with every drop I possessed. My balls emptied in long spurts; wave after wave transferred inside Beth. She moaned in excitement, but I knew she wasn't totally fulfilled. I wasn't the only one who noticed either.

"Oooh, baby. That was hot," said George. "Let me take care of you now, Beth." George rolled off my wife and dove right into her well-used pussy. George licked Beth's clit, while my full load slowly trickled out of my wife's hole. It ran down to her ass, with some of it dripping onto the bed.

"Oh, George. Yes! Eat my pussy. Make me come, baby. Eat it. Eat it!" Beth began to buck like a wild horse, as

George lapped up Beth's lovely cream pie. She had the best of both worlds in her mouth. My wife's pussy, along with both of our offerings, was being consumed by a near stranger. *What a lucky lady*, I thought.

Beth came harder than I had seen in a long time. She yelled so loud that I thought someone would run into our room to see what the matter was. She threw her head back, howled like a wolf at the moon, and let her body go limp. We all collapsed for a few moments before getting dressed.

"So, George. I have to know. Why did you wear the male costume to this party?" I had to ask—I was curious.

"Simple answer? I'm a lesbian. Okay, maybe after tonight, I'm bi. Really, I don't usually do guys, but because you were with Beth and both of you seemed so nice, I figured okay. Besides, you guys are about as horny as I am." That made all three of us chuckle.

"Glad you had a good time. I know I did," added Beth.

Soon after, we parted ways, but promised to get together again someday. The next day, I made a new friend while playing my fantasy football. He was also from New York and his name was Pat. I wonder if that was really Patrick, or maybe Patricia?

Bon Appetit

by J. Troy Seate

—The Appetizer—

I turned the ignition key. The cold engine growled like a savage beast prematurely disturbed from its slumber, frighteningly similar to the way Madeline sounds when she is in the throes of passion. I'm not complaining, mind you. Madeline has proven to be everything I have ever wanted in a lover, or so I thought, and I take pleasure in recounting her unique talents as I drive to work.

Madeline glows with a year-round tan. She possesses luxurious black, curly tresses. In her blue eyes lie the mysteries of deep waters a man can drown in. Her lips are full and pouty. Her blemish-less torso features perfectly formed breasts with puffy pink nipples. The hourglass figure splits at her velvety triangular swatch of neatly trimmed pubic hair. Her legs are long and her feet are delicate. In a word, she has a body that could launch a thousand ships. In another word, she looks like a breathing version of a Vargas.

Madeline's straightforwardness is a quality most rare.

She told me straight out that she had picked me from a gaggle of other men at the singles' picnic for two reasons: because I have an easygoing personality and because of my cock size.

"When I saw that bulge, I knew you could satisfy me," she explained. "I sense that your cock is a custom fit for me, somewhere between comfort and at the threshold of pain, the way I like it. There are any number of ways you will be able to satisfy me."

Madeline let me have sex with her that very night and I soon discovered that she also sensed how best to satisfy *my* needs. Because of where she has led me, I manage my way through each work day with a smile on my face and a melody in my heart. I'm the happiest I've ever been and look forward to three nights a week of warm embraces.

Madeline has but one requirement: complete honesty, a pledge that we will keep our relationship light and breezy. If one tires of the other, it is okay to say so. Even though sex is a given, I try to keep our evenings together original as well as breezy.

Last week, I ask a buddy to prepare one of his succulent, gourmet dinners for Madeline and me, to be served by candlelight on the roof of my apartment building. "Anything to enhance a buddy's sex life," he said, and promised to prepare a feast.

Madeline arrived at eight. Being a woman who would look fetching in a simple tow sack, her choice of duds always surprised me. On this evening, she was decked out in black stilettos, tight black toreador pants, a ruffled white blouse, and a gold tunic similar to that of a matador.

"*Olé*," I said, and offered her a drink. I brought her a martini and kissed her passionately on those ruby-red, pouty lips. "Are we fighting bulls after dinner?"

"When I was getting dressed, I thought about the other night when you came to bed with your face painted white and black circles around your eyes." She giggled at the recollection. "You did the zombie walk with your arms and your dick sticking out, coming for me."

"It was *The Night of the Fucking Dead*. So?"

"You were good and horny that night and I had a feeling this was going to be an even hornier night, so I dressed appropriately."

"Uh-oh. One of your *feelings* again. Isn't every night hornier than the time before?" I asked.

"But tonight will be different. I think that tonight, our relationship will reach another level."

Her forecasts usually proved true, so I could only look forward to the evening with bated breath. I sat aside her martini glass and took hold of her. A wry, openmouthed smile lit up Madeline's face. I wanted my horn to pierce her sooner rather that later. I pressed her against the wall and pulled down her black pants and panties.

"Not even one pass with my cape?" she giggled.

I dropped my shorts and skivvies to my ankles. "You said you'd make me horny and you were right."

"How bullish you are," my bullfighting *senorita* said.

"You'll have to settle for one horn rather than two," I huffed. "Hope that'll do?"

"Quite an appetizer. Your bull-cock is always a custom fit."

"Better than being gored on the streets of Pamplona, I promise you that." Her legs spread to take me in and I plunged into her enveloping depths.

"Run bull, run," she panted as I pounded her into the wall.

"Just don't cut off my ears when we're done," I groaned.

"Maybe just one, but I'll let you keep your balls," she growled like a savage beast disturbed from its slumber, caught up in the throws of passion. "Gore me deeper before I have to plunge my sword between your eyes, my stud bull," she cried while our imaginary audience again shouted, "*Olé!*"

The metaphor lasted longer than I did.

—*The Dinner*—

"We are dining on the roof, so we can consider it a bullring if you like."

"Wonderful." Madeline shimmied back into her tight pants. "I like doing things out of the box."

We took our glasses and I led her up the stairs. The moon had risen above the rooftops, creating an atmospheric, languid backdrop on a warm night. My good buddy, Marshall, stood behind a sizzling hibachi. He had decorated a card table with a red tablecloth, two lit candles, and bone china. The aroma of barbequing steaks and shrimp found its way to our noses.

"How opulent," the *contessa* exclaimed.

"Only the finest for the Goddess of the Lower East Side." I ushered her to our table for two.

Marshall made sure we were seated comfortably. He took Madeline's hand and introduced himself. She smiled warmly and thanked him for his contribution to our evening.

"I'm going to disappear," he told us, "but I'll be back later to deliver dessert."

Madeline and I were alone on the rooftop with the sounds of the city a few floors below. I watched as her face flickered in the candlelight. Glossy lips red as maraschino cherries flashed around perfect white teeth. Glinting nails played with her wine glass. Her white throat, begging to be kissed, arched from her blouse collar.

She captured each mouthful of food and sip of wine with the gusto of a person savoring every taste as if it were her last. Her gastronomic pleasure carried with it such sensuality that my cock began to stiffen and my libido would have gone through the roof had I not already been there.

I recalled an article devoted to sex and food. Madeline's pulchritude somehow captured the essence of the concept: Good food to be preceded and followed by good fucking: my two favorite Fs.

We enjoyed Marshall's sumptuous dinner while the hanging moon shone and the vehicles below played a haunting rhapsody with their wheels and horns. Watching Madeline devour her meal gave rise to that other craving as my cock stiffened. That appetite had already served as an appetizer and would soon become a succulent nightcap.

—The Dessert—

Good to his word, Marshall returned with two servings of chocolate mousse. I invited him to dish up his own serving, pull up a chair, and join us. I was willing to share my beautiful vixen for the time it takes to spoon down the creamy treat and drink a final glass of wine.

Madeline complimented both of us on the evening meal. After some chit-chat, Marshall removed the dishes and prepared to bid us *adieu*.

"I owe you one, buddy," I told him.

"Why don't you hang around?" Madeline asked him. "Provided it is all right with you, Dillon."

"Sure. I guess," I said, not knowing what Madeline had in mind.

"The meal was wonderful," Madeline continued, "and I have a confession to make, Marshall. When we touched hands, I knew that you, as well as Dillon, possess a special type of gift."

Marshall and I looked at each other and waited for my dreamboat to continue. She took our hands in hers and looked at my buddy. "Your package is just right for something. Don't let it embarrass you when I say that I would like to have you as well as Dillon. The two of you, doing me together and each using your own talents."

Who can fathom the caprice of a sensual woman?

Madeline stood and undressed.

"This may not be your cup of tea, either one of you, but I think it will take all of us to another level if you'll go along with me."

I was downright stupefied at this development, but

Madeline usually knew best. Without another word, both Marshall and I disrobed. All three of us placed our clothes over the chairs. We stared at one another, naked, bathed by moonlight, candlelight, and the faint, reflected haze from the surrounding metropolis.

She appraised Marshall's body. "Hello, gorgeous," she said like Barbara Streisand.

Marshall was well built, but his cock was smaller than mine, a steroid dick, perhaps. She beckoned for us to fondle her. We kissed her face, her breasts, and squeezed her ass while she caressed our respective shafts.

When our organs grew hard, Madeline squatted and sucked our cocks, switching from one to the other every few strokes. "You two are perfect for a sandwich," she told us. "Dillon's a perfect fit for my pussy, and Marshall, you're a perfect fit for my ass. Lick my cunt a little, then you both can fuck me."

I was too hot to worry whether or not I was bothered by sharing my centerfold with a friend. How could I argue with a woman who seemed to know more about pleasure than anyone I had ever met? Marshall and I got on our knees and lapped at Madeline's clit like a couple of thirsty dogs at a water tap. Our tongues shared her sweet spot. Madeline's pubic hair dripped with our saliva, but neither of us cared.

Finally, she ordered us to our feet. "Dillon, pick me up and impale me with your prick."

I obeyed. She slid onto my shaft with a satisfying moan. She wrapped her ankles around my hips to anchor the weight of her body.

"Marshall, slip that beautiful cock of yours up my ass."

I could feel Marshall's knees bump against mine as he positioned himself under Madeline's rump. When Marshall rammed his dick into her rectum, she slid up my shaft an inch or two from the impact.

"Ohhhh," she offered in response. "My two beautiful bulls. You have both hooked me. Now double-fuck me."

We got into a rhythm that allowed Marshall and me to alternate thrusts. I could feel the movement of his penis sliding back and forth on the other side of Madeline's muscular internal wall that separated our two cocks. I had the additional thrill of sucking on a bouncing tit, but could tell that Marshall was not feeling deprived.

We panted and heaved, overwhelming the other sounds in the night. Sex was in four-wheel drive—illicit bumping and grinding with an element of risk. We were out in the open, after all.

Here was the real Madeline. The role-playing with orderly conversation and clothes had ended. She was now free of pretend and busy telling Marshall and me how to please her. She didn't give a damn about convention and neither did we.

Marshall came first. His quiver of delight was transmitted through Madeline's legs. She threw back her head and yelled, "One down and two to go. Let's all get our rocks off." When he pulled free of her, she reached around and wiped the fluid from Marshall's cock onto her palm and fingers. She licked away some of his issue and put her fingers to my lips. I would do anything for Madeline's pleasure and I tasted. "You and me and Marshall, coming together as one. What a turn-on," she growled.

When Madeline emitted that patented animal sound, I knew her orgasm was imminent. We came within seconds of each other. Juices ran down my thighs and Madeline encouraged Marshall not to let such a superb substance go to waste. I felt his tongue on my thighs and balls. And while Madeline's vagina held tightly to my cock, I found the lapping sensation most pleasurable.

Once Marshall's head was clear of our bodies, Madeline's ankles unhooked and she dropped to the roof. "Now that's what I call a spectacular *aperitif*," she said. She threw one arm around each of our necks to form something resembling a small football huddle. We sauntered around in slow dance steps while Madeline hummed a popular dance tune.

I might have expected Marshall and me to be eyeing each other rather sheepishly at this point, but we didn't. We were okay with what Madeline had orchestrated and frankly, my balls still tingled from the feel of Marshall's tongue and day-old beard against my thighs.

During our impromptu dance that had turned into a conga line, an alley cat joined Madeline in song, expressing *his* desires for the evening. We took that as our cue to leave. We dressed and walked down the stairs to my apartment. I poured drinks for Madeline and Marshall and we chewed nothing more than the fat for an hour or so. Finally, Marshall kissed *my* alley cat/matador goodnight and we were again alone for whatever adventure our nightcap might bring.

—*The Nightcap*—

In bed, we sucked each other's genitals for a half hour

before Madeline crawled up to my face to talk. "Thanks for fulfilling my desires," she said while juggling my moist ball sack. She always seemed to know the right gesture to make or place to touch. "I sensed something different would happen tonight. When I touched your friend, I knew how I wanted it to go down. I sensed you got off on it, too."

"Actually, yes, and I wouldn't mind double-fucking you again or even a double-blow," I told her while she was making my flesh covered acorns dance.

"No time like the present," Madeline laughed. "Call your chef back."

"We've been friends for a long time."

"I can tell you that he'll be all for it."

Marshall answered his cell phone and said he would come back over.

"Let's do some more yum-yum until he arrives," Madeline suggested. "In the meantime, you might like the view that Marshall had." Madeline got on her knees and laid her chest across the bed. She reached back and grabbed hold of her butt cheeks and spread them apart so I could study her sphincter. "Fuck my pussy and titillate my asshole until your friend arrives," she ordered.

Can a bull ignore the flash of red from his matador? I teased her bunghole because I didn't need psychic power to know that she wanted my finger or Marshall's dick back inside it. On the road to her sweet spot, my lips made pit stops on the bottoms of her feet, her calves, her thighs, and her puckering anus. I tasted the seed of Marshall, and my cock tightened. I grabbed a handful of her luscious, raven curls, put my thumb in her butt, and pierced her warm, pretty pussy. It was some damn good yum-yum. Once I was properly lubricated, I pulled my cock free and penetrated her ass.

"Oh yeah. Shove it all the way up to tonsil-town," she screamed in the key of C.

My second explosive wad of the evening made her scream, to my delight. "That thing's so damned big, you might need a building permit, Dillon," she said. "We may have to cut back to two nights a week, lover. I still walk to work in the mornings."

After I pulled out, she turned, grinned, and kissed my sweaty forehead. She pressed her body next to mine in a full frontal. "It's been an unusual and amusing night for the both of us and the best may be yet to come."

When Marshall knocked on the door, I got up and let him in. "We decided dessert was the best part of the night and you might as well be part of the nightcap," I told him.

Madeline waited in bed for the two of us. "Honesty is the big part of my relationships and Dillon told me he got off on sharing me with you, so present your weapons, boys," she decreed.

"I'm up for whatever you guys have in mind," Marshall told Madeline and me, "but what's after the nightcap?"

"The morning after, of course," Madeline said with a grin.

—*The Morning After*—

When I woke up, I realized our female participant was long gone. Marshall was still in my arms, however. A whole new word had opened up overnight. I had enjoyed fucking Marshall as much as Madeline.

He stirred and playfully ran a finger around my rectum. "We'll start nice and slow," he said. "It can be as good to receive as to give. I hope the nightcap was as satisfactory as last night's dinner?"

I had to admit it was.

"Here's something good to start a morning after a pleasurable night—protein." He put his mouth around my cock and sucked gently. Marshall's lapping tongue, though different, was as pleasurable as that of my horny vixen. I again tingled from the feel of his day-old beard against my nuts and my thighs.

By noon, I had returned all of Marshall's favors by sucking my first dick and receiving my first cock. And without a vagina in sight, I enjoyed taking sex and giving it, tit for tat, pound for pound.

Madeline called me that evening. "Hey, bi-guy," she said with a giggle.

She was right. Our impromptu *ménage-à-trois* had blazed new trails. I realized I enjoyed playing both parts— matador and bull. It resulted in a revamped, partnering schedule. I have Madeline to myself one night a week. On a second night, I share her with Marshall. A third night is obligated as well. That's the night Marshall and I spend with each other, *sans* Madeline.

I now see the world through slightly different eyes. Every time I bite into a pizza wedge, a piece of pie, anything triangular-shaped, I think of Madeline-the-Magnificent's fiery twat. And every time I partake of breakfast sausages, hotdogs, or any tubular treat, I think of my good buddy, Marshall.

Bon appetit.

The Fragile

by Elizabeth Miette

I hear the whispered voices of the Long Dead crying, and I know that my time is drawing near. I must bring forth the souls of the ones that cry out, but I am frightened. I am frightened by the power that is mine alone to call. I am frightened of the souls that have been gone from this world for so long. But, most of all, I am frightened by the feelings that pulse between my thighs for the pair of exquisite monsters that loom before me in the semi-dark of this room.

I begged for a candle, but the gruff whisper had told me that it would be better if I did not see all that there was to see; I do not know if that is really true. If I cannot see, I tend to imagine, and believe me, I have the most macabre of imaginations. I am no simple goth poser, painting on the whiteness and dark, I live and breathe it. Ever since I gave my virgin's blood on the hilt of a vampire sword, I have lived it. And then came the power.

I had just turned another year older when the power came to me, the ability to draw lost souls back to this realm with my orgasm. I was alone when it happened, so the soul had nowhere to go. Apparently, I am not a receptor, merely the door through which they enter. The poor bewildered apparition had floundered and floated along the walls and the edges of the ceiling before vanishing with a final wail. I was just as freaked out and had barely taken the time to throw on some clothes before getting some help. I am a curiosity here in this compound, a mortal among vampires. It is ironic that most of them fear me, more than likely out of fear of who has marked me, the one who had lapped the maiden's blood from my thighs after he had spilled it.

I raced to the Old One, a wrinkled, sexless vampire that had all the knowledge of the blood drinker at her/his disposal and recounted what had happened. I had omitted the masturbation part, but somehow the Old One knew. Word of my incredible power spread through the compound like wildfire and soon, I was everyone's golden dream come true. Long dead lovers and family members could be brought back they reasoned, but the Old One cautioned it would not be wise, or easy.

We soon found old souls do not always adjust to new bodies very well, and that ended tragically for more than one heartbroken vampire as they were forced to dispatch the soul back to where I had summoned it from. And, we found, that if there was no body to take the place, the soul would wail around the room for awhile and then vanish. The longer the soul had been disincorporated, the shorter the time it would last.

Tonight, I do not want to perform this ritual, a fact

I have made abundantly clear, but no one seems to care. So, I have made up my mind that I just will not come, no matter what. I will keep my lusty and wanton reactions to myself and I will not come, period. I knew it would be hard to do, but I thought that I could. That is, until they brought him in. Him. As in that big, beefy hunk of hot man hulking in the corner and staring at me with an unbridled hunger like I have never seen before. Of course, he might not know who I belong to, who has marked me as his own, I certainly have never seen this creature before. That would explain the bold staring.

I have fucked other vampires before, but they have always gotten permission from my Master first. Sex with an underling vampire is kind of restrained at best, and it is nothing but efficiency. As you can imagine, it makes it hard for me to orgasm, which is the only way I can call forth the souls, so I have to improvise. I have talked to the Master about this: and delivered an ultimatum. If he wants to allow them to make use of me to call forth souls, they have to put some effort into it. Fucking the Undead is bad enough without them acting like dead fish in the process.

I return my attention to the big man, noticing his huge hands and imagining them on my delicate, pale frame. I shiver in fear, in apprehension and something else, something slightly darker. Ah, yes. The hunger. I have craved good sex for some time now. Apparently the Master only got it up for virgins, so that wild and wicked night was a one-shot deal, and now I was left surrounded by those who were too afraid of Him to please me. Thankfully, I had acquired a rather startling array of toys to keep me busy, or I might have attempted to flee before now. I lick my lips thinking that things might just be looking up for once.

The other figure comes out of the shadows that had concealed him and I groan. Fabian had tried once before to resurrect his lover with terrible results. She had detested the body her soul had found itself in and he had openly wept when he slit the throat that would send her back to the Netherworld. I hoped that for his sake he had chosen much better this time, although I doubted that she would be satisfied. Back in a body for only five seconds and she had already started to complain and nag; not a good sign. Fabian was probably better off without her. Of course, the whisperers had said time and time again that he had been the one who had dispatched the little bitch in the first place. I would not be at all surprised.

Fabian was a piss-poor fuck too, I had to note, and the last time I had killed off more than a few batteries trying to get the job done to no avail. I had even panted that he could stick it in my ass if that would help, but nothing seemed to work. My orgasm that called forth his harpy was half-hearted at best.

Whispered warnings be damned, I thought to myself and lit a candle. Screw it. In for a penny, in for a pound, so I lit two candles, placing them on either side of the spare mattress that was set up in this room. Soundproof and bare, this was the ritual room and meant to be used only for this act. There was nothing here except for this bed, my toys, and the chained bodies that would hopefully hold the souls that I called forth. I licked my lips again, silently hoping it would be the big guy who did most of the fucking. Fabian only had to be in the room; he did not really have to take part in any way for the ritual to work. It did not matter to the souls who gave me the orgasm that called them forth, and I didn't care either.

Fabian started to walk toward me, but the big man shoved past him, nearly knocking him down in the process. I froze, suddenly chilled to the bone. This was not an outsider vampire—he wasn't even a vampire.

I was eye to eye with a werewolf.

I have never fucked one before, but I had certainly heard my share of the stories. Legend has it that when a wolf takes a woman not of his species, he splits her in half and devours her from the cunt up. The other half goes to his clan and they feast on the Fragile, claiming that frightened flesh tastes sweeter.

Shivers of apprehension twittered up and down my body, but the underlying heat only intensified for me. The great giant of a beast scented the wind, opening his nostrils wide to breathe in the hot smell of wet pussy. He grinned a dopey, nearly sex-starved smile that revealed his strong white teeth. Again a tiny whisper of warning raced through me, but the molten lava between my legs dictated my movements. I approached him, no longer a pale goth, soul caller. I was all wriggly, wanton carnality and every thud of my Thor's hammer heartbeat was my siren's call for him and him alone.

Fabian reached one thin, paper-white hand toward me, all nervousness and tentative and I brushed it away like a moth, focused solely on the towering mass of male muscle in front of me. He started shucking his clothing, ripping most of it to absolute shreds. I started seductively, although I remember being so shy that I once fucked my partner with most of my clothes on. I slowly shimmied out of my mostly black garments.

I stopped about two feet away from him and stared unashamedly at the swollen cock that was mine to tame. I have never faced something so immense. Vampires, for the most part, have all had thin pricks, nothing to really get jazzed about, but then again, being Undead would probably dictate a limited amount of blood to work with in the first place. I licked my lips yet again and, dear God, I growled. I absently wiped my mouth with the back of my hand, only dimly aware that I was drooling as well.

Fabian made one more half-hearted move for me, for some reason thinking that he should be the aggressor. I growled and bared nonexistent fangs at him and he backed off, as much from relief as from shock. The Wolf reached out to me, but I danced out of his reach, falling to my knees and crawling over to the wavering, waiting cock that seemed to pulsate with his very heartbeat. I grasped it, again reminded of how small a creature I truly was. I barely got my hands partway around its girth and squeezed, watching with some satisfaction as its length went from pink to pale purple. A small tear of pre-come glistened at the head, and I stuck my tongue out to a perfect point and caught it, savoring it. He tried to grab my head to take control but I pulled back. I gave him a fairly stern look and was secretly amused when he acquiesced.

I tasted him, inhaled his musky male scent and felt the

gathering storm raging between my legs. I was so wet I thought I might just drown us all if I didn't get release soon. I opened my mouth wide, almost painfully so and allowed inch by inch of his throbbing cock to slide down my throat. I met with resistance when he was about a quarter of the way in, and I would have been disappointed if it was a human man, but of course he was not. This was a beast, a wild and untamed, unpredictable beast, but judging by the blissful expression beginning to seep across his handsome, but oh so dangerous face and into those gold-green eyes, he was about to be tamed. He did a nice, long, slow blink, signally his eminent surrender to my command and I picked up my speed, adding a little sucking motion to my moves. He groaned, and stroked my hair, wanting, I knew, to grab it and pull, to take back the dominance. *Oh no, my pet.* I thought. *You just let Momma drive. I am the Alpha here.*

He groaned again, licked his lip and I nearly missed a stroke. Now that, my friends, was a tongue to jazz with. Long, thick, wet and soft, I could already feel it lapping at my soft wet pussy, making me writhe and moan beneath him. He wouldn't be gentle and tentative, even with those thick sharp teeth in his mouth. I knew that for a fact. I was fearless and exhilarated with anticipation. I could hardly wait and had to slow myself down, as I started ruthlessly tugging at the thick cock that is filled my mouth completely.

I heard him panting, and then a long rumbling growl as the meaty prick jumped once, twice and then spasmed nearly out of control. Spurt after spurt of hot jizz poured

down my throat. I gulped, hoping I did not end up choking
to death on it before I got a taste of what that tongue
could do for me. I took the last drip, licked my lips and
looked up, my eyes locked on his. Fabian had yet to move.
I don't know if he was mortified or relieved that he was
left out of the ritual.

"You want your loved one's soul, Wolfy? Make me come.
You make me scream and I can pull back anybody your
heart desires." I lay back, spreading my legs and showing
him where to start. The big man did not need to be asked
twice. He pounced, pinning me with one arm and shoving
his face between my legs. There was no hesitation, no
wasted energy or needless actions. He simply grasped my
clit between his lips and started sucking, almost mimicking
my own earlier motions perfectly. I spread my legs even
wider, grinding against his face. He slid one thick finger
into me, slamming me just this side of painful, and I could
not get enough. He opened his mouth wide and practically
inhaled my entire cunt and that was it: I was coming, I was
screaming and the room was spinning like never before. I
slowly became aware I was not the only one screaming in
the room, but I did not care. I opened my eyes to find him
smiling over me, his cock hard and rarin' to go again, and
almost a dozen souls wailing around the room.

"We don't have enough bodies." I panted. "Most of
these will have to go back."

The Wolf shrugged his massive shoulders and pounced,
slamming that monster cock into me. I screamed in pain,
in delight, in molten arousal. I let him buck his hips hard
and fast once, maybe twice and then caught him off guard,

rolling his big frame over and pushing my small hand to his throat. He heard my own rumbling growl and lay back, his eyes never leaving mine as his big paws came up to knead and squeeze my breasts. I rocked slow, in circles, relishing the feeling of that massive organ stretching me and filling me completely. I gripped him with velvet muscles and leaned forward, letting my tits brush his belly, grinding my clit against his pelvis. I forced myself to stay slow, but I was nearing the point of no return yet again.

Fabian came up behind me, his long thin hands lying pale and limp on my shoulder. I hissed, but he ignored me. I could feel his cock, a mere shadow of the one I was currently riding, pressing at my anus and I stiffened. I never allowed anal penetration, and I was not about to start with this particular vampire, nor would it have been possible. There was simply no room for anything else. The Wolf motioned Fabian away, and I resumed my grind, throbbing uncontrollably and hanging on the edge.

I let go, tossing my head back and baying at the ceiling, yet another first for me. I do not believe I have ever howled before, during, or after sex in my entire life. I looked up and was shocked to find not a single soul had come through this time, although this had to have been one of the most intense orgasms I had ever had. I rode the aftershocks, allowing him to thrust hard and fast beneath me. In one fluid movement, he rolled me over, stabbing me with his cock over and over until we both came, shouting and cursing, biting and licking, sobbing and laughing all at the same time.

*

I can still call souls, but only three weeks out of the month now. Every fourth week, I find my Wolf lover and fuck him loud, long, and totally without duty, a sexual vacation that rejuvenates me and nearly destroys me. I crave him now—even when I am being taken by a vampire, I crave the rough touch of the Wolf. I want him like I have never wanted any other man. They call me the weaker sex, because I am a woman. They call me the fragile one because I am a mortal. Why, then, is it that my Wolf lover comes on his hands and knees for me every time?

Searching For the Perfect Mate

by Trinity Blacio

Chapter One

Remi has one thing on his mind tonight: sex. Unfortunately, he can't enjoy his latest plaything near as much as he'd like to. Life can change in a matter of moments, as it does for him.

Remi LeBlathe walked through the crowded street. He spotted two people in an intimate conversation at a bistro style table. Why couldn't he find someone? Not that he had a problem getting laid—hell, women lined up to get a chance to have him because of his size. Along with this advantage came the nicknames, "Mammoth the Beast" being the most recent one. Ever since he killed that drug lord who had trespassed on his land, the new name spread throughout his pack.

He needed intimacy, the emotional kind that his

relationships lacked. Someone who wasn't afraid of him. A woman who could bring peace to his life. Maybe, if he were very lucky, tonight his search would be over.

Would she be his mate? That one person destined for him?

He wanted what his brother now had with his mate Jaycee, but he wouldn't be another man's bitch like Pierre. He'd have his own when the time came.

The Taming Shrew Club came into view when he turned the corner and crossed the street. He had visited the members-only club a few times before. Since his friend Dane was mated now, he hoped Lance was there to play tonight.

Running his card through the slot, the door clicked open and he entered the dark room. On stage, Cleo demonstrated her Japanese bondage on her new submissive.

The heavy metal door slammed shut behind him, and he made his way to the bar. He spotted Lance at the end of it in conversation with a redhead named Kellie, his date and partner for the evening. She was new to the pack.

Good. Lance knows what I want. He slid in behind Kellie and wrapped his arms around her body. A little too thin for his tastes, but she did have a nice ass and he'd loved to slid his long, thick cock into it.

"Hey, baby, are you ready for tonight? Has my man Lance informed you of what we have planned for your sweet body?" He knew his friend Dane had contacted Lance earlier and that all the preparations should be in order. He licked the side of her ear and inhaled her scent, nothing. No reaction to her scent. She wasn't his mate, just another pleasure. He glanced up at Lance. Disappointment reached into his hardened heart at the knowledge. "Is the room ready?"

Lance smiled and nodded, "Dane called and told me to meet you here. He said everything would be set up for your tastes."

"Shall we?" His hand rubbed her back in reassurance. He could read her thoughts, and he knew she was nervous. "Do you want to leave? You don't have to please me just because I'm alpha." His long arms wrapped around her and he turned her to face him.

Her big green eyes stared. "I want to be with you. It's just I've never been with two men and well . . . I've heard you're . . . big!" Her cheeks brightened and her gaze lowered.

He knew many of the women he had been with talked about his size, and in some incidents, he hadn't been able to fit all of himself in. Remi brushed her bangs out of her face and lifted her chin. "I can promise you I won't hurt you, and we'll take it slow so you can get used to us." His lips gently grazed her cheek and his fingers brushed over the side of her breast. He could feel her shiver with sexual excitement.

"I want to be with you Remi. I need to be with you tonight," she whispered and rubbed her cheek against his hand.

His cock jerked at her words, and his arm wrapped around her waist to guide her towards the door. Then, a commotion behind him stopped him in his tracks. "Go upstairs and tell Lance I'll be up in a minute. I want to check something out." He pushed her towards the stairs and turned to face five men who had just walked into the club. He didn't recognize any of them, yet they had access to the club.

Each of the newcomers was dressed in fatigues and carried weapons. He could smell the iron. Out of the corner of his eye, he noticed Frank, the bartender, had scented the same thing. His claws broke out and his nose sniffed the air.

The men made their way towards the bar and ordered beers. They hadn't noticed everyone on alert at the club. Easing his way closer, Remi listened to their conversation. Were they connected to the drug dealer he'd killed last week? He didn't care. He could either fight or have sex. Either way, he would release tension tonight.

"I tell you, that bitch is around here. She's dyed her hair red. If I'd have known she was a slut, I would have given her to you guys sooner. The stupid whore!" one man snapped at the men around him.

For some strange reason, the beast inside of him roared with vengeance. This woman meant something to him and he was determined to find out what these men were going to do.

Frank, listen and find out what you can. Have Ike follow them. I want this woman protected, and notify me when they go in to attack her!

The bartender nodded, and picked up the phone to contact Ike.

With that covered, he knew these men would harm no

one in the bar, but he took one long look at the mouth of the man who had threatened this woman. He wanted to make sure the man knew he was watching him.

The guy's gaze landed on his. Remi held it, never flinching.

"You have a problem with me, Titanic, or do you want some of this?" The man grabbed his crotch and his friends laughed.

The bar music shut off and everyone's gaze turned towards the newcomers. *No one will touch them except me, is that understood?* Remi demanded, sending his order into his pack member's heads, which happened to be all the members of the bar. Frank nodded behind him and knew the others had heard him also.

"Number one, you're too small to be my bitch, and I don't care for men who threaten women. Maybe I do need to show you what it's like to be beaten." Remi inched up into the man's personal space and the man's own men surrounded them.

"What's wrong, little man? Not so brave now that I'm here?" Remi knew the man had weapons on him, but he didn't care. If he pulled one out, or either of his men did, they would be dead in minutes.

"Well, then, let me start this for you." Remi smirked and threw a right punch into the man's nose, sending him flying into the bar, knocking down one of his men in the process.

"There, now you have a reason to fight me. Come on, bitch, get up. Let me give you a taste of what it's like to get beaten." Remi's whole body tensed up as the man rose and rushed him. He drew a knife and tried to slash his stomach.

Remi kicked the knife out of his hand and heard the crunch of bones in his fingers. The man screamed, grabbing his hand when a clicking noise behind him sounded.

"I wouldn't do that, buster." Ike said from behind him.

Remi turned his head and nodded at Ike, and nodded again, drawing his attention back to the man. "If I were you, I'd get your men and head out of town now. I won't tell you again. and if I see you in my territory again, I'll kill you. Don't think I won't be watching, because I'll know every move you make." His gaze never left the men as they backed out of the bar, securitizing everyone's moves.

Remi knew that little tussle did nothing to vent all the pent-up aggression he held. He needed hard rough sex now and made his way up to his private room. Ripping his shirt off, he threw it on the ground. He needed to satisfy the hard ache in his pants and the heat that raced through his system. Just the thought of this redhead being hurt by that jerk made him furious.

Chapter Two

Remi turned the corner. Kellie leaned against the wall, her eyes closed and her hand rubbing her exposed mound.

He stopped in front of her. "Are you waiting for me, Kellie?" His hand replaced hers. She was soaked. He slid two fingers into her tight pussy.

"I knew you would need me," she whispered, her heated gaze met his.

"You know it won't be easy. This will be hard and fast. My beast wants you now." He growled low in his throat. Her nipples perked and stuck out through the see-through blouse she had wore.

She nodded and waited for his next command.

"Open your blouse and let me see those big tits. Then I want you to grab that light fixture above you and don't let go."

He unbuttoned his fly and his thick, long cock poked out of its confinement while he watched her hands shake as she opened her shirt. Her pink nipples made his mouth water. He could smell her heat.

Lowering to his knees in front of her, he sucked her nipple into his mouth. He bit it and, at the same time, he pushed four fingers into her pussy. Her little cries drove him further.

Lance, come watch. Let's see if our playmate likes to be watched while I fuck her.

The door opened to his private suite and Lance stood there, his cock in his hand, rubbing it back and forth. "Look at those nipples—just like candy."

Remi released her nipple and stood, bringing his hand coated in her juices to his mouth. Her eyes grew large as he sucked her juices off his fingers.

"Just like honey. Turn around, baby, and put your hands on the wall. Lower your head in between them." Remi pulled out his cock, still wearing his jeans, and watched her get into position, as he grabbed a condom from his pocket and quickly rolled it on. The two little round globes of her ass were soft to the touch, but they needed to be red with heat. His hand came down, spanking her over and over. Her cries and pleas were music to his ears and when he traced his hand down to her pussy lips, her liquid greeted his fingers. It was time.

He leaned over her and grabbed her breast. His cock rammed into her, lifting her off the ground. Her cry echoed in the hall and bounced off the walls. The beast broke through, his fur-covered body triggering her beast to come out. Growls and whimpers filled the hallway.

His claw traced her nipple and his other hand reached down to her clit. He pinched it. Her body shook and her pussy walls clenched his cock. Her muscles rubbed and massaged his massive cock as sweat dripped off of his forehead and landed on her back. His hips never stopped as he brought her over again.

Remi locked his teeth into her neck, holding her; Lance slid down in front of her and sucked her clit into his mouth..

Remi knew he was close. His body tightened when he felt Lance's hand reach around. grabbing his balls and messaging them.

"Harder!" he demanded.

One, two more thrusts and his body jerked, and he came.

"*Yes!*" His body relaxed, but his cock was still hard. Wanting more, he pulled out and tossed the used condom into the trash can. He lifted Kellie into his arms. "We're not done, baby. We've just begun."

He carried her into the room and laid her onto the

center of the bed and noticed all the sex toys were ready to go.

"Grab the plug." He thrust his jeans down to the ground and stepped out of them and grabbed another condom from the bed stand, rolling it on his cock.

Kellie's gaze grew large when she took in his size. She didn't get to see his whole length in the hallway. She watched his hand stroke his cock back and forth over the condom.

"Don't worry little one, we'll stretch you to take us." He grabbed a dildo off the bed, as Lance flipped her onto her stomach. A pillow was placed under her stomach and Remi spread her legs, pushing her knees into a kneeling position. His hand traced over her wet, pink folds. Her scent filled his senses and his tongue gently licked her outer lips, while his thick lips sucked up the juices that slipped from her wet pussy.

The dildo was well lubed and Remi pushed it into her pussy, stretching her again. He placed two fingers into his mouth, coated them with his salvia, and slid them into her ass at the same time that the dildo entered her pussy.

Her little squeaks were muffled around Lance's cock as he thrust in and out of her mouth. Together, they worked to bring her body closer and closer to peak. Then they would stop, not letting her come. Kellie's whimpers told them she needed more. He took out his fingers and the dildo, cleaned it off with a wipe, and switched places. The toy pushed into her ass, and he could see her open, taking it further into her tight fold.

His own cock ached to fill her, but he knew she wouldn't be able to take him yet.

Remi glanced up, and noticed Lance's gaze as he looked down at Kellie. There was something else going on here, and it wasn't just fucking. "Lance, do you need to tell me something?" He pulled the dildo and his fingers out, then sat back on his legs.

Lance's gaze lifted and he could see the confusion there, "I think she's my mate. No, I know she's my mate." His fingers traced her face with love. Remi rose off the bed.

"I'll leave the two of you alone, then." He reached for his pants.

"No, stay. We want you here with us. Don't we, baby?" Lance asked Kellie.

Kellie gazed back at Remi and smiled, "Please stay. I want this. I've always wanted two men to make love to me." She lifted her pink ass up into the air and waited.

A smile formed on Remi's face, Lance moved under her, the pillow kicked to the side, and slid his cock into her pussy. His teeth latched onto her neck and held her in place. Remi kneeled in behind her; his hands traced her ass cheeks and separated them. He slipped the tip of his condom covered-cock into her ass.

Her muscles tightened, "Relax, baby, let me in." The muscles in her ass relaxed and he pushed further into her tight hole. He held her hips still. Lance held still inside her and waited, waited till Remi was in. Remi's teeth ground together, pushing the rest of the way into her haven. The breath he had been holding released in a gush.

Lance's cock rubbed against his as he pulled out of her pussy. When Lance pushed in, he would pull out. Together, they set the rhythm. Sweat dripped down her spine from their heated embrace. Remi reached down and around their bodies, to stimulate her clit while they both thrust in and out of her.

"Now, Kellie. Let it go. Show your mate how you ache for him," he whispered into her ear, his cock ready to explode.

Her muscles tightened around him, stroking the hardened length of him, and he lost it. His seed filled the condom that covered him. He looked down and saw the two of them kissing.

Pulling his body away from their heat, he rose off the bed and nodded to Lance. Now he would hunt the men he had let go and make sure they did no harm to this woman.

Remi knew the men from earlier were still around and hunting. It was time for him to do the same. Slipping his pants back ,on he walked to the bar where Frank waited for him.

"They went to Pierre's town. They're scoping out the surroundings." Frank growled.

"Looks like I get to visit my little brother and hunt at the same time. Thanks, Frank. Oh, and send up a bottle of champagne to my room. It seems Lance has found his mate."

Remi sat down and laced his boots when Ike brought him his knives. Remi never carried guns. He didn't need to—his claws, power, and knives were all he needed.

"Frank, grab Pete and have him meet us at Pierre's. We're going hunting for blood."

Want more sexy fiction?

September 2012 saw the re-launch of the iconic erotic fiction series *Black Lace* with a brand new look and even steamier fiction. We're also re-visiting some of our most popular titles in our *Black Lace Classics* series.

First launched in 1993, *Black Lace* was the first erotic fiction imprint written by women for women and quickly became the most popular erotica imprint in the world.

To find out more, visit us at:
www.blacklace.co.uk

And join the *Black Lace* community:

🐦 @blacklacebooks

f BlackLaceBooks

BLACK
LACE

The leading imprint of women's sexy fiction is back – and it's better than ever!

Also available from Black Lace:

On Demand
Justine Elyot

I have always been drawn to hotels.
I love their anonymity. The hotel does not care
what you do, or with whom.

The Hotel Luxe Noir is a haven for hedonistic liaisons. From brief encounters in the bar to ménages in the elevator, young Sophie Martin has seen it all since she started on reception. But as she witnesses the dark erotic secrets of the staff and guests can she also master her own desires...?

Welcome to the Hotel Luxe Noir – discretion assured, satisfaction guaranteed.

Praise for On Demand

'Indulgent and titillating, On Demand is like a tonic for your imagination. The writing is witty, the personal and sexual quirks of the characters entertaining'
Lara Kairos

'Did I mention that every chapter is highly charged with eroticism, BDSM, D/S, and almost every fantasy you can imagine? If you don't get turned on by at least one of these fantasies, there is no hope for you'
Manic Readers

Also available from Black Lace:

Wedding Games
Karen S Smith

Emma is not looking forward to her cousin's wedding: the usual awkward guests, the endless small talk, the bad dancing...But a chance encounter with Kit, a very sexy stranger, leaves her breathless.

Without a chance to say goodbye, Emma resigns herself to the fact their incredibly hot encounter will be just a sexy memory, but then she meets Kit at another wedding...

Black Lace Books: **the leading imprint of erotic fiction by women for women**

Also available from Black Lace:

I Kissed a Girl
Edited by Regina Perry

Everyone's heard the Katy Perry song, but have you ever been tempted...?

If so, you're not alone: most heterosexual women have had same-sex fantasies, and this diverse collection of short erotic fiction takes us way beyond kissing.

An anthology featuring kinky girl stories from around the globe and women from every walk of life and culture who are curious and eager to explore their full sexuality...with each other.

Black Lace Books: the leading imprint of erotic fiction by women for women

And available digitally, a brand new collection in our best-selling **'Quickies'** series: short erotic fiction anthologies

QUICKIES: GIRLS ON TOP
Emma Hawthorne

This new collection of sensational, sexy stories will arouse and, occasionally, even shock you. This volume contains brand new stories from women who ignore the rules, unleash their sexual fantasies and find out just how wildly delicious sex can be when you take it to the limit – and, sometimes, beyond....

Includes:

Darkroom – Jen and her boyfriend explore group sex

Doctor in the house – Debbie's visit to A&E results in a romp with a doctor which gives a whole new meaning to the term 'bedside manner'....

Mistress Millie – when Millie meets fit farmhand Jake she knows exactly how to put him in his place...

Juicy – Samantha is about to discover her husband and his best friend are hiding a sexy secret...

Festival Fever – Leanna shares a tent with her friends Dee and Mar. And they get up close and very personal...

Top Brass – She's the boss's wife and Cindy knows she shouldn't say no to any of her demands...

And available digitally, a brand new collection in our best-selling **'Quickies'** series: short erotic fiction anthologies

QUICKIES: SEX TOYS
Edited by Lori Perkins

*Because sometimes a hot partner
just isn't enough…*

Think of this Quickies collection as your erotic toy chest packed with twelve indulgent tales about wonderful devices to be used by good girls and bad boys.

Featuring bedroom staples such as dildos, strap-ons, vibrating panties and leather cockrings to more inventive toys such as sex machines and even futuristic playthings, this collection has everything you need to have a devilish time. Surprisingly romantic and wickedly tempting, you'll find stories from your favourite erotic authors such as Liz Coldwell and Rebecca Leigh.